Praise for Marc Olden

GIRI
'Anybody who loved SHIBUMI and THE NINJA shouldn't miss it'
James Patterson

DAI-SHO
'Fast and furious . . . an intensely exciting story reeking of cold-blooded violence'
Publishers Weekly

GAIJIN
'Top-notch thriller . . . A delicious entertainment'
Kirkus Reviews

ONI
'No one has plumbed the secrets of the Orient with near the imagination'
Clive Cussler

KISAENG
'Tough, realistic, sadistic and erotic, *Kisaeng* combines the traditions of Lustbader and Clavell, but outstrips them with sheer energy of narrative'
Fear

KRAIT
'Olden's exciting successor to *Kisaeng* . . . *Krait* bites hard all the way'
Publishing News

Also by the same author, and available from Hodder and Stoughton paperbacks:

Kisaeng

About the author

Marc Olden is the bestselling author of six powerful and chilling novels: *Giri*, *Dai-Sho*, *Gaijin*, *Oni*, *Te* and, most recently *Kisaeng*. He lives in New York City.

Krait

Marc Olden

CORONET BOOKS
Hodder and Stoughton

First published in Great Britain in 1992 by New English Library Hardbacks

Coronet edition 1993

British Library C.I.P.

Olden, Marc
  Krait
  I. Title
  813.54 [F]

ISBN 0-340-59547-7

Printed and bound in Great Britain for Hodder and Stoughton Paperbacks, a division of Hodder and Stoughton Ltd., Mill Road, Dunton Green, Sevenoaks, Kent TN13 2YA (Editorial Office: 47 Bedford Square, London WC1B 3DP) by Clays Ltd., St Ives plc.

For Diane, queen of creatures
and pulse of my heart

Krait. A small poisonous snake found in the jungles of Vietnam. Its bite can kill within hours.

Do not light the Buddha's lamp until you have extinguished every passion.

Japanese

Marcia Merino was then a member of the Movement of the Revolutionary Left (MIR) . . . Her position as organiser made her one of the most knowledgeable activists about the clandestine cell structure set up by MIR in preparation for the military coup. She had been captured and was now a . . . collaborator. Released prisoners had reported during the past year that Merino had assisted DINA in their interrogation and torture.

Rebel Magazine *on DINA, Chile's secret police*

Prologue

A hair from the head of a woman can tie a large elephant.
Japanese

Southern France, June

At sundown Albert Martins sipped a strong red wine from his vineyard and decided to kill the fat man. It was the only way to protect his wife.

He and the fat man were alone in the vast banquet hall of Martins' castle overlooking the walled city of Avignon. The six-hundred-year-old castle, a medieval maze of chambers and passages, was actually two menacing stone fortresses built around a single courtyard. Martins, a former CIA agent, had purchased it with money stolen while assigned to Vietnam.

His dinner guest was Paul du Carri, an obese fiftyish Corsican with a drooping lower lip and an animalistic craving for sex. Du Carri owned an exclusive private clinic in Marseille through which Martins had been laundering drug money for the past two years.

He watched du Carri stare at a ceiling frescoed with biblical scenes. "She wore a black leather face mask," the fat man said. "Never saw her face. Only her eyes. The most intriguing grey eyes imaginable. Slim thing, she was. Eurasian and somewhere in her thirties. Called herself Zani. No real names at an orgy, you understand."

He was relating the sordid details of a visit he'd made to an S & M club while in Paris for a recent medical convention. Apparently, the club was a monthly orgy held in the

1

Place Vendôme flat of a German film producer claiming to be the illegitimate son of Hermann Goering.

Du Carri had gained admittance through his connections with the French blue-bloods undergoing drug and alcohol rehabilitation at his Marseille clinic. A stay in the clinic didn't come cheap. The fat man was fucking his patients in more ways than one.

Martins' long fingers stroked a hand radio used to summon servants. He watched as du Carri dabbed at his mouth with a napkin then said, "She wore a ring in each nipple. Also wore those cut-out panties, the kind that show a woman's front and rear. Nothing else, except the face mask, of course. I'll never forget those grey eyes. The host brought her to me naked on a chain."

"Thank you for sharing that with me," Martins said in fluent French.

His frigid gaze across the lengthy oaken table should have made du Carri edgy if not downright afraid. It should have made the fat man jump a mile. But the normally shrewd du Carri was concentrating on caviar and fondly recalling the orgy. Engrossed in himself, he didn't notice Martins' eyes.

Nor did du Carri glimpse the six dogs that silently filed into the huge room and sat on a worn stone floor near the spacious doorway. Martins' signal to the animals, a blast on a small soundless whistle, had also gone unheeded.

The dogs were Atlas Shepherds, white wolves with tall pink ears, eyes the colour of dried blood and an air of icy hostility. Beautiful but aggressive, they were from North Africa where they guarded the camps of Berber and Taureg tribesmen. Martins controlled them with silent hand signals taught him by a Russian woman who'd trained guard dogs for the KGB in Moscow.

Well trained and self-possessed, the dogs neither barked nor approached the table to beg for food. No sucking-up in hopes of receiving a pat on the head. Martins admired them for being independent.

Tonight he was pleased to see his dogs concentrate on him with a frightening intensity. Their leader had a cropped tail. He looked around to make certain the others were paying

2

attention to Martins. Satisfied, he resumed staring at his master, aware that his courtyard snooze had been interrupted for a reason.

As du Carri prattled on about the orgy, Martins' green eyes hardened. He checked his wrist pulse. Too fast. He appeared calm, but protecting his wife took its toll on his nerves. When she was safe he'd settle down and enjoy life again.

Until this evening he'd had no intention of murdering du Carri. They weren't close friends but they'd gotten along in business and were making money together. Tonight's dinner was business. No wives, no guests. Not one to combine work and play, Martins had yet to introduce his wife to du Carri.

He ran a courier service, assisted by a thirty-five-year-old Vietnamese whose tongue he'd cut out in Saigon seventeen years ago. The clients were Asian narcotics traffickers who wanted their money moved to off-shore banks. Martins used war veterans, ex-cops and mercenaries from around the world as couriers.

His partner was the fugitive financier Charles Hocq, a Eurasian investment banker wanted for the multi-million swindle of a major Asian holding company. Hocq brought in most clients but Martins' know-how made the service efficient and profitable. He prided himself on conceiving plans and following through regardless of pressure.

He was laundering some money through du Carri who applied it against a fictitious list of patients paying their bills in cash. Du Carri was a prudent money manager and quite adept at hiding other people's assets. But while Martins appreciated the fat man's laundering skills, he found his lechery repulsive.

Four days ago Martins had been hired by the Golden Circle Triad to move thirty million dollars from Bangkok to America. The Triad was secretly negotiating to buy an Atlantic City casino, an investment prompted by the approaching Communist takeover of Hong Kong in 1997. The thirty million entrusted to Martins was bribe money for American politicians, Mafia dons, union leaders and gaming authorities. Without the pay-offs there would be no casino.

While paying Martins handsomely, the Golden Circle had

given him a deadline. He had one month to get the thirty million to America. Triads were the Hong Kong equivalent of the Sicilian Mafia but Martins saw little similarity between the two. Triads were older, better organised, more vicious and infinitely richer. Compared to them, the Sicilians were babes in the woods.

In late spring the Golden Circle had undergone a power struggle. When it finished the old leaders were either dead or had been forced into retirement. Replacing them were younger and more ruthless Dragon Heads, leaders who would neither tolerate excuses nor show leniency. They'd warned Martins that the bribe money must get to America on time or he would be held accountable.

A threat? Most definitely.

Until today he'd been confident he could do it. He had a good organisation and capable people. But this morning he'd received a hair-raising cable. The Golden Circle had given him a new deadline. The job must now be done in two weeks.

Martins didn't have a snowball's chance in hell of making that deadline. Unfortunately for him, the new Triad leaders had to show they were in command. Martins now had to deal with a group of ayatollahs. As Hocq said, "In the war between you and the Chinks, bet on the Chinks."

Hocq had brought the Triad, casino owners and American mobsters together. Today he and Martins had complained to the Triad about the new deadline. A bloody waste of time. The deadline was firm. If the casino sale didn't go through on schedule, the Triad stood to lose millions of dollars in legal fees, non-refundable deposits and previous bribes.

Martins had requested additional money to cover increased expenses of making the new deadline. Request denied. He then tried to back out of the deal. Request denied. The Chinese hadn't time to bring in new players. Martins was riding the tiger and couldn't get off.

Albert Martins was fifty-five, a tall, bony-faced American with green eyes and a faint shadow on his nose where nose tip cartilage had been carved away during surgery. Dyed hair transplants hid white patches where the skin had become inflamed while healing after a facelift. His natural blue eyes were hidden behind contact lenses. Dieting and liposuction had left him pounds lighter than he'd been in Vietnam.

The change in appearance, introduced fifteen years ago, was necessary. He was a hunted man.

"Albert Martins" was an alias, one of several used by the American since he and his wife had fled Saigon after the Communist takeover. Their war had yet to end. Officially they were dead. Unofficially, a Vietnamese general had taken it upon himself to continue looking for them. Martins, called Krait by his pursuers, was a fugitive who trusted no one.

Krait, a nickname picked up in Saigon, was the name of a lethal Vietnamese snake. In the closing days of the Vietnam War Martins had been interrogating a Communist agent whom he had nearly beaten to death. Still, the agent refused to betray his cell.

However, he knew Martins' reputation for brutality. Realising the torturer would eventually win, the reporter bit through a wrist artery and bled to death. Before dying he wrote two words in blood on his cell wall: "Krait" and Martins' real name. The incident had left the CIA agent shaken for days.

Zani. Grey eyes.

Martins' annoyance with du Carri turned to controlled rage. And fear. The fat man's perpetual horniness had become a danger to Fabienne. Which is why Martins had called in the dogs.

"Zani was a tigress," the fat man said. "A bit unstable, but with a strong sexual appetite. I couldn't get enough of her." He chuckled. "Want to know why she picked me? She told the Nazi, 'I want to have sex with the ugliest man here.' Submitting to me was a discipline, you see. A punishment for the pleasure she receives from sex. Punishment, pleasure. In sadomasochism it's the same. She became my slave. We did everything imaginable." He sighed. "Tomorrow morning I'm going to Paris for a meeting with a private detective. He used to be an intelligence agent so he knows his stuff. He'll find my Zani for me."

Martins clenched his fists. He wasn't about to let du Carri

locate Zani. Suppose the private detective traced Zani to Ho Chi Minh City, the Communist name for Saigon. Her trail would surely lead the Vietnamese general to Martins and Fabienne. If du Carri reached Paris, Fabienne was dead.

Gripping the hand radio, Martins rose from the banquet table and looked at the dogs. Dropping his right hand to his side, he made a fist then jerked his head in du Carri's direction. The dogs quietly formed a semi-circle around the fat man's chair.

Du Carri smiled at the animals. "You're a beautiful lot, you are. Come to serenade me, have you?"

He looked at Martins. "I'm still waiting to meet your wife."

"This detective of yours," Martins said. "What's his name?"

"Jean Paul Boussuet. Why do you ask?"

"How much does he know about Zani?"

Du Carri held out a spoonful of rabbit stew to the dogs, who ignored it. "I gave him a brief description but her face mask made it impossible to be more specific. He wants to question the Nazi but he's wasting his time. The kraut can't talk about his guests without putting an end to the orgies."

Martins said, "Did you ask the kraut about Zani?"

"As I said, a waste of time. Offered the bastard money, even a free stay at my clinic. He refused to tell me a damn thing. All I could do was leave my phone number with him. If Zani wanted to see me again she would contact him and he'd get in touch with me."

Du Carri swallowed the stew rejected by the dogs. "I did learn this was her first appearance at the party. I think she's as much of a mystery to the Nazi as she is to me."

"Stand up and move away from the table," Martins said.

"What?"

"On your feet."

"Not until I've had dinner. Let the Chinese wait."

Martins blew on his whistle. The dogs leaped on the fat man, knocking him and his chair to the stone floor. Screaming, he disappeared under the snarling animals.

Martins blew on the whistle again and the dogs backed

6

away from du Carri. "Walk towards that small door," Martins said. "The one on the far side of the banquet hall."

Du Carri angrily pushed himself into a sitting position. "You bastard. You're mad, you know that?"

"I said walk."

"Damn you, those dogs could have killed me. I'm bleeding. Is this some kind of joke?"

"If you don't stand up, I'll turn the dogs loose again."

Breathing heavily, du Carri rose and stood glaring at Martins. "For God's sake, tell me why. We're here for business, not games."

Martins spoke into the hand radio then switched it off. Pointing to the far side of the banquet hall he said, "Lead the way. The dogs and I will be behind you. Run, and they'll tear you apart."

Du Carri touched his face then looked at his blood-stained fingers. He wasn't afraid, just furious and resentful. He hated being made the butt of jokes.

"I won't forget this," he said. "After tonight find someone else to handle your money."

"Start walking," Martins said.

Martins, du Carri, and the dogs silently walked past walls hung with medieval tapestries, crossbows, broadswords and spears. At an old wooden door, Martins ordered a halt. The dogs fixed their shiny eyes on a sullen du Carri.

"Open the door," Martins said. "Just pull the bolt up then back. Good. Now step into the corridor. Bit of history for you. The alarm system in this corridor dates from the fourteenth century. Still works."

"Fuck yourself in the ass," du Carri said. He stepped into a dimly-lit corridor carved from rough-hewn stone. Lost in his rage, du Carri staggered forward.

Ahead, a door bolt slammed shut at the far end of the corridor. Du Carri looked over his shoulder at Martins who was speaking into the radio.

The fat man said, "Well, what now?"

Martins blew on the whistle and the dogs trotted out of the corridor, leaving him silhouetted in the doorway against light from the banquet hall.

"You came too close," he said. He bolted the door.

Du Carri hung his head, wondering how he would explain this evening to his wife. Wondering how he could revenge himself on Martins. Suddenly, he felt a rush of cool air from overhead. He heard the sound of a large winch and the clanking of thick chains. When he heard a thunderous rumble he looked up to see the ceiling at the far end of the corridor pull back. Rocks began falling into the corridor. For a few seconds du Carri watched in fascination as the downpour of rocks crept towards him.

The alarm system.

Back against the wall, a frightened du Carri covered his head with his arms and yelled for Martins to open the door.

The ceiling retracted further, filling the passageway with rocks, tumult, and the dust of ages. Du Carri decided to run for it. He had taken two steps towards the banquet hall when a falling chunk of granite knocked him to the corridor floor.

"It'll look like an accident," Martins said. "Nothing new in France. Everyone in this country drives like a lunatic anyway. His corpse and his car will be pushed off a cliff."

Martins and Fabienne stood at the high-vaulted windows of the master bedroom and looked down at the castle courtyard two storeys below. It was a pleasant evening, cool, and not yet dark. Avignon's battlements, brownish and sun burnt, could still be seen in distant, fading sunlight.

"He almost found us out," Martins continued. "Thank God for the crisis with the Triad. Otherwise I'd never have known about the Paris episode."

"We can talk about it later," she said.

Martins cupped her face in his hands. Her beauty was nearly unbearable. It was nothing less than a gift of God. He sometimes wondered if such radiance wasn't higher than genius.

Her looks had drawn male attention since she was a child in Saigon. Her father had consistently rejected her suitors, one of whom had ultimately shot him to death. Her stepfather's nephew, besotted with her, had crushed the stepfather's skull with a tyre iron. By the time Fabienne was fifteen, three men had died for her.

Martins felt her arms go around him. Her smile, beautifully erotic, set him on fire. His heartbeat quickened. Her smile told him that her one wish was to drown him in her sensuality and feel his delight as though it were her own.

Looking into her grey eyes, he handed her the black leather face mask he'd been holding.

"Show me what you and du Carri did in Paris," he said.

1

Erica Styler thought, I can't keep on winning like this. Sooner or later I'll fall on my ass. She'd been a professional gambler since she was seventeen, long enough to know that it was chicken one day and feathers the next. But tonight was something else. In ten hours of poker she'd won $210,000.

The big loser was Charles Hocq, the dwarfish forty-four-year-old Eurasian financier wanted for stealing $500 million from an Asian bank. He was hosting tonight's game on his yacht moored in Puerto Rico's San Juan harbour. The boat carried his dead sister's name "Rachelle" in large gold letters.

The name reminded Erica that she'd heard from Texas Billy Quinnie, sixty-five years old and bold as brass when he had the cards. He claimed to have run into Miss Rachelle herself, an experience that had left him pucker-assed and scared shitless.

"She's been dead more than twenty years," Erica had said. "Am I missing something here?"

"Six months ago," Texas Billy Quinnie had said, "I was playing five-card stud on Hocq's boat down in Haiti. Dropped fifty K in less than an hour. I needed to think on what I was doing wrong so I went on deck for a stroll. Got the urge to take a piss so I open the nearest cabin door and go looking for the can. Next thing you know I'm face to face with Hocq's sister."

Texas Billy shivered. "She don't look no more than seventeen which is what she was when she died. Beg pardon, I'm looking at her embalmed corpse which is lying in a gold

10

casket with ivory inlay and decked out in a white wedding gown, and a ton of jewellery. And if that ain't enough to frost your socks, I see a table near the coffin with service for two, like she was gonna have dinner with brother Charlie. Turns out I'm in Hocq's stateroom."

Erica hadn't known what to think. It was a geeky story, but so was Hocq. He'd once thrown a party in which guests had to dress up as their favourite dead celebrity. He'd come as Vlad the Impaler.

Each time she'd boarded his yacht her routine was the same: up the gangway, find the card table and do some serious gambling. When the game ended she headed for the airport like a bat out of hell. Hocq was a ruthless, twisted bastard. She wasn't about to spend any more time in his company than necessary.

The only thing attractive about him was his money. He was a fiscal genius but when he sat down to play cards, he became a fool. And like all fools who gambled, he anticipated the law of averages changing him from a loser to a winner. Erica didn't see it happening. In two years she'd taken him for nearly a million dollars.

As a big-time corporate fugitive he should have been arrested the second he dropped anchor in Puerto Rican waters. Instead, the *Rachelle* floated undisturbed in San Juan harbour, anchored within sight of the United States Customs House. Hocq had friends in high places.

Erica knew his secret for moving around without being bothered. Tonight at the gangway she'd had to show her passport to two guys in business suits, both of whom had nice bodies for gorillas. They were plainclothes detectives from San Juan's police force. "Money's like manure," Hocq told Erica. "Spread it around and it'll do you a world of good."

He knew money, that's for sure. Erica had once watched him simultaneously carry on three phone conversations, each in a different language, with Hocq in control of each one. He'd done this during a card game so she'd heard the English conversation. He'd upped the price of a promised arms shipment three times, forcing the customer to overpay

11

or see the guns go to his worst enemy. The deal took less than an hour to complete and had brought Hocq a five million dollar commission.

Tonight he sat at a round table in the yacht's salon, clad in a large towel and white cowboy boots. His bare chest and arms bristled with silver acupuncture needles. A floppy disc hung from his neck on a thin gold chain. The disc supposedly contained data on numbered bank accounts, drug dealings, political pay-offs and Hocq's role in the rebuilding of Vietnam's tourist industry. Erica had never seen him without it.

During the game he'd received B-12 injections from Werner Tautz, a green-eyed, thirtyish German bodybuilder in dark glasses and cut-off jeans. After each injection Tautz kissed Hocq's cheek, leaving the embezzler with the radiant grin of a five-year-old. Tautz, in Erica's opinion, was a slut who'd slept his way to the top.

When not at the card table Tautz assisted a short, smiley Vietnamese in serving food and drinks from the salon bar. The German's official duties were chauffeur, personal trainer, occasional bodyguard. Unofficially, he supplied Hocq with drugs and young boys. Erica was convinced he'd eat food off the floor if the money was right.

Injections and kisses notwithstanding, Hocq's luck remained bad. Erica could read him like a book and knew why he continued to lose. He may have been a financial genius but he lacked the self-control for poker. Gamblers were born, not made. You couldn't teach cool; you had it or you didn't.

Erica Styler was thirty-two, a slender, pretty woman with a permanent tan and a strong jawline. As a gambler she followed two rules: when you had bad cards, get out. And when you had good cards, make your opponent pay. She also stayed alert. She observed other players carefully and watched herself to avoid giving clues or betraying her hand. To keep in shape she jogged and no longer ate red meat. Drugs, except for aspirin and vitamins, were out.

Her turf was the big money games. She played because she liked the action and because she enjoyed proving her courage. Her opponents were always high rollers: drug dealers, disbarred lawyers, Asian bankers, insider traders, Mexican politicians and the Charles Hocqs. She had no interest in their lives outside of poker. Her interest was gambling and its two great pleasures – winning and losing.

She was the only woman at these games and tonight was no exception. It was her and four other high rollers, three of whom she knew. She knew Hocq and Abby Langway, a skinny, fortyish New York attorney who handled much of Hocq's legal work. He'd recently made front-page news by again getting federal drug charges dismissed against Andy Lam, a Chinese businessman in Manhattan. This was the third time Langway had kept Lam out of the slammer.

Erica suspected that Lam was probably dealing drugs. She'd met him on the boat, where he spent most of his time conferring with Hocq and Langway in Hocq's stateroom. Hocq had been linked to drugs, among other things, which undoubtedly gave the three men lots to talk about. As for Langway, he'd be a better card player if he dropped his habit of fingering his chips before bluffing.

Erica also knew Sal Altabura, a stocky, fiftyish Italian-American who ran Philadelphia's largest construction union on behalf of his uncle, a Mafia capo. He played through half-closed eyes, occasionally scratching a hairline that began at his eyebrows. He'd hit on Erica a few times and gotten nowhere. She never dated card players.

She had a man, one she loved because he had more nerve than anyone she'd ever known, herself included. She'd fallen in love with him at first sight. Fallen in love with a man whose nerve made him so erotic that he could have talked her into having sex in a car going over a cliff.

The one player Erica didn't know at Hocq's game was a small, fortyish Chinese named Deng. He wore a suit and tie, never sweated and never smiled. So far he hadn't said a word. Something about him demanded privacy.

As for Hocq, he was his usual self, a charming psycho with a capacity for sudden violence. Erica wasn't concerned with his past sins or lack of righteousness. She knew he was an egomaniac who competed for control because he wanted his way every time. He was incapable of taking the middle path and resisted everything which prevented him from doing as he pleased. But when it came to poker he was her pigeon, a sucker for the taking.

Who cared if "Chuckles", her name for Hocq, ripped losing cards apart with his teeth? Or bit his lips until they bled, especially after losing a big pot. Erica had once called his bluff and he'd nearly swallowed his tongue.

This January in Panama City she'd beaten him for ninety thousand dollars. The loss, she later heard, had left him ticked enough to snap a cat's neck then peel its skin off. This was the same Hocq who was a financial adviser to a half-dozen Asian governments. Who had predicted the last two stock market crashes, saving Erica a small fortune. Who had sent roses on her birthday and a condolence card after her father had been murdered.

Hocq's minimal love of animals had recently forced Erica to rethink their relationship. Losing to a woman obviously bugged him. Unfortunately, the problem wasn't about to go away. Erica's skill made it unlikely he'd ever beat her. But the idea that he might harm her was something she couldn't stop thinking about.

She was as tough with him as she was with any player. Poker was a money game, not a way of killing time. To win, you played for blood. Erica lived in the world that she found, played within its rules and succeeded.

Hocq's yacht was starting to get on her nerves. Fearful of being kidnapped by enemies, he'd turned the *Rachelle* into a floating fortress. At first Erica had been excited about playing poker within sight of armed guards and machine-gun emplacements. The thrill had worn off when machine guns had been test fired while she was trying to catch a full house.

She now detested the closed circuit television cameras, floodlights, alarms, and shotgun-toting guards who patrolled the yacht twenty-four hours a day. Hocq couldn't be faulted as a host, however. Because tonight's game might last for days Erica had been assigned a stateroom where she could change clothes or catnap. Her quarters were lavish – two bedrooms, Asian antiques, and a sunken living room with wall-to-wall

14

rose carpeting and an original Picasso. She could watch CNN and American soap operas, thanks to a telecommunications satellite hook up.

The *Rachelle* also had a gym, mini-hospital, movie theatre and a discotheque dominated by a large oil painting of Hocq's deceased sister. On a ship's tour Erica had seen Rachelle Hocq's photograph in every cabin, something she'd found a tad scarey. The tour had not included the room where Rachelle supposedly lay in her coffin.

Erica had been in her cabin changing for tonight's game when the phone rang. *Hocq.* At once he fell into his habit of speaking about himself as though he'd just left the room. "Getting even is the story of Charles's life," he'd said to her. "It's childish but I insist on it. Tonight we will continue playing until Charles wins. No matter how long it takes, we are going to play until I win."

Erica hung up and stared into the vanity mirror. She couldn't stop grinding her teeth. *Until Charles wins.* No way. Chuckles could shove a gerbil up his ass before she let him see she was intimidated.

The creep didn't own her. If he wanted a toy, go to K Mart. Chuckles didn't know it but he'd just decided their future together. Erica was about to pull the plug on the little reptile. Tonight's game would be their last.

In the salon Erica's two aces beat Hocq for eleven thousand dollars just after dawn. She showed no emotion winning or losing. Gamblers called her "Ice Princess", the chilly lady who never gave you a break. Princesses didn't play poker for fun.

The sun could be seen through a porthole, an orange blaze rising over El Morro, the great sixteenth-century fort built by Spain. In San Juan's old town, atop a hill leading from the harbour, the new day was greeted by church bells. A cruise ship departing the harbour boomed its horn three times. When Erica walked off the *Rachelle* after the game, she was going to shout, too.

Langway announced he was dropping out. He'd lost fifty thousand dollars, enough for one night. He said to Hocq,

15

"What time are we sailing tomorrow? Or should I say today?"

"Noon," Hocq said. "I never stay too long in one place."

"What about this game?"

"What about it?"

The lawyer shook his head. "Someone has to be awake during the meeting. Suppose the others don't make it here by noon. We sail without them?"

Hocq peeked at his hole card. "Punctuality is their responsibility. Now if it's all right with you I'd like to get my money back from Miss Styler. The game will be over before we sail. Sleep sweet and sound, counsellor."

Erica thought, glory hallelujah. Six hours and she was out of here. She wasn't about to cruise the seven seas until Chuckles' luck changed. If he didn't get even within the next six hours, tough. Erica wasn't going to get blocked arteries over it.

The grim-looking Mr Deng left next, walking away with eighty thousand dollars in winnings. Hocq disliked seeing anyone quit while ahead but apparently Deng was the exception to the rule. Erica watched Chuckles virtually bow down to the departing Chinese, ordering two white-jacketed Vietnamese stewards to show him to his cabin and attend his every need. Did Hocq fear Deng or was Erica imagining things?

A half-hour later Altabura announced he'd had it. Erica wasn't surprised to hear him say he'd lost seventy-five thousand dollars. He didn't play well. However, she was surprised to see him toss a dig at Hocq.

Altabura said to Hocq, "Ice Princess took me for a few beans but it don't compare to what she's done to you. How many years since you won a hand against her? Christ, she owns your skinny butt, don't she? You probably lost enough to pay off the national debt of fucking Guatemala."

Erica stared at her cards. Keep me out of this. You dorks fight it out. Altabura had gotten the nerve to speak up because with his money gone and no reason to remain sober, he'd just belted down three pina coladas in quick succession. He was also a made man in his uncle's crime family. He was used to

16

pushing people around. But he was a long way from home. And he was dealing with Charles Hocq.

Palms on the table, the red-faced embezzler sighed. "Thank you for the game, Sal. I find your unbridled sense of observation quite provocative. It makes me wonder why we haven't established deep emotional ties before this. My advice is not to analyse my gambling losses too closely. In fact, my advice is to shut your wop mouth before I pluck out one of your eyes and mail it back to your uncle."

Erica watched Altabura blink, then nervously wring his hands before looking through the porthole at the rising sun. He swallowed twice, then smiled at Hocq and said, "Lighten up." Turning his attention to Erica, he invited her to come to his cabin and tuck him in. She didn't respond.

"Well, since I can't have you, Sweet Cheeks," Altabura said, "I'll have to make other arrangements." He winked at Hocq who nodded as if to say, I understand.

There were several hookers on board, all imported from the States as sweeteners for Hocq's business deals. Earlier Erica had seen some doo-doo-brain bimbos sunning themselves on deck. Since Altabura wanted company, a working girl would now be dragged from a deep sleep and ordered to report for duty.

Erica and Hocq were now the last two players left. She was up nearly two hundred and fifty thousand dollars. Chuckles had less than twenty thousand. If her luck held, she would put him away in minutes. They were playing table stakes. Lose what you had showing and you were history.

He'd given her the edge with his reckless playing, his insistence on being in every pot. How soon before he went belly up? Two or three hands, max. Erica had to make it expensive for him to play those hands. The sooner he folded, the sooner she could head for the airport.

She sipped a Perrier and watched Hocq call for a new deck. Would that change his luck? No way. He'd switched decks eight times and gotten nowhere. He'd keep on losing until he learned to stay out when he had nothing.

In high-stakes games gamblers didn't deal the cards. A non-playing dealer kept players from cutting the cards to their advantage. Tonight's dealer was Frank, a balding, middle-aged Haitian from a San Juan casino. He'd also been the constant target of Hocq's frustration, enduring outbursts and racial slurs from the embezzler who took out his losses on the Haitian. Erica disliked losers who whined.

She was swallowing the last of her Perrier when Hocq cursed Frank in Vietnamese then said, "You understand what I said?"

Frank, looking like a rabbit caught in the headlights, shook his head.

Hocq said, "You don't understand Vietnamese, is that what you're telling me? You're a feeble-minded, black bastard, you know that?"

Snatching an ashtray from the table he threw it at the Haitian, missing his head by inches.

Erica's anger overruled her fear. Caution was forgotten. "You stupid son of a bitch," she said to Hocq. "What in hell's the matter with you? You could have killed him. If you can't control yourself stay away from the card table. What are you, some kind of moral imbecile? Do that again and I walk and if you never get even, I don't give a damn."

She wasn't brave but this unhinged little queen had just tried to kill somebody and she wasn't about to play dummy.

A grinning Hocq smacked himself gently on the wrist. "Bad boy, Charles, bad boy. Erica, *mon chou*, you are absolutely correct. Frank, I apologise most humbly. My actions were insulting and inexcusable. I offer you my regrets and beg your forgiveness."

He tossed a pair of hundred dollar chips in Frank's direction. "A bonus. Cash in when you're finished."

He signalled the smiley Vietnamese bartender. "Tuan, a glass of champagne for Frank." His voice was all apologies and regrets.

Winking at Erica, Hocq pressed a beeper lying on the table beside him. Across the salon Werner Tautz, sleeping on a green leather couch, stirred and shut off his beeper. Seconds later he hovered over Hocq, listening as the embezzler whispered in his ear. Finished, Hocq kissed the tip of Tautz's nose and said, "Go."

Before leaving, the German gave Erica a smile that frightened her. What had Chuckles whispered to the kraut? Erica wished she had her gun. She carried a .357 Magnum as protection but had been forced to hand it over to Hocq's security. The gun would be returned when she left the yacht.

She watched as Tautz slid open a glass door, stepped on deck and walked to the railing to stare at a Brazilian freighter anchored at the adjoining pier. He lit a cigarette, inhaled, then jerked his head in a signal, motioning someone closer. A Vietnamese guard armed with a shotgun stepped out of the shadows and the two huddled before the guard returned to his post.

Tautz took another drag on his cigarette, flipped it overboard and strolled in the opposite direction. Erica nervously fingered a stack of chips, sensing the kraut had been talking about her. The thought crossed her mind that she might have trouble getting off the boat. In the end she decided she was imagining things. What would Hocq gain by keeping her here?

Time to bury Chuckles.

The game was five-card stud. First card face down, the remaining four face up. In a sudden run of bad luck, Erica started losing. Hocq's two kings beat her pair of tens, costing her fifteen thousand dollars. He won the next two hands. In ten minutes she dropped almost forty thousand.

Next hand. Hocq had deuces showing. Feeling cocky, he bet wildly. Erica stayed with him, not raising, just matching his bets. When he drew a jack of diamonds his eyes nearly left their sockets. He shoved chips into the pot with both hands. Twice he peeked at his hole card, biting his lip in a poor attempt to conceal his excitement.

Erica didn't need to be hit over the head. Chuckles had matched the jack or deuces. Figure him for two pair or three of a kind. Erica had the three, five, seven of clubs showing. Nothing. Her hole card hadn't been touched since the first round of betting. One peek, then she'd ignored it.

On the surface Hocq had her beat. She should have folded. Backed off and let him have the pot. But she wanted to end this game, even if it meant losing some of her winnings. And there was her pride. She wanted to end Hocq's winning streak. Meaning, she'd have to break the rules.

"Deuces bet twenty thousand," Hocq said.

"Your twenty and twenty more." Finish it, she thought.

Hocq waggled a forefinger at her. "Not this time, Princess. This is one pot you're not going to steal. Charles sees your twenty and raises ten."

"See your raise." *Finish it*. She'd just bet fifty thousand dollars on a possibility. Not smart.

Last card. An uneasy Frank dealt a second jack to Hocq who whooped then folded his hands in prayer and went quiet. Erica thought, Jesus, no. She'd just shot herself in the foot. Hocq now had two pair showing. And a matching hole card for one pair.

Erica fought to maintain her composure. She ignored Hocq. Instead she stared calmly at Frank's nose as he peeled off the top card, eyed it briefly then dealt it to her. *Four of clubs*. She had the three, four, five, seven of clubs showing. She felt thirsty, a sign of nerves. She circled her neck to ease the stiffness in her shoulders. She ignored her hole card.

Hocq blew into his cupped hands. "I've two pair showing and you're all possibles. Possible straight, flush, straight flush. Poor Charles. All he has are these pathetic two pair. How sad."

He'd given up trying to control himself. "Like the wise virgin, I save myself for what matters. This hand matters."

Erica worked saliva into her dry mouth.

"Twenty thousand to you," Hocq said.

"Call." She kept her voice level.

Hocq said, "No bluffing Charles this time. I have fifteen thousand left. Bet it all."

"Call," Erica said. She counted out the chips.

Hocq turned over his hole card, a third jack. He had a full house. He squealed and applauded. "Charles is persistent. That's the secret of his success. Charles wins, Charles wins."

Erica turned over her hole card. Six of clubs.

"Straight flush," she said. She'd just won the biggest pot of the night.

The salon plunged into an ominous silence. Erica waited

for Hocq to go ballistic. She felt the boat sway beneath her feet and heard seagulls shrieking. She tensed, expecting Hocq's outburst any second.

A harbour patrol helicopter passed over the yacht then banked left and headed inland. Behind the bar, the smiley Vietnamese stopped drying a glass and froze before turning to stare into the bar mirror. Frank tugged nervously at his watch strap. Erica waited.

Hocq went rigid in his chair. As Erica watched he shook his head as though denying he'd lost. After several seconds he pounded the table with clenched fists, toppling drinks and stacked chips. He began to drool. He pulled an acupuncture needle from his chest and inserted it between the knuckles of his pinky and ring fingers. A shaken Erica wanted to run. But that would have meant leaving $300,000 behind.

Frank cringed, expecting to be butchered at any moment. Erica decided that helping him would give her courage. She touched his hand. "We can share a cab," she said. He nodded, too terrified to speak.

Hocq whispered, "You win, I suppose."

Erica thought, Is there something wrong with your brain? Of course I win. "There's a ten-thirty plane leaving for Miami. I'm supposed to play in the Atlantic City World Series of Poker day after tomorrow. I could use a day's rest before it starts."

Hocq nodded. "Yes, of course. I quite understand. Thank you for the game. I'll see you again. Soon."

Erica smiled. "Of course."

Hocq said, "Frank, would you please help Miss Styler to cash in? And Frank, don't forget your bonus."

The Haitian nodded. "Yes, sir."

At the bar Erica and Frank silently filled her shoulder bag with cash. She'd won close to three hundred and fifty thousand, her best for one game. She was getting more elated by the minute. Thank you, Chuckles, and goodbye, you little prick.

Hocq sat alone at the poker table, his back to Erica and Frank. As the morning sun crept into the salon he removed acupuncture needles from his body and shoved them point

21

down into the table. When they were all upright, he slowly tore his losing cards into small pieces then sprinkled them over the needles. "It's snowing," he said. Erica's instincts said leave the boat *now*.

She glanced at Frank. He was on the verge of collapse. She'd have to be strong for the both of them. Smiling, she cashed in his bonus then added a thousand dollars from her winnings. His eyes teared. He glanced at Hocq's back then took Erica's hands in his, squeezing hard. "Thank you," he whispered.

"I'll see you soon, Erica," Hocq said.

"So long, Charles," she said.

Heart thumping, she followed Frank out of the salon and on deck into the first sun. She patted the shoulder-bag, feeling the comforting weight of the money. For a few seconds she considered heading straight for the gangplank. Leave her clothes and jewellery in the guest cabin. Buy new stuff in Miami and Atlantic City.

She rejected the idea. She'd brought some great things with her. And there were the coral earrings from her lover. She couldn't leave them behind. She told Frank to wait for her on the dock. "Won't be long," she said. "Just have to grab my things and we're off. Would you ask one of the guards to return my gun?"

"Yes, Miss Styler. You won't be long?"

"I'm as anxious to leave as you are. Why don't you line us up a cab?"

But when she returned to the gangway with her suitcase Frank was nowhere in sight. Not on the dock, not on the ship.

Increasingly uneasy, she headed for the gangway. Maybe he was looking for a cab. Not many on the pier this hour of the morning. She also noticed something else. The two detectives guarding the dockside end of the gangway were missing.

When she reached the gangway two Vietnamese with shotguns blocked her path and refused to move. She wasn't to leave the ship, they said. Erica started to panic.

She hated being told what to do. To keep from coming apart, she yielded to her anger. "What the hell is going on here?" she said. "Get out of my way before I –"

"Oh, princess."

Hocq. Behind her. His voice was casual and slightly amused. Erica took her time turning around. In the silence, the yacht scraped against the dock then strained at its mooring lines. She clung to the rail for support, reminding herself to stay calm.

Near a lifeboat, Hocq and Tautz stood casually drinking strong Cuban coffee. Tautz also held the remains of a croissant, the fag doughnut a gambler once told Erica. She took two steps towards Hocq and stopped. If she wanted to survive, she'd have to watch her every move from now on.

She decided to act as though the last few seconds had been a misunderstanding. All she had to do was stroke Chuckles then she was off the boat. No problem. "Charles, there's some confusion here. They won't let me off the boat. Would you straighten this out?"

Hocq looked up at the sun. "I said I'd see you soon, didn't I?"

He sipped his coffee then said, "You called me a moral imbecile. Charles found that embarrassing. Abusing a man in front of others is gauche. If Charles is an imbecile then Charles isn't responsible for his actions, is he?"

Tautz snickered.

Hocq said, "You're staying until Charles wins. Letting me win doesn't count. Now off to your cabin and rest while you can. We'll be playing cards soon."

In his stateroom Hocq, dressed in a blue mini-robe and espadrilles, stood before a full-length mirror holding a silk shirt in either hand. It was nearly 12.30 in the afternoon and the *Rachelle* was twenty miles out of Puerto Rico, heading west towards Cuba. He always felt better when he was well dressed. He'd probably be the most stylish man at the meeting which began in half an hour.

"Black or green?" he said to Werner Tautz who lay on a large, round bed watching a soccer match being televised from Milan.

Eyes on the screen the German said, "Black. Matches your heart."

23

"Black with a beige jacket and cream-coloured slacks –"

There was a knock on the door.

Hocq said, "Yes?"

"Albert," said a male voice.

"Come in."

Albert Martins entered the stateroom dressed in a tan leisure suit, dark glasses and a straw hat worn low on his forehead. He carried a woman's handbag in one hand and a wallet-sized photograph in the other. Switching off the television set, he gave Tautz a contemptuous look, then sat down on a sofa with an excellent view of the ocean.

He placed the handbag and photograph on a bamboo coffee table, lit a Gitane and blew smoke at the window. For a few seconds he stared at the ocean which under a fiery sun glistened like polished glass.

He appeared calm. But a throbbing vein on his temple and an extended wait before speaking implied he was thinking carefully before deciding to speak. His silence was also a warning against approaching him. Hocq laid the shirts on the bed, sat down beside them and crossed his legs. He knew his partner. When Martins was about to nitpick or quibble, he adopted a sour look.

Martins picked up the photograph. "As if we don't have enough trouble," he said.

He looked at Hocq. "We've got problems with this Chinese casino deal, and you insist on adding to our burden. Because of you we now have to contend with someone I hoped I'd never see again. A man who's more dangerous than you can possibly imagine."

"You've met Miss Styler," Hocq said. "That is her handbag you're carrying. Or have you turned into one of those sensitive men American magazines love to write about."

Tautz said, "Who told you she's on board?"

Martins rose and walked towards the bed. "Her stateroom's near mine, in case you've forgotten. Hers has an armed guard in front of it."

Tautz looked at his fingernails. "And naturally, your curiosity was aroused."

Ignoring him, Martins handed the photograph to Hocq.

24

"Miss Styler and I had a brief chat. I led her to believe I'd help her to escape. You don't go in for girls and she's not like those tramps you use as marketing tools. I assumed heterosexuality wasn't your motive in keeping her on board. When she told me the real reason, I couldn't believe it. Are you out of your mind?"

Hocq looked at the photograph then handed it to Tautz. "He's quite handsome," Hocq said. "I don't usually go for blonds, but I'm willing to make an exception in his case. Who is he? I assume he's connected with Miss Styler."

"They'd love him in a Turkish prison," said Tautz. "I wouldn't mind loving him myself."

Pocketing the photograph Martins said to Hocq, "You shouldn't have invited her here, let alone kept her on board against her will. If I'd known she was a regular at your games, I'd have spoken up sooner. She can hurt us."

"You are the chivalrous one," Hocq said. "I suppose this is what comes of living in a castle with your very own queen. How is Fabienne these days?"

"Miss Styler has seen Altabura, Langway and Deng," Martins said. "We've got a deal going to bring the biggest Triad into Atlantic City and suddenly here's a woman who knows the players. Does this make sense to you? Because it sure doesn't make sense to me."

Hocq rose from the bed. "She knows nothing. No one discusses business at the card table. Besides, she's used to consorting with riffraff. Who else has the time or money to play cards? I seriously doubt if she has the slightest interest in anything other than poker. She's here because she needs to be taught a lesson."

Martins said, "She's *my* problem. She's seen my face."

"What's that supposed to mean?"

Martins looked at a grinning Tautz as Hocq said, "Werner knows about you and Fabienne. I trust him with my life. He knows if he leaves me you'll kill him because he knows too much."

Returning to the couch, Martins stubbed out his cigarette and stared at the ocean. "All this over a poker game." He looked at Hocq. "You asked about the blond guy. He's Erica Styler's lover. He'll come for her."

Hocq and Tautz exchanged looks then burst out laughing.

Martins waited. When they'd finished he said, "His name is Simon Bendor. He and I were in Vietnam together. Miss Styler's carrying his photograph in her wallet."

Hocq nodded. "I see. This wouldn't have anything to do with the exquisite Fabienne, would it?"

A silent Martins fingered his wedding ring.

Hocq smiled. "Correct me if I'm wrong. You're afraid Simon Bendor will come looking for Miss Styler and in the process discover your whereabouts. Let me put it another way: back in Vietnam you sold him out. You double-crossed him in order to get Fabienne. Albert, Albert. The things you've done for that woman. Shocking. Fabienne's the reason you're tearing your hair out over Erica Styler, isn't it?"

Tautz said, "Simple Simon doesn't seem so tough to me. He looks like a sissy."

"He can take you out in two seconds," Martins said.

Tautz cupped his scrotum. "I'm shaking in my boots. Next, you'll be telling me he has a big red 'S' on his chest."

Martins studied the photograph. "Hasn't aged a day. Always did look like a high-school surfer."

Hocq said, "Exactly what did Golden Boy do in Vietnam?"

"Sucked his thumb," Tautz said.

"He killed people," Martins said.

In the silence that followed, the boat dipped and rose on the sea. Tautz froze in the act of lighting a cigarette. A frowning Hocq chewed his thumbnail.

Martins said, "He was attached to a secret CIA unit created by something called the Health Alteration Committee. Check the records and you'll find the committee actually existed. As for the secret unit, Congress still doesn't know about it. Everyone assigned to it was a killer. Bendor and his crew were in a class by themselves."

He looked at Tautz. "Bendor was their martial arts instructor. He taught them to kill with their hands."

Tautz blinked. Martins was pleased to see the kraut put down his cigarette without having lit it. Tautz was a wise-ass.

26

"The man knew his stuff," Martins said. "Even I wouldn't take him on. He was also a courier, bodyguard, and burglar. His speciality was wet work. Executions. Trust me when I tell you he was grade A."

Hocq stepped forward. "I refuse to piss my pants over someone I don't know. Someone I will never meet. This yacht is a fortress. Its impregnable. There's no way he can get to me."

Martins said, "You're not going to turn her loose?"

Hocq shouted, "*I have my pride!* And don't think about sneaking her off the boat. Try it and someone's going to get hurt."

Martins looked out at the ocean. He expected Hocq to be bullheaded but not over something so insignificant. Hocq was a financial genius, able to put together great deals in his sleep. However, there were times when he was little more than a grown-up child, unwilling to control his impulses. Martins had never met a man so brilliant yet so determined to avoid reality.

The casino meeting was only minutes away. It would be self-defeating for Martins to upset his partner's fragile ego. Hocq had brought together the Triad and Sal Altabura's Philadelphia Mafia family which owned a major interest in the casino. No Hocq, no deal. If the deal collapsed, Martins would have a problem with the Chinese and be out a small fortune. A two per cent finder's fee was waiting for him and Hocq when the deal was finalised.

Hocq was also the key to their courier service. He brought in most of the clients, some of whom retained him as an investment counsellor. A stressed-out Hocq was bad for business.

Hocq said, "An army couldn't touch me out here. And you expect me to worry about one man?"

Martins said, "I'm telling you, turn her loose."

"The answer is no. Bendor's one man. You're getting yourself worked up over nothing. With all due respect, Albert, Fabienne seems to bring out a certain tension in you."

"You don't know Bendor. I do."

"We agreed to stay out of each other's personal lives. Miss

27

Styler needs an attitude adjustment and I'm here to see that she gets it. She insulted me publicly, something I will not tolerate. The woman's won a million dollars of my money which I intend to win back. Let me ask you something: after all this time, what makes you think Bendor is still dangerous? Vietnam was fifteen years ago."

Martins said, "The average age of American soldiers over there was nineteen. Bendor couldn't have been more than twenty-one when we met. Maybe younger, I'm not sure. He doesn't exactly look decrepit in this photograph. Back then he was a physical fitness freak and the most cold-blooded bastard I'd ever met."

Hocq snorted. "That was then. This is now."

"Miss Styler tells me Bendor runs a health club in Hawaii," Martins said. "That spells physical fitness to me. She's aware of your tendency to buy police so she'd rather not have her fate in their hands. She prefers that I bring in Bendor to deal with the problem."

A smirking Hocq said, "He's to come running to her rescue, is he? *On ne badine pas avec l'amour.* 'Love is –'"

"'Love is not to be trifled with,'" Martins said. "My French is excellent."

Tautz said, "I think Mr Martins is very happy in his castle and doesn't want to start running again. Isn't that so, Mr Martins?"

"How'd you like me to get a dozen bricks from the Berlin Wall," Martins said, "and shove them up your ass?"

Tautz snorted. "Terminate me with extreme prejudice, you mean. Isn't that how you people put it?"

Hocq chuckled. "Careful, Werner. When it comes to Fabienne our Mr Martins is mad, bad and dangerous to know."

Martins said, "Bendor thinks I'm dead. I'd like to leave it that way. Trust me on this. As soon as we dock, send Styler on her way."

"She doesn't know who you are," Tautz said. "How can she tell Bendor *anything*?"

Martins said, "Unlike you, Bendor thinks. Without meaning to, Styler could easily put him on to us. One wrong word, that's all it takes. And before you know it, Bendor's asking questions."

"What do you expect?" Tautz said. "You killed six men to get Fabienne and two were Bendor's friends. Why shouldn't he want to get even? Personally, I think he's forgotten all about you. Incredible. I mean you love a woman enough to kill six men for her. From what I hear, Fabienne's worth it."

Tautz rolled his eyes towards the ceiling. With the boss behind him, he could say whatever he damn well pleased. And it pleased him to put the needle into Martins. "Just between us, Mr Martins," Tautz said, "did Fabienne and Bendor ever have an affair?"

Martins wasn't going to let himself be provoked by this fruitbar with the smart mouth. Without Charlie, Tautz wouldn't have the balls to smart-mouth anybody. For now, Martins had to bite the bullet. He could give Tautz a ton of grief but Charlie would get pissed and that was bad for business. But one of these days, friend, one of these days . . .

Martins said to Hocq, "Have you told anyone she's on board?"

Hocq folded his arms across his chest. "I've told nobody. And I know you'll keep your mouth shut because you don't want more trouble with the Golden Circle. Miss Styler stays. You've got your queen and now I've got mine."

"Tautz is all the queen you need. Let Styler go."

"Miss Styler is my own little Scheherazade. Only she isn't going to tell me stories for a thousand and one nights. Instead, we'll play cards."

Hocq aimed a forefinger at Martins. "If Bendor becomes a problem I'll return Miss Styler to him one piece at a time. For now, she stays on board. You aren't about to give up your woman. Why should Charles give up his?"

Hocq and Tautz burst out laughing, with the German pointing at Hocq and saying, "*Your woman.*"

Hands behind his neck, Martins stared up at a crystal chandelier. Then he said, "She tells me Bendor is supposed to meet her in New York this weekend. When she doesn't keep their date, he'll want to know why." He rose and stared at the sea. "Our only chance is for me to work up a pre-emptive strike."

Tautz frowned. "Pre *what*?"

Hocq smiled. "Oh, Tautzie."

He fixed his gaze on Martins. "Albert, I think you should avoid letting Bendor take over your life. Fear has a smell, you know."

The embezzler looked at the German. "Pre-emptive, Tautzie. It means do unto others before they do unto you. Albert is going to kill Simon Bendor before Bendor kills him."

2

The ancient Hawaiians had words for snow, rain, and wind, but no word for weather. Since Hawaiian weather was nearly perfect there was nothing to talk about. Winter temperatures average in the seventies, summer in the low eighties. All four seasons are identical, thanks to year-round trade winds.

Hawaii's climate, however, is modified by altitude. Mountain weather often turns chilly, producing head colds, the need for sweaters, and a cosy fire. The mountains also attract moist winds that build rain clouds and bring permanent dampness. Each of the eight main islands receives rain daily. Five hundred inches of mountain rain each year make Hawaiian rainfalls among the heaviest in the world.

As usual the June downpour on Mount Tantalus, Honolulu's highest residential area, brought the danger of mud. Vehicle breakdowns were routine and Simon Bendor, jogging from the peak towards the sea, spotted a few: a dune buggy sidelined with a broken axle, a poncho-clad backpacker repairing a motorbike, and three dripping surfers pushing a stalled van. He watched a bus filled with Japanese tourists skid downhill before sliding into a water-filled ditch.

He saw two female collegians in West Oahu College sweatshirts walking bicycles up the mud-clogged road instead of turning back. Weather forecasters had predicted today's rain would last until evening. Tantalus would be a sea of mud for days to come.

He left the road and ran inland, along a hiking trail leading into the huge tropical forest covering the mountain. The downpour kept away hikers, campers and other joggers but

31

he saw signs they'd been in the forest on other occasions. Abandoned aluminium tent poles, sleeping-bags, foam pads, beer cans and flashlight batteries. An ugly picture when you loved the land as Simon did.

He preferred the hiking trail which was lined with orchids, plumeria, passion fruit vines, and koa trees, the wood used by old Hawaiians for dugout canoes and surfboards. But today the trail was ankle deep in mud and impassable. Abandoning it, he headed deeper into the forest, towards cliffs and ravines. He ran towards the firm footing of hardened lava beds.

He leaped into a shallow pond dug by wild boars who'd torn up the forest floor, speeding through muddied water. He wore a hooded poncho, sweatpants, and combat boots. Running shoes were no protection against *a'a'*, the Hawaiian name for the jagged lava that tore up anything but the toughest foot gear. Named for the pained cry of those who'd fallen on it, *a'a'* cut through running shoes like a hot knife through butter. It was as deadly as the reef coral that had broken Simon's legs seventeen years ago, when he'd first surfed the deadly Banzai Pipeline, the great curling tube of a wave off Oahu's Ehukai Beach.

He was in excellent shape. He trained two hours daily — weights, running, boxing, karate. At thirty-four he retained the same wiry build he'd had as a California high-school gymnastic champion. His blond good looks and friendly smile concealed an iron will and formidable self-confidence. Only his cold green eyes hinted at an ability to fascinate and terrify.

He was a professional thief. In the past fifteen years he'd stolen nearly $200 million in cash, bonds, jewels and antiques. He stole for excitement, not money. He was incapable of living without danger.

He worked alone, preferably at night, and avoided confrontation. He never carried weapons since they led to violence which drew police attention. He had no criminal record, not even a traffic ticket. He'd never left behind a fingerprint. He robbed the wealthy, not out of any social sense, but because they were the ones with money.

Simon never stole in Hawaii where he shared a cliffside

home on Mount Tantalus with his sixty-seven-year-old widowed mother. Hawaii was his refuge, the place where he sat on his sundeck and enjoyed the beauty of huge rainbows across the valleys below his home. Where he motorbiked across windy cliffs sculptured by centuries of battering by the ocean.

He stole only on the mainland, usually the east coast, with only an occasional west coast job. New York cops, admiring his ability, had nicknamed him "The Magician". They'd also added to his legend by crediting him with burglaries pulled by others. "That's fame for you," his mother had said. "Keeps the memory of your deeds alive even among the gullible."

He'd invested his loot wisely. He owned a Honolulu home, a Manhattan condo, Hawaiian and mainland real estate, plus a blue-chip stock portfolio chosen by his mother. He'd also financed her Waikiki book store and a friend's Honolulu antique shop. For tax purposes he operated two successful health clubs, one in Honolulu, the other in Manhattan.

He began to sweat as he jogged onto shiny black lava forming a strip in the middle of a valley dense with bamboo, ginger, eucalyptus trees and giant philodendrons. Like many Hawaiian valleys this one ran up, forming a narrow incline between two bamboo-covered ridges. Encircling the valley were *palis*, stone cliffs carved by wind and falling water into columns forming beautiful patterns.

The rain had turned the *palis* into narrow waterfalls, dropping hundreds of feet in a dense, humid forest. Simon loved the forest's stillness. He ran here daily, not just for fitness but because the forest supplied a peace not found within himself.

He ran across hardened lava, towards a stone trail leading to a *pali* with an excellent view of Waikiki beach and the ocean. Several yards ahead two scrawny wild pigs feasted on the small white flowers of the kopiko shrub and the remains of a dead bat. Hearing Simon, they stopped eating and fled towards a bamboo-covered ravine, squealing their annoyance at being interrupted.

Seeing the dead bat reminded him of how much Erica hated bats. Her skin crawled at the sight of them hanging upside down from trees or flying across a darkened Hawaiian sky. Hawaii's tree snails, king-sized cockroaches and mosquitoes bothered her. But not like bats. "They're ugly," she said. "Ugly beyond belief."

She was playing poker with Charles Hocq in Puerto Rico. Crazy Charlie who managed to make the supermarket tabloids almost every week. Simon wondered if it was true that Hocq had clubbed a servant to death for putting a jar of jam and a newspaper on the wrong side of his plate at breakfast. Sooner or later Erica would have to stop playing cards with him.

He hadn't heard from her in three days which didn't surprise him. When she played cards, the world could end and she wouldn't know it. "Poker is not a matter of life and death," she said. "It's much more serious than that." Simon would hear from her after she'd walked off with more of Hocq's money.

She'd recently told Simon, "Chuckles has been giving me that vulture look lately, the one that says he wants to eat my heart out. It's like being stared at by Ted Bundy. The money's nice but there are other games."

"It's your call," Simon had said. She had wanted him to listen not lecture. She would solve the Hocq problem herself. Simon wasn't going to make the mistake of trying to run her life, one that had been hectic and strenuous before she'd met him and which showed no signs of changing.

She was attracted to dangerous people but Hocq was *too* dangerous. Recently, a Hong Kong gold merchant who'd lost millions to Hocq had hired mercenaries to kidnap him from his Manila home. Three mercs had been shot to death by Hocq's bodyguards. The rest now faced long prison terms, thanks to Hocq's political connections.

Simon loved Erica more than he had loved any other woman. He loved her because she threw herself into the moment with complete abandon, because she was committed to whatever she undertook. She could be stubborn, often refusing to back down in the face of overwhelming odds. But she was honest, with no hidden agenda. And as a gambler, she

34

was utterly fearless. He'd never met a more exciting woman in his life.

Before Erica he'd lived with a deep-seated feeling of loneliness which he'd hidden even from his mother. Erica had relieved that loneliness. In her absence, the loneliness always returned. In his heart there was room for only her. Her needs were as important as his own. He'd made mistakes in his life but it was no mistake to have loved Erica.

He was alone on the lava slope after the departure of the wild pigs. A wild turkey in an overgrown canyon called for its mate and a trio of rowdy amakihi birds flitted about the branches of a koa tree in search of insects and fruit. Leaving the lava slope, he jogged through a steady rain and onto a narrow stony path nearly hidden by thick undergrowth. The path was slight, a hodgepodge of rocks and pebbles in danger of being swallowed by the jungle any moment. But it beat running in mud up to his knees.

He slowed down, not wanting to twist an ankle on the stones. The rock trail snaked its way between the bamboo ravine sheltering the pigs and a *pali* where a rain-created waterfall plunged into a rocky gorge. Simon wouldn't be jogging to the summit today for a view of Honolulu and the Pacific Ocean. Dirt trails were washed out.

Rain also loosened boulders, sending them crashing down the *pali*'s trails. When it rained Simon kept his eyes peeled around cliffs rather than be flattened by a flying boulder. This was no time for a fractured skull. He was to meet Erica in Manhattan five days from now.

He avoided *panini*, the tall prickly pear cactus on either side of the narrow rocky path. *Panini* meant "very unfriendly", a reference to the sharp needles covering the flat leaves. The cactus, resembling the ones found in America's south-west, had pear-shaped fruit which turned into beautiful yellow and orange flowers. The fruit was delicious but came with yellow bristles that pierced the skin and tongue. Simon hadn't touched it in years.

He neared the waterfall, eyes peeled for falling boulders. He spotted two wild pigs running from the bamboo-covered ravine some thirty yards away. He wondered if they were the same pair who'd been eating the dead bat.

Running behind them was a trio of wild goats. Suddenly dozens of birds flew from the same bamboo-covered gorge – grey terns, yellow-eyed mynas, sparrows, owls and fiery red *i'iwis*, screeching as they scattered across the darkened sky. Bats, birds, pigs, and goats were on the move at once. Something had disturbed them. The bats amazed Simon most of all. It took a lot to unnerve them.

He heard a splash behind him and turned to see rocks from the *pali*'s summit drop into puddles hidden throughout the undergrowth. They'd been loosened by a waterfall thundering down the cliff's face and into a rocky gorge. The rocks could have cracked his skull. He'd be better off standing somewhere else.

He took a step, heard a *pop* come from the bamboo ravine to his left, and then something struck a tall cactus just behind him. His instincts kicked in immediately. *Bullet.* Someone in the ravine had nearly killed him.

The shot was still echoing across the rain-forest when Simon caught sight of a gun flash in the ravine. A second later a bullet ripped through his poncho, passing harmlessly between his left arm and ribcage. He crouched behind the undergrowth, his outward calm hiding a cold hostility.

He stared at the ravine, anxious to locate the shooter. He saw nobody. But as he crawled left to peer around a eucalyptus tree, two puffs of white smoke appeared side by side in the ravine and then bullets ripped the cactus near Simon. He dropped stomach down, the rocky trail digging into his chest and thighs. At least two gunmen were shooting at him.

Forget about going for them. They had rifles, probably with high-powered scopes. They'd pick him off before he'd gone twenty yards. As it was they weren't missing him by much. His one choice was to run.

He dived towards the cliff, clearing a clump of giant philodendrons and landing in muddy water. He rolled towards the waterfall as bullets ripped into the philodendrons' glossy leaves. Then he crawled through mud and wild vegetation, until a large rock blocked his path. He scrambled around it, skinning his hand on a rusty bucket which lay to his right.

A terrified partridge leaped from the bucket, brushing Simon's face with beating wings. The bird had been hiding from the rain. It rose from the ground and immediately took a bullet in the chest, exploding over Simon's head, spraying him with gore and bloodied feathers. He knocked the bucket aside and continued his fast crawl forward. He felt a strong tug at his foot but didn't look around. A bullet had just sliced the heel from his boot.

Ahead lay a small pond, surface covered with trash, broken vines and tree branches. Jumping to his feet Simon dived for the water, hurdling wild grass, entering the pond with the grace of the high-school diving champion he'd once been. He vanished below the surface. Behind him, a bullet struck a decayed log hidden in the grass, sending wood chips spinning in the air.

He rose in waist-deep water and waded across the pond, gulping air. A light mist hid a nearby *pali* but he heard the roar of water racing down its face and crashing into the gorge. He let the sound guide him.

His nostrils were sour with the pond's stench, his mouth gritty with mud. He was soaked to the skin. He'd torn his poncho and sweat pants on rocks and bamboo shards hidden in the mud. He spat to clear his mouth.

He wiped his face with his poncho. Who wanted him dead *this* bad? Could be it was payback. Maybe he had robbed the wrong guy. Such as the former Iranian secret police chief now living in Washington. Simon had taken the wife's $4 million necklace. How about the Cuban travel agent and money launderer who'd lost $750,000 when Simon had hit his Fifth Avenue agency. Or the cranky boss of a Manhattan leverage buyout firm whom Simon had taken for a million in bearer bonds.

Each had the money and tenacity to find Simon and have him killed. He'd stepped on his dick, no doubt about it. Otherwise why were shooters trying to drop the hammer on him? He was no longer safe in Hawaii. Any hopes of living a peaceful life in his beloved islands were gone. The thought left him bitter and sad.

He blamed himself for not having chosen his jobs more carefully. *But he was careful.* He knew everything about being a thief. He worked with only one fence, reducing the chances of being ratted out. And the fence, a former New York City detective named Joe D'Agosta, had proven reliable. Until now, anyway.

Had Dag given him up? Simon doubted it. Dag had always been a stand-up guy. Without Simon – they split the take down the middle with Joe handling expenses – Dag would be out a ton of money. Dag hadn't given him up. But someone had.

He'd always calculated his options, anticipating opponents' moves so that most confrontations were battles he'd already won. He was clear-headed and didn't allow his emotions to screw up his thinking. *But he had screwed up.*

Poncho in one hand, he stumbled from the pond then pushed his way through tangled vines and wild orchids until he reached a small clearing. He raced across it and up a soft lava knoll topped by a grand jacaranda tree. As he threw himself behind the big tree shots tore into the knoll. He landed in a pile of litter and junk. Fifteen yards away was a flooded gorge.

He sat against the jacaranda's thick trunk, staring at the bloodied hands he'd torn on cactus. His sweatpants were also torn. His expensive diver's watch was missing.

Poncho over his head against the rain, he peered around the tree. Near the rocky trail he'd abandoned he saw three men in camouflage pants, ponchos and bush hats. They were dressed like a Marine fire team. One was limping. He recoiled each time his right foot touched the ground.

Bad Foot, as Simon called him, had probably cut himself on razor sharp lava. Apparently the shooters didn't know the forest. Meaning they weren't from Hawaii.

Bad Foot and a small, round man Simon called the Jockey carried long rifles wrapped in camouflage rags. The third shooter was a giant who used a telescope to peer at the jacaranda. He carried no visible weapons, but there was a green canvas bag hanging from one shoulder. Simon figured Jumbo for the leader.

Bad Foot and the Jockey fired at the jacaranda, keeping Simon in place. Jumbo was the spotter, using his telescope to direct their fire. Simon watched him say something to Bad Foot and the Jockey. Immediately the two began shooting lower, concentrating their fire on the base of the jacaranda. Simon ducked behind the tree. He was being hunted by pros.

Bullets tore away the jacaranda's bark as Simon assessed his situation. He was pinned down. Couldn't retreat, couldn't go forward. He was between the shooters and the waterfall. Apart from the tree there was little cover. And there were no stone paths.

He could stay put and wait for them to move in and kill him. Or he could run. However, mud would slow him down, making it easy for them to pick him off. Jumbo and friends had a single-mindedness about them. They wouldn't leave without capping Simon.

He stared at a grey sky dotted with black clouds. In good weather he could've sprinted to the top of any *pali* then disappeared in one of a dozen caves. If he didn't find another way to disappear, he was history.

Then he heard the explosion. The earth shook beneath him. The poncho over his head split under the sudden weight of mud, leaves and sheets of muddy water. *Grenade*. He peeked around the tree and saw Jumbo take another grenade from his green canvas sack. Simon threw himself face down in the mud.

The grenade exploded in front of the jacaranda, stinging Simon's bare arms with mud. A third grenade showered him with more mud and violet-blue blossoms from the jacaranda. When the mud stopped flying, he peeked from under the poncho. The tree was taking a beating. It couldn't stand up to grenades for much longer.

Rain fell on the grenade flames, sending a thick, black smoke rising from the ground. Bullets whacked against the jacaranda. Bad Foot and the Jockey were good shots.

Using rainwater, Simon bathed his eyes which had been

stung by grenade smoke. That's when he noticed that the knoll was now covered by a sooty, wet mist created by rain and grenade flames. He couldn't see the shooters and they couldn't see him.

Time for The Magician to do the impossible. Time for him to grab the wolf by its ears and hang on. Simon's adrenalin was pumping. *Showtime*. He crawled into the black smoke, towards the sound of the waterfall.

3

In pouring rain Mickey Henry seated himself on a boulder in the Mount Tantalus forest shortly after 9.00 a.m. Behind him a waterfall plunged down the rocky face of a cliff, flooding the gorge at its base. Hanging from his shoulder was a Heckler & Koch 300 rifle with a telescope mount. He had to sit because his right foot was killing him.

Using an abandoned tuna can, he scraped mud from his injured foot then removed the running shoe. The shoe was blood soaked, its sole slashed. The foot was worse: blood poured from an inch-deep gash near the heel. Mickey Henry had stepped on hardened lava which had sliced through his running shoes faster than shit going through a tin goose.

He extended his leg, letting rain wash blood from his mangled foot. When the foot was cleaned he wiped it with Simon Bendor's poncho. Bendor had just been iced by Mickey Henry and two more shooters. One had travelled from Africa especially for this hit.

The other shooters were Joe Dean LaBudd, a huge forty-year-old Georgia redneck, and Anton Mulder, a little twenty-nine-year-old Dutchman so cross-eyed he could see his own head. All three were couriers for Albert Martins which wasn't a full-time job, allowing them to work other jobs as well. LaBudd was a security officer for a major Atlanta hotel. Anton Mulder was a mercenary who lived in Zaire with three black wives.

Mickey Henry, from Key West, Florida, now lived in London where he did bodyguard work for corporate executives when he wasn't working for Albert Martins. A desire

41

for excitement left him continually impatient and dissatisfied. That's why he worked for Martins. The money wasn't bad either.

Bendor had run them ragged until they'd finally wasted his butt. One of Martins' Hawaiian contacts had supplied them with intelligence on Bendor's movements but had failed to mention how cold this mountain could be. Mickey Henry was freezing his nuts off.

Bad as the rain was, the mud was worse. Even with two good feet thirty-nine-year-old, chubby-cheeked Mickey Henry found it hard getting around the mountain. He hadn't been in weather this bad since Vietnam, where he'd served as an Intelligence NCO.

He and the other shooters weren't dressed for racing through Hawaii's jungles. They weren't wearing combat boots, warm clothing, nor did they have a compass. Bendor hadn't helped things by making a last-minute change in his route. They'd almost lost him in the rain.

Mickey Henry tore a strip from Bendor's poncho and wrapped it around his injured foot then pushed the bundled foot into the carved-up Reebok. It wouldn't go. Too much wrapping.

He removed the wrapping then gingerly inserted his foot into the Reebok. To keep out the mud he wrapped the poncho strip around the shoe. He wasn't looking forward to walking. But he'd have to since he couldn't fly to the car, which was parked a mile away.

On Martins' orders he'd killed informants, rip-off artists, bad cops and never lost a night's sleep. That was business. Bendor wasn't business. Mickey Henry knew who Martins did business with and Bendor wasn't a player. This was personal. Very personal, since Martins hadn't said why he wanted the guy wasted.

Mickey Henry squinted into the pouring rain at LaBudd and Mulder who were several yards away, arguing over which of them had killed Bendor. Meanwhile they were getting soaked to the skin. Bendor was dead. Martins wouldn't care who did it so long as it was done.

LaBudd had trashed Mickey Henry and Mulder for failing

42

to kill Bendor with their first shots, forgetting that rain and mud had been working against them. When LaBudd had insisted they locate Bendor's body Mickey Henry, thinking of his bad foot, had gotten pissed. He'd yelled at LaBudd, saying that Bendor was in the gorge under tons of water. No good. LaBudd had demanded a confirmed kill.

They'd looked behind koa trees, behind rain-slicked boulders, in bamboo groves, and under patches of thick vines. They'd plodded through puddles up to their knees, in a cold rain that damn near scraped off their skin. The sound of the rain was driving Mickey Henry wacky.

Minutes ago LaBudd had called a halt, announcing Bendor's body was at the bottom of the gorge. They'd done their job. Bendor was history. Mickey Henry, foot hurting more than ever, leaned back against a boulder, rain coming down in buckets and him wondering how much Semtex it would take to explode one king-sized redneck.

"Back to the car," LaBudd said. "Keep to the rock trail Bendor used." With a grouchy Mulder on his heels, the big man began high-stepping his way through the mud. Mickey Henry wasn't going anywhere. He'd taken one step then realised he'd tied the poncho strip too tight around the shoe. He couldn't put any weight on his bad foot.

LaBudd and Mulder had their minds on getting to the car, not on Mickey Henry. Which left him feeling uneasy. He didn't like tramping around the woods by himself. Being alone had one advantage, however. He wouldn't have to listen to LaBudd bragging that his grenades had blown Bendor to kingdom come.

He peered through the rain at LaBudd and Mulder who'd just reached the tall cactus lining the stone path. They were still arguing over the Bendor kill. Give it a rest, for Christ's sake. Sliding off the boulder, Mickey Henry settled his bad foot in the mud and stood up. He decided to pee before moving out.

Simon watched them split up — two men walking away from the gorge, one staying behind to tend an injured foot. All three had passed within inches of his hiding place. Eyes gleaming,

43

he observed their every move. His enthusiasm for the game began to grow.

He was hiding in the flooded gorge, clinging to a stone wall by his fingertips, toes perched uneasily on a narrow granite ledge. His body was submerged, his head concealed beneath an upended plastic cooler floating among rotting leaves and bamboo shards. Both arms trembled with the effort of holding onto the slippery wall. Beneath the plastic cooler, a dead rat floated inches from his face.

Ignoring the rat he focused on his enemies with relentless concentration. He maintained an unbroken calm. He was no longer the target. He was the hunter, ready to strike when his prey was most vulnerable.

Martins. Simon burned the name into his brain. Could he have lost sight of an enemy who was that dangerous? Memory was a tricky thing, but you didn't forget anyone who wanted you dead. To understand why he was being hunted Simon would have to resurrect his past.

Mickey Henry zipped his fly, thinking about his new problem. The rifle strap was cutting into his shoulder and screwing up his balance. He unslung the weapon, and that's when he noticed the beat-up, plastic water cooler. It had moved. It wasn't in the water any more.

He squeezed rain from his eyes with thumb and forefinger. He'd just seen the cooler floating in the gorge. Did the damn thing have legs? He propped his rifle against the boulder then limped towards the gorge for a closer look, wondering if an alligator had pushed the cooler there while crawling out of the water. *Alligators in Hawaii?* Scarey.

The cooler on the bank was the one he'd seen in the water. He recognised the broken handle, the scratches on top. And the bullet holes put there by him and Mulder. *How did it get on the bank?*

An antsy Mickey Henry looked in the direction of LaBudd and Mulder. They'd disappeared. Probably behind the cactus plants lining the stone trail. He took a deep breath. No need to sweat bullets just yet.

He slipped a hand under his poncho, and cupped the butt

of a silenced Smith & Wesson .22 tucked in his waistband. Holding his breath, he stared at the flooded gorge. His heart speeded up, his eyes began a non-stop blinking. Was he looking for alligators or a dead man who wasn't dead? The once beautiful waterfall suddenly appeared menacing. He cleared the .22 from his belt and eased the safety off.

He looked behind him. Scoped everything in sight, from hanging vines to leaves floating in the gorge. The area was clean. His narrowed eyes swept the area again. Everything appeared in order. He put the .22's safety back on. He was getting pucker-assed over nothing. Bendor was dead.

He limped towards the boulder, wishing he didn't have to carry the rifle. But if he left it behind, LaBudd would jump all over him. Mickey Henry could hear that redneck now: *A bad foot ain't no excuse for junking your weapon. A real soldier would cut off his dick before abandoning his rifle.* A real soldier might but Mickey Henry wouldn't.

At the boulder he looked for the rifle. It was gone. The camo cloth was still there, lying on the ground collecting rain. But no rifle. He spat in disgust. What else could go wrong. The rifle was around, he was sure of that. Probably dropped into the mud and sunk halfway to China.

He looked around for a stick. A length of bamboo. Something to go poking into the mud with, so he wouldn't have to get down on his hands and knees. He stared at the gorge. Lots of junk over there. Like that rusty tent pole near the water's edge. He took a step towards the gorge then froze. *Christ.* A man was staring at Mickey Henry from no more than four feet away.

The guy stood beside the boulder where Mickey Henry had been sitting only minutes ago. He was slim, well-muscled, and wasn't wearing a poncho or rain hat. Son of a bitch was soaking wet, not that it seemed to bother him. His sweat pants, tee-shirt, and bare arms were mud smeared. The guy hadn't made a sound.

Bendor. Mickey Henry recognised him from a photo LaBudd had.

He held Mickey Henry's missing rifle at port arms, finger on the trigger. The guy was *cold*, with an attitude that left

Mickey Henry shit-scared to the bone. For the first time in years he felt real fear. He was looking at the man they'd come halfway around the world to kill.

He was angry at himself for having let the guy get this close. Never should have happened. Anger diminished his terror; he was raring to take on Mr Simon. Time for a gut check. Let's see what Bendor was made of.

Mickey Henry flexed his fingers, getting ready. Bendor had used the water cooler as a diversion. Nice. But he should have killed Mickey Henry when he had the chance. Mickey Henry's confidence was coming back.

"You Bendor?" Mickey Henry tried to sound like he wasn't nervous.

No answer.

Mickey Henry flashed his country-boy grin. The rain started coming down harder. He had to raise his voice. "You don't want to shoot me. Otherwise, you'd have done it already. I say we work this out. Pull that trigger and my friends will hear the shot. They'll be all over your ass. What say we talk, you and me?"

Mickey Henry searched Bendor's face, looking for clues. Looking for something that said the guy could be taken. No help there. Bendor was an ice cube. No shakes, no shivers. Watching him gave Mickey Henry the creeps.

He wondered if Bendor wasn't, well, stupid. Maybe the guy was keeping quiet because he didn't have sense enough to tie his shoes. Bet he didn't have the stomach for murder either. Most people didn't. Mickey Henry only had to get him to lay the rifle down. Then he was going to kill him.

Suddenly Bendor made his move, taking Mickey Henry completely by surprise. Happened like a bolt out of the blue. He tossed the rifle to Mickey Henry. Just gave it away. *Unbelievable*. Mickey Henry thought, fucking retard. You deserve to die.

Bendor didn't exactly toss the piece. He underhanded it, almost tossing the rifle over Mickey Henry's head. Eyes on the rifle Mickey Henry backed up, feeling the pain in his bad foot. The foot was killing him but if Bendor wanted to turn over the rifle, Mickey Henry was going to take it.

His hands were about to close on the rifle when he spied Bendor speeding towards him. Here comes trouble. Bendor was barrel-assing through the mud, coming at Mickey Henry like a heat-seeking missile. Leaving him goose bumpy, with his asshole sucking wind.

Mickey Henry caught the rifle, slammed the butt against his thigh and pulled the trigger. Aimed for Bendor's belt buckle. Stevie Wonder could have hit the guy from this distance. Mickey Henry felt on top of the world. He grooved on killing people.

He tensed for the expected recoil. It never came. *Bendor had thrown him an unloaded gun!* Made him use it instead of using the handgun. Mickey Henry felt sick. He'd been *had*.

He saw Bendor's face, finding it youthful and cold-blooded. The eyes were the most frightening. They were wolfish, unfeeling, and gave Mickey Henry the cold creeps. He felt an overwhelming terror. In his panic the roaring waterfall seemed more menacing than ever. He thought, use the .22.

And then Bendor was on him.

Simon drove his boot heel into Mickey Henry's left knee-cap, tearing ligaments and crippling the shooter. Mickey Henry screamed. The .22 was forgotten. Arms spread, he fell back into the mud, knee on fire with pain. Clutching his damaged knee to his chest, he thrashed about in the mud. Mud covered his face, his ears, his nose. The mud, a stinking slime, became the fright of his life.

He tried to stand but couldn't. His cracked knee couldn't take his weight and gave way, dropping him back into the mud. In a frenzy, he twisted and turned in the mud, squeezing the knee between his chest and arms to ease the pain.

As Mickey Henry struggled to a sitting position Simon crouched behind him, slipped an arm around his neck and pulled back, forearm crushing the shooter's throat. Mickey Henry gagged. He couldn't breathe; his head felt ready to explode. He clawed at Bendor's forearm with muddied hands. Blood trickled from a corner of his mouth.

Simon suddenly released his choke hold. Mickey Henry coughed violently, swallowing air down a pained throat. He was going to live. He was thinking about life's sweetness

47

when Simon shoved his face into the mud, immersing Mickey Henry's head and shoulders in the ooze.

Mickey Henry sank deeper into the mud and died.

LaBudd was mad enough to spit nails. He was standing under a tree, in mud up to his knees and drowning in rain because a couple of jerkoffs were lagging behind. Fat-ass Mickey Henry had a hurt foot and could hardly walk. Mulder was acting pokey because LaBudd had accused him of being a piss-poor shot. Well, bless my ten toes, but if you shoot at a man three times and miss, we're talking fuck-up.

LaBudd shaded his eyes with a large hand, grunting when he finally saw Mulder through the downpour. It was raining pitchforks; you could barely see your hand in front of your face. The Dutchman was maybe twenty yards away, poncho wrapped around him, and probably still pissed off.

It wasn't wise to push him too far. The Dutchman wasn't above settling a score by shooting you in the back. He and LaBudd had left the waterfall together, arguing all the way. Eventually LaBudd had ended up in front by himself. As long as he could look around and see Mulder, no problem. But the Dutchman had dropped out of sight, leaving LaBudd a tad jittery. He decided to wait for the little prick to catch up. It was always good to know where the Dutchman was at all times.

Turning his back to the approaching Mulder, LaBudd leaned against the giant koa tree and rubbed sleep from his eyes. He'd give a week's pay for a cup of black coffee laced with Jack Daniels. Removing a chunk of Red Man chewing tobacco from his shoulder-bag, he bit off a wad then hung the bag on a koa branch. Goddam rain.

He spat tobacco juice on the tree then looked over his shoulder. Mulder was only feet away, poncho hood hiding his face and making it impossible to tell what the little squirt was thinking. LaBudd grinned, remembering the African roulette joke. *You go to bed with three black women and one of them is a cannibal.* Better not lay that on Mulder right now.

LaBudd said, "Seen Mickey Henry? Can't be waiting on

him all day. I'd sooner let him buttfuck me in church before I carry him out of here on my back."

He spat, intentionally aiming at Mulder's feet. The tobacco juice landed just inches from Mulder's muddied combat boot. LaBudd grinned at the Dutchman. Man's got to have a little fun, right? Then he took a second look at Mulder's feet. *The Dutchman was wearing boots.*

LaBudd looked up to see Mulder bring a silenced .22 from under his poncho and without a word shoot him in the right hand. Bug-eyed, LaBudd backed into the koa tree, screaming "The hell you have to go and shoot me for? God is my witness, I'm gonna kill you."

He leaned against the tree. The pain was terrible, down-right bodacious, but it would take more than one bullet to bring him down. He wasn't about to leave Hawaii until he'd squared accounts with the Dutchman. Sure as God made little green apples, he was going to waste Mulder's nigger-loving ass.

He glanced at his canvas bag. He only needed one hand to throw a grenade. One grenade could blast the Dutchman back to Africa. LaBudd reached for the bag then stopped when Mulder waved the .22, warning him off. LaBudd glared at him.

Except he wasn't looking at Mulder.

Simon fired the .22 again, shooting LaBudd in the left thigh and dropping the big man at the base of the koa tree. Sitting in the mud, a stunned LaBudd watched as rain washed blood from his leg. He shook his head violently. His arm and leg hurt like hell, God knows they did. Bad as the pain was, the anger at being tricked by Bendor was worse.

Three shooters and still Bendor had managed to outfox them. They'd had him outnumbered, outgunned, but it hadn't done any good. Getting shot triggered off memories of Nam in LaBudd. Suddenly he had the taste of ham and beans in his mouth. The last time he'd eaten C-rations had been in Nam.

Crouching over LaBudd, Simon jammed the .22 under his chin. The big man's hostility radiated from his wide, sun-coarsened face. He was a bad-ass redneck. Two bullets

49

in him and he was still dangerous. Still capable of killing Bendor if he got the chance.

Simon patted LaBudd down with one hand and found no weapons. He rose, took the canvas bag from the tree branch and looked inside. He saw the grenades, smooth-bodied M26s like those he'd seen in Vietnam. There was also one smoke grenade, an M34 that even strong men could barely throw far enough to avoid being burned by its spray of burning phosphorus.

The bag also held a Colt semi-automatic, a big gun for a big man. Other items: a map of Honolulu with Simon's neighbourhood circled in red, chewing tobacco, breath mints, a pack of cigars, car keys, a wallet. And an unsealed white envelope.

Simon checked the wallet ID then moved on to the envelope. To avoid the rain, he kept the envelope inside the bag. Removing two pages from the envelope, he unfolded them in the bag. He was looking at a computer printout of his daily movements. Jogging route, island and mainland addresses, unlisted telephone numbers. His bank accounts, favourite restaurants and vehicle identifications. Time and place of his gym workouts. Simon had been under surveillance.

Breath control was the key to curbing anxiety. He inhaled deeply, drawing air into his lower lungs then exhaling slowly, letting air flow from his upper lungs. He felt calmer immediately. He relaxed his shoulders and straightened his back.

The surveillance report was first class. Martins, whoever he was, had power. People like that inspired fear. Simon was having one hell of a day. It couldn't get any worse. He was wrong.

He looked at the last item in the envelope. Caught off guard, he flinched. A vein throbbed on his forehead. Closing his eyes, he took a deep breath until he was once more clear-headed. Opening his eyes he stared at a wallet-sized photograph of himself. A month ago he'd given it to Erica.

That's how the shooters had found him.

He shoved the envelope, with its contents, in his waistband. Then removing the Colt from the bag, he thumbed off the safety. His gun hand hung at his side.

He said to LaBudd, "Is Erica Styler alive?"

LaBudd looked away. "Never met any Erica Styler. I ain't about to forget you put two bullets in me."

Placing the Colt inches from LaBudd's right ear, Simon pointed it at the ground and pulled the trigger. The shot echoed throughout the forest. LaBudd's skull was filled with an unbearable pain. The muscles of his neck stiffened with an excruciating tension. Half-conscious, he sagged down into the mud, wondering if it was day or night. He was sure his eardrum was gone.

Simon placed the Colt beside LaBudd's other ear. "Is Erica Styler alive?"

LaBudd was as tough as they come. He could take pain, but oh baby, this was rough. The ringing in his ear was hellacious. And he had a monster headache to boot. But he wasn't knuckling under to this prick. He spoke through clenched teeth. "Telling you, I don't know no Erica Styler. Punch out both my ears if it makes you happy. Answer's still gonna be the same. Never heard of the woman."

"Is she with Albert Martins?"

"How would I know?"

"But you know Charles Hocq, Martins' partner."

LaBudd's eyes narrowed. "How'd you learn 'bout Hocq?"

"It was the last thing Mulder told me before he died."

"Before he *what*?"

"You have a photograph of me which belongs to Erica Styler. Last time. Where is she?"

LaBudd sat up, his poncho spotted with blood. His head felt like hammered shit. He was strong as a bull, 6' 7" in his stocking feet, and bench pressed four hundred and fifty pounds. But he wasn't bullet proof. Time to talk some trash. Stay alive so he could get this sucker.

LaBudd said, "If I could help you with your lady, I would. I suggest you ask Hocq. Martins never mentioned her. That's the God's honest truth. Anyway, I don't ask questions. Martins says jump, I jump. Tell me something. You really clip Mulder and Mickey Henry?"

"Erica flies off to play cards with Hocq, and his partner sends three shooters after me. Why?"

"Mister, that's something you got to take up with Martins. He's down on you, I know that much. You want to know why, ask him. My leg ain't all that bad but my hand is killing me. You're a piece of work, you know that? Walk right up to a man and shoot him without a word."

"Did Martins ever mention Erica Styler?"

LaBudd spat tobacco juice. "No, sir. Don't do me no good to lie, now does it?"

"Mulder thought the hit was personal. Thought maybe it might have to do with Martins' wife."

LaBudd grinned. "You know her?"

Simon shook his head. "No."

"Saw her at Martins' home once. Very pretty lady. Guess we're both out of luck. I don't know Erica Styler. You don't know Fabienne Martins."

Simon stopped listening. A whisper deep in his brain rapidly became a scream. *Fabienne alive?* He shook his head. She couldn't be.

But even as he thought, *hoped*, it was someone else, he instinctively knew the truth. A long-buried anger returned so strongly that he began to shake. *How had she gotten out of Vietnam alive?* The answer was Martins.

Overwhelmed by dark memories Simon stared unseeingly at a nearby *pali*. Past agonies, long suppressed, turned into new pain. A minute became a long time. He spoke softly. "What did you say her name is?"

LaBudd chuckled. "Who we talking about, your woman or Martins' wife?"

A mistake. LaBudd had smart-mouthed the wrong guy. One minute Bendor was staring off in the distance. The next he was crouched over LaBudd, angry as God on judgement day, the Colt jammed against LaBudd's balls. "Don't jerk me around," he said.

LaBudd turned serious. "I hear you, buddy. Stay cool. Fabienne. Name's Fabienne." His eyes narrowed. *Bendor knows her.*

Simon stood up. "Is she Eurasian? Very beautiful?"

LaBudd nodded, eyeballing this very weird specimen of humanity. "A knockout. Half French, half Vietnamese. Aces,

52

as my old man would say. You see her once, you ain't likely to forget her."

"I haven't forgotten her."

LaBudd chuckled. "With all due respect, friend, if you're involved with Fabienne you're throwing the meat to the wrong lady. Martins will have your balls."

Simon's eyes were glazed. "I know how he feels about her."

A surprised LaBudd said, "You know Martins? Now why didn't he tell me that?"

"We were in Vietnam together. Except his name wasn't Martins then."

LaBudd grinned. "Man, I knew you weren't a civilian. You're good. Thing is, you have no idea who you're up against. And I don't mean just Martins. Talking about the people behind him."

Using his good hand LaBudd pressed down on the bullet hole in his thigh. He had to shake up this citizen. That way, he'd come to know he needed LaBudd's help. After that it would be easy for LaBudd to kill the son of a bitch.

He spat out his chew. "Martins and Hocq are in with some heavy people. People as high up as you can imagine. I'm talking movers and shakers. The kind that walk tall every day of the week."

He held his grin a long time. "Uncle Sam's working hand in glove with Martins and Charlie Hocq. Uncle's helping us every step of the way. That's why nobody's able to stop us."

He waited for Simon to be impressed.

"Go on," Simon said.

"I don't want to see you get in over your head. All you want is your woman back. I can get behind that. So here's the deal. You get me to a doctor and I'll call Martins about your lady. Might be I can straighten out things between you and him. Least let me try."

"Mulder said Martins lives in southern France, in Avignon."

LaBudd winced. "My hand's killing me. Yeah, him and Fabienne have this big old castle there. Help me up so's we can get started on finding out about your woman." LaBudd thinking, one arm ought to be enough. Get close enough, friend, and you can kiss your ass *buenas noches*.

Simon looked into LaBudd's eyes. The big man tensed, praying treachery wasn't written on his face. Then Bendor tucked his gun hand under his poncho and a grinning LaBudd was beside himself with joy. He'd snap this pilgrim's neck in no time. One hand. Wouldn't need anything else.

He said, "So you and Martins was in Nam together. Did three tours over there myself. Loved it. Had me a time and a half. War break out tomorrow, I'd be on the first plane back."

Simon extended his left hand, his right still hidden. LaBudd licked his lips. Turn out the lights, the party's over. "You mentioned Martins had another name in Nam. What was it?"

"Krait," Simon said, firing through his poncho and shooting LaBudd in the head.

4

Albert Martins felt relieved, his usual reaction on leaving a place as depressing as Cuba. This afternoon he stood alone at the *Rachelle*'s stern, filing his nails as the yacht pulled out of Havana harbour. Soon he'd go below deck to the communications room, hopefully to receive a fax saying Simon Bendor was dead.

He turned his back to Havana's waterfront and began trimming the cuticle on his pinky. Nail grooming was a continuing fixation as was a preoccupation with neatness that found him bathing three times a day. Martins did not connect cleanliness to godliness. He had absolutely no interest in God. He was simply very concerned with his appearance.

Havana. It was no longer the glamorous city he'd first visited as a college undergraduate, Martins spending one weekend fucking like a crazed monkey, determined to marry the fifteen-year-old black whore with whom he'd become intoxicated. The Cuban capital was now rundown and dilapidated beyond recognition, fiercely Communist, and surrounded by a countryside with miles of billboards quoting Castro. It had lost contact with the universe.

The city possessed no shopping to speak of. Martins had bought Fabienne a straw tote bag and a *Cuba Si* T-shirt. Not much of a fashion statement, but there was little else to choose from. The country was dirt poor; Cuban women wore earrings made from the cardboard lining of bottle caps and pendants made from melted toothbrushes. Vendors dispensed ice cream in empty Coca-Cola cans with the tops cut off.

He'd come to Cuba on business. The *Rachelle* had stopped

here to pick up François DuChamps, a bow-legged forty-year-old ex-French Legionnaire, and one of Martins' couriers. DuChamps had flown from Bangkok with three million dollars in Triad money for the Atlantic City deal. The *Rachelle* would take him to the Dominican Republic where an American airliner would then fly him to Miami.

In two days couriers had moved ten million dollars of Triad money into the States. Not bad, but not good enough. Martins had just twelve days left on his deadline. Twelve days to smuggle twenty million dollars past DEA agents, the FBI, and rip-off artists, not to mention US customs and bank inspectors. Never again would he submit to this kind of pressure.

In Havana the *Rachelle* had also picked up Hocq's security chief, a tall forty-four-year-old Cuban named Jesse Borrega. Borrega, ex-army sergeant and former heavyweight boxer, had spent a week with his wife and children. He'd fought wars in Angola, Guatemala, Nicaragua and Peru. He'd been a Castro bodyguard. He was steady and calm, at ease wherever he happened to be.

An unassuming man, he refused to allow Hocq's outlandish behaviour to get to him. A year ago in Macao he'd taken a bullet meant for Hocq, killing the shooter before passing out. Martins admired Borrega's quiet professionalism but for some reason they'd never hit it off. Twice the Cuban had rejected generous offers to head security at Martins' castle, giving no reason for his decision. Borrega's reluctance to warm up to Martins was a disappointment, since the Cuban was the only man around Hocq worthy of respect.

Also in Havana, Martins and Hocq had attended a meeting between the slight, poker-loving Deng, one of the Golden Circle's new leaders, and Edmundo Colina, a plumpish thirty-eight-year-old bureaucrat from Cuba's official tourist agency. Cuba wanted to rebuild its tourist trade and Deng's people had millions of dollars to invest in the West. Hocq had set up the meeting, noting God Himself couldn't have ordained a more perfect union. The sooner both sides fell into bed, the sooner Martins and Hocq collected a five million finder's fee.

During the meeting Deng had been alert and watchful. He'd have to be thoroughly convinced before agreeing to anything. Forcing a course of action on him was impossible. Martins couldn't recall ever having met a stupid Triad leader.

As for Colina, the Cuban couldn't have been more accommodating. With Cuba desperate for hard currency, he'd promised Deng everything but the moon with a fence around it. For years he'd personally seen Martins' couriers safely in and out of Cuba. For a price Colina could be relied upon.

But at the conclusion of today's meeting there'd been no agreement. No reason to uncork the champagne and pass out those twisted black Cuban cigars Martins loved. Deng had the traditional Chinese mistrust of foreigners. He wasn't rushing into any deal until he'd exhaustively gone over every detail. He hadn't risen to the top of Hong Kong's underworld by being over-eager.

Martins had watched him listen politely, occasionally nodding his small head and, as usual, living at his own rhythm. Colina had offered to speak English but Deng had pleaded ignorance of the language. He would speak in Cantonese; Hocq and Martins would do him the courtesy of translating into English and Spanish. Both Martins and Hocq played along. Deng's English was perfect.

So was his Spanish, French, Russian, German and four Chinese dialects. He worked through interpreters because it was to his advantage. During translating and rephrasing, he'd size up the opposition, observe weak points and determine who was naughty or nice. Martins had to admire him. Deng was clever and smart enough to hide it.

Colina had salivated over the thought of Triad money pouring into Cuba. He was also dreaming of his end of the deal. Castro, his brother Raul, their generals, intelligence officers and secret police, were getting fat doing business with the Colombian drug cartel. But it was civil servants like Colina who did the work. Human nature being what it was, Martins was sure Colina was skimming some of the Colombian take for himself. The Triad millions offered a glorious opportunity to skim more.

Cuba's most important men, Colina promised, would safe-guard Triad's investments. These same men were protecting Chinese money and heroin passing through Cuba on the way to America. Cuba prided itself on taking care of its friends.

However, the cautious Deng had put the deal on hold, causing Martins to grind his teeth in disappointment. Forget Colina's promises of a rosy future. Deng was not going to make any arrangements until he'd had time to study the overall potential of Cuban tourism. And not before his Atlantic City deal had been completed.

"A wise man does not chase two rabbits at the same time," he said. "Any choice involves the possibility of error. One must minimise such possibilities. It is best to follow the gradual approach, to take one step at a time."

One step at a time. Martins' stomach had turned queasy. Was Deng addressing Colina? Or was he telling Martins and Hocq to concentrate on getting the thirty million into America. It wouldn't have surprised Martins if Deng knew Erica Styler was still aboard the *Rachelle*. Deng had the ability to guard his own secrets ferociously while knowing everything about everybody else.

He was no longer on the *Rachelle*, thank God. After the Colina meeting he'd left for Mexico City, travelling alone and appearing as innocuous as a puppy. From there he was to fly to New York for a meeting set up by Abby Langway with American and Chinese businessmen fronting the casino deal.

Before disembarking Deng wanted a status report on the smuggling of the bribe money. Just a spot quiz while he, Martins and Hocq stood on deck saying their goodbyes. Martins knew how distrusting the Triad could be so he'd warned Hocq to be ready. Charlie, bless him, had come through with flying colours.

"Now that the Americans have taken Noriega prisoner," Deng said, "are you still bringing money through Panama?"

Hocq shook his head. "We stopped using Panama before the American invasion. The country's a mess, especially the banking system. Without Noriega's protection banks have fallen apart. We saw it coming and advised our clients to make other arrangements."

Deng said, "I understand some Colombian drug dealers can't get their money out of America. Without Noriega, there's nowhere for them to go. Is this true?"

Hocq's smile was confident. "I warned them. In America these Colombians must now stand guard over millions of dollars hidden in their homes. They're frightened of American banks but with Noriega gone, they don't know where to send their cash."

Deng said, "And you still think it unwise for us to send any casino money directly to our Chinatown banks in New York and San Francisco?"

"Yes," Hocq said. "Your front men are under a microscope. American gaming commissions, the FBI, police, the media – each will go over your people with a fine-tooth comb. Any hint of suspicion and the deal is dead. Leave the casino money to us."

Martins said, "The FBI knows some Chinatown banks are Triad fronts. They could be watching your banks. You don't want the FBI to see you moving large amounts of money just as you're preparing to buy a casino."

"Exactly," Hocq said. "That's why I feel that once the money is in America, it must pass through legitimate businesses. Trust me."

Deng smiled. "We're all thieves here, Mr Hocq. Has there ever been trust among thieves? One should trust the friends of today as though they will be the enemies of tomorrow."

Before disembarking in Puerto Rico Abby Langway, Hocq's lawyer, also raised a question. He'd learned, courtesy of the gossipy Werner Tautz, that Erica Styler was being held prisoner on board the *Rachelle*. Martins had watched Langway's jaw drop and his face change colour. And he'd watched Langway try to convince Hocq to release Styler at once.

"Your opinion on law matters," Hocq had told the lawyer. "Your opinion on my personal life does not matter. It's never a good idea to provoke me. You should know that by now."

Martins had seen it coming. That slightly cross-eyed look Charlie got just before he went gaga. Langway recognised it too; he backed off in a hurry. Later when they were alone he said to Martins, "What the hell did she do to him? She's

59

locked in her cabin, under guard. What do I say if someone asks me about her?"

Martins smiled. "You lie. Saves long explanations. As a lawyer, you ought to know that."

At the ship's railing Martins looked over his shoulder at Castillo de la Fuerza, the four-hundred-year-old fort that was Cuba's oldest building. An impressive sight. Neither as fluid nor as graceful as forts in France, but impressive nevertheless. A giant Soviet oil tanker began entering the port, blotting out the view. The sea air was suddenly overpowered by the disturbing smell of oil.

Nails cleaned, Martins returned the file to a small leather case containing nail clippers, pen-knife, a small pair of scissors, and a spare file. He owned a dozen cases, usually travelling with three or four in his luggage. He'd always enjoyed the sleek look and solid feel of steel; its cold precision appealed to his exacting nature. Steel produced clean nails, to Martins' mind a mark of status.

From his shirt pocket he took out a pocket watch, a hundred-and-fifty-year-old Hampden, its gold-plated back and front engraved with roses and laurel wreaths. A short gold chain was attached to the stem. He pressed the stem with his thumb and the dial cover popped open. Almost five o'clock. His fax with the good news about Bendor should have arrived by now.

He closed the watch cover then turned the timepiece over and used a thumbnail pry to open the back cover. Inside the cover was an inscription: *For Albert from Fabienne. 25–12–75*. Her gift to him on their first Christmas together. He thought of what it had cost him to love her. *Love is too young to know what conscience is.*

He returned the watch to his shirt pocket, then used a silk handkerchief to wipe sweat from his neck. He was refolding the handkerchief when he saw Jesse Borrega walking towards him. The Cuban, curly-haired and nearly Martins' height, marched with long strides, oblivious of the ocean's sway and the June heat. An Israeli-made Desert Eagle .357 Magnum with a fourteen-inch barrel hung upside down from his shoulder holster. Somewhere on him, he carried two more handguns and a knife.

Stopping three feet away from Martins, Borrega leaned on the railing, watching from behind mirrored sunglasses as Havana receded in the distance. "Communications just beeped me. Fax coming in for you downstairs."

"Thanks. You look in on Miss Styler?"

Borrega stroked his thick black moustache. "Not my business. It becomes my business when her boyfriend sets foot on this ship."

"I see you've been talking to Tautz."

Borrega walked away without comment.

Martins thought, He knows she shouldn't be here. He knows Charlie's having one of his stupid moments. Borrega and Martins had one thing in common: they were both being forced to suffer a certain fool gladly.

On the sundeck, nail file in hand, a grim Martins sat in a deck chair and watched Hocq read the fax in silence.

Finished, Hocq handed the fax to Jesse Borrega then looked at Martins. "You sure you didn't decode it wrong? You could've made a mistake."

"He took out three guys," Borrega said. He nodded, one professional admiring the work of another.

Tautz, a Margarita in hand, reached for the fax. "Let me see that."

Borrega ignored him. Tautz let his empty hand fall.

"I have to check security," Borrega said to Hocq. "See if we need to make changes."

Hocq bit a thumbnail. "Think he'll come here?"

Borrega handed the fax to Martins. "He's a step closer, isn't he?"

Martins felt suddenly weary. "I've confirmed the fax. Bendor did kill three couriers. After that, he and his mother disappeared. No one seems to know where they've headed."

"He's heading here," Borrega said. "He's coming for his woman. And you."

Hocq folded his hands. "He can't get *me*, can he, Jesse? Can he?"

"You've hired me to see it doesn't happen. And that's what I intend to do."

Martins folded the fax. "I've told my people in the States to be on the lookout, to kill him on sight."

Tautz licked salt from the rim of his Margarita. "You bit the dog," he said to Martins, "and now the dog's coming to bite you."

Hocq rose and headed towards a staircase leading to the upper deck. Martins frowned. "Where're you going? We've things to go over. Bendor – "

"I'm going to play cards with Erica," Hocq said. "This business with Bendor is very stimulating. I'll be in her cabin. Don't disturb us."

Tautz leered. "Don't do anything I wouldn't do."

He turned to Martins, "You know, maybe Bendor isn't a dog after all. Maybe he's an elephant. Elephants have great memories, you know."

Borrega eyed both men then shook his head in dismissal. Seconds later he was on a staircase leading below deck. Tautz was now alone with Martins. And nervous. Quickly finishing his drink, he leaped from his chair and hurried below deck.

Alone, Martins looked out at the ocean. How easy it was for memory to drag one back to the past. He'd spent years building a safe life for Fabienne and himself. Years fighting off enemies. To survive, he'd become a wolf among wolves. Now he felt old and sad. For fifteen years he'd tried to escape the person he once was. And he'd tried to escape Simon Bendor.

He'd failed to elude either man.

5

Detroit, 1942

On a cold December dawn in a deserted alley a bony-faced black vagrant paused in the act of drinking from a discarded milk carton. He'd just heard the sound of a window-pane being broken. Over his shoulder he saw a naked white woman yelling in a cheap basement room. Getting beat on by her man, probably.

There was blood on her tits so maybe she'd been knifed too. The vagrant, an ex-jockey named Smokey Pendergrass, watched the woman yank on the window bars and holler up a storm. Wasn't Smokey's problem. Nigger shouldn't get mixed up with white women.

He saw a husky white man yank the woman away from the window and punch her in the face. Smokey wanted no part of this. He crouched between two garbage cans, merged with the darkness, and stared into the bedroom. He'd watch these two fools and that's all.

The husky white man was Willard Crews, a thick-necked thirty-year-old Detroit trolley driver, who minutes ago had removed a baseball bat from a closet, and entered Mary Morell's bedroom in the basement of a rundown rooming house facing the Detroit River.

The bat was split at one end, and if the drunken Crews hadn't been so eager to kill Mary Morell he might have taken time to search this rat-infested cubby hole for a more stable weapon. But dedicated as he was to killing the slender twenty-six-year-old barmaid, his ex-lover, Crews failed to notice the imperfections of the bat he'd given their nine-year-old son Edwin for Christmas.

Crews struck Mary Morell on the head as she lay sleeping, the naked Edwin cradled in her arms. The end portion of the bat broke off and flew onto a nearby dresser. Mary Morell woke up screaming, forcing Edwin to sit upright, suddenly wide awake as he stared at his father in bug-eyed horror.

In desperation a nude Mary Morell grabbed a blood-stained pillow and swung it at Crews, knocking the remains of the bat from his hand. Then she rolled out of bed screaming, one step bringing her to a curtain hiding a barred window. She tore away the curtain, hoping to catch the attention of beggars sleeping in the alley behind the rooming house. She quickly lifted the window, leaving bloody handprints on the panes.

Pulling her away from the window Crews drove a fist into her nose, breaking it. Another facial blow dropped the barmaid to the floor. Crazed with pain, Mary Morell fought for her life. She kicked out with her bare feet, pushing Crews into the dresser where he lost his balance.

Scrambling to her feet she grabbed a hand mirror and struck Crews in the face. Mouth bleeding, he backed into the bed then stared at his blood-covered palm. "Bitch!" he yelled at Mary Morell. "Want to play rough, we'll play rough."

Mary Morell raced towards the bedroom door. Run upstairs, she thought. Wake the other boarders. Or run outside and get help from workers unloading trucks at the meat market across the street. Damn Willard Crews for being a drunk and for being too quick to hit women.

For her part, she was too quick to take up with men. Her mother had warned her about taking up with any pair of pants that crossed her path. Mary had left Canada to get away from that sanctimonious old bitch.

Mary was near the bedroom entrance when Crews grabbed her shoulder and pulled her to the floor. Crews had only one thought in mind, to punish this tramp for having sex with Eddie. Straddling Mary's chest, he punched her in the face and banged her head against the floor. Seconds later she stopped moving. Her face was swollen and puffy. She wasn't so pretty now.

She moaned. Bitch wasn't dead, not by a long shot. Then

she lay still. She was still unconscious when Crews used a lamp cord to strangle her to death.

Strangled her for defiling Edwin, their son. Her own flesh and blood.

Until he was a teenager Edwin Morell lived with Mary Morell's widowed mother in Canada, in the southern Ontario city of Windsor on the Detroit River. Like Detroit, located a mile away, Ontario was an automobile-producing town, turning out Canadian-made Fords, Chryslers and GM vehicles.

Edwin's grandmother ran a boarding house for auto workers. She forced him to earn his keep by cleaning guest rooms, serving diners, chopping wood. She spoke only French and was obsessed with personal cleanliness, a fixation passed on to Edwin.

At sixteen he stood well over six feet and weighed more than fourteen stone. He worked part-time in a Ford plant and played high-school football. He was easily bored, insensitive, and enjoyed intimidating people. Having gone through an abundance of pain, he thought nothing of making others suffer.

Sex was his obsession. For him, there was no greater pleasure. His relationships were casual, limited to prostitutes, waitresses and barmaids, women to whom he felt no emotional attachment. He kept notebooks on his sex-life, describing each woman and his sexual relationship with her in detail. His tastes often ran to the shocking and forbidden.

When he was seventeen his grandmother inspected his room in his absence and turned up the notebooks. What she read left her disgusted. The boy needed to be straightened out before he ended up in the electric chair like his father.

Wrapping the notebooks in newspaper, she hurried to the kitchen. This smut belonged in the fires of hell. For now her wood-burning stove would have to do. In the kitchen she locked the door to keep from being disturbed.

Rage had blinded her to caution. She never saw flames from the stove touch the sleeves of her dressing gown. When she noticed that her clothing was on fire, the flames had spread along one arm. The sight of her burning gown caused the old woman to panic.

She leaped backwards, away from the stove, and bumped into a butcher's block, overturning a pot of cooking grease onto herself. Grease fed the flames on her gown. Her screams attracted boarders but before they could break down the kitchen door she was severely burned. Two days later she died without regaining consciousness.

Immediately after his grandmother's funeral, Edwin returned to Detroit and to a country more suited to his aggressive temperament. Canada was lifeless, its weather endlessly cold, the people tiresome. He'd cleaned his last toilet and worked on his last automobile assembly line. As the bus left Windsor he began cleaning his nails, removing the last of Canada from his life.

In Detroit he attended a junior college where he studied history, psychology, and sought to improve his French, a language in which he was already fluent. He also played football, starring as an offensive tackle until a broken collarbone forced him to quit. The three thousand dollars from his grandmother's estate didn't last long. Still, with a growing confidence in his intelligence, Edwin committed himself to finishing school.

The police department and its cadet programme solved his money problems. They paid his tuition and most of his living expenses. In return he performed clerical work at a precinct house, took criminology courses, and pledged to join the police force after graduation. Impressed by police camaraderie he eagerly kept his pledge.

As a beat cop he delivered babies, broke up cockfights, was shot twice, and endured the unforgettable odour of decaying human flesh when he found abandoned corpses. He dealt with crazies, druggies, beggars, drunks. As protection against filth and disease, he carried two pairs of surgical gloves and cleaned his nails after every tour of duty. A job perk was the sex he received from prostitutes in return for letting them work unmolested.

He made detective in three years, was assigned to homicide, and capitalised on a wealth of experience as a beat cop. He had learned a lot about police work, about crime, and even more about human nature. Nothing shocked him.

His wife, however, was more easily floored by destiny and happenstance. Morell's marriage to a nightclub dancer ended when she arrived home unexpectedly to find him in their bedroom with two prostitutes. He was naked from the waist down; one prostitute was naked, handcuffed and blindfolded. She was also bruised and weeping. A second prostitute, a teenage black girl, was gagged and tied to a chair.

A calm Morell said to his stunned spouse, "*So?*"

He developed an obsession for information, becoming an expert at collecting and analysing it. Physical evidence could only help to secure a conviction; to put a perp away you needed a witness who'd seen the crime and was willing to tell all. Ninety per cent of criminal cases were solved with the help of informants. The better the informants, the better the detective.

He used his informants, taking care not to let them use him. The average informant was a spiteful little weasel out for number one. He or she wanted revenge, money, power, or the turn-on that came with being around cops. Women made the best informants because revenge was usually the only weapon left to them.

In his mid-thirties Morell was approached by Maggie Seay, an energetic, red-haired twenty-two-year-old who'd been a prostitute since she was fourteen. He found her to be sensual, playful, and earthy. He'd seen enough working girls to know this one was cream. Trashy cream, but cream nonetheless, and with a world class butt.

She'd come to Morell because two Arabs had tried to kill her and she expected them to try again. Why Morell? Because he had a reputation for taking care of working girls.

"That's because working girls take care of me," he said.

She held his gaze. "First, let's talk about how I got jammed up. Then we'll discuss what your help's going to cost me, and whether or not I think it's worth it."

She worked for Starlight Escort Service, major credit cards

accepted, and business accounts welcome. Two weeks ago the agency had sent her to a Woodward Avenue hotel for a date with George Bishara, a small fortyish Arab. Bishara smelled, didn't know what he was doing in bed, and took forever to do it.

Maggie had been ready to leave when Bishara rushed to answer a loud knocking at the suite door. She thought, vice detectives. She could lose her earnings to a greedy badge and be forced to give him free head as well. The caller turned out to be Bishara's brother Anwar, a roly-poly fifty-year-old with oily skin.

The brothers started quarrelling over money, with Anwar complaining he'd been cheated out of his share in an insurance scam. Maggie knew she'd heard too much. Smelly George knew it too, and refused to let her leave. He backed off when she reminded him the agency's girls travelled with an armed driver. Hers was waiting in front of the hotel and if she didn't come down, he'd come up. She wasn't bullshitting. In exchange for half the girls' earnings, the agency also furnished security.

"I wasn't going to rat them out," she told Morell. "You think I want cops poking around my life? But right after this, I nearly got killed by a hit-and-run driver. Then somebody pushes me in front of a trolley. I know its those scumbucket Arabs. Can you get them off my back?"

Meanwhile, George Bishara continued to call the agency and ask for her. Maggie kept turning him down. Morell asked for her phone number, saying he'd see what he could come up with.

They went to bed two days later, when he had something to tell her.

"The Bishara brothers own two Detroit restaurants," he said, "as well as video stores in three states. Not bad for two ragheads from Marseille who've only been here five years. In that time they've filed a dozen insurance claims for fire and burglary, collecting nearly two million dollars. Nobody's caught them dicking the insurance companies, which doesn't mean they're not doing it. Did you know Detroit has the largest Arab population in America?"

Maggie said, "Can't you arrest them because of what I heard?"

"Your word against theirs. And you don't have any corroboration. Given your record you'd have trouble getting the DA to believe Nixon's still President."

"My record?"

"You've been popped for prostitution, credit card theft, drug possession. Getting back to the Bisharas, everybody's got civil rights these days. Blacks, fags, long-haired dopers protesting the War. I can't arrest the Bisharas because one doesn't change his underwear and the other's got pimples. Takes more than that. Could be they're watching you, which means they've seen you talking to a cop."

"That's good, isn't it?"

"Yes and no. Might scare them off. Or make them antsy enough to ice you so they can stay out of the slammer. Be very careful about your dates." Morell enjoyed sharing a woman sexually involved with other men.

Maggie Seay was an intriguing combination of sex goddess and lost child. She was like Morell in some ways – complex, moody, and a loner with an insightful mind. She appeared to understand his aversion to bleeding hearts and wise-ass lawyers who were putting criminals back on the street. He still liked his job, but it was becoming depressing. Maggie was a welcome change at the end of a hard day.

She treated Morell to the first Christmas tree he'd had in years. They decorated it together then made love on the floor, bodies illuminated by blinking tree lights. Later, she purred like a kitten as he filed her nails.

Three weeks after they met Morell waited for her in his apartment. He had a gift for her, a black leather jacket lined with rabbit fur, a five hundred dollar buy a fence let him have for fifty. After she arrived they'd order Chinese food.

Tonight she was an hour late. Morell telephoned the agency; they hadn't heard from her either. Apparently the driver, Paul Rovin, was missing as well. Morell, known to the agency as Maggie's cop friend, got the client's name and the address of the hotel where the date was taking place.

At the hotel, he by-passed the elevator, walked up six flights of stairs and after listening at the client's door and hearing nothing, he slipped the lock with a credit card. Gun in hand, he entered the room then closed the door behind him. The light was on. He leaned against the door and listened, fierce eyes taking in everything.

The room was empty. There was an unmade bed, a stuffed chair with frayed armrests, an empty closet, and a small desk in front of the only window. On the night table a half bottle of vodka rested on a Bible. A woman's handbag was atop a black and white television set. Maggie's. She was here.

He found her in the tiny bathroom. Her nude body, a pair of panty hose tightened around the neck, hung from a shower head. Her clothes were scattered on the bathroom floor. Morell found no signs of a struggle. Eyes closed, he slumped against the door jamb. This wasn't dead meat. This was Maggie.

He left the hotel room, not worrying about fingerprints. Detroit was shivering under a record January freeze so he'd worn gloves. Outside he walked the streets absentmindedly. Eventually he found a bar and made an anonymous telephone call to the police, giving the location of Maggie's body.

Then he returned to the hotel, where he took up a position across the street, waiting in twenty below zero cold. When he heard the wail of a police siren he whispered, "Goodbye kid," and left.

An autopsy ruled Maggie's death as suicide. She hadn't left a note, but most suicides didn't.

Unfortunately, the coroner was an incompetent rummy who would have been bounced years ago if he hadn't had city hall connections. He was a seventy-year-old boozehound who'd bungled his way through a quickie postmortem on Maggie, misreading all available evidence. Morell knew someone had murdered her and made it appear as if she'd killed herself.

The body of Paul Rovin, Maggie's forty-eight-year-old driver, turned up three days later, stuffed in the trunk of his limousine. Someone had pumped two bullets in his heart, stripped the car and dumped it in a black ghetto. Rovin had been an ex-con and known druggie. Police assumed he'd got ripped off making a buy.

On his own time Morell investigated Maggie's murder. No one at Starlight Escorts had met her last date, a first-time customer named Dudley Ganz. A local real estate agent Ganz had telephoned the hotel for a reservation, pre-paying in cash via messenger.

When Morell confronted the balding, forty-year-old Ganz, the real estate agent denied knowing Maggie. He had a valid alibi for the night of her death. The Ganz family had been in Ontario on a skiing weekend, a fact confirmed by Morell. Ganz and Starlight Escorts had been used to lure Maggie Seay into a trap. Morell asked if Ganz knew the Bishara brothers.

The real estate agent knew them. He'd recently dropped the Arabs as clients, having gone to court to collect back rent, and to stop them from making unauthorised renovations on his properties. Few real estate agents dealt with the Bisharas more than once.

The quickest way to get information on anyone, Morell knew, was to follow the money trail. If the Bisharas were stealing, it meant they needed the money. He learned they owed back state taxes and money to restaurant suppliers. They were also heavy gamblers. Where were they when Maggie died? Supposedly at George's house, working on tax returns with wives and children as witnesses.

Morell persisted, telephoning Marseille police and in fluent French asking if the Bisharas had a record over there. No, said police. Legally they were as clean as a whistle. However, the rest of the family was another story.

Daddy had operated a hot car ring active along the Riviera during the fifties. Gang members, French and Arabs, specialised in snatching the latest model sports cars for resale in North Africa. Mother had kept the gang's books, skilfully depicting the family's auto repair business as a legitimate undertaking. Brothers George and Anwar had worked for the car ring as thieves and enforcers.

But according to Marseille cops, neither brother had a criminal record. On three separate occasions witnesses about

71

to give evidence against them had been found dead. Two had been found hanging from bathroom shower heads.

Six years ago Mr and Mrs Bishara had been killed in Tunis by a car bomb believed to have been planted by Corsican gangsters. The family had been passing counterfeit money along the Riviera, with habitual gamblers George and Anwar dumping the phony cash in mob-owned casinos. To avoid their parents' fate the brothers had emigrated to America.

Morell wanted the district attorney's office to exhume Maggie's body and have it examined by a different coroner. To do that he called in a marker from King Somerville, a short, forty-year-old Irishman and ambitious district attorney. Morell had squashed a shoplifting charge against Somerville's wife. The mick owed him.

After exhuming Maggie's body Somerville assigned a younger coroner to conduct a new postmortem. This one found evidence indicating she'd died from a punch to the throat. She had been killed prior to being hanged. Maggie had been murdered.

The motive, Morell told Somerville, was a fear she might blow the whistle on an insurance scam. Somerville, no fool, asked about Morell's relationship with the dead girl. She was an informant, the detective said. Just another snitch. Somerville grinned. "She must have been some piece of ass."

"She brought me a Christmas tree once," Morell said.

Then he asked another favour: permission to interrogate one of the Bishara brothers, two men with a motive for killing Maggie. Morell suspected the hot-tempered George of having committed the murder, but chose to ignore him for the moment. Instead he zeroed in on Anwar who'd been angry at being short-changed by his brother.

Morell broke Anwar in less than an hour. He began by placing a telephone book on Anwar's head then pounding it with a blackjack. The Arab was left with a bad headache, a fear of Morell, and no scars he could point to in court.

"I know about your last scheme," Morell told Anwar. "The one involving a burglary at your Fort Wayne restaurant. A phoney robbery set up by you. The one where George cheated you out of your share."

Anwar blinked. Gotcha, Morell thought.

"George has been fucking you all along," the detective said. "He's been taking the lion's share of your scams and you never knew it. Think I'm lying? Take a look at this."

He showed Anwar letters from insurance companies offering the real figures on these phoney claims. Figures indicating that brother George had been holding out on Anwar and paying him less than the claim was worth. Anwar's face grew redder by the minute. Morell filed his nails. He'd made up the figures himself.

Desire for revenge and fear of Morell prodded Anwar into pointing the finger at his brother. He signed a statement naming George as the killer of Maggie Seay and Paul Rovin. Anwar claimed he hadn't killed anybody.

But he had stolen Dudley Ganz's credit card number and helped George break into Ganz's office when they knew the real estate agent would be in Canada. In Ganz's office George had tinkered with Ganz's call-forwarding service, programming the call from Starlight Escorts to Anwar who was at another number. Anwar then pretended to be Dudley Ganz.

At the hotel, when Maggie tried to escape, the volatile George had punched her in the throat, killing her instantly. Anwar also pinned Paul Rovin's murder on George but admitted his complicity in helping to make Maggie's death look like a suicide.

The Bishara case made headlines in Detroit, offering murder, sex, and money, along with a crusading district attorney who'd bucked the system and won. George Bishara received life in prison, his brother Anwar a ten-year sentence in return for having cooperated with the authorities. With Morell's approval, Somerville took most of the credit.

A week after the trial Morell was offered a new job. He was interviewed by two well-dressed men claiming to represent the federal government but who remained deliberately vague about which agency. The older of the pair, a long-faced man calling himself Pfeil, said the job included foreign travel, required a knowledge of at least one foreign language, and involved working closely with the US State Department.

His companion was Leveen, a flap-eared man with glasses,

who claimed their agency appreciated men good at interrogation. Morell was known to be adept at getting suspects to tell all.

"How'd you hear about me?" Morell said.

Pfeil tugged at a hairy ear. "This Arab thing. The FBI gets fingerprints from every major case in the country which includes the ones you work on. Any time they come across something we might be interested in, they pass it on. You reopened a closed investigation, worked with the French police, then finished things off with a first-class interrogation on a camel fucker. Don't tell us about Somerville. He wouldn't be where he is if he hadn't married a judge's daughter. You've got a future. But not as a cop."

Morell looked at his nails. "You know something I don't?"

Pfeil said, "With luck, you might make lieutenant but that's as high as you'll go. Your background and your interest in bimbos works against you. You've levelled off, whether you know it or not."

"You telling me I should pack it in?"

Big-eared Leveen said, "Detroit's a mess and getting worse and you know it. Three years ago, 1967, you had the worst race riot the country's ever seen. Whites can't get out of this town fast enough. Sooner or later you're going to have a black mayor, black city council and a black police commissioner. When that happens, bunky, you're dead."

Morell nodded. City Hall was spending nearly its entire budget constructing highways out to the suburbs so that the whites could travel between their jobs and safe all-white neighbourhoods. Forget about money for police salaries.

Pfeil said, "We'll start you at twice your current salary."

"So nobody likes my choice of women," Morell said. "You guys are thorough, I'll give you that."

"We get the job done," Leveen said. "You'll have a free hand working for us, something you don't have now."

Morell folded his hands in his lap. He loved watching government types act like their counterparts in the movies. They probably ran films at home and practised making faces in the mirror.

"Why is working for you such a joy?" he said.

74

Pfeil beamed. "Because we get to make up the rules as we go along. You might say its our job to see that no organisation becomes bigger than we are."

"I don't remember that being in the constitution," Morell said.

"The constitution's what we say it is," Pfeil said.

"So I've heard," Morell said. "I suppose your offer beats eating off the floor. Me and the CIA. Who'd have thought it?"

6

Saigon, March 1975

Simon Bendor's ultimatum mentioned Morell's affair with a female prisoner, making the ultimatum both embarrassing and menacing. Bendor had interrupted this morning's CIA briefing by threatening to kill Morell because of this affair.

Morell didn't like ultimatums. But he'd heard this one out. Bendor commanded attention. Only yesterday he had slipped past armed guards protecting a Chinatown villa, slit the throat of a Saigon banker running money couriers to the Vietcong in Cambodia then escaped unseen.

Morell now considered himself at risk from Bendor, a slim nineteen-year-old from Hawaii and the agency's top assassin in South-east Asia. In the past four months Bendor had killed twenty-two people on CIA assignment. You didn't take on someone like that unless you had a sure way of killing him. Morell had given the matter some thought and was convinced he could liquidate Mr Bendor. Tomorrow Bendor was going to die.

From a window of his American embassy office Morell eyed the mass of Vietnamese lined up outside the compound for exit visas. He tightened his fist around a necklace of small blue pearls. The necklace belonged to Fabienne Bao, the enemy prisoner with whom he was having an affair. She was eighteen, half his age, and the most beautiful woman he'd seen. He'd been drawn to her like a needle to a magnet.

She was a member of Unit B-36, the mysterious North Vietnamese intelligence service that had penetrated South

Vietnam's government and intelligence services at the highest level. Morell had connived to block her return to the Communists because he'd fallen in love with her, a love he could neither control nor overcome. He'd also kept Fabienne to prevent North Vietnam from executing her as a collaborator.

He was a CIA agent assigned to South Vietnamese intelligence and one of 1100 Americans still in Saigon two years after US troop withdrawal. Officially Americans were advisers to the South. Unofficially, they worked with any South Vietnamese agency fighting the Communists.

Morell's job called for him to interrogate the most prominent enemy prisoners. In five years with the agency he'd instructed the secret police and intelligence services of a dozen countries in interrogation techniques, counter-intelligence, and in maintaining internal security. He'd also trained government death squads.

He saw himself as a patriot helping free nations to defend themselves from terrorism and anarchy. It didn't bother him that interrogation was another name for torture. Torture was the best way to maintain an orderly society while sending a message to the opposition. In Saigon Morell had delivered this message so effectively that he was known as "Krait", after the Vietnamese snake whose deadly bite killed in seconds.

Fabienne Bao wasn't the only prisoner the Communists wanted to retrieve immediately. They also wanted Quang Bai, a sweet-faced twenty-year-old Saigon photographer who Morell had beaten into revealing his true identity as an enemy agent. Quang was the only son of a founder of the Vietcong, a general who'd lost most of his family in the war. With a Communist victory a foregone conclusion, the general wanted to share this triumph with his beloved Quang.

In exchange the Communists had offered four American POWs, one of whom was Pete Sanchez, the chunky thirty-year-old Texan who was Simon Bendor's commanding officer and close friend. It was Sanchez who two weeks ago had stayed behind to cover Bendor's retreat from a Central Highlands village with a wounded American colonel who'd been the CIA province adviser. Bendor and the colonel had made it to the Air America helicopter just as the North Vietnamese overran Sanchez' position.

Bendor had delivered this morning's threat in front of several agents who'd backed off from Morell as though he'd dropped his pants and shown his haemorrhoids.

"You've blocked this exchange at every turn," Bendor had said. "First you convinced the embassy we weren't being offered enough in exchange for the Bao woman. Then you claimed we couldn't let her go because she was giving us valuable information. You're stonewalling because you're fucking her. Pete Sanchez took a bullet for me. Either hand Bao over to her people or I'll kill you."

A shaky Morell thought, no, buddy boy, *you're* dead. Tomorrow it's your ass.

Bendor was a contract agent, a freelancer attached to an ultra secret CIA unit unknown even to Congress. The unit, a brainchild of the agency's Health and Alteration Committee, had no official name. Someone had tabbed it the Merry Pranksters and the name stuck. Name aside, the unit was little more than an execution squad. In Saigon, the members took their orders directly from the CIA Station Chief or his number two man.

Simon Bendor was the stand-out among the dozen or so group members, considered little more than lunatics with a death wish. As their martial arts instructor he was unbeatable; as a killer, he was even more effective. He was fearless, cold-blooded, and when not on the job, he kept to himself. It was expected he would die violently.

His interest in a POW exchange had begun the minute he'd learned the North wanted the return of Fabienne and Quang Bai. Anticipating a collision course Morell had become interested in Bendor. First move: access Bendor's file for a hurried assessment of his character.

Bendor, Simon. Born 1956 in California, where he was a high-school gymnastic champion and amateur boxer. Father Shea Bendor flew with British RAF during World War II. Mother Alexis Bendor taught English literature and foreign languages at Santa Monica College. Also worked briefly as WWII code-breaker for OSS. Family moved to Hawaii when young Bendor was sixteen. Father flew for various airlines and mother taught at Hawaii U. Both continued to take assignments for the CIA.

Simon Bendor became Hawaii's top high-school athlete, receiving dozens of track scholarships to island and mainland colleges. Around this time he suffered a serious surfing accident when his legs were nearly sliced off by razor sharp coral. Doctors had recommended amputating both legs to save his life. Mrs Bendor opposed them and arranged for naval surgeons to operate on her son, saving his legs.

More bad luck for the Bendor family. Shea Bendor was killed flying guns to Indonesia at the agency's request. Mrs Bendor then set up house with a Honolulu local named Victor Yashima, a forty-four-year-old Japanese-American fish exporter and grower of prize-winning roses. Agency investigators listed him as her long-time lover.

Yashima's family history was uncommon, to say the least. For starters, his real name was Kanna and he was wanted for murder. During World War II the family had been sent to a California internment camp. After months of imprisonment the family had made an attempted breakout. All, save one, had been shot to death.

John Kanna, alias Victor Yashima, had been the only survivor. He'd managed to escape from the camp, killing two guards in the process. Later he added another victim, a San Francisco lawyer who'd been entrusted with the family land. The lawyer, it seems, had turned out to be a thief. He'd sold the Kannas' land then pocketed the proceeds. Fearing retribution, he paid guards at the internment camp to kill the Kannas.

The lawyer's fear of reprisal was not misplaced. The peaceful appearing Kannas were descended from *ninjas*, Japan's fabled medieval spies and assassins. They also followed the Mikkyo school of Buddhism, a combination of martial arts, black arts and supernatural healing. Victor Yashima had passed on this knowledge to Simon Bendor who'd turned out to be a stellar pupil.

Yashima himself wasn't teaching much these days. A year ago in Honolulu a crazed Vietnam vet, thinking he was attacking a Vietcong stronghold, had shot up a Buddhist temple, killing Yashima and three others. Morell had a similar fate in mind for Bendor.

The CIA agent decided that Bendor could best be disposed of by using his training against him. Morell saw Bendor as an adrenalin junkie, a man hooked on excitement and ready to gamble with his life at a minute's notice. Why not set a trap and bait it with the one thing Bendor found irresistible, namely danger?

In his embassy office Morell touched a plastic window and felt the vibrations caused by Communist artillery shelling the city's outskirts. The eastern perimeter had just come under attack by American fighter-bombers, captured aircraft manned by North Vietnamese pilots. Sixteen North Vietnamese battalions – 140,000 men – were moving to encircle the city. South Vietnamese generals, corrupt and incompetent most of them, were claiming they could win the war if given more American money. This theory was too feeble-minded to merit a response.

On the desk behind Morell was a telephone he'd just taken out of a locked desk drawer. This was his private line, its number unknown to the embassy and most agency personnel. He expected a call momentarily, one concerning his participation tomorrow in a robbery. He didn't know all the details but he knew he stood to make a bundle. In Saigon anyone in a position to get rich was doing it while they could.

He planned to make his escape immediately after the robbery, taking Fabienne with him. He didn't like leaving American POWs in enemy hands but he saw no other way of holding onto Fabienne. Morell knew if Pete Sanchez died in captivity, Bendor would hound him into the ground. But a dead Bendor couldn't hound anybody.

To calm himself Morell began filing his nails. *Fabienne*. Seductive and moody, vulnerable and distant. Above all, addictive and, in the end, undefinable. With her, passion had entered his lonely life for the first time.

He'd never seen anyone more beautiful. She was Eurasian, the daughter of a wealthy French importer and his Vietnamese mistress, both killed in the war. As a staunch Marxist, she was committed to Ho Chi Minh's plan to eliminate all Western influence in South-east Asia. Her cell operated in Saigon, collecting intelligence while liquidating South Vietnamese VIPs.

Her beauty was Fabienne's power. To expose double agents she'd become the mistress of a South Vietnamese intelligence officer earlier this year. When she'd learned all she needed to know, the intelligence officer and the doubles were eliminated. She had seduced a South Vietnamese code clerk into defecting; she'd charmed a Vietnamese interpreter into giving her information on Communist prisoners being held in South Vietnamese interrogation centres.

Morell stopped filing his nails and picked up her pearls. If Fabienne hadn't been so beautiful she'd never have been captured. She'd attracted the attention of a French diplomat who'd learned her true identity through Communist contacts. When she'd resisted his advances he'd betrayed her to South Vietnamese intelligence.

Revenge, however, brought the diplomat an unforeseen complication. Fabienne's cell had castrated him then hacked off his head.

Morell had set out to turn Fabienne into a traitor. His goal: force her to identify enemy agents who had infiltrated the South's presidential cabinet. Anyone in covert work was afraid or paranoid; the breathtaking Miss Bao was too young to be as audacious as she believed herself to be. Morell decided to alternate psychological pressure with physical torture.

He spent three days interrogating her for long hours, allowing her to sleep, only to wake her minutes later. He placed a heavily moistened black bag over her face, bringing her to the point of suffocation. She panicked. He removed the bag, watching as she sucked in air. She was starting to get the message. So was Morell who noticed her sexual response, something she frantically tried to hide.

He switched to the unexpected. He removed her from a

small prison cell, one in which she'd only been able to sit or lie down curled up. She was then placed in a hotel across from the Presidential Palace. This left her even more fearful. She was now surrounded by luxury.

Morell had booked her in a two bedroom suite overlooking a courtyard restaurant. She had new linen, fresh flowers, a closet of stylish women's clothing, baskets of fresh fruit, and a well-stocked bar. Two Vietnamese maids stood by awaiting instructions. One handed Fabienne a cassette recorder and several tapes.

Morell spoke to the stunned Fabienne in French. "If you want anything there are busboys on duty around the clock."

She trembled, not knowing what to say.

Morell smiled. The Vietnamese were suckers for affection. Show them a little kindness and they turned into puppies. They were traditionally brutal to their enemies and expected the same treatment when captured. A little tenderness went a long way.

"We're in the same boat," Morell said to Fabienne. "We both take orders. Understand, what I did was business, not personal. I like you, as a matter of fact."

She found her voice. "You do?"

"I respect you for not breaking."

Bullshit. Sooner or later, Krait broke them all. He could have pushed her into a nervous breakdown without any trouble. In Brazil he'd worked on a female journalist for thirty-six hours straight, only to have her go insane.

Intuitive and selfish, Fabienne quickly sized up the situation. As an agent she'd found it difficult keeping her guard up all the time. Now it appeared she could relax. The American's eyes were glued to her.

Morell said, "I don't think you want to be an agent. Don't get me wrong. You did well but it's time to consider the future. What are you going to do when the war ends?"

He lit a cigarette. "After your armies get here, Saigon's going to be dangerous for a woman. Were I to let you walk out of here, you'd have a hard time convincing your people

82

you haven't talked. I have a reputation for breaking prisoners. Your side's going to assume the worst."

Fabienne said, "Are you offering to protect me?" Perhaps it was time to think about the future.

"I enjoy taking care of women," Morell said.

She held his gaze. "Do you?"

"Why don't I call room service and have them send up some food? You like champagne?"

Their affair began the next day, Morell believing there were no more sexual surprises only to learn he was wrong. *She lay on her back, legs wrapped high around his back, and gently guided his testicles between her vaginal lips. With the shaft of his penis resting against her clitoris, she set the pace, gently rotating her hips as she sucked his fingers. Where did you learn that, he asked. My father, she said. Before Morell could say anything he ejaculated, an orgasm so strong he nearly passed out.*

Her only desire was her own pleasure but she accepted pain willingly, a sign of submission Morell required in his women.

Within a week she had told him everything: codes, safe house locations, the name of her paymaster. She gave him the names of her cell members who were then captured or killed. She gave him the names of prominent South Vietnamese officials who were double agents. Another successful interrogation for Krait.

Morell had turned Fabienne. At the same time, he'd met a woman who'd awoken an unbelievable passion in him, one who could provoke him into doing anything. North Vietnam branded Fabienne a traitorous whore, adding her name to a blood list of those to be executed after the war. She was *hoi chanh*, a defector.

"You've nowhere else to go," Morell said. "Your place is with me now." Eighteen years old, and she had him thinking they had a future together. He didn't feel rational any more.

And Fabienne?

"For me everything is clear because I love you," she said. "You will make everything all right."

*   *   *

When his private embassy phone rang Morell squeezed his nail file until it dug into his palm. Then he picked up the receiver and waited for the caller to speak.

"Edwin? It's Charles."

"Charlie. We still on for today?"

"Five this afternoon. My villa." Charlie Hocq was in his late twenties, a small Eurasian dismissed by most Americans as a homosexual half-wit in a white linen suit. Morell knew better.

Hocq was a financial genius with a talent for turning schemes into money. He was one of Saigon's most prominent investment bankers and among other things he laundered CIA money on the black market. He could have left the city at any time but chose to remain, seeing the chaos around him as an opportunity to get rich.

Morell gripped the receiver. "Is our little project on for tomorrow as well?"

"Of course. Charles knows what he's doing."

That third person crap again. Charlie was an oddball whose weird habits included speaking of himself in the third person. He was also paranoid, conniving, and sometimes downright diabolical.

"See you at five." Morell hung up. Last chance to pull out. But he couldn't. Not if he wanted Fabienne. He looked at her pearls. When in doubt, play to win.

Charles Hocq fingered a thin gold chain hanging from his neck. "With any luck you'll leave Saigon with something like twenty million dollars."

Morell whistled. Incredible. He had expected to make money from Charlie's deal but nothing like this.

Morell said, "Twenty million dollars. You sure?"

"Twenty million dollars for twenty minutes' work, maybe less. A million dollars a minute. Uncommon wages, wouldn't you say?"

The two were in Hocq's villa, in a sunken living room facing Saigon's waterfront. Through a picture window a Russian freighter could be seen hauling anchor in preparation for sailing on the evening tide. Morell had just three hours to

84

get back to his hotel before evening curfew, announced by three thirty-second blasts on the city's sirens.

Hocq said, "I get even. You get rich. Actually, we both get rich."

Morell blew cigarette smoke at a wooden ceiling fan. Charlie was feuding with one of Saigon's power brokers, an assistant to South Vietnam's president. Feuds were nothing new over here; arguments went on forever between religious groups, political parties, families and individuals. Outsiders like Morell were asking for trouble if they became involved. But for twenty million dollars he'd get involved in anybody's feud.

Through Charlie he'd made money selling dollars on the black market. Charlie had also been his guide through the corruption, chaos, and excitement that was Saigon. Charlie knew everything about everybody, qualifying him as a first-class informant. In return for information about Saigon's movers and shakers, Morell passed on CIA intelligence for Hocq's business use. Hocq was also allowed unrestricted use of CIA owned airlines, allowing him to travel securely and in secret.

As an added bonus Morell furnished identification papers Hocq needed to by-pass roadblocks in and out of Saigon. Their relationship worked because each knew the value of mutual exploitation.

"Twenty million is your share from the robbery," Hocq said. "I also have the half million in cash you requested for expenses. Take that with you when you leave this evening. Since the robbery was my idea everything else is mine."

"I can live with twenty million," Morell said. "My men are ready. I just have to tell them where and when."

"Excellent. You'll earn your money. You'll be putting your life on the line."

Morell thought, first Bendor and now Charlie tell me to watch my ass. And all because he wanted Fabienne.

"I know the risks," Morell said, "but I'm still going through with it. I can't afford to hang around Saigon much longer." He especially didn't want to be here when people started inquiring into Simon Bendor's death.

85

"Did you contact your doctor friend?" Morell asked.

"Everything's arranged. You'll have the operation on his Brazilian ranch. You'll recuperate there as well. He's good, so it'll cost you plenty."

"Plastic surgery's only the beginning. I'm going for a complete renovation. Weight loss, new name, the works."

"Does this mean you'll be a virgin again? Speaking of the untouched and the unspoiled, when may I expect Fabienne?"

Morell carefully stubbed out his cigarette. "Tomorrow before the job. I'll bring her here, as agreed."

Charlie had insisted on *protecting* Fabienne until Morell completed his part in the deal. Morell, however, knew the real reason Charlie wanted Fabienne near him tomorrow. He was protecting himself against a double-cross.

Charlie survived because he trusted no one. He'd come a long way from the little boy whose Chinese father had been institutionalised with mental problems and whose French mother had abandoned him and his sister. There was more to Charlie than just being a social climber.

Morell enjoyed watching him weasel his way into the lives of Saigon's rulers. Charlie telephoned them daily, courted them with bribes and expensive gifts. He had them to his lavish villa for parties and dinners. In return he took advantage of their weaknesses and benefited from their mistakes.

His game plan usually worked. That is until recently, when he'd been outfoxed by a Vietnamese politician whose connections made him dangerous. Dangerous for everyone except Charlie. The robbery, Morell knew, was Charlie's way of getting even.

Not long ago a presidential assistant named Van Tien Cao had bought a tract of land outside Paris. Through friends he'd arranged for it to be appraised at more than its true value. With the land as collateral he'd then borrowed ten million dollars from Hocq's bank. He was now refusing to repay the loan.

Cao's job, plus being first cousin to South Vietnam's president, gave him enormous clout. Cao also had judges, generals and local strong men in his pocket. Charlie Hocq could kiss his ten million dollars goodbye. Well, not exactly.

He said to Morell, "A month from now the Communists will have taken over this city. Smart people are moving their money out while they can."

Bingo. Morell felt a chill. Now he knew what kind of robbery Charlie was planning and why he could afford to cut Morell in for twenty million dollars.

Hocq steepled his fingers under his chin. "I am about to teach Mr Cao that one doesn't screw Charles and get away with it. He's going to pay for *everything*."

Everything meant the incident with Rachelle, Hocq's late sister. She'd been a seventeen-year-old beauty with dreams of becoming a pop singer. Earlier this year she'd drowned in Hocq's swimming pool, a victim of a lifelong problem with asthma. Hocq had avenged her death by dynamiting the pool then covering it with cement. He still kept her room intact, with clothes, cosmetics, and books exactly as she'd left them. The room also included her carefully preserved corpse, lifelike in a gold coffin that was surrounded by fresh flowers and burning candles.

Ten days ago masked thugs had invaded Hocq's villa, and poured gasoline on Rachelle's corpse. If Hocq didn't renounce all financial claims on Van Tien Cao, Rachelle was going up in flames. He'd quickly signed papers saying that Cao had repaid the ten million dollar loan in full.

"Cao thinks he's beaten me," Hocq said to Morell. "He's about to learn how wrong he is. I'm getting my money back with interest."

He tapped his temple with a forefinger. "Killing Cao won't give Charles back his money. One must think in a different way."

Morell listened to bells from a nearby cathedral. Reminds me of a funeral, he thought. Mine, if I'm not careful.

He lit another cigarette. "Let's hear about my twenty million."

Hocq placed his empty tea cup on a rattan coffee table. "Tomorrow morning eleven women will leave here for Tan Son Nhut Air Force Base outside of town. They're scheduled to board a South Vietnamese military jet for a private flight to Hong Kong. These eleven ladies are the cream of Saigon society. Their husbands are cabinet officials, bank presidents, generals, and, of course, drug dealers. You and your men will hijack their plane while it's on the ground. My pilot will then fly you to Thailand."

Morell frowned. "Be serious. If you intend to hold these women for ransom, you're crazy. Their husbands have dozens of mistresses. Vietnamese men can't keep their pants on. These guys won't notice their wives are gone."

Hocq held up a forefinger. "I'm not interested in the wives. I want their luggage. Every suitcase, handbag, valise, shopping bag, packing case. In the next few hours these women will have cleaned out Saigon's banks, safe deposit boxes, wall safes. They're couriers, Edwin. They have to get their husbands' money out before it's too late. We're talking a bloody fortune. And all that's standing between it and us are eleven women."

Morell whistled. There it was. Charlie's revenge and Morell's future. "They clean out the banks then we take it from them. Nice."

"These women constantly fly out of Saigon on shopping trips. Because of their husbands they're never bothered by customs, police or even your CIA."

Morell nodded. "No roadblocks, no hassles. For these ladies, it's one straight line to the airport. You're right. The airport's the best place to pull it off. Wait until the luggage is loaded on the plane then grab the plane."

Hocq said, "There'll be millions in dollars, francs, piastres, gold bars. Much of it's drug money, no surprise if you know Saigon. The ladies will also be carrying antiques, jewellery, and, of course, kilos of heroin which is as good as gold if not better. And let's not forget the millions in diamonds, a popular currency in Asia."

Hocq nervously chewed a thumbnail. "I want any papers, files, and records as well. I'm especially interested in all records belonging to General Tung. That old fart's made a fortune dealing drugs. His records list his customers, partners, wholesale suppliers, smuggling routes. A smart man could turn this information into cash."

"Two smart men working together," Morell said, "might do even better."

"I'm thinking of using this data to start a courier service specialising in moving drug money around the world."

"Good idea."

"Banks leave a paper trail and that's trouble. At some future date, perhaps, you and I will sit down and discuss my courier idea. For now let's concern ourselves with these eleven ladies. Would it surprise you to learn one of them is Mrs Cao?"

Morell grinned. "No, it wouldn't."

"Damn woman drinks too much which makes her talk too much."

"How else could you have learned about the money?"

"Which men are you using?"

"Freelancers. Saigon's full of them."

Freelancers. Former American GIs, French Legionnaires, South African policemen, English and Israeli commandos. All of them in Saigon because they were anxious to escape from the problems of peace. All ready to chase the Angel of Death.

"They're pros," Morell said. "As long as they're paid, they'll do anything. I don't think they should know how much money's involved. Might prove tempting. I'll tell them we're grabbing some money but that most of what we're after is data."

Hocq's smile was malicious. "Oh, before I forget. Would you care to see Marianne?"

"Where is she?"

"Upstairs resting. Your kindness has left her ecstatic. She can't get over your decision to take her with you tomorrow. For that matter, neither can I. You seem to be surrounded by women these days."

"Must be my new after-shave."

"Most Americans leaving Saigon dump their Vietnamese loves and never look back. Not you. Here you are, just hours away from a colossal undertaking, yet you find time to rescue a young woman from advancing Communist hordes. A delicate flower like Marianne wouldn't survive incarceration in a Communist re-education camp." Hocq stared at him from under hooded eyes. "Edwin, Edwin. Something tells me there's more to this Marianne business then you're letting on. Are you sure you don't want me to take her *and* Fabienne to Thailand? I'd love to watch the two of them compare notes."

Morell chose his words carefully. "Leave Marianne to me. Tomorrow morning I'll pick her up here when I drop off Fabienne. Taking her out of Saigon is my way of repaying her for the good times."

"She says you're a superb lover though prone to extremes at times. I believe the word she used was *demanding*. And to think, it was Charles who brought you two lovebirds together."

"Did she follow my instructions?"

"I assume she did. Swears she told no one she was leaving Saigon, just as you ordered. Arrived on my doorstep an hour or so ago, carrying one suitcase, and weeping copiously while blessing your name for saving her life." Hocq frowned. "Have you noticed the close resemblance between her and Fabienne? Same size, same cat-like eyes, same long, black hair. They could pass for sisters."

Morell looked at the ceiling. "Tell her I said hello and that I'll see her tomorrow."

Hocq's eyes were as narrow as dimes. "Yes, of course."

Morell and Hocq locked eyes, Morell concentrating on the sound of water slapping against the harbour's stone walls. Charlie was giving him the barracuda look, the one indicating his shrewd, sly mind was operating on all cylinders. Morell's slight headache got worse.

Hocq said, "Charles wants to know *everything*. Everything about your plans for Marianne."

Morell thought, stay calm. "There's nothing to tell. She's coming with me – "

Hands behind his head, Hocq stared at a silver framed photograph of his sister which rested atop a nearby grand piano. "I'd hate for anything to go wrong tomorrow because of your fixation with Fabienne. You're obsessed with her, Edwin, and if I've learned one thing about people in love, it's how treacherous they can be. A man in love will do

90

anything to attain his heart's desire. You'll lie, cheat, even step on people's feet." He looked at Morell, a satisfied smirk on his face. "Did you really think I wouldn't figure it out?"

"Figure what out?" Morell's throat turned dry.

"When you grew tired of fucking Marianne you dropped her like a hot rock. Now suddenly you want to do her a good turn."

"What are you getting at?"

"There's sweat on your upper lip, Edwin. Very Nixonesque. I chose you for this project because I thought we understood each other and because as a CIA agent you have the run of Tan Son Nhut. But, if necessary, I can make other arrangements."

Suddenly a screaming Hocq was on his feet, arms flailing. *Scaring the shit out of Morell.* "You're out as of now unless you tell me why you're rescuing Marianne Bong. Never be devious around me. Never."

Morell's heartbeat was out of control. Charlie had nailed him and there wasn't a thing he could do about it. Except spill his guts.

Hocq closed his eyes. "Tell Charles about Marianne or kiss Fabienne and twenty million dollars goodbye."

Tan Son Nhut Air Base
Morell and his ten men rushed into the dilapidated hangar. Except for him, all had their faces darkened by camouflage paint, their hair hidden under watch caps. Krait's face inspired fear which restrained the guards from questioning him.

His mind was free-falling from amphetamines taken to give him courage. He focused on each noise with drug-heightened perception. His hair follicles seemed to snap their way through a skin warmed by an invisible fire. He heard combat boots scraping a cement floor. Heard a woman scream and a round being chambered into a .45 Automatic. His eyes saw into every shadowy corner, into the abandoned helicopters and broken jeeps around him.

They had surprised eleven well-dressed Vietnamese women and guards exiting limousines, jeeps, and two army trucks. A trio of Filipino mechanics had also been caught unawares.

91

Morell's men quickly took command, sealing off the hangar from the inside, disarming guards, and lining up the terrified women near a school bus that was to take them to the plane.

Luggage and packages were hastily removed from limousines then transferred to the army trucks. The Vietnamese women, aged mid-twenties to mid-sixties, watched in entranced horror. A politician's wife begged for mercy until the look on Morell's drug-twisted face forced her into silence.

He suddenly became a giant eye, filling the vast hangar with his God-like presence, seeing everything with awesome clarity. Seeing a solidly built thirtyish American shove handbags and carry-on luggage into duffel bags. Seeing a lanky Australian, Uzi hanging from his belt, drag two full duffel bags across the oil-stained floor to the trucks. The eye also saw a tubby little Scot on guard at a front window, binoculars to his eyes, an AK-47 Assault rifle cradled in his arms.

The giant eye took in the three Filipino mechanics kneeling near a fork-lift, fingers locked behind their necks. Behind them a South African aimed a silenced .22 Hush Puppy at their heads. The eye sped to the school bus, to a slim woman sitting alone in a front seat, her face hidden by dark glasses and a scarf. Also on the bus were two Vietnamese males, a slender young Army major handcuffed to the steering wheel and a smooth-faced, energetic man who sat chain-smoking near a front exit. His name was Ly, and he was Hocq's pilot. A short, sun-burnt Englishman guarded the bus. He sat on the bus steps, a shotgun across his knees.

Located north of Saigon, Tan Son Nhut handled the bulk of South Vietnamese military and commercial air traffic. Morell's men couldn't stay here long without arousing suspicion. Amidst barracks, terminals, runways, barbed wire and warehouses stood the luxurious villas of Vietnamese generals guarded by Vietnamese Marines. Morell was stealing their money and heroin. If caught, he'd be killed on the spot.

Someone touched his arm. A jittery Morell whirled, hand on a .45 Automatic tucked in his belt. An American, Felix Chapin, flinched, then said he'd finished stuffing the duffel bags. Morell's rabbit-sharp hearing picked up Chapin's breathing, the clink of his dogtags, the creaking of the leather strap on an Uzi hanging from his shoulder. A former Marine corporal, Chapin was roughly Morell's size and age.

Morell had used him before, finding Chapin dependable but not too bright. He would make the flight to Thailand as backup, earning an extra $10,000 for keeping an eye on Hocq's pilot, the jumpy Mr Ly. The other freelancers were being left behind; no one else was needed on the plane. Besides, all wanted to return to Saigon in hopes of making more money in the city's last chaotic hours.

"Bags loaded," Chapin said.

Morell nodded. "Follow me."

At the school bus Morell, voice sputtering inside his head, spoke to the little Englishman, a former SAS sergeant named Colin Hayes. "Anyone tried to contact the major?"

"Negative," Hayes said. "Quiet as a graveyard in our little corner. You bloody lot are making all the noise."

Hayes held up a hand radio. "Our Major Vien's not received a message from the plane, the control tower or Saigon. I speak Vietnamese so I don't anticipate any trouble getting him to inform the plane you're on your way. How goes it with the ladies?"

Morell glanced over his shoulder. "Wetting their pants. Soon as all the luggage is on the trucks, we're gone."

He looked at Hayes. "As planned, you'll have two men with you to guard the soldiers and the mechanics. After I'm aboard the plane, the other men will return with the women and Major Vien. Cuff them and leave them here in the hangar. Then all of you exit the base together."

Morell took a safe deposit box key from his shirt pocket and handed it to Hayes.

Hayes examined the key carefully, found the initials and secret mark he'd scratched on it, then nodded. Last night, Morell had paid his men half their money in cash. The rest had been deposited in Hayes' bank, to be collected by him and the others when the job was finished. Collecting the rest of their fee was another reason the mercenaries preferred to remain in Saigon.

Morell said, "We appreciate your help on this one."

93

The freelancers had been told they were on a CIA operation, one of many happening around Saigon. The objective, according to Morell, was to confiscate stolen property and records being shipped out of the country by Communist double agents. As for the lone woman guarded by Colin Hayes, she was a Communist defector being flown out for her safety.

Hayes pointed to the trucks. "They're loaded. Time for Major Vien to alert the plane."

Morell looked at Vien. "If he acts up, kill him."

He pointed to a pair of Germans, both ex-Legionnaires and slight enough to pass for Vietnamese from a distance. "Change into sentries' shirts and helmets then drive the trucks. Everyone else, on the bus. Bring the women."

When Major Vien had contacted the plane Morell said to Chapin, "You, Vien, our pilot and the lady go with me in the white limousine." Morell entered the car first, taking the passenger seat, and watching as the sobbing women were herded on the bus. Four mercenaries followed the women onto the bus, lying in the aisles where they couldn't be seen from outside.

Prodded by Felix Chapin, an edgy Major Vien slid behind the wheel of Morell's limousine. Chapin took the jump seat behind him. Ly, Hocq's pilot, and the Vietnamese woman in dark glasses sat in the back seat. Morell pushed the car horn. Ahead, two men pulled the hangar door open. The white limo left first, followed by the school bus and the Army trucks.

It was a half-mile to a 747 waiting for the women and their cargo. A half-mile past burned buildings gutted terminals, and security guards edgy about Communist infiltrators. Past small A-1 fighter-bombers cruising low around the perimeter of the base, waiting for Communist gunners to reveal themselves. Past trucks of ragtag, armed Vietnamese soldiers worried about escaping Saigon alive.

Hands shaking, Morell reached for a small bottle in his shirt pocket. The drugs were wearing off. Fatigue threatened to devour him. Uncapping the bottle, he swallowed more amphetamines.

The 747 sat on a grassy runway pockmarked by rocket

attacks. Six Vietnamese Marines and a pilot in a yellow jumpsuit smoked and chatted around a jeep parked under an airplane wing. All turned to watch Morell's convoy. When the limo came to a stop Morell placed his .45 in a flight bag hanging from his shoulder. He said to Major Vien, "Warn your friends and you're dead." The warning was coming from Krait. The Major nodded.

"Out," said Morell.

Vien left the limousine, followed by Morell who kept a hand in the flight bag. He'd never felt more sure of his powers.

Chapin, Uzi hidden in a folded newspaper under his arm, followed Morell and Vien towards the jeep. Remaining in the limo were Ly, Hocq's pilot, and the mysterious Vietnamese woman. Meanwhile, the Vietnamese wives, prodded by ex-Legionnaires in Vietnamese army shirts and helmets, silently left the bus and walked towards the plane. Morell heard their footsteps, sensed their terror. He suddenly felt himself to be in danger.

Because the feeling of oppression was real, he pulled the .45 from the flight bag, rushed forward and clubbed the yellow jump-suited pilot on the head. As the pilot lay bleeding at his feet, Morell experienced a surge of relief. Recognising Krait, the Vietnamese Marines were paralysed with fear.

Morell's men raced from the bus, joining the Legionnaires in covering the Marines. Felix Chapin drew his Uzi from under the newspaper and stood beside Morell. A frightened Major Vien, arms over his head, dropped to his knees shouting, "Don't shoot! Don't shoot!"

A wild-eyed Morell aimed the .45 at Vien's head. "Order the guards to put everything on the plane."

Then he looked at the white limo. "Fabienne! On the plane! Hurry!"

An hour out of Saigon Morell left Felix in the cockpit with Ly, and walked towards the rear of the plane. He had a whopper of a headache, one aggravated by bumpy flight and the roar of the plane's motor. He walked past rows of empty seats before sitting down beside a smiling Marianne Bong.

"Headache's killing me," he said.

He touched her face. Delicate, soft spoken, vulnerable Marianne Bong. One of Saigon's classier bar girls. A moody, changeable, twenty-two-year-old beauty seeking a protector and provider. Her dependence had fed Morell's need to feel important. No complaints about their sex life. It had been totally uninhibited, unshackled. Eventually he'd grown tired of her whims and moods. He'd dropped her without looking back.

She placed her head on his shoulder. "I am so happy you take me with you. It was a wonderful surprise to hear from you again. You won't be sorry you take me with you."

She slipped a hand inside his shirt. "When we get to Thailand am I to continue being this Fabienne person?"

Morell took her face in his hands, kissed her gently, and felt her mouth open to his tongue and when she went to embrace him, he seized her throat then quietly strangled her to death, fingers crushing her larynx, grinding a thin gold chain and crucifix into her soft skin.

As the dead woman sagged in her seat Morell reached into his flight bag, removed Fabienne's blue pearls then hung them around Marianne's neck. A handbag belonging to Fabienne was dropped on Marianne's lap. Leaving his seat Morell walked to the cockpit and knocked on the door. "Felix!" he shouted. "Open up. I need your help."

The big man opened the cockpit door. Morell pointed to the rear of the plane. "It's Fabienne. I think she's passed out. Could be an oxygen problem. Help me get her into the aisle then we'll look for an oxygen mask."

Chapin nodded. "You got it."

Morell stepped aside to let Chapin precede him down the aisle. At Marianne's seat, Chapin slipped an arm around her waist and lifted her from the seat, thinking the lady had tits that wouldn't quit. He'd lie face down in her dirty bath water any day. He stepped in the aisle where Morell, still behind him, drew his .45 and clubbed Chapin on the head. Chapin dropped to his knees, letting Marianne Bong's corpse slip from his arms.

Morell struck Chapin repeatedly, remembering Charlie's reaction to his plans for Marianne.

Charlie had said, "Anything to make you happy, is that it? You're a barbarian, an absolute barbarian. Good luck with your little scheme and let me know how it turns out. I want to know everything."

From his flight bag, Morell removed a passport with his name and photograph then tucked it inside Chapin's shirt. Morell's wallet and CIA identification were shoved into Chapin's pockets.

Finished, he collapsed in a nearby seat and gripped the arm rests. Abdominal cramps sliced into him with fanatical savagery. He'd blindly followed his desire for Fabienne. He closed his eyes, thinking of the power she wielded over him. He was fooling himself if he thought their relationship would run smoothly.

He drifted into a troubled sleep, wondering if he'd ever fear Fabienne and the power she had over him. At least he wouldn't have to spend his life looking over his shoulder for Simon Bendor. If he wasn't already dead, he soon would be.

At 10.15 that night Simon Bendor, carrying a shotgun, entered Chase Knox's office in the American Embassy, and sat on a leather couch beside an American flag. Knox was seated behind a cherrywood desk, a black briefcase in front of him. He was a slight man in his late thirties, with small ears on either side of a long head which was dominated by blue eyes that looked deceptively amiable. He was second in command of the CIA's Saigon station.

Knox said nothing as Simon laid the shotgun beside him on the couch then absentmindedly touched the web belt around his waist. Hanging from the belt was a holstered .45 Automatic and K-Bar knife. The belt and Simon's shirt were spotted with blood.

"It was a trap," Simon said. "Morell set me up to be killed. They were expecting us."

"I heard. The bastard seems to have gone berserk all of a sudden. This won't look good on my record. I was the one who sent you on his say-so. I understand you had casualties." He sounded impatient, as though wishing this interview were over so he could do something less trying.

"We went in with a four man team," Simon said. "One dead, two wounded, one pretty bad. When we saw it was a trap, we shot our way out. They chased us through Chinatown. Eventually we got behind them and took them out."

"Sounds as though you've had quite an evening. How'd you outflank them?"

"Made them think they'd killed me. That's when they got careless."

Knox smiled, impressed. "Remind me not to play poker with you. How'd you learn it was Morell who set you up?"

"I made one of the shooters talk. Morell hired six freelancers, shitheads who hang around massage parlours getting stoned on cheap opium. Where's Morell?"

Knox folded his hands on the desk. "Before we run amok, let's slow the pace a bit. There are some things you should know."

"Where's Morell? Nobody around here wants to talk about the guy. Mention his name and everybody's suddenly dumb, deaf and blind."

"One step at a time." Knox removed a cablegram from the black briefcase and held it out to Simon.

"Morell's dead," Knox said. "Him and Fabienne Bao. Their bodies were found an hour ago in the wreckage of a hijacked 747 which apparently exploded on landing in Thailand. Both bodies were burned and mangled beyond recognition. Thai police made a positive identification from passports, jewellery, personal papers."

Simon read the cablegram then shook his head. "Son of a bitch. This kills Pete Sanchez. Without Fabienne Bao, there's no hostage deal. All we've got is Quang Bai."

"We don't have him either. He's dead."

"He's *what*?"

"Morell killed him this morning before leaving Saigon. One shot in the back of the head."

Knox shrugged his shoulders. "For the life of me, I can't figure out why. Makes no sense. You'd think he deliberately

98

set out to kill Sanchez. Morell was the last one to see Quang alive so we know he killed him. As for Miss Bao, apparently Morell's relationship with her was, shall we say, somewhat subjective. Dead or alive, he's caused us a few complications."

Knox took another page from the briefcase and held it out to Simon. "There was a robbery this afternoon at Tan Son Nhut. A gang got away with a fortune in cash, gold, and God knows what else. They're supposed to have walked off with nearly a hundred million dollars belonging to some very important Vietnamese. Morell was positively identified as the gang's leader. He flew out with the loot."

Simon looked at the page. "I heard about the robbery as I came in. Is that why he and the Bao woman were killed?"

"What else could it be? He double-crosses us then gets double-crossed himself. That's what I mean by complications. Right now the Chief of Station's on the phone with the presidential palace, trying to mollify the president who claims to have personally lost over ten million dollars in the robbery. The president claims the robbery was a CIA operation and wants us to make restitution. Now do you understand why everybody's so tight-lipped around here?"

Simon moved to a window overlooking several Quonset huts erected alongside the main embassy building. "I had doubts about working for you people. My mother talked me into this deal because we needed the money. When I showed up at Langley, some people didn't like the idea of a kid coming out of nowhere and cutting them out of a job. I had to prove myself."

Knox wrinkled his nose in distaste. "I heard. You sent two of our unarmed combat instructors to the hospital. Was that necessary?"

"They thought if they hurt me, I'd quit. Pete Sanchez was a CIA officer but he took my side. Saved my job."

Simon turned from the window. "When we went after those Vietcong sappers who were blowing up half of Saigon, Pete stopped a bullet meant for me. That's why I wanted this job tonight. I wanted a hostage to trade for Pete."

"I thought we'd get one," Knox said. "According to Morell,

we could capture Paris Kelly, if we showed up at a certain Chinatown restaurant this evening. Kelly's the most wanted American defector of the war and I don't have to tell you why. He didn't just go over to the Vietcong, he went to work for them. When he's not broadcasting propaganda out of Hanoi, he's sneaking into Saigon to kill Americans. If there was one guy we wanted to get our hands on, it was him."

Simon said, "There was an American in the restaurant but he wasn't Kelly. He was a decoy. He let his guard down when he thought I was dead." Simon touched the K-Bar. "He was the one who told me Morell set up the ambush to get me."

"Why you?"

"Because I knew that he'd stopped a prisoner exchange in order to hang onto Fabienne Bao. I told Morell if Pete Sanchez died because of her, I'd kill him."

Knox touched his ear. "Yes, well, that's not the sort of thing the agency wants to see on the front page of the *New York Times*. You bring in any prisoners?"

"No."

"I see. Probably just as well. One less complication for the Chief of Station. He's got enough on his plate as it is. Lots of ruffled Vietnamese feathers out there. Losing that money infuriates them more than losing to the Communists. Our ambassador and the State Department are also getting involved. We need to keep the Vietnamese happy if we want a shot at winning this war."

"The war's lost. Morell knew that, which is why he ran. Anyone actually see him and Fabienne fly out of Tan Son Nhut?"

"We have at least twenty witnesses. The women who were robbed and their security guards. I'm sorry you feel our efforts are being wasted over here. I realise you're quite young, but one would think the time you've spent with the agency would have convinced you how important it is to fight Communism wherever you find it. Would you rather fight them in Honolulu? Because that's what will happen if we don't stop them here."

Simon returned to the couch. "Let me ask you something. When's the last time anybody took a shot at you?"

100

Silence.

Simon said, "That's what I thought. I may be young, but I'm not dumb. We're over here because we think we're better than these people. As for Communism, it sucks and so does the agency."

A red-faced Knox said, "I'll have to report what you've just said."

"Do I look like I give a shit? What about Morell's heist team? Anybody go after them?"

"That's the responsibility of the Vietnamese police. We don't have the manpower to investigate every freelancer in Saigon. I should add that witnesses heard Morell call Fabienne by name before she boarded the plane."

Simon clasped his hands behind his head. "Convenient."

"You have something to say, say it."

"My mother knows more about intelligence than you people will ever know. She says you only get a few pieces of information to work with. Ninety per cent of that can't be verified as to validity or reliability. You have to look at all sides. You look at the indicators, the mosaic. It's difficult to put it all together."

"What's your point?"

"Morell had to pick up Fabienne Bao then meet his men and go to the airport for the robbery. Yet, he takes time to kill Quang Bai, something completely unnecessary. And during the robbery, he doesn't hide his face. Wants everybody to see him. The other guys are wearing camo cream, but not him. Doesn't that make you curious?"

Knox shook his head. "If you're saying Morell's still alive, you're fantasising. His corpse was positively identified. The official policy of this embassy is that Edwin Morell and Fabienne Bao are both deceased. Do you have any idea of the problems if the Vietnamese believed he's still alive?"

"He's killed Pete Sanchez and he tried to kill me. I'd like to make sure he's dead."

Knox tugged at an infinitesimal earlobe. His patience was running thin. "If it makes you feel any better, go to Thailand, dig up Morell, and kill him again. But for now, I expect you to get on board. Just follow orders. That's something else your mother should have told you. Morell's dead. That's the party line."

"Suppose he isn't dead."

Knox returned the papers to his briefcase. Who was this snotnose to challenge him? "You're being debriefed tonight. Tomorrow morning you'll be on the first plane back to the States. The war's over for you, mister."

"Suddenly I get the feeling I'm not wanted any more. You guys planning to hand over a hundred million dollars of American tax money to the drug dealers who run this country?"

Knox slammed both hands down on his desk. "We can still win this war, but not if people like you alienate our allies."

Knox stood up, signalling the meeting was over. "Sorry about what happened to you tonight, but that couldn't be helped."

Simon heard the door open and turned to see four armed American Marines enter the office. He grinned at Knox. "Buzz three times in case of trouble, right? Maybe one of these days we can have another discussion about Morell."

"Escort Mr Bendor to the conference room," Knox said. "Keep him there until we're ready for his debriefing. When it's over escort him to his quarters. Make sure he stays there until it's time to take him to his plane. On behalf of the agency, Mr Bendor, I thank you for your efforts. As for Edwin Morell he no longer exists."

7

Santo Domingo, June

Inside the Cathedral of Santa Maria de la Menor Albert Martins walked away from a marble and bronze sarcophagus said to contain the remains of Christopher Columbus. He was angry.

An abrasive woman had just interrupted his sight-seeing, forcing him to move to another part of the four-hundred-and-fifty-year-old church. She was a French-speaking guide, a big-chinned fortyish Dominican who was leading several French sailors on a noon tour of the cathedral, the oldest in the Western Hemisphere.

Her French was atrocious. She was butchering every sentence while pointing out the cathedral's altars and delicate carvings, its unlimited gold and silver treasures. Martins, knowing the language fluently, shared the French contempt for those who spoke it incorrectly.

He'd left the *Rachelle*, docked in the harbour, for a bit of peace and quiet. Since seven this morning he'd been working at getting his couriers into the States, doing it without help from Charlie. Charlie had been too tired to talk business today, having spent the night playing cards. All he wanted to do now was sleep. He'd been in a foul mood, which meant Styler was still taking him to the cleaners.

This left Martins responsible for checking faxes, telexes, telephone calls, and radio dispatches from couriers communicating from various checkpoints as they made their way to the States. An hour ago he'd escorted François DuChamps, the ex-Legionnaire they'd picked up in Havana, off the

Rachelle with three million in Triad money. A limousine and armed guards had been waiting dockside to take DuChamps to Santo Domingo's Las Americas International Airport for a two-hour flight to Miami aboard a CIA owned airline.

From Miami, DuChamps would catch a commercial flight to New York and turn the money over to Abby Langway, Hocq's lawyer. Langway would launder the cash before using it to buy the Atlantic City casino for the Golden Circle Triad. Later this evening the *Rachelle* would sail for the Cayman Islands to pick up more couriers and get them into the States. Martins had only eleven days left on his deadline.

In the cathedral he sat in a carved oak pew, inhaling incense as he watched a small altar boy in a black cassock light a pair of tall white candles on a gilded altar. The cool stone floor beneath his feet, the darkness, and solemn quiet were a pleasant change after being around Charlie. He watched the altar boy genuflect, cross himself, then move onto another altar.

Maybe Martins should light a candle and let God deal with Simon Bendor. Whatever God did, He did well. Almost as well as Bendor who'd taken out three of Martins' best men. And all because Fabienne had forced a promise from Martins a lifetime ago.

Saigon, 1975

On the morning of the Tan Son Nhut robbery a brooding Fabienne, about to leave her hotel suite with Morell for Hocq's villa, finally broke a long silence. "I want you to kill Quang Bai," she said. "It will bring us closer together."

Morell was shocked. Was she crazy? What did she have against Quang Bai?

"If you love me," she said, "you'll do it."

"What has love got to do with killing a prisoner?"

"Quang Bai is no ordinary prisoner. His father – "

"I know who his father is. I don't have time for games. Not this morning. I've got to drop you at Hocq's, pick up my men, and get out to the airport."

She'd never looked more beautiful. "I cannot go back to my people. If you were to leave me, I would have nothing."

104

"I don't plan to leave you."

"I've burned my bridges. Now you burn yours. Kill Quang Bai and his father will kill Pete Sanchez. When that happens, your people will never forgive you. Kill Quang Bai and neither of us can turn back."

Morell fumbled for words. "What if I refuse?"

She stared at him for a long time, letting him imagine the worst. Imagine that she wouldn't be in Thailand when the 747 landed. That she would talk Hocq into letting her go free.

"If I kill Quang Bai," he said, "your people will do more than kill Pete Sanchez. They'll hunt us down. And so will the Americans."

"Do it for me."

He took her in his arms, wondering if he didn't love her too much. Wondering when her love would again push him into being cruel.

"For you," he said.

In the cathedral, Martins looked at his watch and decided it was time for lunch. He saw himself relaxing at a sidewalk café with a rum punch and a plate of sliced mango. He'd have to cross the square, making his way through tourists, beggars, pickpockets, street performers and soldiers in dark glasses.

After lunch he'd shop on Calle Las Damas where the fifteenth-century architecture made it one of the most beautiful streets in the Americas. Ten years ago, as Edwin Morell, he'd trained the Dominican Republic's secret police in interrogation techniques. As Albert Martins he could now travel anywhere unrecognised. In his new incarnation, he was his own king, his own guide.

On the cathedral steps he flinched in the sudden heat of a hot sun, allowing his senses to adjust to the smells and sounds of a teeming Columbus Square in front of him. He put on his sunglasses then looked around for the church cornerstone, said to be laid by Diego Columbus, Christopher's son. Columbus was the heart of the tourist industry, having landed on the island in 1492. Martins found the city's history fascinating. Ponce de Leon, Cortes, Balboa, de Velazquez had all set out from here to explore and conquer Spanish America.

The tall Martins, a standout in his new summer gaberdine suit, was a target for beggars, lottery ticket sellers and fruit peddlers. He fended them off, finding their body odour more repellent then their sales pitches. He was also reminded of how baseball mad Dominicans were. Young and old wore tee-shirts bearing photographs of Juan Marichal, Cesar Cedeno, and Pedro Guerrero, Dominican-born players who'd made it in the American major leagues.

Many Dominicans carried transistors tuned to local baseball games. Martins sometimes checked the *International Herald Tribune* for Detroit Tiger scores, but he wasn't as wild about the game as he'd been years ago.

As tourists filed in and out of the cathedral, he turned from Columbus Square and let his eyes search for the church cornerstone laid by Diego Columbus. What happened next caught him completely off-guard.

At the sight of a man standing in front of the cathedral, Morell immediately recoiled in horror. Lounging alongside the cathedral entrance, blond, tanned and fit, arms folded across his chest and eyes hidden behind mirrored sunglasses was *Simon Bendor*.

Martins felt himself grow dizzy. Hit by a sudden cramping abdominal pain, he swayed briefly before bracing himself, feet apart. His heart quivered at breakneck speed.

How had Bendor tracked him down? Martins froze on the spot, he and Bendor eyeing each other, Martins tensing for Bendor's attack. Less than six feet separated them. To Martins's utter relief and surprise, Bendor's eyes moved on. Martins turned his back. *The bastard doesn't know what I look like.*

Martins faced Bendor again. Saw him look at his watch then glance around the Square. He was expecting someone. *He didn't know what Martins looked like. Martins could walk up to Bendor and kill him.*

Martins wasn't carrying a gun. Too risky in a foreign country. He was carrying a passport identifying him as George Page, a French olive-oil salesman living in Marseille. If Dominican police sent Martins' fingerprints to Marseille, they'd learn the real George Page was dead.

He was carrying a weapon, however. Hands shaking, he removed a small leather case from a jacket pocket, opened it and took out the largest nail file. He began filing his nails.

He watched Bendor turn his back and peer at the crowds towards the north end of Columbus Square. Martins was strong. He had six inches height on Bendor, and was holding enough steel in his hand to gouge out Bendor's throat. And he had the element of surprise. One second would be time enough to do the job.

Nail file in his fist, Martins pushed his way towards Bendor.

8

Alexis Bendor had flown to Santo Domingo to help her son rescue Erica Styler. A morning flight from Miami had brought her here in only two hours. To a land where boom boxes played *merengue* music loud enough to make her ears bleed.

She was in the city's old quarter, walking past the House of Cord, where Sir Francis Drake had been bribed to cease burning down the city block by block. She was late for a noon meeting with Simon at the Cathedral of Santa Maria de la Menor, the oldest church in the new world. Just thinking about challenging Charles Hocq had turned Alexis into a bundle of nerves. To get to Erica, they would have to go through enough armed men and guard dogs to chew off every leg in Finland.

Simon also intended to confront Albert Martins, Hocq's enigmatic partner. Two days ago Martins had tried to have Simon killed. Alexis detested anyone who'd harm her son. She'd left Hawaii several hours after Simon but not before checking on Martins' ties to the intelligence community at Simon's request.

As an OSS agent in World War II, she developed psychological profiles on traitors, defectors, and double agents, a tribe whose treacherous behaviour fascinated her. "Outsiders", she called them. Always at war with themselves. Albert Martins was an outsider and since he was trying to kill Simon, he was now at war with Alexis.

Having kept her ties to the intelligence community, she'd learned a good deal about Mr Martins with a single telephone

108

call. She'd made the call to a former OSS agent now a member of the *Wise Old Men*, a senior informal advisory group which advised the President of the United States on espionage matters. Alexis' contact was a seventy-year-old widower whose wealthy family had had the political foresight to back the state's first black governor.

The widower had recently proposed marriage to her, backing his request for Alexis' hand with a promise of a certified cheque for five million dollars on their wedding day. She'd turned him down, explaining that people who wanted to marry should see each other more frequently than once every ten years. Meanwhile, he had faxed some colourful data on Martins which she couldn't wait to share with Simon.

This was Alexis' first trip to Santo Domingo, a city whose attractive colonial architecture was spoiled by narrow streets jammed with people and traffic. Columbus and Pizarro may have raced through these age-old thoroughfares but slow moving buses, parked cars and thousands of pedestrians had prevented Alexis' cab from doing the same. She'd left the cab and now hurried towards Columbus Square on foot.

Alexis Gladys Bendor was in her mid-sixties, a tall, sharp-faced woman with grey eyes, and dyed blonde hair combed to cover scar tissue where her right ear used to be. During the closing days of World War II a member of British intelligence had betrayed her OSS team to the Japanese. Three fellow agents had been tortured to death. Alexis, who'd lost an ear to her torturers, escaped after killing two of them.

In Honolulu she owned a book store specialising in first editions and rare prints. She was energetic, demanding, and because she couldn't stand failure, drove herself to attain her goals. Her energy level was formidable and she used every bit of it. Having suffered an appalling captivity herself, she sympathised with Erica Styler's plight. Being caged had left its mark on Alexis; it would do the same to the younger woman. But for all of her empathy for Erica, the truth was Alexis disliked her.

Erica Styler had been a professional gambler from the age of seventeen, an occupation making her character and conduct highly suspect. A gambler spent time in the company of hoodlums. Her father, also a professional gambler, had been murdered by a New Orleans Mafia Don for cheating at poker. So what did this say about Erica?

Perhaps her biggest offence was being young. Her cheekbones and long legs could produce an explosion of jealousy in any woman of uncertain age. Alexis was prepared to reject this mini-skirted cardsharp for reminding her that time was a woman's worst enemy. Old age could definitely be a crown of thorns.

Simon had said that Erica wasn't a cheat, that she won because she had the guts to act on what she believed. Alexis had said, "Never forget that much of the world's troubles are caused by fools acting on the courage of their so-called convictions."

Still, she had to admit that Erica had a certain pluck. Such as when she'd dumped her husband, a flamenco dancer who'd left their second anniversary party with a Desert Inn showgirl in search of more ice, only to stay away for a month. Or when she'd shot a Mexican handyman who'd attempted to rape her in a Phoenix motel. Or when she'd put a bullet in a mugger who'd attacked her in a Chicago parking lot.

Alexis was in Erica's debt because she had saved Simon's life. Last October on a warm New York night, she had excused herself from a poker game and gone to the bathroom to freshen up. A sudden tapping at the window left her in shock. The bathroom was eight storeys above the street and twelve storeys from the roof. No fire escapes or ledges to speak of. But someone was at the window.

Magnum in hand, Erica had opened the window and found herself staring at a masked figure clinging to an extremely narrow ledge by bloodied fingertips. Guess who?

Alexis had gotten the rest of the story from Simon. Erica had allowed him to climb into the bathroom, then accused him of being a thief. He'd admitted it, impressing Erica with his candour. He'd been cracking a safe in a venerable Manhattan club when a second burglar had slipped onto the premises, setting off a silent alarm. Burglar number two immediately caught three bullets in the chest from a security guard.

A SWAT team had responded to the alarm, bringing along enough weapons to kill Simon ten times over. Trapped between security guards and cops, he'd taken the only way out which was to climb the front of Erica's high-rise. With hands torn and bleeding from the bricks, he'd expected to slip and fall to his death.

Sour grapes not withstanding, Alexis was forced to give Erica points for what she'd done. Simon had climbed as high as his mangled hands could take him. Had Erica not opened the bathroom window, he'd have died and that's why Alexis was in Santo Domingo.

In Santo Domingo Simon's plan was to have Alexis create a diversion while he disabled Hocq's yacht with explosives, forcing all on board to disembark. The plan wasn't foolproof, but it seemed safer than taking on Hocq's goons and the Dominican police. And as Simon pointed out, even if he could get on the yacht, learning Erica's exact location wouldn't be easy. His one chance was to trick Hocq into bringing her ashore.

Alexis had suggested they meet in the cathedral and go over Simon's plan. "This harebrained scheme of yours needs all the help it can get," she'd told him. "There's no better place to kick it off than in the mansion house of the omnipotent God." In church they'd just be tourists come to stare at Columbus' bones and buy a limestone statue of Jesus from the souvenir stand.

On Calle Isabel la Catolica, she asked a policeman for directions in fluent Spanish then stopped at a sidewalk café for a quick Coke which she swallowed with a Halazone, a pill that made water potable. The blistering Caribbean sun called for stronger sunglasses, so she bought a pair from a street vendor, bargaining him down from ten US dollars to five.

She understood Simon's need for excitement, his need to be a free spirit. *But did he have to steal for a living?* Each burglary took ten years off her life. Whenever he set forth to plunder, a nervous Alexis found herself unable to sleep until he returned safely. How calmly he risked his life. How certain he was of his courage when eluding police or cracking someone's safe.

111

He'd listen when she said thieving was dangerous, agree with her, then do as he pleased.

There were no formal goodbyes at these times, no warm wishes for success. She loved her son too much to see him off to his death. On certain mornings she'd awake and the house would feel empty and she would know he'd gone. Not to the health club or on a five-mile run, but to the mainland to put his life on the line.

She'd slip into her robe and walk to his room, finding it empty, with his personal papers on a white wicker desk. The papers included Simon's will, property deeds, chequebooks, insurance policies, safety deposit box keys. There was also a letter to his attorney appointing Alexis co-executor of his estate. At those times, her prayer was always the same. *Dear Lord, don't let him die.*

Before leaving for Santo Domingo he'd been forced to kill three men in self-defence, a disclosure that nearly caused Alexis to jump out of her skin. He'd hidden the bodies in the forest where they wouldn't be found for a long time.

"The man who sent them after me will try again," he said. "We're being watched. It's best we leave the islands for a few days."

A stunned Alexis said, "Are you serious?"

Simon handed her a letter-sized envelope. "I took that from one of the men I killed. They knew our every move."

"Who's behind this?"

"A man named Morell. We were in Vietnam together fifteen years ago. Calls himself Albert Martins now. He and Hocq run a courier service for drug money. Hocq's keeping Erica prisoner on his yacht which is now in Santo Domingo. Martins is afraid I'll come for her and make trouble for him. He's got that right. He might try to get at me through you. That's why you've got to leave Hawaii."

Alexis looked up from the report. "Morell. Didn't he try to kill you in Vietnam over some woman? You told me they were dead."

"I thought they were. But according to one of the men I killed, Morell and his lady are very much alive and living in southern France. The shooter described Fabienne Bao perfectly. Said she's married to someone who sounds very much like Morell."

Alexis said, "Call him Martins. I doubt if anyone knows him as Morell. He was also called Krait, wasn't he? I remember now. He was our torture virtuoso in Saigon."

"That's the man."

Alexis felt a sudden sadness. "He got Pete Sanchez killed. Peter was a dear, dear boy."

"It wasn't just Pete who died. Four more American POWs were executed after Martins killed a Vietcong leader's son. He did it to impress Fabienne."

Alexis' hand went to the hair hiding the scar tissue on her head. "The evil in this world never goes away, does it?"

Simon put his arm around her. "Sorry I brought this on you. You know how I feel about making trouble in the islands."

"Don't be ridiculous. This thing started because Martins wanted that woman. Besides, you're my son. Am I supposed to crochet samplers while someone puts a bullet in your head?"

Simon took her hand. "I want you to leave for the mainland right away. Don't tell anyone you're going. Not the servants, not your jogging club, not anyone at the book store. Keep away from Hawaii until this thing's cleared up."

Alexis held up the report on Simon. "Whoever put this together knows the islands. No outsider could have done this in the short time Erica's been gone. You did say they came for you right after Miss Styler flew off for her usual skate on thin ice."

Simon said, "Check out Martins but use a public phone. I want to know if he's got friends in the CIA or if his man was lying to me. Draw ten thousand dollars out of the Oahu National account for expenses."

He held up a forefinger. "Don't close the book store. Just tell the staff you're staying with a sick friend and that you'll be back soon."

"When do I leave?"

"Right away. We fly out of Honolulu in separate planes. Just bring a shoulder-bag and buy whatever else you need. If

113

someone's watching the house, I don't want them to know we're pulling out. I'll need your help in Santo Domingo."

"You've got it. What about Joe D'Agosta, your friendly neighbourhood fence? Isn't there something he can do?"

Simon nodded. "He's lining up explosives for me in Santo Domingo. He knows wiseguys who're shipping stolen cars to the Caribbean. Joe's getting the explosives through them."

"I have a question," Alexis said. "Next time, can you arrange to fall in love with someone less *unusual?*"

Columbus Square

Alexis pushed her way through tourists, money changers, lottery ticket vendors, and fruit juice sellers clustered in front of the Cathedral of Santa Maria de la Menor.

As a religious sceptic, she was uncomfortable around the heavy-handed grip of Catholicism which was everywhere in this country. She was checked into a hotel opposite the National Pantheon, a mausoleum for prominent Dominicans. Walking to the cathedral she'd passed convents, vendors hawking silk paintings of saints, and numerous pigeon-anointed statues of the Virgin. The Antichrist had his work cut out for him around here.

Pausing near a group of Japanese tourists photographing each other on the cathedral steps, she shaded her eyes with one hand and pulled her blouse away from her sweat-soaked chest. The sun was murder. She was starting to feel like a baked apple. Dominican flies and insects were hanging around her like cannibals after missionaries. The sooner she entered the cathedral, the better.

She stood on tiptoe, peering through the Japanese for a sight of Simon. Ah, there was her boy leaning against a pillar flanking the entrance. Dressed in jeans, white polo shirt, and looking like a rock star. Joe Cool himself. Oblivious to women eyeing him as they passed in and out of the cathedral.

He was also oblivious to a man who'd caught Alexis' eyes. The man was fiftyish, grey-haired, and quite tall. He wore an expensive summer suit, and a Rolex. He was closing in on Simon's back as though stalking his prey.

Alexis felt cold. Her heartbeat turned violent and she was out of breath. She had a photograph of the tall man in her shoulder-bag, courtesy of the widower. He was Albert Martins and there was a nail file in one fist. *He was about to kill Simon.*

Alexis screamed, "Simon, behind you! It's Albert Martins!"

She pushed her way through the Japanese, scattering them left and right. One hand was in her shoulder-bag, fumbling for the only weapon she had, a Sony Walkman. She threw it at Martins who'd turned to stare at the woman who knew him by name.

The Walkman was a formidable projectile. Alexis aimed for Martins' head. His arms came up as a shield and the Walkman struck him in the elbow. Alexis was fearful and angry at once, but there was a wild joy in her heart when she saw the shock on Martins' face. God, how she wanted him dead.

She raced towards him then yelled in pain as she collided with a chunky Japanese woman photographing teenage girls on the cathedral steps. Alexis and the woman went down in a tangle of arms and legs, Alexis screaming Simon's name, and the Japanese woman grunting as her spine hit the concrete and the camera left her hands.

Simon turned to see his mother on the ground, arms and legs flailing. Something was wrong and not just with Alexis.

He saw a tall, grey-haired man backing away from him, a man who seemed to know Simon, whose eyes held a look of recognition. The man feared him, which made no sense. Simon had never seen him before. *Or had he?*

They locked eyes, neither looking away, and the tall man nodded his head as though saying *next time*. Without a word, he slowly fell back into the mass of tourists and Dominicans, moving deliberately, never turning his back on Simon who thought, This guy's a stone killer. Something about the man said that he was more dangerous than a cornered rat. Except he wasn't about to let himself be cornered.

Simon concentrated on him, seeing his long nose, sharply creased trousers, the beads of perspiration on his forehead, the fist tightly clenched around a nail file. The longer he stared, the more familiar the man seemed. He was staring at the nail file in the tall man's fist when he heard Alexis yell, "Simon!"

Alexis. She was still on the ground, surrounded by Japanese tourists attempting to lift her and the chubby woman. Simon hurried to her side. The tall man who'd disappeared inside the cathedral was forgotten.

9

Santo Domingo Harbour

At 2.32 that afternoon a short, pistol-packing Vietnamese with unruly hair escorted Erica Styler into the salon of the *Rachelle* and to the poker table where Charles Hocq was eating fresh pineapple. Erica seated herself across from him.

Hocq dismissed the guard then spent the next few minutes dipping pineapple chunks into a small glass of vodka and popping them into his mouth. The pineapple lay on a pewter platter stolen from a London museum by a pale-eyed Welshman who frequently supplied him with antiques and other art treasures.

Finally Erica said, "Why did you wake me?"

"We must do something about your feeling of self-importance."

"We aren't supposed to play again until this evening."

Hocq speared a piece of pineapple. "Charles has a theory about winning. It's like making love. You enjoy it so much, you can't wait to do it again."

They eyed each other in silence knowing that the less sleep she had, the better Hocq's chances were of beating her. Three days as a prisoner had taken the edge off her game. Three days were more than enough time for frustration and rage to eat away at her insides.

Two hours ago, towards the end of a twelve-hour game, Hocq had gotten outrageously lucky and taken Erica for fifty grand. She'd said nothing, figuring the loss would put her that much closer to getting away from this loony-bin. There'd been a point in the game where he'd thrown money around with the

117

audacity of the ignorant. His frantic confidence had tipped her off. He'd cheated but she couldn't figure out how.

He'd won these hands easily, applauding himself and setting Erica's teeth on edge with his cackling. She'd been fleeced by this little shit because she'd been too dog-tired to stop him.

The *Rachelle* was docked in Santo Domingo, its second stop since leaving Puerto Rico. Erica and Hocq had started playing when the ship arrived in port last night, finishing at noon. If Hocq had his way they'd play until sailing for the Cayman Islands this evening. The Caymans was a centre for hot money. Erica guessed that Hocq and Albert Martins were going there to launder money.

When not playing cards she was confined to quarters. Her ship-to-shore phone had been disconnected. She still had an inter-com phone but the only people she spoke to were Hocq or a cook who prepared her meals to order. Hocq summoned her by having a guard pound on her stateroom door with a gun butt. If she didn't answer, the guard was under orders to forcibly bring her to the salon.

The loss of her freedom was crushing. She was in hell; being a prisoner had left her frightened, uncertain, and full of rage. At the beginning she'd had no appetite, slept sporadically, and paid little attention to her appearance. But the determination which made her a gambler also made her resolve to survive. She decided to establish a regular routine and follow it whether she wanted to or not.

She forced herself to eat three small meals a day, dress for each game, and take a daily twenty-minute walk about her stateroom before going to bed. Walking allowed her to unwind; it tired her enough to allow her to catch a little sleep. She was now the only woman on board, the hookers having been escorted ashore when the ship docked this morning. For Erica being locked up suddenly became preferable to being leered at by armed men with too much leisure time.

Usually she and Hocq were alone at the poker table, one shuffling while the other dealt, both playing in silence until his beeper went off. Then he would speak into a cellular phone, conducting business in one of several languages.

To work the circulation back into her legs, and avoid the appearance of eavesdropping, Erica would leave the table and pace the salon.

She did manage to overhear Hocq speak about a big-time deal he and his lawyer Abby Langway had going with some Philadelphia wiseguys and Hong Kong Chinese. Which explained the recent presence on board of Sal Altabura and the mysterious Mr Deng.

As for Werner Tautz, when he wasn't injecting himself with steroids or maxing out Hocq's credit cards by ship-to-shore phone, he'd deal poker. Hocq and his kiss-ass bodyguard shared the comfort of friendship, among other things. Which didn't stop Tautz from coming on to Erica in front of Hocq who found the German's bisexuality amusing if not provocative.

At the beginning of her detention she'd deliberately lost several hands, hoping Hocq's ego would be satisfied and he'd put her ashore. That tactic had backfired. Hocq had caught on, and freaked out, throwing cards and food all over the salon, making it clear that kowtowing to him was unacceptable. He must achieve victory through his own powers.

All he needed was time and with Erica on board the *Rachelle* indefinitely, he had all the time in the world. Time, he told her, was now suspended. He warned her against more contrived losses.

"Play me for a fool again," he said, "and I'll have you stripped naked and handed to the crew. I'll also have Tautz film your getting raped and add it to my collection of adult cinematic masterpieces. Did I ever show you my copy of Joan Crawford's fuck film? She made it when she was a young starlet trying to break into Hollywood. It's nearly seventy years old, a black and white print that's not very good but you can still make out her face. Cost me a quarter of a million dollars."

"You've made your point," Erica said.

"You're learning, princess."

On these occasions she thought of Simon more strongly than ever. Albert Martins had returned her handbag while

119

keeping Simon's photograph. Erica had wondered why until she'd witnessed Martins and Hocq arguing over her presence on the boat. Martins had wanted her put ashore at once. Hocq had refused; he never backed down when his ego was at stake. Erica had to pay for humiliating him.

Martins hadn't liked his partner's decision but he'd refused to press the issue, frustrating Erica who would have preferred a heated debate that ended with her being kicked off the boat. She was in for a surprise. Martins was quite anxious about an upcoming confrontation with Simon. *Confrontation with Simon?*

"Styler is a gun pointed at my head," Martins had told Hocq. "Bendor won't rest until he gets her back."

"Don't you feel embarrassed at being so cautious?" Hocq said. "Well, I'm sure we'll all benefit from your warning. Now drop the subject before you bust a blood vessel."

At their first meeting Albert Martins had told Erica he'd get her away from Hocq, and like a fool she'd believed him. Martins had turned out to be a lying son of a bitch who'd conned her into thinking she'd be turned loose at the next port. Instead he'd taken Simon's photograph from her wallet, pumped her for information then sent men to kill him.

This morning she'd learned of Martins' attempt on Simon's life from Werner Tautz who enjoyed dumping on Martins. Martins had shown up at the game in an attempt to persuade Hocq to forgo poker and devote time to business. Because he was winning Hocq had refused to budge, kicking off another battle over Erica.

Tautz had joined the quarrel by taunting Martins over a bungled attempt to kill Simon. A shocked Erica had leaped from her chair, sending poker chips flying across the table and drawing Martins' unwelcomed attention. His cold eyes had terrified her so much she'd nervously begun picking up cards scattered at her feet.

Martins turned his attention to Hocq. "Tautz's defective understanding is beginning to wear thin. He should try using his mouth for something besides sucking cock."

Erica, cards in one hand, rose from under the table to see a smirking Tautz stick out his chin as though saying to Martins,

"Up yours." An amused Hocq winked then told Tautz to stop needling Martins and get them all fresh coffee. A shaken Erica gripped the back of her chair for balance, too unnerved to move or say a word. *Why had Martins tried to kill Simon?*

He announced his intention to go ashore for a walk, all the while giving Tautz a murderous look. As Martins turned to leave Tautz had said, "Women are a trouble and a worry, aren't they, Albert?" Martins never looked back but Erica sensed Tautz had struck a nerve. She assumed *the woman* meant her until Tautz called out to a departing Martins, "Give my regards to Fabienne."

Hocq then spoke to Tautz in a tone that Erica took to be both serious and sarcastic. "I should remind you of something, Tautzie. Albert does not possess an indefinite supply of forbearance. Nor is he too inclined towards showing mercy. Push him too far and you'll have to live with the agony."

Tautz snorted, flipped the absent Martins the finger, then took one of Hocq's cigarettes from the table, and lit it. After a deep drag he placed the cigarette in Hocq's mouth, kissed him on the cheek then flashed Erica a boyish grin that said Daddy's standing between me and the world.

She said, "Who's Fabienne?"

"Mrs Martins," Tautz said happily.

"What's her connection with Simon?"

"She's the reason Albert tried to kill your boyfriend in Saigon fifteen years ago. Looks like Albert plans to keep on trying until he gets it right. Your boyfriend's one lucky guy, princess, but his luck won't last forever. Albert has plenty of friends in the CIA, guys who love playing Cowboys and Indians."

He slipped an arm around Erica's waist. "Sooner or later, they'll put your Romeo out of business. Then maybe you and me can watch the sunset together from my cabin."

She pushed him away. "I don't think so."

Hocq grinned, cupped a hand to his ear, and tilted his head towards Erica. "Well now, do I hear a possible wager in the making?"

"What do you mean?" she said.

"How much faith do you have in your boyfriend's ability

to survive? True, he's won the first round but the match is far from over. Would you like to bet on his chances of staying alive against Albert and the CIA?"

"That's one of the sickest things I've ever heard. I'm not about to bet on Simon's life, not with you or anybody else."

Hocq nodded. "It does make us sound like degenerates, doesn't it?"

"*Fucking* degenerates describes us better," Tautz said. "I'll bet our Erica's done some degenerate fucking."

"Learn a new word," Erica said and reached for a cigarette. She'd smoked more in the past two days than she had in weeks.

"So you're not interested in betting on your lover," Hocq said.

Tautz raised his hand. "I'll bet with you. Gives me something to do. But I want odds."

Hocq chuckled. "Well, I can't be seen betting against Albert, so I'll take him and give you fifty to one. How's that?"

"Done. A thousand dollars says Bendor kills Albert. Not that I believe he'll do it, but watching him try helps pass the time. Should he survive the next few days and somehow manage to kill Albert, there's always Albert's CIA friends. They'll kill Bendor for sure. I'm having second thoughts about this bet, Charles."

"Tautzie, Tautzie. You want the moon with a ribbon around it, don't you? All right. If Bendor kills Albert, you win. If Bendor stays alive for ten days, you also win. How's that?"

The German grinned. "Done."

Erica examined Hocq and Tautz carefully, despising what she saw. She hated seeing these fruits behave as if everyone was a dumping ground for their fantasies. Knowing that Simon worked alone, that he would be facing Martins and the CIA by himself, she turned to hide her tears.

In the salon, she watched Hocq push the remains of the pineapple aside then wipe his mouth with a napkin. Watching him eat reminded her of a python swallowing a live pig inch by inch. Hocq was devouring Erica the same way, taking away her freedom, her peace of mind, her health, as well as any hope of rescue. Martins' eagerness to see Simon dead and Hocq's cold-blooded indifference to the matter had increased the danger to Erica. If these freaks were willing to kill Simon, they'd kill her just as quickly.

She wondered how much longer she could play cards under these conditions. Her game would soon fall apart. Being imprisoned had left her unable to concentrate properly. After she lost, what then? Hocq wanted to break her, to destroy her confidence. She now believed he wanted to kill her or drive her to suicide.

"I'd like some coffee," she said to Hocq.

"Julio." Hocq raised his hand and a black-browed fifty-year-old Peruvian behind the bar said, "Si, Mr Hocq."

"Julio. Café, *por favor. Para la senorita.*"

"Si, Mr Hocq."

Erica massaged the back of her neck, then pounded the base of her skull with a fist to clear cobwebs from her head. Her shoulders were knotted from tension. She needed a massage and a hot bath, followed by hours of uninterrupted sleep. If she was rested, she could pick up on Hocq's cheating in a heartbeat.

She hadn't realised she'd dozed off until she smelled rich Cuban coffee and opened her eyes to see a steaming cup in front of her. Near the coffee lay a platter of sliced mango, pineapple, guava, and papaya, along with a dish of grated coconut sprinkled with nutmeg. Hocq was saying he liked her earrings, which apparently reminded him of a pair he'd seen on the statue of a Sri Lankan fertility goddess.

He reached over to touch her left earring then froze, his attention caught by something on deck. She saw him frown, then squint as though to get a better look. Erica glanced over her shoulder to see Martins pull back the sliding glass door and rush into the salon. He looked a mess. His tie was lopsided and his usually well-groomed hair was now in disarray. Close on his heels were Jesse Borrega and Willie

Ahn, the pudgy-faced forty-year-old Chinese captain of the *Rachelle*. Werner Tautz, in cut-off jeans and chewing on a raw carrot, brought up the rear.

Erica couldn't take her eyes from Martins. He was red-faced with excitement and anger. She watched him march up to the table and stare at her with hatred in his eyes. A frightened Erica wondered if he was going to kill her.

Martins turned to look at Hocq. "I warned you, but you wouldn't listen. Bendor's here in Santo Domingo. That's right, Charlie, the man's here. I've just had a run-in with him and his mother in front of the cathedral. I was this close to killing him when she warned him. Thanks to you, the Bendors now know what I look like."

Hocq held up one hand in a stop signal. "Albert, slow down. You say Bendor *and* his mother are here in Santo Domingo?"

"She knew my name. Knew what I looked like. It was incredible. Bendor stared right at me and never recognised me. He was dead until that mother of his showed up."

Erica squeezed the arms of her chair. Martins' voice came to her as though in a dream. She struggled to remain composed, to avoid being carried away by fear. Or hope. *Simon in Santo Domingo. And Alexis had prevented Martins from killing him.*

Erica thought, Thank God for the mother of all mothers. Alexis deserved all the credit in the world for recognising Martins in time to save Simon's life. She made a mental note to never again dismiss Alexis' cloak and dagger stories as the ramblings of some old war-horse.

Martins placed both hands on the table, leaned past Erica and glared at Hocq. He stared at the financier for long seconds, then glanced at Erica before turning back to his partner. When Martins spoke, his voice was soft, without inflection, and so chilling that Erica pushed her chair away from the table.

"I suggest we sail for the Caymans immediately, before Bendor prevents this ship from ever sailing again. I tried explaining the situation to your Captain and to Mr Borrega, but they insist I take the matter up with you."

124

Hocq examined the platter of leftover pineapple. "They take their orders from me. You're looking flustered, Albert. Too much sun, perhaps. What happened to that nice pocket handkerchief Fabienne gave you? Did you lose it making your getaway?"

Borrega stepped forward to stand beside Martins. Erica sensed that Borrega disliked Martins but was hearing him out because the yacht's security was at stake. The Cuban said, "He says Bendor's come to Santo Domingo for his woman. He thinks if we stay there might be trouble."

Hocq used a fork to pick at the pineapple. "And what do you think, Jesse?"

"Three dead shooters say Bendor's no amateur. Figure he's going to come at us one of two ways: he shoots his way onto the boat. Or he does what I would do."

Hocq mashed a small piece of pineapple into pulp. "Which is?"

"Blow the boat. Make everybody come ashore where he's got better odds."

Hocq let the fork slip from his fingers.

Borrega said, "If I'm him, I'm thinking any shooting might get my woman killed. So I'll fix things to keep the boat from going anywhere. I'll make them bring her to me."

Hocq bit a thumbnail. "You're saying we should let this mystery man run us out of Santo Domingo? This man who's only been seen by Albert."

Borrega jerked his head towards Erica. "Bendor's not down here for his health. He wants her. And he's a killer. He can make our lives miserable until we catch him. I say we leave for the Caymans right away."

Hocq snorted. "What do you think about Albert running into mother and son at the cathedral."

The Cuban shrugged. "Coincidence, nothing more. When Martins left the boat, he didn't know where he was going. So how could Bendor know? My guess is the Bendors showed up at the cathedral same time he did."

He looked at Erica. "Turn her loose and maybe Bendor backs off."

"She stays," Martins said.

Hocq grinned. "Tautzie, did you hear that? Why the sudden change of heart, my friend?"

Martins placed a hand on Erica's shoulder but spoke to Hocq. "Bendor wants to kill me. I saw it in his face back at the cathedral. Giving Miss Styler back won't help me in the least. He has an old score to settle – "

"He's got a new one to settle too," Borrega said. "You just tried to kill him again, remember?"

Martins took a nail file from his pocket and began trimming the cuticle on a pinky finger. "Miss Styler is my bargaining chip."

Hocq giggled. "How quickly life changes. *Your* bargaining chip, you said."

Martins rubbed his pinky nail against his jacket lapel. "Charlie, do you have any idea how much Chinese money we've managed to move into the States so far?"

Hocq's eyes narrowed.

Martins slipped his nail file back into its leather case. "Do you know where our couriers are at this moment? Or that an emergency meeting has been scheduled between our New York people and our contact on the New Jersey gaming casino commission? Or that the wiseguys are trying to hold us up for more money?"

Palms on the table, Martins leaned towards Hocq. "Suppose something happened to me and you had to run the business by yourself. Do you think the Chinese would be upset if you failed to get the money stateside on time? Personally, I wouldn't want to tell Deng I fucked up his deal because I was busy playing cards with a lady."

Martins folded both arms across his chest. "On the other hand maybe you think you don't have to explain anything to the Chinks because they can't get to you here on the boat. Do you really want to bet your life on that, Charlie?"

Hocq sighed. "You've made your point. Miss Styler stays because *we* want her to. Captain, how soon could you be ready to sail?"

Before Captain Ahn could speak Borrega said, "I want divers to check below the water line in case Bendor's already attached explosives. Then I want to have the harbour police

126

keep an eye out for anybody asking about our destination. They can radio the ship if anyone's been checking on us."

He looked at Martins. "You still have intelligence contacts here?"

"Yes, but I don't deal with them any more. I've turned them over to Charlie."

Hocq said, "In his new incarnation, he prefers to remain anonymous."

Borrega looked at Hocq. "Doesn't matter. I want intelligence and Dominican police looking for Bendor and his mother."

Martins nodded. "I've copies of a Bendor photo but nothing on his mother."

Borrega said, "Give me a description and we'll go with that."

A frowning Hocq chewed a thumbnail and looked at Borrega. "You'll need cash. Albert's old spy contacts and the police don't work for nothing. Captain?"

The pudgy Ahn, cap in hand, bowed then said, "We're still refuelling but if we leave now there's enough to get us to the Caymans. I'll need a pilot to take us out of the harbour, and oh yes, we're taking on provisions and some of the men are still onshore – "

Hocq looked up at the ceiling and thought about his potential problems with the Triad. "Fuck the men onshore," he said. "And fuck the food. Just get us out of here."

Suddenly he leaned towards Erica who trembled at the violence in his face. "It's all your fault," he whispered. "Someone get this woman out of here! Get her out of my sight."

In her bedroom Erica swallowed more vodka. She sat on a four-poster bed canopied in flowered silk, staring at a setting sun through an open porthole. Beneath her the *Rachelle* rose and fell on a choppy sea. On television, the home shopping network offered a complete hair care system, shampoo, conditioner, and combs for $34.50, half the manufacturer's list price. The yacht was an hour out of Santo Domingo and bound for the Cayman Islands.

Between what she'd just witnessed and what she'd deduced on her own, Erica knew why they were cruising the Caribbean. She knew why the Chinese drug money was being brought into the States. She knew about the Philly wiseguys, politicians, and gaming officials who were being paid off so that the casino deal would go down. She swallowed more vodka. Hocq and Martins were planning to kill her. Had they planned to let her live, they wouldn't have talked so freely.

Her eyes welled with tears. To have Simon come so close then have that miracle not occur had nearly destroyed her. How would he find Erica now? She was close to falling apart.

She finished her vodka then listened to the low hum of the ship's engine. She'd always understood the madness of gambling. Or so she thought. However, this experience with Hocq was a reminder that she'd failed to understand an important part of the madness – the violence that went with gambling.

She should have understood this because it had killed her parents. Her father, a soft-spoken gambler with an anthropology degree and a talent for stride piano, had taught her everything there was to know about poker. But despite having won thirty million dollars he'd died broke, a victim of the violence which could no more be separated from gambling than heat could be separated from fire.

Towards the end of his career her father had lost his nerve. He became afraid to bet any hand, good or bad. Rather than stop playing he'd joined a card mob, a group of poker cheats working as a team. During California's racing season the mob had broken into a warehouse and substituted three cartons of marked cards for legitimate ones. When the marked cards appeared in hotels, private games, and stores, Colly Styler and the other cheats got rich.

Soon the marked cards' existence became known and a member of a New Orleans crime family, who'd been taken for half a million dollars, put out a contract on the card mob. Erica's father and mother had died when dynamite wired to the engine of their car exploded in the driveway of their New Jersey home. Men like Hocq were

128

quick to use this same violence, quicker than Erica would ever be.

For all these years she'd seen herself as the golden girl of gambling. In truth she'd always been at a disadvantage because she'd underestimated men like Hocq. Even if she survived this ordeal, her confidence could be destroyed forever.

The vodka was taking effect. Erica's eyelids weighed a ton. It would be nice to nod out for a while. She wasn't used to drinking hard liquor. She'd done a little Scotch and vodka but after meeting Simon, she'd kicked the hard stuff and gone in for Evian water and the occasional glass of champagne. Simon had warned her against playing cards with Hocq but had left the final decision to her. She'd made the wrong one. As the ship rose high on a giant wave Erica, weighed down by regret and despair, fell back on the bed and sank into an uneasy sleep.

She awoke instantly. Outside the porthole the sun was still shining. Her watch said she'd only been asleep for minutes. Her instincts said she was in danger. Both feet were bare. Her tired, befuddled mind knew this was wrong.

She forced herself to sit up on the edge of the bed. She shook her head violently, desperate to clear it and as her eyes cleared she saw Tautz kneeling at her feet, Tautz smiling up at her, his tongue waggling lasciviously, and then he returned to sucking her big toe. Erica kicked at him, and he fell back laughing.

Two men were with him, a thin, tough-looking Chinese who'd been guarding the front door of her stateroom, and a balding, jowly Brazilian who held a camcorder in one hand.

An angry Erica pushed herself unsteadily to her feet. "What are you doing in my cabin? Out. *Now*."

Tautz scratched his head. "Charlie says you've been the cause of much anxiety. He says he's too busy to play cards right now because he and Martins have business to attend to. But he wants your lessons in humility to be continued. So me and the boys are going to teach you not to be so proud. And we're going to film the whole thing."

He grabbed Erica's ankles in a painful grip. "Party time, princess. Take off your clothes. If you don't, we're going to help you. I said, take them *off*."

129

10

Simon Bendor appeared at Abby Langway's Madison Avenue law office that Wednesday afternoon at 12.35, when the firm's three attorneys and most of its secretaries were out to lunch. He wore a brown wig, a blue jumpsuit with the building maintainence logo on the pocket, and non-prescription rimless glasses. He chewed bubble gum.

A badge reading *electricians do it free of charge* was pinned to his tool belt, courtesy of Alexis. "If you're going to swim in the ocean of the commonplace," she said, "go all the way."

After inspecting electrical outlets and wiring, he found himself in the ante office used by Wynona Jackson, the ultra-slim, fortyish black woman who was Langway's private secretary. It was Mrs Jackson who'd stayed behind to man the phones while everyone went out to lunch. Simon had interrupted her lunch of tuna salad and Evian water, prompting her to be snippy while showing him around the empty offices.

He finished making notes on a clipboard then smiled at Mrs Jackson who stood in the doorway connecting her office to Langway's. Instead of returning his smile she wrinkled her nose. "Guess that's it," he said to her.

He removed the bubble gum from his mouth. "You have a waste basket?"

"Under my desk. Will that be all?" She sounded pissed off.

"Yes, ma'am, that'll be all." Simon laid his clipboard on the desk, near Mrs Jackson's personal computer and atop an empty audio cassette container. Then he dropped the gum into the waste basket.

When he stood up he noticed Mrs Jackson's flaring nostrils and hooded eyes. She'd reached the boiling point. He reached for his clipboard, picking up the empty cassette container at the same time. He lifted a hand in farewell. "Everything looks fine. No problems as far as I can see."

"Next time you drop in without notice, I'm going to get on your supervisor like a dog on meat. You hear me?"

"Yes, ma'am. Have a nice day."

"It'll begin the minute you leave."

At 1.33 that same afternoon Alexis Bendor, sitting in a Fifth Avenue hotel suite, hung up the phone and clapped once in triumph. Then she exchanged smiles with Joe D'Agosta, a stubby, balding, forty-eight-year-old retired New York City detective who stood beside her chair. "Victory puts us on a level with heaven," she said.

She watched D'Agosta lift a thumb in agreement. He was Simon's fence and selected his burglaries. He ran a coin shop in Queens where he lived with a drunken and mentally unstable wife whom he'd refused to divorce because of the Catholic Church. Life had crapped on him a second time by afflicting an only child, a teenage daughter, with Multiple Sclerosis. Without the money from Simon's burglaries, medical treatment would have been unaffordable.

He'd never mentioned his troubles to Alexis. It was Simon who'd told her about Dag's thirty-two commendations for valour, and how he'd been kicked off the force after being framed by a drug informant. She counted on him to keep Simon alive, to bring a certain judgement and prudence to her son's fixation with larceny.

Dag turned down burglaries he considered too dangerous. He dealt only with Simon, lowering the risk of being betrayed. Nor would he keep stolen goods any longer than twenty-four hours. Buyers were lined up in advance, allowing Simon to steal to order. If a customer backed out of a done deal, Dag found another buyer quickly or threw the item away.

Alexis wasn't surprised by his willingness to help Simon rescue Erica. "Worrying about her is going to affect his confidence," Dag told Alexis. "Without confidence he's just

131

another heist artist with big dreams. Till he gets her back, he won't be good for shit. If she dies," he said, "he'll blame himself for sure. There goes his confidence. And without that he'll make mistakes. Either he gets her back or he has to stop stealing. A dead Erica means a different Simon. His head won't be on straight and he could get us both killed."

Alexis had agreed. Alive or dead, Miss Styler had her hooks in Simon. If she died, that grip would become permanent. Carved in stone. A tombstone, to be exact.

In the Fifth Avenue hotel Alexis sat behind a writing desk making notes on hotel stationery. D'Agosta stared silently out of a window at the skating rink in Central Park ten storeys below. When Alexis finished she said, "Simon?"

"In a minute." He sat on a camel-back sofa, bare feet resting on a leather ottoman as he made notes on the clipboard he'd carried into Abby Langway's office. Seconds later he slipped the clipboard under his arm and walked over to his mother. D'Agosta turned from the window and faced them.

Alexis said, "I've just spoken with a Miss Margaret O'Keeffe of Lebedeff-Goldsmith Realty. Her company manages the building where Abby Langway has his law office. She informs me there are several vacancies on the premises. At my request, she gave me floors, suite numbers, and amount of space. She'll be delighted to show these vacancies at my convenience."

"Nice." Simon seemed pleased.

D'Agosta nodded. "Gives you a choice of hiding places until you hit Langway's office tonight. I checked building security. Clara Alvarez came through for me."

Dag was a regular at a Queens bar popular with Puerto Ricans, Cubans, Colombians, and Dominicans who were enrolled as night students at nearby Queens College. Ignoring the men, he chatted up the women, many of whom were maids anxious to learn English. Dag had also enrolled at Queens College for evening courses in art appreciation, ballroom dancing and Spanish for beginners. He learned to do a fair *merengue* and speak passable Spanish, making it easier to meet the maids who could do him and Simon some good.

Maids worked for people with money, and often needed money themselves.

"You remember Clara Alvarez," Dag said to Simon. "She got us into that Central Park South penthouse belonging to the guy who got rich off all those travel books. The guy who went on the Johnny Carson show and told everybody he'd once been attacked by a polar bear while at the North Pole."

"I remember. I came away that night with a little Chinese Buddha that went for almost half a million."

"Right. Clara's now working a couple of co-ops on the West Side. Until a month ago she cleaned offices in Langway's building. From what she tells me security there is nothing special. You can walk in until around six in the evening. At six you sign in and out. That's also when every access to the building is locked except for the front entrance."

"There'll be one, maybe two guards in the lobby, unarmed, as usual. Rent-a-cops knocking down four bucks an hour while listening to the ballgame. Getting out, you just sign the logbook in the lobby."

D'Agosta folded his arms across his chest and looked down at his shoes. "You could still run into a problem."

Simon rubbed the back of his neck. "Such as."

"Some of these shysters work around the clock. The office goes twenty-four hours non-stop. Langway's got two associates. If one of them's working late you could be in for a long night."

Simon hung his head, thinking. Finally he said, "There's no other way to play it. Langway is Martins' bagman. The Dutchman who tried to cap me in Hawaii said they bring the money to Langway and he passes it on. Sometimes to a guy in Chinatown, sometimes to bankers and other businessmen. I plan to steal some of Martins' money and use it to get Erica back."

D'Agosta sat down on the window-sill. "Chinks won't like getting ripped off."

"It's not whether you win or lose," Simon said, "but where you lay the blame."

D'Agosta grinned. "I should have known. You're not going to trade the money for Erica. You've got something else in mind."

Alexis said, "Let's say you get into Langway's office. What exactly will you be looking for?"

"This," Simon said, holding up the empty cassette container he'd taken from Mrs Jackson's desk. "Belongs to Langway's secretary. Holds a tape used to save data in personal computers."

"I use a PC," Alexis said, "but I save with diskettes, not tapes."

Simon handed her the empty tape box. "This is for people who are security conscious, who have something to protect. It prevents computer theft. Keeps out the hackers. At the end of the day, you remove it from your PC and suddenly the machine has amnesia. All data, all instructions, everything's gone. Store it overnight in a safe. Insert it back into the PC in the morning."

"Temporary amnesia," said D'Agosta. "I like it. I know Hocq's wanted for stealing but I'm fuzzy on the details. What makes him a Class A felon instead of a chump change artist?"

Alexis chuckled. "Don't call him a chump, whatever you do. After Saigon was overrun, he skipped to Hong Kong with nearly sixty million dollars' worth of other people's money. In Hong Kong he meets Benny Leong, a Chinese mutual fund salesman who's dreamed of going into business for himself."

"But who didn't have the money," said D'Agosta.

"True. Little Charlie helped Benny set up his own mutual fund. The money rolls in and pretty soon Benny wants to expand which he does by setting up a holding company called OII, Overseas International Investments. It owns banks, insurance companies, real estate, mutual funds, and God knows what else. Leong does pretty good until he again has a cash-flow problem. This one's a whopper because he's expanded too fast."

D'Agosta grinned. "I can see it coming."

Alexis winked. "Which makes you smarter than Benny.

134

Again Charlie bails him but not before greasing the skids under him. Charlies starts a rumour that Benny's cash-flow problem is bigger than Benny's letting on. Next, Charlie bribes police in a half-dozen countries to close down OII offices to make Benny look bad. The closings are illegal, but who's going to argue with cops carrying machine guns? Charlie also bribes journalists to write that Benny's company is being mismanaged and internal scandals are being covered up."

Alexis sighed. "The worst was yet to come. Around that time the market collapses. Overnight OII stock drops like a stone. People can't dump their shares fast enough. Benny's in quicksand and sinking fast. At this point Little Charlie steps forward with a loan which turns out to have more strings than Nixon has excuses. Benny can have the cash providing he meets certain conditions."

D'Agosta put both hands behind his head. "Hocq sounds like he'd piss on you and tell you it's raining."

Alexis said, "He wanted Benny and his people out, and his own people in. Benny fought but circumstances were against him. In the end he took ten million dollars for his stock and walked away from the company he'd built with his life's blood. Six months later he tucked a shotgun under his chin and pulled the trigger."

"How long did it take Hocq to rape the company?" D'Agosta said.

Alexis chuckled. "In less than six months he took Benny's company for nearly five hundred million dollars. He set up his own shell companies and used them to borrow OII money which he had no intention of repaying. He forced OII to buy expensive stock in companies he set up solely for that purpose. Needless to say, the stock wasn't worth the paper it was printed on.

"The loans and proceeds from the stock swindle were run through a series of dummy corporations. Charlie shifted the stolen money from one phoney company to another. To complicate matters, he'd shut down his shell companies without warning. Following the money trail became impossible. In effect a half billion dollars vanished into a black hole in

135

outer space. You could say Charlie has a lot of respect for property. He just wants your property to become his so that he can respect it even more."

D'Agosta nodded in appreciation. "Five hundred million. Meanwhile, he's on his yacht getting tanned and nobody can touch him. I read where he carries his sister's corpse every place he goes."

He looked at Simon. "You going to do anything about those guys in front of your apartment and the health club?"

"Maybe I'll send them my hotel bill," Simon said. "You got their licence numbers?"

"One drive by was enough to make them. I could have the plates run if you want."

"Just watch yourself. If we're lucky Martins hasn't connected you to me. Stay clear of him. He and his so-called CIA friends play rough."

D'Agosta said, "So-called?"

Alexis shook her head sadly. "I hate to say it, but intelligence ain't what it used to be. The problem is with the two-gun cowboys who've read too many paperbacks. The meathead who'd rather play spy than take out the garbage."

Simon nodded. "That's Reagan for you, speaking of drooling loonies. You voted for the man."

Alexis closed her eyes and shivered. "Bonzo and the CIA agreed that the privatisation of intelligence was an idea whose time had come. According to them, anyone in America could run a network of freelance agents. Can you imagine? Suddenly agents who'd been kicked out of the CIA for incompetence were back in business. Agents who'd retired for reasons of physical or mental health were allowed to return to the game."

Simon grinned. "Bonzo had the psychos dancing in the streets and why not? He'd given them permission to cook up one harebrained scheme after another, so long as they did it in the name of patriotism."

D'Agosta shook his head. "Jerkoffs like this shouldn't be allowed out of the house. Instead they're playing John Wayne with real guns."

Alexis nodded. "And causing no end of problems for the

136

rest of us. Carter didn't like cowboys. Reagan, on the other hand, loved them. Whenever he had a crackpot scheme he used these cowboys rather than go through Congress. That's how we ended up getting involved with the Afghan rebels, the Contras, and dabbling in the Iranian–Iraqi war. Things we should have avoided like the plague. Thanks to Bonzo we've got an underground intelligence network that's accountable to nobody."

"Great," D'Agosta said. "So when these shitbirds aren't posing as patriots, they're working as hitmen and couriers for Martins."

"Beats pumping gas or selling insurance," Alexis said.

Simon said, "Tell Joe what you learned about Martins. She knows some old dude in Washington with White House connections and who's worth three-quarters of a billion dollars. He wants to marry her but she's not interested."

D'Agosta shrugged. "For that kind of money, I'll marry him."

Alexis looked at D'Agosta. "The widower, as I called him, is twenty years older than I am. I'm not about to marry a man whose upper plate falls out every time he eats corn on the cob. Give him credit, his mind's still pretty sharp. He says Martins has ties to the Random Group which claims to be a consultancy service but is actually a private intelligence company with offices across the country. Whatever it digs up it passes along to various Washington agencies, the CIA being one. Their intelligence is first-rate, I'm told, with some of the best stuff coming from Martins and Hocq. They get it from their customers who turn out to be government officials trafficking in narcotics.

"Random repays Martins and Hocq for these juicy tidbits by furnishing couriers and private planes to carry their drug money around the world. Random's government connections allow it to guarantee the planes won't be touched by US customs. The man behind Random is a rightwing nutcase named Hugh Henson who's made a fortune from razors, cosmetics, toiletries and God knows what else. He's richer than Croesus and makes Genghis Khan look liberal."

D'Agosta scratched his forehead. "Henson, Henson. Didn't

I see him on TV recently?" He snapped his fingers. "Couple days ago there was this flood in Santo Domingo. Some village almost got washed away. Over a hundred people drowned. The town had no electricity, no drinking water, and cholera had broken out. Henson flew down there with a load of food and medical supplies. He owns this airline that specialises in disaster relief."

Alexis nodded. "The airline's called *Always There*. Floods, earthquakes, revolutions, Henson or his people are always there handing out blankets, hot coffee, children's toys, quinine tablets and tiny American flags. The man's a super patriot. Loves to see his name in the papers. He's been invited to the White House, Moscow, the Vatican, Buckingham Palace. His charity's supported by some big names, among them the Vice-President and his wife."

Alexis shook her head. "Now let's discuss life's harsh realities. Mr Henson's *Always There* is an intelligence front. It carries agents, guns and military advisers all over the world. It also brings drug money into the country for Hocq and Martins. Some CIA people know this, but don't care so long as Martins and Hocq produce useful information.

"Get this," she said. "In 1981 Israel stopped Iraq from developing a nuclear bomb by smashing a reactor at a place called Osirak. According to the widower Saddam Hussein is still trying to build a bomb but he's spread the project among five separate locations to protect it from another pre-emptive Israeli strike. Random was the first to pass this on to the CIA. Guess where Random got it from?"

"Hocq," said D'Agosta.

"Right you are. He's laundering drug money for one of Saddam's cousins. Information like this is worth its weight in gold. That's why Henson and the CIA play footsie with Martins and Hocq."

Simon took a sheet from the clipboard and handed it to D'Agosta. "I'll need this for tonight. Don't buy at one store. Spread it around and pay cash. No plastic."

Dag looked up from the page. "How soon you want it?"

"An hour and a half from now, tops. Two hours from now, I hope to be walking into Langway's building. I'll find a place to hole up, catch a nap, then hit his office later tonight. Providing it's empty."

Alexis held out her hand for the list. After studying it for a few minutes she said, "Too much for one person to do." She tore off the top third and handed the remainder of the list back to D'Agosta. "Two people can do the job in half the time."

She looked at Simon. "Stop frowning. I'll be fine. If we're going to help Erica you have to get into Langway's office. Suppose Dag gets caught in traffic and doesn't get back here in time."

Simon said, "Suppose Random has a photograph of you. You could run into some of their people on the street. We know they're watching the Manhattan health club and my apartment."

"I'll wear that tacky wig you bought me in Santo Domingo. Look, you need all the help you can get. I'll wear the wig, dark glasses, and think positive thoughts. Don't worry about me. Old age and cunning beats youth and strength every time."

She smiled at D'Agosta. "Haven't told you how Simon and I made it out of Santo Domingo. Couldn't have done it without the Pope. Never did find out his real name, but it doesn't matter. He came through for us. Next time you contact your bent-nosed friends, have them send my regards to the Pope, will you?"

Albert Martins was not impressed by people who demonstrated courage under torture. Such pluck, he knew, was merely temporary and no more effective than treating cancer with a band-aid. People resisted only when they hadn't suffered enough.

In any interrogation Martins looked for the *pay-off*, that moment when a victim's eyes went soft with submission, when he or she realised that resistance was useless. The eyes said, *I'm helpless. I'll tell you everything.* This look always reminded Martins of half-dead animals caught in a trap, unessential little creatures stubbornly clinging to existence while their lives ebbed away. He couldn't understand why anyone held on when there was no hope left.

139

This evening in Los Tres Ojos (the Three Eyes), a beautiful country area ten minutes outside of Santo Domingo, Martins and four members of Dominican intelligence were in the basement of a small villa on the edge of a wooded grove. Los Tres Ojos were three subterranean lagoons of salt, sweet, and sulphur waters fed by an underground river and ringed by rock formations and lush vegetation. The villa, made of white marble, belonged to the highest ranking agent present, a goggle-eyed man whose drug money Martins had been laundering for years.

With the four agents as onlookers, Martins had almost concluded his interrogation of Guzman Sosua, an overweight forty-year-old Dominican police captain. Sosua had thought of himself as a tough guy, cursing Martins and vowing to kill him the first chance he got. Martins never took this macho nonsense seriously. Fifteen minutes and he could turn any tough guy into silly putty. Captain Sosua, with his big belly and flabby arms, was at the silly putty stage now, ready to shoot off his mouth. A few more questions then Martins would head to the airport for a flight to the Cayman Islands and the resumption of his lively cruise with Charlie.

He wiped his bloodstained hands with a damp towel then dropped the towel on a small table beside a pair of surgeon's scalpels, pliers, hypodermic needles, and two vials of a colourless liquid. Speaking in Spanish he said, "Captain Sosua, I understand you helped Mrs Bendor and her son escape to the States."

A naked, bleeding Sosua, his hands and ankles cuffed to a steel chair bolted to the cement floor, looked up at Martins with glazed eyes. "I helped, yes."

"What did you do, exactly?" Martins wrinkled his nose. The odour of sulphur from the lagoon had permeated the damp, stone walls. Also, tough-guy Sosua had lost control of his bowels. The stink in the basement was stifling.

"Took her to the airport," Sosua said. "Walked her past customs and the police. She, she was wearing a wig."

"A wig. Why not a false nose and moustache? And her son?"

"He left on his own. His mother said he had several

140

passports." Sosua coughed up blood. Martins, studying his nails, never looked at him. But he was aware of the attention being paid him by the Dominican intelligence officers. They were impressed, having just seen a master at work.

Martins said, "You said a New York Mafia family asked you to line up explosives for Simon Bendor. I want the name of the individual who contacted you."

"Torchia. Mikey Torchia. He's with the Runfolo family."

"What's the connection between Torchia and Simon Bendor?"

"No connection. They don't know each other. Torchia, he was doing somebody a favour."

"And who is this somebody?"

"I didn't ask. I was getting paid, that's all I had to know. Ten thousand dollars in advance, another fifteen when I delivered the explosives." Closing his eyes, Sosua gasped for breath.

Martins rubbed his unshaven jaw. "And the Bendors paid you the full price as a reward for helping them to get out of the country. Nice of them, wouldn't you say?"

"Yes."

"Unfortunately, you boasted about your new riches to a lady who is an informant for secret policemen whom we pay quite handsomely. I'll have someone contact Mr Torchia and find out who put in the order for Bendor's explosives."

Borrega was right, Martins thought. The boat's not safe in port. Bendor can blow a hole in it any time he damned well pleases. Martins would be better off in Avignon, behind his castle walls.

He said, "Tell me something, Captain Sosua. Why are you called the Pope?"

"I have many children. That's why I need the money."

Martins picked up a scalpel. "The Holy Father himself. Many children, you say. Exactly how many?"

"Fifteen." Sosua's head flopped back on his shoulders, exposing his neck.

"Be glad you're getting away from them," Martins said, and cut Sosua's throat.

11

Jesse Borrega stood outside Erica Styler's stateroom, waiting for the *Rachelle* to ride out a high wave. When the deck was again steady under his feet he slipped a key into the lock. Then he pulled his Magnum from its shoulder holster and slowly opened the door, entering the foyer on tiptoe. Inside he stared at the red-carpeted corridor in front of him. He saw no one.

Behind Borrega, the foyer walls were hung with wood block prints of nude African women, reminding him of Angola where he and other Cuban soldiers had fought under Russian officers as Castro's repayment for Soviet loans. At the end of the hallway a sliver of afternoon sunlight marked the stairs leading down to a sunken living room.

Why had he come to the woman's stateroom? To maintain control of his men, he told himself. Or was it because of his wife and three daughters. Were they to be violated he would kill whoever was responsible. Kill him painfully, using the machete as he'd been taught by the old Indian when they'd chopped sugar cane together in Oriente province.

But it was important that Borrega view the matter of Erica Styler from his position as ship's security chief, not as anybody's saviour. The guard on Erica Styler's door, Ho Tse, had left his post without Borrega's permission. That was Tse's mistake.

When he'd accepted this job Borrega had called the guards together and laid down his rules. There were only two. He was the boss and under no circumstances was a man to leave his post unguarded. Stand guard until you're relieved, he told them, or you'll wish you had.

Ho Tse had left his post to get laid. Let him get away with that and Borrega would lose respect. Better to clamp down now, before every man on board stopped work and lined up outside Styler's quarters looking to get lucky.

Bendor wanted his woman back and Hocq was determined to hold onto her. The yacht could turn into a battlefield at any minute. Until Bendor was taken out, everyone on board the *Rachelle* was skating on thin ice. Bendor was fearless and totally unpredictable. That made him dangerous.

He sounded like a crazy man but when Borrega thought about it, Bendor had been a soldier and how many soldiers were normal? Soldiers were the scum of the earth, and Borrega ought to know. There were times when he'd been more afraid of the men he served with than of the enemy. That's why he ruled the *Rachelle*'s guards with a firm hand.

The guards were hired killers, many of them ex-soldiers who got a hard-on just thinking about putting a bullet in somebody's head. Borrega had kept them in line with his fists, his gun, and occasionally, a kind word. But he'd done it mostly by kicking ass because you couldn't rule this bunch by reading from the Bible.

In the corridor, cool air from overhead vents chilled his neck and shoulders. To avoid making a noise, he removed a key-ring from his belt and the coins from his pockets, placing them on the carpet. Then he thumbed off the Magnum's safety and walked along the hallway, leaving the stateroom door open behind him. Despite rough seas, he kept his balance without touching the walls. As a boxer, he prided himself on moving gracefully.

He'd reached the end of the hallway when he stopped and listened. *Voices.* Not from the living room but off to the right. From the bedroom. He heard men laughing. And Erica Styler screaming in pain.

Borrega jogged across the empty living room then flattened himself outside the doorway to the master bedroom. The door was open. The Cuban carefully peeked into the bedroom. He shook his head in disgust.

Werner Tautz, naked except for a sailing cap, sat on the edge of a four-poster bed peering through the viewfinder on a camcorder. In front of him two men – Mateos, a chunky Brazilian, and Ho Tse, who'd been guarding the stateroom door, were trying to push a nude, shrieking Erica Styler to the floor. The Cuban tightened his grip on the Magnum.

Tautz laid the camcorder on the bed then threw up both hands in frustration. "Damn, she's only a woman. Can't you bastards get her on her knees for Christ's sake? Break her arm, pull her hair. *Do something*. I want this bitch on her knees."

The German rose from the bed. "Ho, give me your knife and take the camera. Just point it at me and her. When I give you the signal, press that red button. That's all you have to do. We're going to make our own deep throat. When she's finished doing me, you boys are next."

He pointed Ho Tse's switchblade at Erica. "And you, you little whore. Keep fighting and I'll carve my initials on those nice tits of yours."

Borrega casually entered the room, rotating his head to loosen his neck as fighters did before the sound of the bell. The gesture was one of contempt for the men in front of him.

He zeroed in on Mateos, walking up to his back. The Brazilian was a tough customer, an ex-cop who'd served on a death squad hired by São Paulo merchants to kill youthful thieves driving away tourists. Despised by much of the crew, he'd raped one of the *Rachelle*'s bartenders, a teenage Vietnamese boy who under Borrega's questioning had denied the attack. Borrega had known the boy was lying, but understood why. The kid had his pride.

Mateos. Borrega brought the Magnum's barrel down on the Brazilian's head, knocking him into Erica and sending both of them sprawling at Tautz's feet. Tautz quickly leaped backwards, as though Mateos could infect him with a touch. Dazed, Mateos rolled over and sat up. He was shaking his head when Borrega backhanded the Magnum across his face, knocking the Brazilian unconscious.

Caught by surprise Ho Tse, a bony twenty-two-year-old Hong Kong streetfighter wanted for the rape-murder of a

144

ten-year-old girl, had stood frozen while Borrega clubbed Mateos senseless. Unsure of his next move, Ho touched the butt of the Colt Python in his belt, thinking, The Cuban's going to kill me.

Borrega wore the look of an unmerciful executioner, a look Ho had seen on an *Hung Kwan*, or Red Pole, the Triad strong arm man responsible for meting out punishment to members who broke the gang's rules. Terrified, Ho wondered if he should try to kill Borrega or play it safe and run for his life.

He was using precious seconds to deliberate when Borrega kicked him in the knee, driving him backwards into Erica's dresser. Ho landed face down on the dresser's glass top, knocking cosmetics to the floor. His back was to Borrega who punched him in the kidneys, a short vicious left hook with power behind it. Borrega called that punch "the pisser". He'd hit men with it and they ended pissing blood. Ho dropped screaming to the rug. Borrega kicked him in the balls then quickly spun around, Magnum aimed at Tautz's head.

The terrified German eyed the gun. He still held the switchblade which he pointed at Borrega with a trembling hand. At his feet, a shaky Erica covered herself with the dress she'd been wearing. A quick glance at her, then Tautz said, "Butt out, greaseball. Charlie knows I'm here. He sent me."

Borrega slipped the Magnum back into its shoulder holster. "I don't like being called greaseball. Hocq told you to do this?"

"That's right, *greaseball*. And you work for him, not her. Wait until he hears how you screwed things up."

"Why don't we tell him together?" Borrega looked down at Erica. "Get dressed, Miss Styler."

He extended his hand and she took it, hers a small, soft hand that reminded him of the magic in women. *Bonita*, he thought. *Such beauty could set ice on fire.* To a woman like this, a man could show his soul. Borrega's throat tightened. He forced himself to look away. He said to Tautz, "Let's go talk to Hocq."

"Know what we call people like you in Germany?" Tautz said. "*Bloder Trottel.* Useless imbecile."

He threw the switchblade aside then tapped his temple with

one finger. "*Schwachsinnig*. Mentally retarded. That's you, my garlic-eating friend. You're nothing but a hired gorilla, you know that? You need to be reminded who's boss around here. Yes, we'll see Charlie. And after he sets you straight, I'm coming back here and finish what I started with this whore."

Erica, now in her dress, froze. She'd started towards a guest bedroom but now stood rooted to the spot, back to Borrega. He couldn't see her face, but he sensed her dread. Sensed the pain she felt in anticipation of future degradation. He watched her shoulders slump with the weight of fear. She reminded him of the women he'd seen in Angola, war victims whose faces seemed to be contorted in a never-ending scream.

What he did next wasn't professional. He knew that but didn't care.

He hooked a right to Tautz's stomach, a classic sucker punch the German never saw coming. Pop-eyed, Tautz doubled over and prepared to vomit. He was gasping for breath when Borrega sidestepped and hit him twice in the ribcage with his left then crouched and again went to the stomach, a right hand with all of his power behind it. Tautz flew backwards, landing on Erica's bed where he threw up, his nude, muscular body jerking repeatedly as his stomach disgorged its contents, and when his stomach was empty, he wept as he sucked air through his mouth.

Grabbing the German's ankles, Borrega yanked him from the bed and onto the floor. "Touch her again," Borrega said, "and I'll kill you. Hocq won't know because it'll look like an accident. You might fall overboard with your throat cut. Or maybe a steel drum slides across the deck and breaks your spine. Maybe you'll slip and fall into the ship's propellers, or maybe you'll drown in a thousand pounds of diesel oil. But you bother Miss Styler again, and you die out here on the ocean. You got my word on that, *compadre*."

The Cuban looked at Erica. She'd been watching him and Tautz, her sad, red-rimmed eyes moving from one to the other. Barefoot in a sleeveless dress, hair wild around a tear-stained face, she appeared fragile yet strong. And so beautiful in her vulnerability that Borrega stared as though

146

seeing her for the first time. She'd been a visitor to the boat for the past three years and they'd nodded politely, finally reaching the stage where they'd said hello and goodbye. She'd made it clear she was here for poker, nothing else. And Borrega was married to a wonderful woman.

But now he was seeing Erica Styler for the first time. And as he did, it occurred to him there was nothing more overpowering than a beautiful woman in danger. He thought, There is something wonderful and strange about this one. Her tears reminded him of the day his eldest daughter came home from school weeping because she'd lost a role in a school play for being too tall.

Except Erica Styler was nobody's child. Their eyes met and Borrega knew that if he allowed himself, he could love this woman passionately. Love this woman whose lover he would kill because that was his job.

He watched her turn and race to the second bedroom. When the door slammed behind her, the Cuban thought, Don't let that woman invade you, *compadre*. Walk away from her before you forget common sense and follow your desires.

"Clean yourself," he said to Tautz. "You stink. When you've finished, there's something I have to do before we see Mr Hocq."

Charles Hocq didn't like computers, calculators or any piece of hardware designed to think for you. The *Rachelle*'s computer system was fine for his accountants, but he preferred to calculate figures on an abacus rather than pricy doodads that often broke down without warning.

As a rule he worked alone, sitting in a deck chair in the glass-enclosed veranda of his duplex stateroom. But when Jesse Borrega rang him this afternoon on the intercom, Hocq had put aside his work on the casino deal and agreed to a meeting, wondering why the Cuban had insisted on seeing him immediately.

Usually they met in the morning and over breakfast dis cussed security problems, although with Borrega in charge problems were few and far between. Hocq found himself thinking how right the Cuban had been about Simon Bendor maybe blowing up the *Rachelle*. Hocq thought about it as he walked down the veranda staircase, clinging to the railing, remembering a fall during a hurricane that had resulted in a broken ankle.

Borrega's call might have to do with Bendor, a matter Jesse was treating as though it were World War Three. Hocq couldn't understand why anyone was serious about Bendor, who hadn't come close to harming anyone except those three couriers who hadn't been prudent enough. Still, it never hurt to be cautious. Wasn't that why he'd hired Jesse?

The greaseball, as Werner called him, had goaded Dominican Intelligence into capturing the policeman calling himself the Pope. A job well done. Albert, the old worry wart, had agreed. He was now in Santo Domingo where he was inflicting excruciating pain on the Pope in hopes of learning the whereabouts of Simon Bendor. The concept of showing mercy and leniency to his enemies had never entered Albert's head.

In a deep-carpeted entrance hall, whose walls were covered in *shoji* screens, Hocq lit a Turkish cigarette and waited for Borrega's knock. He pulled a tobacco strand from his tongue then flicked it aside, thinking perhaps he should listen to Werner and stop smoking. When Werner had told him to read the facts on smoking, Hocq had replied, "I'd rather give up reading."

Werner kept his gorgeous body by pumping himself with steroids. When *his* dependency had been pointed out to him, he'd flashed stunning teeth that had cost Hocq a fortune and said, "This stuff isn't addictive, *liebchen*. I ought to know, I've been doing it for years."

Hocq stubbed out his cigarette in a stone ashtray and was about to light another when he heard a knock at the door. Opening it, he saw Werner doubled over in pain. His hair was untidy, his clothes dishevelled, and he smelled. He'd been weeping.

The next thing Hocq noticed was Borrega, standing beside Werner with a determined look on his face. Hocq blinked, noticing for the first time how callous the Cuban's eyes could be.

"Jesse. Werner. What's this all about?"

Borrega scratched his nose. "Sorry to disturb you, but I thought it best we sort something out immediately."

"Of course. Come in, come in."

Hocq led the way to the living room where a large bay window offered a stunning view of the ocean. "Werner, is there something wrong? You look as though you've been hurt." Hocq motioned his visitors towards Chinese Chippendale chairs arranged around a lacquered low table.

Tautz said, "Just leave me alone, OK?"

Hocq and Tautz sat down, with Tautz turning his back to Hocq and staring across the room at a portrait of Hocq's sister that hung over an empty fireplace. Borrega remained standing, eyes on the sulking German. Hocq felt the tension between the two. He lit another cigarette and waited for Werner or Jesse to speak.

"The problem concerns ship security," Borrega said to Hocq. "It's something I'd like settled once and for all."

"Of course, Jesse. But I don't see the problem. Security's your area. You're being paid to keep me alive and you've done a first-rate job. What's this got to do with whatever's going on between you and Werner?"

Borrega told Hocq about stopping the attack on Erica Styler, omitting any mention of Hocq's involvement. As for Tautz's participation, the Cuban simply said they'd had words about the attack, and punches had been thrown, nothing serious. When Borrega finished talking, Hocq reached over and laid a hand on Tautz' forearm. "Werner, is this true?"

Tautz sensed his role in the play. And he wasn't happy. His role called for him to take the blame and keep Hocq out of it.

Hocq turned to Borrega. "Jesse, I swear I had nothing to do with this despicable episode. I would never submit a woman to such an indignity. To me, a woman is nothing less than a creature between man and the angels. The reverence I have for my sister, I have for all women."

Tautz spun around in his chair and glared at Hocq, the German angry enough to speak out now. He was prepared

149

to when he felt the vibes coming from Hocq who still refused to look at him. Felt the vibes and pain as Hocq mercilessly dug manicured nails into Tautz's wrist. An amused Borrega thought, get ready, *compadre*. Big song and dance coming your way.

"Jesse, Jesse," Hocq said. "I may be a bit capricious when it comes to poker but I would never order anyone to mistreat Miss Styler. Hospitality is sweet courtesy and she is my guest after all." Hocq suddenly looked misty-eyed, as though too sensitive for this world. Borrega stared at the floor.

He knew Hocq was lying but tell the little queen that and he'd go *loco*. Better to ignore Hocq's crocodile tears and hope he didn't get angry with Borrega for punching out his favourite *maricon*. The beating didn't show. Borrega had deliberately avoided banging Tautz in the face. Let Hocq see a couple of black eyes on lover-boy and Jesse could be out of a job.

Hands behind his head, Hocq gave Borrega a probing smile. "You're saying the attack on Miss Styler has affected the ship's security. How so?"

"News of the attack was all over the ship. That's how I learned about it. Guys were asking how come Mateos and Ho Tse got to rape her. Why couldn't the rest of them get in on a good thing. Suddenly nobody's thinking about Simon Bendor any more. They just wanted to get laid."

Hocq suddenly seemed more jovial. "And what did you say?"

"If I want to keep you alive, I must control the men. But I can't do that if they leave their posts without my permission and if they have their minds on rape. One man attacks Miss Styler and the rest won't be happy until they get a shot at her. If they're thinking about her, they're not thinking about you."

Hocq nodded slowly. "I understand. You're concerned with my safety. Charles likes that, Jesse. He really does."

"On your orders, I've had a man in front of her door around the clock. Keeps her in, and keeps the crew out. When I give an order, it must be obeyed. If I tell them to die for you, they'd better do it. We can start by making sure no man leaves his post without permission."

Hocq nodded repeatedly. "Absolutely. If you tell them to die for me, they have to do it. And do it with their whole heart."

Borrega knew he had the little queen going. "If Ho Tse was guarding you, and left his post without permission, I'd punish him for that. Just as I punished him for leaving his post to rape Miss Styler."

Hocq nodded in agreement. "Of course. What else could you possibly do? My goodness, Werner, did you hear what stupid Ho Tse tried to do? My God, that poor girl. If Jesse hadn't come along when he did, who knows what would have happened?"

Tautz rolled his eyes up into his head.

Hocq looked at Borrega with the appreciation of a puppy blessed with a kind owner. "You're someone I can rely on, Jesse. There're no restrictions on protecting me. None whatsoever."

"That was my understanding."

"That's how Charles wants it and that's how it's going to be. Jesse, you're the first security chief I've had who can control these guards. Your predecessor was cowardly, we called him chicken of the sea. You deal with Miss Styler's attackers anyway you see fit. I'll call and offer her my apologies. Perhaps send flowers or a bottle of perfume. As for Werner, you leave him to me."

Tautz shifted in his chair, wincing at the pain. "Mr Borrega has already dealt with Miss Styler's *attackers* as he saw fit."

Hocq grinned, pleased to see such efficiency on his behalf. "Really? Excellent. Simply excellent."

"He shot them in the head," Tautz said, "then threw their bodies overboard."

Hocq's grin vanished instantly, and he appeared to be thinking about what he'd just heard. He swallowed, then shrugged. "A bullet in the brain *is* persuasive. Justice for the unjust, I suppose you could say."

"My job isn't to keep the guards happy," Borrega said. "It's to have them ready. I suppose when Tautz saw the door to Miss Styler's quarters left unguarded, he simply walked in to see if she was all right. Maybe I misunderstood why he

151

was there. You know how things happen in the heat of the moment."

Tautz said to Hocq, "You going to let him get away with what he did to me?"

"What did he do to you, Werner?"

"Beat me. Threatened me. Told me never to bother that whore again."

Borrega's voice was menacing. "She's not a whore. Don't ever call her that."

In the long silence that followed, a smirking Hocq twiddled his thumbs and stared at the ceiling. Then, "She's not a whore, Werner, and don't you forget it. And you say Jesse hit you?"

"Yes. Not the face, just the body."

"Not too low, I trust. Next time, try running away. At least have the courage to escape your convictions. Did you offend Jesse in any way? Did you interfere with him in the performance of his duty? You know you're not supposed to call him names, don't you?"

Tautz frowned. "I did as I was told, that's all."

Hocq folded his arms. "And exactly what were you told, Werner?"

The German looked away. "Forget it. Just forget it."

Hocq smiled at Borrega. "Our Latin knight in shining armour. Jesse, from now on I want you to personally see that Miss Styler is not disturbed."

"I'll do my best. Have to get back to work now."

Hocq held up a forefinger. "Question: won't the loss of Mateos and Ho Tse leave us shorthanded?"

"No problem," Borrega said. "I've radioed Havana. Couple guys I served with in Angola are flying out to the Caymans. They'll meet us there. They're good men."

"If you say so, that's good enough for me. Let me ask you something. You guessed right on Bendor and the explosives. Any idea what he'll do next?"

The Cuban thought about it for a while and then shook his head. "He knows we're on to him so for now, he'll stay away from the boat. Look for him to do something crazy, to show up where you're not looking for him."

"I see. Thank you, Jesse. And I'll tell Miss Styler she's in your care from now on."

Alone with Hocq, Tautz said, "How could you do that to me? You let that greaseball think you had nothing to do with what happened to that whore."

Hocq wiggled a forefinger at him. "I suggest you eliminate the words *whore* and *greaseball* from your vocabulary. At least around Jesse. As for what that greaseball thinks, he's too sharp to swallow the doo-doo I just threw in his face. He knows the truth. If he were stupid, I'd never have hired him."

"So what's this game going on between you two?"

"He wants to keep his job, and I want to keep him around. He also despises Albert, which is something I intend to capitalise on."

"I don't understand."

Hocq sighed. "Haven't you noticed? Albert's taken a sudden interest in Miss Styler. She's become *his* bargaining chip, it would appear. *His*, not mine. You heard him. If Bendor gets too close, he intends to use her in *his* defence, and to hell with Charles."

"I've noticed. So?"

"So where does this leave Charles? What happens to me if Albert attempts to make a deal with Bendor and save his own skin?"

Tautz grinned. "So you want the greaseball to stop Albert from taking Miss Styler away if things get bad."

Hocq touched his nose. "Charles knows. Wouldn't surprise me if Jesse hasn't begun to fancy Miss Styler. I detect a certain warmth in his tone when he spoke of her. Especially when he insisted you not call her a whore."

"He's a fucking gentleman."

"A gentleman is somebody who won't hit a lady with his hat on."

"I didn't notice him being all that nice to her."

"I'm the poker player, not you. One look, and I can tell if a man has the balls to do business with me. Jesse is leaning in Erica's direction. Perhaps it's those long, lonely nights at sea. His attraction for the lady might inspire him to try harder to eliminate Bendor."

153

Yawning, Hocq stretched his arms overhead. "All this amorous chit-chat has Charles in the mood for cheap thrills. Go upstairs and get my special video tape. Now's a good time to refresh my memory, to remind myself why Jesse hates Albert so much." He grinned. "Outside of you and me, Jesse's the only one who knows about this tape. He came to my quarters on business one day and I happened to be watching it. Naturally, I switched it off but he'd seen enough. Enough to make him hate Albert forever from what I can see. I know what you're thinking, but not to worry. In Jesse's business, you keep secrets or you're out of work."

Tautz rose gingerly from his chair. "How long have you and Albert been partners?"

"Fifteen years. Why?"

"Fifteen years. In that time you guys probably made a lot of money together."

"Why the sudden interest in my finances?"

"Millions or no millions, if Albert ever finds out about that tape he'll kill you."

"Probably," said Hocq, settling back in his chair and smiling sweetly at Tautz. "If he ever found out about it."

The voice was soothing, but the eyes were threatening and Tautz knew he was flirting with disaster. He quickly tried to extricate himself from the danger posed by his mouth. "He won't hear about it from me, that's for sure."

"I find that reassuring," Hocq said. "Let me ask you, Werner. Why wouldn't you turn this tape over to Albert? You just might come in for a lavish reward."

"Forget it. The minute he saw that tape, he'd kill whoever brought it to him for knowing too much. You know, like in the old days when the king would cut off a messenger's head for bringing him bad news."

Hocq thought over what he'd just heard, and then winked at the German in approval. "I've always enjoyed knowing more about people than they know about me. That tape gives me an edge on Albert. You never know a man, Werner, until you watch him and his wife on film doing something naughty. Very, very naughty."

154

12

At 8.55 p.m. Simon Bendor stepped to a window in a vacant Madison Avenue office and dialled Abby Langway's office on a cellular phone. As Langway's phone rang one floor below, Simon stared down at a darkened mansion whose windows were so blackened by Manhattan's polluted air that a late sunset failed to penetrate them.

He'd spent three hours in an empty, refuse-littered office, napping on a sagging sofa until awakened by his wrist alarm. The office's previous tenant had been an Indian psychiatrist who'd combined a private practice with work as a psychiatric consultant for a dozen city agencies. The shrink was now serving a three-year prison term for taking cash and drugs to fix disability cases for city employees.

Twenty minutes ago Simon had dialled Langway's office, speaking to a rough-voiced, Latino secretary who'd sounded unsettled and fatigued. He'd quickly fabricated an excuse for calling by asking if this was the state unemployment insurance agency. Angry at answering a wrong number, the secretary had called him a jerk then hung up. As he listened to the phone ring, he hoped she was on the elevator now descending towards the lobby. He listened for two full minutes before pushing down the cellular antenna. *Showtime.*

Tonight he wore a grey suit, matching tie, pocket hankie, crewcut wig, and surgical gloves. "You look absolutely spineless in that outfit," Alexis had said. "But I suppose that's the point."

An attaché case rested on the window-sill in front of him, alongside the remains of a salad that had been his supper. He shoved the remains into a plastic bag then locked the bag and cellular phone inside the case. He looked around for anything incriminating he might have left behind. He'd left nothing.

At the office entrance, he placed an ear against the frosted glass door and listened. *Voices*. He flattened himself against the wall. Directly in front of the office, an argument was in high gear. Two Haitian cleaning women were squabbling in a French patois, voices echoing along the empty hallway. Simon leaned against the wall and folded his arms. He could only wait this one out.

Minutes later the women entered an office to his left, pulling a cleaning cart behind them. One slammed the door, rattling the glass door in Simon's office. He shook his head. At least the dispute ended before they started swinging machetes. He picked up the attaché case, cracked the frosted glass door and peered into the shadowy corridor. Empty.

He crossed the corridor and stepped through an exit door onto a small, dusty landing. He waited until his eyes had adjusted to the stuffy, semi-darkness. Then he walked down to the next landing and cracked the exit door. All clear.

He walked past deserted offices and a bank of elevators towards Abby Langway's office. When it came to stealing, he was ice on ice. But this time he didn't feel the usual rush that came with doing a job. This time he was thinking about Erica. He refused to think she might be dead. To be at his best, he had to keep her alive in his mind.

Building security was pretty lame. Had management asked Simon's opinion he would have told them that most security was worthless, that when people finally decided to take precautions they did too little. The average citizen had too high an opinion of himself and his ability to protect his property.

In front of Langway's office he touched the door with a gloved hand. Solid wood, one inch thick. Closed flush against a solid jamb. All hinges were inside, preventing removal of the door. Door frames enforced by steel strips. Not bad. Give the man a B plus.

Instead of a lock Langway had installed a digital alarm panel, with a touchtone-like dial. Keys weren't necessary.

To turn off the alarm and enter the office, simply punch in a four-digit number. Crack addicts would pass up this door in favour of a softer target. Dope fiends could afford to choose another prey. Simon couldn't.

From the attaché case he removed a random digital selector, a small computer twice the size of his hand. After looking around to make sure he was still unobserved, he connected a selector wire to the alarm panel. Then he aimed the selector at the door, pressed his thumbs on a pair of red buttons, and watched the selector's small screen.

The selector kicked in immediately, probing the alarm panel and forcing it to send thousands of four-figure combinations speeding across its screen. Picking the proper combination wasn't Simon's worry. The selector would do that for him. Twenty seconds later the lightning quick passage of numbers came to a sudden halt, leaving a four number combination – *1963* – on the small screen.

A security number was usually chosen because of its significance in people's lives. For Langway, 1963 could be the year he'd graduated law school or gotten married. It was also the year John Kennedy had been assassinated, the year the Beatles hit it big in America, the year Stan Musial had retired. Maybe Langway was thinking of a time when he was more innocent and less corrupt.

Simon punched the number into Langway's alarm panel, opened the door, and disconnected the selector wire. Inside, he closed the door behind him, returned the selector to the attaché case then put on a pair of night vision goggles. He looked around. Much better.

Seconds ago he'd been standing in darkness. With the infrared NVs he could now see clearly even if everything did have a greenish tinge. He was in the reception area which contained a desk and two small leather sofas. Between the two sofas was a coffee table topped by magazines and sporting a bowl of Hershey's Chocolate Kisses. Simon popped a couple of kisses in his mouth, dropped the tin foil wrappings in his pocket, and went looking for an escape route. It was his first move on every job.

He checked Langway's office, the associates' offices, and

the law library which also doubled as the conference room. He came up empty.

Then he got lucky. He found a tiny balcony outside the window of Langway's private office. From here it was a six-foot leap to a balcony facing a different office window. His escape route.

He returned to the reception area, took two magazines from the coffee table and placed them on the receptionist's desk. He climbed on the desk, feet on the magazines, and with a small screwdriver unscrewed the cover of a smoke alarm in the ceiling. Removing the alarm battery, he dropped it in his jacket pocket. Then he inserted a dead battery in the alarm and replaced the cover. Sprinklers? *No problema.* There weren't any.

Returning the magazines to the coffee table he picked up the attaché case and walked along a carpeted hallway to the law library. He'd located its smoke alarm earlier today, atop a floor-to-ceiling bookcase. He removed his shoes, stood on the arms of a wooden chair, and again exchanged the alarm's battery for a dead one. He put his shoes back on and walked to the office of Langway's secretary, the testy Mrs Wynona Jackson.

Case in hand, he entered Langway's office and stopped in front of the wall safe. Simon silently thanked Mrs Jackson for having pointed out the safe to him. Not that he wouldn't have found it eventually.

It was to the left of Langway's oak desk, hidden behind a print of a Van Gogh self-portrait. Simon remembered how Mrs Jackson had become even more tight-assed when he'd stopped in front of the picture. She might as well have shouted, *Here's the safe, dude.*

Removing the print from the wall, he stroked the outside of the safe. Nothing to write home about. It was seven or eight years old, making it obsolete in today's high-tech world. It had a solid steel body, inaccessible hinges, and hardened steel plates over the lock mechanism to make it drill resistant. For Simon, it wasn't a challenge.

He did have one worry. Langway might have backed up the safe with its own alarm or smoke sensor or even a vibration sensor. Chances were he hadn't. Any man dumb enough to stay with this turkey didn't have the smarts to add the extras that might keep out thieves

He peered closer at the safe, searching for its rating. He found it engraved on the manufacturer's nameplate, courtesy of Underwriters' Laboratories. *TL-15*. Was Langway serious? TL-15 was the lowest burglar-resistance rating a safe could get. It meant the safe could resist an attack from ordinary burglar's tools for fifteen minutes. Fifteen *whole* minutes.

The nameplate also contained a second coding rating: *TR-B*. TR, for torch resistant; B, for ten minutes. The safe could hold out against a torch for ten minutes. Was Langway serious or what? A dedicated thief was ready to put in a lot more than ten minutes. Langway probably hadn't been robbed since he'd bought it, allowing him to develop a false sense of security. Into each life some rain must fall, and Mr Langway was about to get hit with a downpour.

Simon took a special stethoscope from the attaché case, fitted the earpieces to his ears and placed the diaphragm against the safe's dial. He was using a Tonoscope, a medical stethoscope with a diaphragm sensing unit and built-in one hundred times amplifier. To clear the dial, he turned it five times to the left. Then he switched direction. The combinations on these models all began with a right turn.

Halfway through the first revolution, he heard a click. We're getting there. This was the last number dialled to open the safe. He continued turning to the right, slowly, carefully. Listening. Seconds later he knew the number of tumblers he had to deal with.

He began gathering the tumblers, moving them collectively in rotation with the dial. Two more minutes of dialling and the opening lever and cam were in position to open the safe. But because the tumblers weren't in line, the safe wasn't ready to open.

He shook the dial gently, listening as the lever clicked against the tumblers. Soon he had manipulated the cam into picking up the tumblers. He had the combination numbers. But not their order. *No problema*.

He had turned up four numbers. The first two were *19*

and 63, numbers obviously dear to Langway's heart. The remaining two numbers had to be added in proper sequence. Simon turned the dial, starting with 19 and 63, then added the leftover numbers. The safe wouldn't open. The sequence was wrong.

He switched the last two numbers, re-dialled the combination, and turned the handle. He heard a hard click through the earpieces. He whispered, "*Yes!*" The safe was unlocked. He opened the door. Some men were born good, some made good, and some made off with the goods.

The computer tapes were in the front. He removed all nine and counted them twice, making sure he had the number correct. Then he placed them on the floor and from the attaché case removed a plastic bag of similar tapes. He counted out nine, placing them in the safe.

Next, he checked the safe's remaining contents. He found nearly four thousand dollars in cash and thought about pocketing the money. He rejected the idea; theft could disrupt his plan. The safe also contained a petty cashbox, business contracts, correspondence, the office lease, signature plates for the cheque signing machine. He took some of the contracts and correspondence then returned the rest to the safe.

Time for the finale. He adjusted the NVs for more light, took a small propane torch from the attaché case and trained the flame on the safe door. He scorched the dial, handle, door. Flying sparks bounced off the NVs. He didn't stop until he'd torched the outside of the safe for twenty minutes. Until he'd turned the contents into ashes.

Finished, he removed several extension cords, plugs, hair driers and a small radio from the attaché case. Two extension cords and three plugs were connected to Langway's air-conditioner, lights, and small refrigerator before being plugged into a single electric outlet. Simon then turned on every electric switch in the office. Nothing happened until he turned the fridge thermostat up to high. That's when the overloaded wall outlet blew and sent flames creeping along the extension cords.

Not bad for starters. The fire needed a boost, however. Simon lit the propane torch and touched its flame to the office drapes and papers on Langway's desk. He set fire to the rug and to the wall where the safe was located. When he decided the smoke was getting too dangerous, he left the room.

In the law library he used extension cords and another hair drier to overload a single socket and increase its power usage. The socket blew immediately. To cover his tracks, he torched the hair drier until it was a melted mass of plastic. Before leaving the library, he set fire to the rug, drapes, and law books.

In the secretarial area, he set his third and last fire. He connected three computers, a hair drier, and a radio to a single socket. All three fires burned brightly.

The smoke detectors were silent. *And there were no sprinklers.*

In the lobby a baby-faced security guard sat at a small desk, eyes glued to *Hustler* magazine's joke page. He never looked up as a slim man in a grey suit hovered over the signout book. The guard didn't notice that the man didn't write his name. Instead he used a pencil stub to underline the last signature.

As the grey-suited man walked to the building entrance the guard smiled at the joke comparing President Bush to a tampon because the President was in the best place at the worst time.

13

It was almost 11 p.m. when Albert Martins shoved Lisa Rizal, a chubby seventeen-year-old Filipino prostitute, onto the bedroom floor of a mountain villa north of Manila.

He kicked the half-naked teenager then removed his lightweight, embroidered overshirt, a garment favoured by Filipino men instead of jackets in the tropical heat. The shirt was sprinkled with Lisa Rizal's blood. Her blood also dotted the mosquito netting surrounding a large bed.

The sobbing prostitute crawled towards the bedroom door. An excited Charles Hocq squeezed Tautz' forearm and leaned forward in his chair to watch the teenager's face. He applauded when Martins removed his belt and viciously whipped Rizal. Hocq squeezed Tautz' hand to get his attention then pointed to a second woman near a darkened fireplace.

She was naked, thirtyish, and exquisitely beautiful. Letter opener in one hand, she advanced towards Martins and the prostitute. Hocq lit a Turkish cigarette and blew smoke at the second woman. "Fabienne, *ma petite lapin*," he said. "You're looking gorgeous as always." He waved to her while Martins continued whipping Lisa Rizal, the dark-haired college student who moonlighted as a prostitute.

When Fabienne reached Martins' side, she smiled at Rizal. "Stupid little tramp. You're going to pay for being so hardheaded." Tautz said to Hocq, "Here it comes. Lessons in good behaviour from your Auntie Fabienne."

As Fabienne held Rizal down, Martins raped her. Kicking and screaming, the teenager bit Martins' hand. Angered, he punched her in the face while Fabienne stabbed her with the letter opener. When he tired of hitting her, Martins lay back on the floor and watched Fabienne continue attacking the girl. The teenager's screams were piercing.

Hocq, a look of annoyance on his face, stuck both index fingers in his ears. The irritated expression was replaced by a smile when Fabienne began performing oral sex on the dying girl. After a few minutes, Fabienne lifted her bloodied face and smiled at Martins. Tautz said, "Fabienne gets a ten. She's got style."

And as Lisa Rizal whimpered in agony just inches away, Martins and Fabienne had sex on the floor. "I love a happy ending," Hocq said.

Minutes later, Martins and Fabienne lay in each other's arms, oblivious to the last agonies of Lisa Rizal. When Fabienne whispered something to Martins, Hocq said he wished she'd speak louder. He watched Martins walk towards the bathroom. Fabienne strolled to her dresser where she picked up a bottle of perfume, and a can of hairspray.

When she turned Martins was pouring after-shave lotion on Rizal. Fabienne joined in, dousing the girl with perfume and then wetting her with hairspray. When she finished Martins dropped a flaming lighter on the teenager. Rizal shrieked and twisted wildly before making a last effort to rise from the floor. But her ordeal proved too weakening. Wailing as flames blackened her flesh, she fell into a fetal position.

Eyeing her with a chilly calm, Martins and Fabienne backed away from the smoke.

Tautz removed the video cassette from a VCR atop a television set in Hocq's master bedroom aboard the *Rachelle*. "This could send Martins to prison for life," he said.

Kicking off his slippers, Hocq settled into a lotus position on a red leather couch. He closed his eyes and held both hands palms up in the centre of his body. A radiant sunset had turned a calm sea a bright crimson.

"Meditation expedites your concentration," Hocq said.

"No shit," Tautz said.

"Without concentration one has no peace. Our Fabienne

lacks peace. Otherwise, she wouldn't be the homicidal little whore that she is. She crucified the Rizal girl and never showed the slightest remorse. Fabienne does what she pleases then denies she did anything wrong."

Tautz turned the video tape around in his hands. "Martins always has cunt on the mind, that guy. Once a month he probably gets a nosebleed. Did you know they were going to kill the girl?"

Eyes still closed, Hocq shook his head. "No, but I wasn't surprised. Their idea of a hot time left me dumbfounded. Miss Rizal was even more stunned."

He smiled sweetly. "I still keep a hidden camera in that guest room but I've yet to see anything as colourful as the Martins in action. You learn a lot about a man when you observe him at his pleasures."

Tautz turned the cassette around in his hands. "I'd hate to see this sort of thing become a trend."

Hocq said, "Fabienne wanted to destroy something she couldn't be any more, which is young and innocent. Relatively innocent, in Miss Rizal's case. Albert and Fabienne are wolves who view the rest of the world as woolly lambs."

Hocq took several quick breaths then exhaled for a long time. "Poor Lisa. She was only whoring for money to complete nursing school. Albert and Fabienne spared her the high cost of tuition." Hocq smiled mischievously. "When Albert asked me for someone unspoiled and disease free, I immediately thought of Lisa. I'd used her before and never had a complaint. I thought Albert wanted her for himself. I had no idea he was planning a *menage à trois* and neither did Lisa."

"How old is this tape?" Tautz said, settling himself on the couch beside Hocq.

"Four years. Which doesn't lessen its impact. Filipinos are violently opposed to their people being sexually exploited by foreigners. Foreigners come to their country to take advantage of Filipino poverty. They rape children and turn nice girls like Lisa into whores. Filipinos don't like that."

Hocq closed a nostril with an index finger. "Any foreigner convicted of a sex crime in the Philippines can expect no

164

mercy. I told police Miss Rizal had fallen asleep while smoking in bed. However, if police see this tape, my partner could find himself extradited for murder. Unless he chooses to run for his life."

Tautz smiled. "Albert's dick is safely tucked away in your back pocket."

Hocq cocked one eyebrow. "Why do you and Albert dislike each other?"

"He called me a whore."

"You are a whore."

"That still doesn't give him the right to say it. Not when *he*'s married to a slut himself."

"Werner, Werner. You're not supposed to know too much about Fabienne, remember?"

"I don't have to take shit from that guy."

"Listen to Charles. Be careful. Albert can be ruthless."

Hocq opened his eyes, uncrossed his legs and pointed to the tape. "Put that away before Albert shows up. Tonight he and I will be working on the Golden Circle deal until the wee hours."

Tautz looked at his watch. "Less than forty-five minutes before we dock in the Caymans. The tape will be hidden long before he comes on board. You think he and Fabienne do things like this all the time?"

"You mean strip whores naked and test their pain threshold?"

Tautz nodded.

"I suppose they misbehave now and again. When it comes to women, Martins has always marched to a different drummer. And Fabienne's no schoolgirl either. Incestuous relationship with her father. Bizarre affair with a Vietcong leader who used to make her strip then get down on all fours. Then there was her work for Communist Intelligence, much of which she did on her back. If they ever starred her as 'Mary Poppins', she'd stick the umbrella up her ass. I've had difficulty buying presents for Fabienne. What can you give a girl who's had everybody?"

"She killed people in Vietnam, didn't she?"

Hocq lit a cigarette. "Men did her killing for her. She was

165

quite good at getting them to degrade themselves. Albert lets her go with other men from time to time. Excites him to hear about her adventures."

A frowning Tautz chased a thought in his mind. "This Vietnam big shot still wants to get his hands on her."

"Phan Bai, you mean. The old Vietcong hero whose son Albert murdered. He's never accepted the idea that Albert and Fabienne died in a plane crash. He's pursued them with the same determination he showed in driving the French and Americans from his country."

"And there's a reward for Fabienne's capture?"

"Fifty thousand dollars. Not much by Western standards, but a bloody fortune in Vietnam."

"Speaking of money, don't forget our bet."

"When it comes to money, Charles doesn't forget a thing. A thousand dollars at fifty to one that Bendor kills Albert."

"Or that Bendor stays alive for ten days."

"You have a week left. Which is also the same amount of time we have to get the Golden Circle's money into the States. Now go put that tape away before Albert bites our heads off."

Werner Tautz returned the tape to Rachelle Hocq's coffin, hiding it in an interior panel and following Charlie's instructions exactly. *Never touch Rachelle's corpse. Never smoke or eat around her. Remove your shoes before entering her room. Be respectful in her presence.* Tautz thought, you'd think she was the Princess of Wales instead of cold meat.

Her coffin was in a two-room cabin adjacent to the master bedroom. A frigid temperature which prevented her embalmed corpse from rotting left Tautz feeling colder than an Eskimo's butt. The cabin was off-limits to everyone, not that the crew was anxious to view a cadaver. Rachelle's coffin was a perfect hiding place for Charlie's tape.

One room contained her clothing, stuffed toys, and cosmetics, along with her guitar and bamboo flute. The second room, the icebox, allowed Rachelle a bit of privacy. Her corpse was displayed in an open cedarwood casket with a brilliant lacquered finish enhanced by gold dust and cracked ivory inlay. A large bronze Buddha, housed in a teakwood pagoda, kept watch on the corpse.

Rachelle's youthful face had been given a shy smile by a wizened, ninety-year-old Chinese mortician who touched up the corpse twice a year. He'd dressed her in white silk, with gold and diamond rings on all of her fingers. A pink spotlight shone down from the ceiling, making Rachelle seem lifelike. Tautz didn't know whether to fuck her or take her dancing.

For him, death was simple. You laid down one day and you didn't get up, and that was that. Charlie viewed the matter differently. For him, Rachelle wasn't dead; she was napping.

Tautz had been around – Rome, the Riviera, California, and Rio de Janeiro, living off young women, old women; young queers, old queers. Living off anyone rich enough to afford his body. He thought he'd seen it all until he'd taken up with Hocq, a weirdo who carried his sister's corpse everywhere. If the money and perks hadn't been so good, Tautz would have jumped ship long ago.

He returned the tape to the coffin and looked around to see if he'd dropped anything on the floor. Once he'd accidentally left a bit of raw carrot near the coffin, and had caught hell from Charlie. He never wanted to go through that again.

He looked at Rachelle's corpse, at her custom fitted gown and jewellery. All this luxury wasted on a frozen little cunt. He felt his sore ribs. Borrega had a punch like a mule's kick.

As he massaged his ribs Tautz considered his future. Sooner or later, Charlie would lose interest in him and go after someone younger. Tautz also had to worry about Borrega beating him again or even killing him. He had to worry about Martins hurting him when Charlie wasn't around. And he was still reeling over Charlie's suggestion they marry each other when this Golden Circle shit was finished. *Werner Tautz married to a man?*

He'd been born to a prostitute in the Reeperbahm, Hamburg's famed redlight district, and hadn't the slightest idea who his father was nor did he care. Charlie had given him a taste of the good life which Tautz wasn't about to give up. But did he want it bad enough to *marry* Charlie?

167

This thing with Erica Styler and her assassin-boyfriend could get out of hand. Tautz might have to abandon Charlie without so much as a goodbye kiss. But why go empty handed? He stared at Rachelle Hocq's rings, emerald necklace, diamond and gold bracelets, jewel pendants. These little knick-knacks could set up Tautz for life.

All he had to do was fill up his shopping-bag, and stroll off the boat. He knew places in Germany where Charlie would never find him. He smiled, thinking of how he could protect himself against Charlie. The tape of Albert and the missus in action could very well end up in Albert's hands, courtesy of an anonymous donor.

A quick viewing of the tape and Albert would know who to blame. *Goodbye, Charlie*. And Tautz would be free to live without looking over his shoulder.

Was Charlie serious about killing him if he tried to leave? Charlie was Charlie and a master trickster. However, he'd first have to catch Tautz. Which wasn't going to be easy.

The German blew a kiss to Rachelle's corpse and left her cabin, determined to survive at all costs.

14

At 2.20 a.m. Erica Styler, escorted by Jesse Borrega, left her quarters on the *Rachelle* and began walking along the open deck towards Hocq's stateroom.

Hocq claimed to be too fatigued to leave his quarters for the salon. He also didn't want to expose his sinuses to the steamy night air. Would Erica mind coming to his stateroom for a few hands of five-card stud? Did she have a choice?

The encounter with Werner Tautz had left her too frightened to sleep. Valium, cigarettes and vodka had failed to calm her nerves. Since the yacht's arrival at the Grand Cayman Islands, she'd waited to be summoned by Hocq. In that time she'd paced her stateroom until finally she'd collapsed on her bed in tears.

On deck a bright moon had turned the yacht's lifeboats, gun emplacements, and helicopter into frightening apparitions. Shadows lengthened as Erica approached them. She saw no safety anywhere.

The guards appeared more heavily armed than usual. More watchful, more edgy. Tonight they didn't laugh, drink on duty or listen to transistor radios. Guard duty was being taken more seriously than ever. The number of guards had also increased. It depressed Erica to see the ship so impregnable.

While the guards were concerned with Simon, Erica sensed their fear of Borrega. This time as she walked past the lookouts posted on deck, no one leered at her. Nor were lewd remarks passed. Erica had attained instant respect, thanks to Borrega's shooting of two would-be rapists.

She was in his debt. He'd showed guts punching out Tautz.

At the same time she knew he'd kill Simon without batting an eye. Nothing personal. It was just business.

She and Borrega walked in silence. Erica had the shakes. Opening and closing her fists helped keep her trembling from being too obvious. She felt the humidity. Rain was on the way. Something else to depress her.

When they reached Hocq's stateroom, she and Borrega stopped to look at the empty pier where a bespectacled, young black slowly drove a fork-lift towards a warehouse. She was reluctant to leave Borrega; she felt safe around him. Unless she was imagining things, he wasn't anxious to leave her either. She remembered the look in his eyes after the attack in her stateroom. Her heart began beating faster. Simon, she thought. I must remember Simon.

"I'd like to thank you again for what you did today," she said.

Borrega, elbows on the railing, waved his hand until he caught the attention of a guard on the pier. The guard acknowledged him with a wave then tapped a smaller guard on the shoulder and whispered in his ear. Both guards, who were Cubans, waved to Borrega who pointed to the fork-lift driver. The Cubans nodded. Immediately they walked towards the fork-lift driver. Borrega, *el jefe*, wanted him checked out.

Borrega fished a cigarette from his shirt pocket. "I had to stop the discipline problem before it got bigger."

Erica shook her head. "That's not the whole story."

"Makes my job easier, Miss Styler, when the guards stay in line."

"Erica."

Borrega smiled, looking handsome in the warm moonlight. Erica's heart jumped. She fumbled in her handbag for a cigarette.

Borrega said, "Martins says Tautz is dumb. Says he can't figure out the dosage on One-a-Day vitamin tablets."

Erica smiled. She felt relaxed around Borrega. Too relaxed.

The Cuban nodded. "It's the one thing Martins and I agree on. We can both do without Tautz."

"You don't like Martins either," Erica said.

170

Borrega stared at his cigarette. "I don't like the way he treats women. I walked into Hocq's quarters one day when he and Tautz – " He broke off and brought the cigarette to his lips.

Erica said, "I only know one other man who could have taken on three men and beat them."

Borrega looked at her. "I hear he's pretty good, your guy. They say he was doing some serious things in Vietnam when he was only nineteen. I started boxing when I was eight. Some kid stole my new bike. I complained to a cop who told me I'd better learn to fight unless I wanted to keep on losing bikes."

"Same thing happened to Simon," Erica said. "He was working in a California supermarket after school. One day he tried to stop some kids from stealing beer. They beat him pretty badly. That's when his mother took him to a boxing coach."

Borrega blew cigarette smoke at a Finnish cruise ship berthed nearby. "Smart woman. Martins doesn't like her, that's for sure."

"What did he expect? He tried to kill Simon. God knows what Alexis would do if she hears about the bet Hocq has with Tautz."

"What bet?" Borrega said.

She told him.

Borrega shook his head. "Mrs Bendor isn't the only one who'd be upset. I don't think Martins would appreciate people gambling with his life."

Erica placed a cigarette in her mouth and Borrega lit it, firing a wooden match with his thumbnail. In the flickering glow of the flame their eyes met. "You think the bet is wrong but you'll still try to kill Simon," she said.

Borrega thought, I could become lost in her eyes. He looked away as casually as possible. "I wouldn't be doing my job if I didn't try to stop him. I'm sorry you're here but that's not my doing. Your man isn't stupid. He understands the situation. He'll try to get you back and I'll try to stop him."

Erica angrily flicked her cigarette overboard. "Manly men doing manly things. You're all too willing to kill for the sake

171

of women and children. But you never ask us how we feel about it."

"No, I guess we don't," Borrega said.

Erica closed her eyes. "God, what did I just say? If it hadn't been for you, who knows what Tautz would have done to me? I can't think straight any more."

"There're no easy answers. I find it hard enough to understand life, let alone make judgements."

"I'm sorry for what I just said."

"Don't worry about it. You've had a few things on your mind lately."

She smiled at him. They looked at each other for a long time. Finally Erica said, "I've got to go. Don't know if I can play cards after what happened, but I guess I have to try."

"Play to win. Like you always do."

She offered her hand and Borrega took it. He was ready to take her in his arms, out of sympathy or because the two of them were alone in the dark. Sensing this, she slowly pulled away from him, not trusting herself to speak. Borrega opened the door, watched her step inside, and then softly closed the door behind her. He thought, Keep telling yourself you're not killing her man because you want her.

He headed for the gangway without looking back.

A minute later the door to Hocq's stateroom opened to reveal a darkened foyer. After a few seconds Albert Martins stepped on deck, quietly closed the door behind him then walked to a nearby lifeboat. He concealed himself behind the lifeboat, out of sight of Borrega who stepped from the gangway and onto the dock. Granny was right. Eavesdroppers never hear good spoken of themselves.

Martins and Charlie had just concluded hours of work on the Golden Circle deal. They'd been in touch with couriers by phone, fax, and radio. Here in the Caymans the *Rachelle* had picked a courier carrying two million dollars of Triad money. Day after tomorrow the courier would be dropped off the Florida coast, to be picked up by a shrimp boat and taken to Tampa. Then he'd be driven to New York where the two million would be turned over to Abby Langway.

Martins and Hocq had also spoken with Abby Langway

in New York where up to now things were going smoothly. Tomorrow Langway was expecting another four million dollars. This was Triad money coming in from Toronto, to be counted before being passed on to front men in Chinatown. Langway had been warned not to mislay a single dollar. Not unless he wanted to encounter the wrath of Martins and the Golden Circle.

With Charlie concentrating on business, he and Martins had accomplished much in just five hours. When they'd finished Martins had announced his intention of going to his cabin and sleeping. Not Charlie. He'd wanted to play poker with Erica Styler.

Speaking of Miss Styler, Martins had learned of the attempted rape from Manuel da Gama, a gaunt, young Portuguese radio operator who was his paid informant. Da Gama had related a complete account of Borrega's timely rescue, followed by his execution of two guards. Martins had been incensed. Charlie had acted stupidly. Styler might have been killed, leaving them without a hostage.

And now there was Charlie's bet, the details of which Martins had just overheard. This bit of eavesdropping had left Martins incensed and bitter. Charlie had betrayed him by toying with his life.

Martins shouldn't be surprised. Betrayal followed Charlie around like a shadow. Sooner or later he betrayed everyone he worked with. He'd screwed people in Vietnam, Hong Kong, and God knows where else. Martins should have known the day would come when he'd get it up the ass from Charlie.

Charlie was Eurasian and the Chinese side of him believed it was better to exploit than be exploited. The bet had been a selfish whim on Charlie's part, the act of a wicked little boy. It had also changed Charlie and Martins' relationship forever.

Charlie believed in getting the edge on people. Martins had more than a few criminal acts to his credit and Charlie knew about them all. But why worry, Martins had told himself, Charlie needed him.

Simon Bendor's entry into the game had changed things. Charlie, it appeared, had thrown loyalty out of the window. He could well be planning to hand Martins and Erica

Styler over to Bendor. Charlie's problems would be over and Martins' just beginning. In Granny's words, *If I were you, Edwin, I'd be worried about my future.*

Learning of the bet now pushed him into a decision. He must get Charlie before Charlie got him. He remembered Borrega had seen something in Charlie's quarters which had turned him against Martins. Something that made him dislike Martins because of his attitude to women.

Martins turned from the pier, leaned back against the lifeboat and stared up at the moon. Concentrate, he told himself. Be Charlie for the next few minutes. Become that little prick. Get inside his head and look around.

Charlie's edge. What could it be? Women were Martins' weak spot. Always had been. Suddenly his eyes glistened from the thrill of having made a spectacular discovery.

"Lisa Rizal," he whispered.

At dawn an exhausted Erica pushed ten thousand dollars in chips into the pot. "I call."

She was playing poorly. Hocq was beating her without cheating.

The ship bobbed gently at anchor. In Hocq's living room a picture window glowed crimson with an early sunrise. Erica sipped black coffee and watched Hocq shake his head. "What, no raise?" he said. "Shows a lack of fortitude, if you ask me."

He turned up his hole card, the ace of clubs. "Caught the flush. Charles wins again."

Sensing Erica's physical and emotional weakness, Hocq had gone for the jugular. This game had cost her seventy thousand dollars.

She'd lost her nerve and was making mistakes. Fatigue had dulled her reflexes and robbed her of all energy. Instead of playing to win, she was trying not to lose. She was ignoring Hocq's errors and committing too many of her own. For the first time ever, he was bluffing her out of pots.

Franklin Chao, a juicy-lipped thirty-year-old Chinese accountant, dealt another hand of five-card stud. Chao had been pressed into service as a dealer, a task not to his liking. At

174

best he was adequate, managing to handle the cards without dropping them on the floor. He'd also avoided antagonising Charlie, no mean feat.

Hocq's earlier cheating was no longer a secret. Erica had figured out he'd done it through the use of "trims" slipped into the game by Werner Tautz. Trims were marked decks, cards trimmed according to rank. The way she was playing now, Hocq didn't need them.

"Allow me to apologise again for what happened today," Hocq said. "Blame Tautz' behaviour on steroids."

"It wasn't Tautz' idea, it was yours."

"Are you saying I ordered Tautz to attack you?"

Anger gave her courage. "You're an asshole, Charlie."

"It's a gift."

"Next time Werner wants to get laid, tell him to crawl up a chicken's ass and wait."

"I most certainly will. By the way, how long does Borrega have to wait?"

"I have a question for you. What are you going to do if Borrega kills him?"

Hocq nodded. "I'm going to break you, princess. I'm going to turn you into a loser."

Erica watched as Franklin Chao dealt Hocq a second deuce. She drew a trey, matching one she had showing. She bet cautiously. Too timid, she thought. Too calculating. Another time she'd have run Charlie's butt out of the game. Not now.

She caught a seven matching her hole card. Two pair. Sevens over threes. She bet twenty thousand dollars. Hocq saw her twenty then raised ten thousand. Erica matched his bet. Her last card, a jack of spades, was useless. Hocq caught a four, giving him two pair showing, fours over deuces. Unless he had a matching hole card, Erica had him beat.

Concentrate, she thought. Remember Charlie's betting habits. His weak points. Her brain, however, refused to function.

"Your bet, princess." Hocq casually tugged at an ear-lobe.

Play it safe. "Call."

175

"Raise thirty thousand," Hocq said.

Erica swallowed. Her hands were sweating. She forced herself to see his raise. But she didn't bump it. "Call."

Hocq turned over his hole card. A third deuce. Erica had lost eighty thousand dollars.

Hocq blew her a kiss. "How does it feel to be a loser, princess? Charles would like to know."

15

Avignon, France

In a telephone call from the Cayman Islands Martins ordered Fabienne to remain within the castle compound until further notice. She assumed the order had to do with du Carri's murder. She was mistaken.

"Charlie could be planning a double-cross," Martins said. "Stay close to home where it will be hard for him to get at you."

Fabienne closed her eyes. "I feared this would happen one day. But he can't run the business without you. *He needs you.* And what about Simon Bendor? Does Charlie want to take him on alone?"

"Logic and Charlie don't always go together. He's acting more selfishly than usual. Self-preservation makes men do strange things."

Martins told Fabienne about Charlie's bet on his life. He also told her of his suspicions that Charlie might use the Lisa Rizal killing against him. This could mean their extradition to the Philippines on murder charges. An extradition order could also lead the Vietnamese to Martins and Fabienne.

"Charlie's got something else to hit me with," Martins said. "He can hand Erica Styler over to Bendor and leave me to fight my battles alone. And if I get killed Charlie wins his bet."

"After all these years he acts this way," Fabienne said.

"You know the Chinese as well as I do. They're out for number one, and Charlie's part Chinese. I have the feeling that if Bendor gets too close, Charlie will cut me loose. Self-preservation, remember?"

"And Bendor knows we're alive."

"He saw me in Santo Domingo. And I'm assuming he interrogated the men I sent to Hawaii before he killed them. He knows."

Fabienne was afraid. In Vietnam Bendor had been a legend, a mythical assassin who could approach the most well-protected victim without being detected. He was a kill-crazy maniac who had never showed remorse. The more things change, the more they remained the same. Bendor was still a killer. And he was determined to murder them.

Martins said, "Charlie's always bragging about having the edge on anyone he works with. We needed each other, so I never thought of our relationship in those terms. Seems I was wrong."

"What are you going to do?"

"Nail him before he nails me. I'm sorry it has to end this way but he doesn't leave me much choice."

"Charlie can be ghastly at times."

"That's why I want you to stay put. If you're in Paris or Milan, he could easily — "

"I understand," she said. "I'll do as you ask."

"Tell Trach that from now on the castle entrance is to be locked and guarded around the clock. And he's to be very careful about who comes inside. Check all IDs — workmen, delivery people, cleaning women, everybody."

Trach Dai was a birdlike thirty-five-year-old Chinese/Vietnamese who assisted Martins in running the courier ring from the castle. He had strong contacts with Golden Triangle druglords he'd met while in Communist Intelligence during the Vietnam War. He also served as Fabienne's bodyguard when she went on her sexual adventures.

He and Martins had been bitter enemies in Vietnam. Martins had captured his spy cell and executed everyone but Trach Dai, whose tongue he'd cut out. Both men now maintained an uneasy truce based on common business interests and a mutual obsession with Fabienne. Trach was asexual but devoted to Fabienne. His passion for her, while not sexual, was nearly as violent as Martins'.

He'd been a starving orphan, foraging through garbage

178

in Saigon alleys when she'd taken him home with her. Aware of her powers even as a child, Fabienne had no trouble convincing her father to let the sickly orphan live at their home. Trach Dai had eaten table scraps and slept on the kitchen floor with the dogs but he'd never forgotten Fabienne's kindness.

He'd become her second self, a friend who understood and forgave. Fabienne had been his defence until he'd become strong enough to protect them both. Before and after the Vietnam War he had killed to save her life. As friends they thought as one. Trach Dai knew everything about Fabienne and continued to love her.

With Saigon about to fall, she'd saved him again by having Martins put him on one of Hocq's planes bound for Hong Kong. Trach was a part of her, she told Martins. To kill him was to kill her. Needless to say, Martins found the relationship between his wife and Trach Dai irrational. But to please her, Martins let her have her way.

In time, he came to see he'd made the right decision. Fabienne lived on a sexual tightrope. Her addiction to the shocking and forbidden made her vulnerable to danger. Trach was a formidable bodyguard. He was quite capable of dealing with anyone who would harm Fabienne on her sexual forays outside of the castle. Their relationship, Martins decided, was far from traditional.

But then so was Fabienne.

She wore blue and silver this evening – blue silk trousers, tank top, diamond choker with matching earrings. Her belt, sandals, and bracelets were silver. She wore no make-up, only lipstick. She looked incredibly beautiful.

She and Trach Dai walked across the spacious castle courtyard now darkened by twilight shadows cast by the castle's massive towers. It was just after sundown and still warm. Fabienne was accompanying Trach who'd almost completed his security check. He spoke to her in sign language, combining lip-reading with the manual alphabet. When guards needed to be given orders Fabienne spoke for Trach.

179

Their destination was the gatehouse, the most vulnerable part of the castle because it contained the entrance and drawbridge. They passed the kennels where Trach waved to the wolf-like Atlas Shepherds who ignored him and continued devouring fresh horsemeat. At the gatehouse he pointed to a pair of defensive turrets made of granite, then to the surrounding granite walls whose pink tinge came from a fire set two hundred years ago by supporters of the French Revolution. He signed to Fabienne. *The walls are seven feet thick. Hocq can't break them down.*

Fabienne nodded. The castle's position was strong: it sat alone atop a large outcrop of rock that had made it invulnerable to battering and sappers. Powerful towers, a lack of windows, and the presence of murder holes – wall slits used by bowmen – conveyed an air of invincibility and menace. Fabienne should have felt safe. Instead she felt intimidated by the castle's mystery and power.

Intimidated because she was now a prisoner.

She stared through the rusted portcullis and down the cliff at neat rows of cypress trees lining an empty dirt road leading through fields of olive trees, lavender, poppies and grapevines. She watched a heftily-built female cyclist, a loaf of bread strapped to the bike rack, peddle towards the spires of Avignon two miles away. In the castle's dry moat, a scrawny Frenchman with a walrus moustache slowly rode a power mower in lazy circles. Two nobodies, Fabienne thought. And each with more freedom than I.

"I love this land," she said to Trach. "The vineyards, stone farmhouses, waterfalls, Roman ruins, the market gardens. But I must be free to come and go as I please."

Trach quickly spelled out his words. *Dangerous to leave. Hocq might abduct you as he did Erica Styler.*

Fabienne nodded. "In Saigon he held me hostage until Albert committed that big robbery. I'm worried about Albert. You have to be so careful around Charlie. He flies off the handle at a moment's notice."

Trach resumed signing. *The wise man takes advantage of his enemy's poor judgement.*

"'Do not fight defensive,'" Fabienne said. "'Success comes

only with being offensive.' I remember. But how can Albert take the offensive while on Charlie's yacht?"

Lure Hocq here.

"You mean get Charlie to leave his boat and come to the castle."

Trach nodded. *Trick the tiger into leaving its lair. Albert knows the tiger. He will know what bait to use.*

"Perhaps I should tell him that."

This is his only chance. On the boat, Hocq is strong. Away from the boat he is weak.

Fabienne squeezed his hands. "I'll call Albert now and tell him what you said."

I did it for you, not him.

"I know," said Fabienne. Trach's animosity towards her husband was so well hidden that Martins appeared genuinely unconcerned in the little man's presence. Vietnam was fifteen years ago and long forgotten. Or so it seemed. But Fabienne knew that Trach was Chinese and capable of waiting years for revenge. The best she'd been able to do was make him promise not to harm Albert while she was alive.

In the courtyard guilt seized her. Guilt over what Albert had done to Trach in Saigon. So she did what she always did at these times. She took Trach in her arms and called him her beloved little brother.

They walked towards the banquet hall where they were to eat a supper of Vietnamese food cooked by Trach. Martins hated Vietnamese cuisine; Fabienne could only have it when he was away. She said to Trach, "Why can't Bendor and Hocq wipe away the past and get on with their lives?"

Trach Dai signed, *Because for some men the past can only be washed away with blood.*

He delivered his message with a cold smile.

"Would you wipe out your past that way?" she asked.

No, Trach Dai lied. *I would not.*

181

16

He would have to remain unknown, undetected. He must draw no attention to himself or his purpose. Let him use the enemy against each other. Feed them false information, to be discovered on their own. His own tactics must remain hidden and unpredictable.

Abby Langway stepped from his Madison Avenue office building at 4.20 p.m. to find a cop in mirrored sunglasses and helmet standing beside his limousine, night stick tucked under one arm as he wrote up a ticket. Langway stopped in place. This city was impossible.

Norman Lins also saw the cop and halted in front of Langway. Lins was a thin-lipped, fortyish Texas courier who was escorting the lawyer and four million dollars to Chinatown in lower Manhattan. The Texan had a hand in his jacket pocket around the butt of a Browning automatic. The other kept a tight grip on the handle of a metal suitcase. Langway carried a similar suitcase.

"I'll do the talking," Langway said. "Where the hell is Jody, by the way? He's supposed to be with the car."

"Copping some z's in the back seat, looks like," Lins said, removing his hand from his jacket pocket. "Him and me's both been travelling on damn little rest. Meanwhile that cop's got his cute little scooter in front of the car, blocking our way."

Langway pushed his suitcase against Lins' muscular thigh. "Keep walking. We're talking traffic ticket, not a damn AIDS test."

182

"My ID is from out of state," Lins said, his tone making it clear he didn't like surprises.

"I said let me do the talking. Now, would you mind moving your ass?"

Langway looked at the cop who'd stepped to the front of the limousine to copy down the licence number. Just one more break from my everyday wonderful life, he thought. Two days ago a fire in his office had destroyed tapes, office records, and cash, not to mention personal items that couldn't be replaced. Because he was in an old building without sprinklers, the insurance company was talking tough about paying off. Langway just might have to go to court.

A preliminary fire department report said the fire had been caused by defective electrical wiring. But Langway's secretary claimed the wiring had been inspected the very day of the fire and pronounced in good shape. Langway had checked with building management and been told no one had been sent to his office.

A minute later management had changed its tune. Someone *might* have come up to Langway's office. Management wasn't sure because its records weren't up to date. In other words, management didn't know what the hell was going on.

Langway had enough on his mind without the fire and some cop giving him a ticket. He was putting in fifteen-hour days on this casino deal, plus working weekends. Thank God he was being well paid because he needed the money. His ex-wife wanted an increase in child support and his Sutton Place co-op was boosting his maintenance fifty per cent. He had a new cabin cruiser on order. Just the thing for weekends on Long Island Sound with a blonde dental technician who loved to unzip his fly with her teeth.

When Langway and Lins reached the limousine the cop, slender and moustachioed, flashed the grin of a man happy to be sticking it to somebody. He held out the ticket between thumb and forefinger. "Who wants it?" His voice was cheerful enough to make Langway want to put his foot up the guy's ass.

Langway handed his suitcase to Lins. "Throw them on the back seat." Then he looked at the cop. "I'll take it. What is it

183

this time – moving violation? Meter expired? Except the meter hasn't expired as far as I can see, or does that matter?"

Smiley, as Langway thought of the cop, handed him the ticket then stepped aside to allow Lins to pass in front of him. Lins' back was to Smiley. Langway, anxious to get in the limo, was about to follow Lins when Smiley stiff-armed him in the chest. It was a powerful blow from a guy who wasn't all that big. As Langway staggered backwards, thinking Smiley had lost his mind, the cop clubbed Lins on the head with his nightstick, knocking him to the ground.

Lins landed on his back, an arm flopping against the limo, and as he started to rise Smiley kicked him in the head. Lins slumped to the pavement and didn't move. A frightened Langway knew that Jody wasn't coming out of the car to help. Smiley had taken care of him too. Langway's only thought was how to stay alive.

By now several people had stopped to watch the action. But not to interfere. Not in New York where cops did as they pleased. Along with Langway the crowd watched Smiley calmly hang the metal suitcases on the scooter's handlebars then mount the scooter and kick start it. A second later he was driving north on Madison Avenue, skilfully weaving through traffic.

Langway nearly screamed when someone bumped him from the rear. Christ, a homeless black man. Thin, stinking, crazy, and nearly toothless. A battered wooden picture frame hung around his neck. Langway recognised the guy, a local headcase who called himself Captain Nice after a Saturday morning cartoon. Nice was a creep who'd get in your face, his head in that crappy-looking frame as he shouted, "I been framed." Then his hand would come out, soliciting payment for his tacky performance.

Now he stood beside Langway and chewed on the remains of a hamburger plucked from a nearby trash basket. Suddenly Nice pointed to the fallen Lins and cackled with the satisfaction of someone convinced he'd been right all along. "Y'all be making a movie, right? Hey, put me in there. Ain't got to pay me but five dollars. Five dollars and I be in your movie."

184

17

It was just after dark when Joe D'Agosta drove his Ford van from Manhattan into Astoria, a small section of Queens whose semi-detached houses, coffee-houses, and ornate churches were home to more Greeks than any city outside of Greece.

He stopped the van on Ditmars Boulevard and purchased two boxes of fresh Greek pastry from a deli whose sidewalk was crowded with elderly Greek men in lawn chairs. Dag went for *chocolatinas*, a cream pastry made of chocolate and whipped cream. This stuff was delicious but fattening. Soon he'd have to oil his butt to put on his pants.

In the parked van he offered a *chocolatina* to Alexis who sat in the passenger seat disguised in sunglasses and a dark wig which she claimed made her look like Cesar Romero. They were heading for D'Agosta's home just minutes away. Alexis would stay there while Simon took care of business in Manhattan.

"This neighbourhood is fascinating," she said to D'Agosta. "It really is a little Athens."

D'Agosta swallowed a mouthful of pastry. "Greeks live here their whole lives without speaking a word of English. When I was born it was all Italian. Greeks started taking over in the sixties, so the Italians moved out. Except for my old man, may he rest in peace. Nobody was going to push him out of *his* neighbourhood. He used to own a wine supply shop on the end of this block. Sold grape presses, kegs, extracts – whatever you needed to make your own wine." D'Agosta shook his head. "He hated Greeks. Used to tell everybody the five toughest years for a Greek kid were the second grade."

A laughing Alexis nearly choked on her pastry, forcing D'Agosta to pat her on the back. Finally she said, "That's not politically correct, but it's funny. This stuff's delicious but no more for me. Don't want to spoil my appetite."

She was looking forward to her first decent meal since Honolulu. D'Agosta, who'd taught himself French cooking, was going to cook Châteaubriand in the style of the European chefs of the thirties – grilling the thick, centrepiece of fillet steak between two pieces of sirloin.

"Sure your wife won't mind my staying with you?" Alexis said.

D'Agosta removed another *chocolatina* from the pastry box. "Depends on how much she's had to drink and whether or not she's taking the expensive medicine I'm paying for." He pointed to Alexis' shoulder-bag on the seat between them. "First we stop at my coin shop and put those copies of Langway's tapes in the safe."

Alexis stared at the restaurant. Through its glass front she could see a wall mural of the Parthenon by moonlight. She looked troubled.

"Simon knows what he's doing," D'Agosta said.

Alexis took D'Agosta's hand. "If anything goes wrong he's dead."

D'Agosta smiled. "You listen to Simon sometimes and you can think the guy's as crazy as catshit. But if anybody can put those tapes to work for us, he can."

Alexis patted her shoulder-bag. "Just having them in our possession can get us killed."

"Don't I know it. They're hotter than the weather."

Alexis and D'Agosta had viewed the tapes on a computer in an East Harlem pawnshop owned by Alayne Spertell, a former policewoman who'd taken early retirement rather than be questioned about a missing kilo of confiscated cocaine. Spertell hadn't asked what the tapes contained or why they were being copied. Among cops, favours were granted without undue inquiry.

Alexis said, "Martins and Hocq would kill us for knowing that these tapes contain the sordid details about their little casino deal."

She closed her eyes. "Triads, Mafioso, corrupt politicians and gaming officials. These tapes are dynamite. And let's not forget the participation of the very affluent Hugh Henson who loans intelligence operatives to Martins and Hocq for use as couriers of drug money. I may have trouble sleeping tonight."

D'Agosta licked cream from a thumb. "Next year's a presidential election, right?"

"Unfortunately, yes."

"Polls says the President can't lose. Now suppose it gets out that someone close to the President is on the board of directors of Henson's airline which just happens to be smuggling drug money into the country."

Alexis sat up straight. "There'll be hell to pay. Get this information to the right person and we might do ourselves some good. I know just who to talk to."

"The widower?"

"He could save the President's butt and help us at the same time."

D'Agosta took another piece of *chocolatina* from the box. "Whatever happens I want to see Andy Lam go down. He's Langway's Chinatown contact. Wasn't surprised to see his name on the tapes. When I was on the force, he was always calling me a racist. Kept giving me this shit about white cops stereotyping Asians as criminals. All the while he was laundering drug money, and smuggling illegal aliens into the country. He just never got caught. Back then he owned one bank. Now he owns two, and half of Chinatown besides."

Alexis nodded. "And you say he's got clout at City Hall?"

"Dines with the mayor, sits on city commissions, and gets himself a good citizen award every year. Supports both political parties and gives money to all the right causes. The guy's always been dirty but nobody's nailed him."

"These tapes could hang him."

"Sure could. They tie his ass to the Triad *and* the Mafia. Anyway, let's drop them at my shop and get home. I'm hungry. Beats me why people diet. What's the sense of starving so you can live longer. I don't call that living, do you?"

*   *   *

187

D'Agosta's coin shop faced the bocci courts in the park on Steinway Street. It was nearly 9.30 p.m. when his van pulled into a parking space in a block of Italian bakeries, Greek delis, and oriental dry cleaners, all of which were closed. The darkened block was deserted except for two Vietnamese teenagers bouncing a basketball in front of a Vietnamese restaurant, the one place of business still open.

As D'Agosta and Alexis left the van he said, "If my old man thought Greeks were bad he'd shit if he saw these Asians. In Sicily, where he was from, you were loyal to your village. Everyone outside the village was your enemy. Believe me when I tell you there weren't any yellow people in his village."

At the shop entrance he said, "Won't be long. Safe's in the back room. Been here twelve years and haven't washed the windows once."

He caught sight of the blue and white car from a corner of his eye. The squad car pulled up behind the van, and three men got out. All wore plain clothes. They headed towards him and Alexis, spreading out to cut off any avenue of escape.

"Trouble," D'Agosta said.

"They're cops," Alexis said. "We haven't done anything, so why should there be trouble? I thought you knew every cop in Astoria."

D'Agosta's teeth were clenched. "Never seen these guys before. Besides, plain clothes don't travel in squad cars.

The leader was a light-skinned black man, broad-shouldered with pudgy faced good looks. He was thirtyish, smartly dressed in a white summer suit, and had the easy smile of a man convinced of his own charm. He flashed his tin at D'Agosta and Alexis.

"Mrs Bendor, Mr D'Agosta, I'm Detective Cleveland. The men with me are Detectives Crisp and Brendal. Sorry to disturb you, but we'd like your help regarding some stolen property. Stolen coins, to be precise." He smiled without showing his teeth.

Crisp was small with spiky hair. Brendal was balding, with jowls that could have come from a bloodhound. The June heat seemed to be bothering him.

"You had my place staked out," D'Agosta said.

Cleveland smiled.

D'Agosta took a deep breath. "I'd like to see some identification."

"We just showed you our badges," Cleveland said.

D'Agosta said, "You showed me your badge. The other two haven't shown me anything. I'd also like to see a photo ID from everybody. You wouldn't mind if I called the precinct and spoke to your watch commander, would you?"

Cleveland stared at his nails. "To be honest I would mind. Now we can get on with our business in a mannerly fashion. Or we can show you the downside of being a wiseass. Up to you, my man."

He opened his jacket revealing a gun tucked in his belt. D'Agosta noticed the gun wasn't too big. The well-dressed Cleveland hadn't hurt the line of his suit.

D'Agosta looked at the ground.

"A sublime move on your part, dude," Cleveland said. "You just bought yourself and the lady with the bad wig a few minutes more of this precious life. Oh, before I forget, regards from Mikey Torchia and the Pope. If you're looking for perfect friends in this world, well, what can I tell you?"

18

Scotch and soda in one hand, Abby Langway stood at a window in his Sutton Place duplex and stared down at a townhouse belonging to the Secretary-General of the UN. It was nearly 10 p.m. and black-tie guests were still arriving for the Secretary's dinner party.

Langway drained his glass and was reaching for the bottle when the phone rang. He picked it up on the first ring.

"It's me," Hugh Henson said. "Just got off the phone with Martins."

In the six hours since the robbery, Henson and Martins had done little else except burn up the long-distance lines between the *Rachelle* and the Waldorf Towers where Henson kept two suites. Langway was Hocq's lawyer while Henson had attached himself to Martins. This split had only been intensified by the robbery. When it came to laying blame for the loss of the money, it was Langway and Hocq v. Martins and his spy groupie, Hugh Henson.

"Albert's in a bad mood," Henson said. "Losing four million dollars has left him kind of snippy. I'm glad there's an ocean between us."

Henson, a wide-nosed sixty-five-year-old industrialist, was fascinated by danger but refused to take risks. Unable to stomach corporate boredom he'd founded Random Consultants Ltd, a private intelligence agency that allowed him to become involved in what he called the "down-and-dirty". He hated Communists, the US Congress, the IRS, women, movies with subtitles, MTV, and environmentalists whom he called shit-eating tree-huggers.

He was worth two billion dollars and had enough clout to get Norman Lins and Jody Brill admitted to a posh private hospital. Smiley had given Lins a skull fracture and a broken cheekbone. Jody Brill, unconscious through it all, had a broken arm and nose. Langway hadn't suffered physical injury but his nerves were shot to hell.

"Martins and I feel the thief was Simon Bendor," Henson said. "Who else has the balls to pull off something like this?"

"Hugh, your opinion is whatever Martins tells you it is. Neither of you wants to believe that maybe a courier sold out."

"Albert thinks we'll be hearing from Bendor with a proposition. The money for his girlfriend. When that happens, we're to let Albert know."

Langway looked across the living room at his wearied reflection in a smoked mirror over a fireplace. An eighteenth-century Chinese lacquer screen hid the fireplace hearth. His wife wanted the screen as part of the divorce settlement. Losing her was no big deal. Losing the screen was.

"Pinning this thing on Bendor is convenient," Langway said. "Stops us from looking any further. Forget about the others whose motives were as good as Bendor's if not better."

"The other players." Henson sounded resigned to hearing something he'd just as soon reject.

Langway said, "Start with the Philadelphia wiseguys who want a bigger piece of the pie. Then there are rival Triads who are fighting the Golden Circle to see who'll get established here first. How about the customs people we're paying off? Maybe they decided we weren't paying them enough." Langway paused. Then, "Finally we have your people, Hugh."

"Wondered when you'd get around to that."

"Your couriers, your pilots, your *intelligence* service. They knew about the money. What's to stop them from grabbing it."

Henson sighed. "Martins is replacing some of the missing money. If Bendor took it, that means your client Mr Hocq is responsible because he brought him into the picture."

191

"Telling Charlie about the robbery was the hardest thing I've had to do since becoming his lawyer. He went nuts, absolutely nuts."

"You'd go nuts too," Henson said, "if you had to give the Triad four million dollars by tomorrow morning. What did you tell Andy Lam?"

"I said our couriers are having trouble getting across the Canadian border. Told him our customs guy wasn't on duty and we're having to make other arrangements. There won't be a problem if we can square things with the Triad by tomorrow. This thing is breaking my balls."

"Albert says the Chinese aren't stupid. Lam could still have heard about the robbery. Since this is an emergency I'm offering Albert some assistance."

"Figures. How much?"

"Two million. That's his fiscal liability. Hocq has until noon tomorrow to find his two million. My couriers were involved so I feel somewhat responsible."

Langway closed his eyes. "You didn't call to tell me you're giving Martins two million dollars. Why did you call?"

"Albert thinks the fire in your office could be tied to the robbery."

"He *what*? Jesus. Hugh, if you keep listening to assholes, you're going to get AIDS through your ears. Martins is crazy and you can tell him I said so."

"I'm just passing on what he told me. He says the two events coming so close together have to be related."

Langway tightened his grip on the phone. "I smell panic. Martins needs a scapegoat. Something tells me Charlie and myself have been elected. The way I figure it, Martins could have grabbed the money. He pays back half, he's still up two million. Get real, Hugh. I wouldn't put myself through this shit for any amount of money. Martins is fucking out of his mind to suspect me."

Henson cleared his throat. "You can tell him in person. He's coming to New York tomorrow."

Langway went rigid. "He's what?"

"I have a plane on call for him in Tampa. He's notified all couriers to sit tight until they hear from him. No more

192

travelling until he gives the word. All remaining courier runs are to be rescheduled. You, Martins and I will do that as soon as possible. He also wants to check Random's internal security and your internal security as well."

Langway swallowed the rest of his Scotch. His stomach heated up immediately. He felt sick. "Martins coming here tomorrow?" he said. "Christ, I really need that. I really need that."

"Until Bendor's out of the picture Albert wants us to keep in close contact."

"So now the great spy master is spying on me. Wonderful."

Henson sighed. "Be careful how you talk to Albert. I wouldn't describe his present mood as Christlike. Just remember – a kind word is like a spring day."

"Right. And a wet bird never flies at night."

"What's that mean?"

"Nothing."

"I see."

Langway massaged his eyes with a thumb and forefinger. "I lost four million dollars of someone else's money and my office looks like the Iraqi Army's just marched through it. And Martins thinks I'm ripping him off. The guy's all heart."

He slammed down the phone. Then he went to a second-floor bathroom, leaned over the toilet bowl, and threw up.

Downstairs in the living room, Simon Bendor rose from behind the lacquered screen in front of the fireplace. He wore a black ski mask and leather gloves. He carried the metal suitcases he'd taken from Langway six hours ago.

He walked to a Frank Stella print on a far wall, moved it aside and dialled the combination of a wall safe. He'd had the safe open when he'd heard Langway entering the apartment. A few more minutes and he'd finish what he'd been doing when he'd been interrupted. He looked over his shoulder. No sign of Langway.

So Martins was coming to New York. Interesting.

He finished with the safe, closed it and replaced the print. Then he picked up the suitcases, walked to the front door and removed his mask. He quietly let himself out of the apartment. Behind him the telephone, which he'd bugged, began to ring.

19

It was nearly midnight in the *Rachelle*'s conference room as Charles Hocq listened to Martins' theory on the robbery and Langway's fire. He listened without interruption.

Showing a rare self-control he waited until Martins had finished, before saying, "You're inventive, if nothing else. You're claiming Bendor learned of the couriers through Abby. By your thinking Abby's accountable for the loss of the money which I don't think is right."

"I don't like surprises," Martins said. "I'm flying to New York to make sure we don't get hit with any more."

"The men you sent to kill Bendor could have told him about the money. That is, assuming Bendor is our thief."

"Charlie, you brought Bendor down on us, remember?"

Hocq began tugging at a brass button on his dressing gown. "Let's go back in time, shall we? Your desire for Fabienne preceded this crisis. Seems to me there's more than enough blame to go round. And while we're handing out blame, I wish you'd consider replacing Henson. His men failed to defend Langway and failed to kill Bendor in Hawaii."

"If you suspect Henson of the robbery," Martins said, "all I can say is you're sadly mistaken. May I point out he's too rich to steal?"

"Perhaps. But his men aren't rich."

Hocq yanked the button off his gown then looked at Borrega. "Jesse, your counsel will be greatly appreciated."

The Cuban said, "If Bendor pulled the robbery, why haven't we heard from him? Why hasn't he tried to make a deal for his woman?"

Hocq smiled at Martins. "Yes, Albert. Why *haven't* we heard from Mr Bendor?"

"What makes you think we won't?" Martins said. He almost said, Bet you we hear from him soon. No cracks about betting. Not until he'd learned if Charlie had anything to do with the robbery. Martins had become obsessed with Charlie's bet. The more his obsession grew, the more suspicious he grew of Charlie's every action.

Suppose Charlie had pulled the robbery with the intention of blaming Martins. Four million dollars was reason enough to stab anybody in the back. With Martins out of the way, all proceeds from the casino and Cuban tourist deals would go to Charlie. Furthermore, a dead Martins could be blamed for everything that went wrong.

Fabienne and Trach Dai were right. Better to deal with Crafty Charlie from behind the sturdy walls of Martins' castle than confront him on this floating loony bin. Better to deal with Bendor from the castle as well. And to do that Martins needed Erica Styler under his control.

Borrega said, "Bendor's not the type to give up. If he pulled the robbery, he's bound to get in touch. So far he hasn't. That bothers me."

Martins began shredding a napkin with his nail file. "Bothers me as well. I wonder if he's gotten in touch with Langway?"

Hocq shook his head. "I'm telling you Abby's no thief. I trust him. I rely on him. We haven't heard from Bendor because he doesn't have the fucking money."

Borrega stroked his moustache. "Bendor's sharp. Even if he deals for the money, he has to know nobody's going to let him get away with stealing. You, the Mafia, the Triad, everybody will come after him. Exchange or no exchange, he's a dead man."

Martins frowned. "What are you trying to say?"

"I'm saying that snatching the money is a temporary solution at best. After he gets his woman back, Bendor still has to stay alive."

Hocq gnawed on the brass button. "Did you hear that, Albert? Bendor doesn't gain anything by stealing our money.

As I've been trying to tell you, someone else took it."

Martins was about to reply when Manuel da Gama, the radio operator, entered the conference room with a cablegram. He handed it to Martins who read in silence while da Gama waited for a reply.

When Martins finished he passed the cable to Hocq. He read it then handed it to Borrega. Hocq shook his head. "I can't believe it. Henson has actually done something right. He's captured Bendor's mother and the dynamite man."

"Another reason to go to New York," Martins said. "I will personally interrogate her. When I'm finished, she'll tell me where Bendor is. And she'll tell me if he took the money."

He began filing his nails. "If I've learned one thing over the years it's that no one lies under intense pain. And who should know this better than Mrs Bendor? She underwent some nasty torture at the end of World War II. Lost an ear. Time she lost the other one."

20

Alexis Bendor, cuffed hands in her lap, sat beside the window of a shabby Queens motel, staring at La Guardia Airport just yards away.

A 707 had just taken off from the Marine terminal, an Art Deco extravaganza built for the 1939 New York World's Fair. Two police boats, almost invisible in the sticky night, slowly cruised the darkened water, leaving whitecaps in their wake. Behind the boats a seagull, a black dot in the moonlight, skimmed the water's surface in search of food.

Alexis, Joe D'Agosta, and their three captors were in a threadbare room, waiting for one of Hugh Henson's planes to land at the airport. Alexis and D'Agosta were to be taken aboard the plane which would depart immediately. As the aircraft circled the sky, they were to be interrogated by Albert Martins.

Dag sat beside Alexis on a metal folding chair, cuffed hands wiping perspiration from his neck. Alexis was frightened and assumed he was too. He didn't look scared, which she put down to his police training. Alexis, meanwhile, had to squeeze both wrists to keep her hands from shaking.

She looked at Cleveland, the white-suited black man who seemed to be running things. He sat in the room's only stuffed chair, pillow case on his lap as he cleaned his wingtip shoes with Evian water and a paper towel. Finished, he put his shoes back on, tying the laces into precise bows. Very prissy, Alexis thought. Cut him open and you'd find disinfectant in his veins.

Cleveland threw his damp paper towel at the chunky

197

Brendal who lay on a sagging double bed, absorbed in a TV newscast. "Eddie fucking Murphy," Brendal said, tossing the paper towel on the floor. Steady beer drinking had him shuttling back and forth to the toilet. Alexis had watched him swallow cans of Coors Gold, hit the john, then return to the bed and another six pack.

He excused his drinking by claiming the heat was getting to him. He didn't like the air-conditioner either; it was giving off more warm air than cold. In any case, he drank because he enjoyed it. Crisp, the third man, enjoyed smoking. An ashtray on a nearby night table was overflowing.

The run-down motel was on a deserted lot in a section of Queens called Jackson Heights. Jackson Heights, said the chatty Cleveland, was the largest South American community in the country. He made no secret of his distaste for Hispanics, describing them as lazy, uneducated, and with no respect for the law.

"The first thing you learn at a Puerto Rican driving school," he said to Alexis, "is how to open a car with a coat hanger." A Puerto Rican American Express Card, he told her, was a knife. Strange, Alexis thought, how we all need someone to look down on.

She and Dag had been driven to the motel in Dag's van, handcuffed and face down on the oily floor. The spiky haired, skinny Crisp had sat across from them, a .45 Automatic held loosely in one hand. He spent the trip listening to Patsy Cline on his Walkman, keeping time by waving his .45. His bulging eyes reminded Alexis of a weasel in heat.

The perspiring Brendal had driven the van. Cleveland, ever protective of his snazzy appearance, had driven the squad car. One look at Dag's van and he'd refused to set foot inside, claiming the van smelled as if someone had just cracked a fart. "Your ride is a cesspool," he told Dag. "Do all Italians live this way, or is it just you?"

"Just me. And some flamingos I know."

"Flamingos?"

"They say when flamingos get married they put a couple of cast-iron Italians on the lawn."

Cleveland smiled. "Cool. I like that. Shows grace under

pressure. And you are under pressure, homeboy. Copious pressure."

In the motel Alexis stared ahead, along a small hallway and into a cramped bathroom where Crisp could be seen crouched over a basin, hands cupped under running water. He'd urinated without shutting the door, grinning over his shoulder at Alexis who'd turned away in disgust. Now he was complaining about bugs, which were everywhere including under Alexis' feet.

Crisp dried his hands with paper towels. "Roach heaven back here," he said to no one in particular. "Each time we come here it's SOS. Same Old Shit. Dirt, no sheets, and bugs up the ass. I'd rather drink muddy water and sleep on a hollow log than set foot in this dump again." He returned to the bedroom. "Bug spray back there is useless. Spray roaches and all they do is give you the finger."

He asked Brendal for a beer. Brendal, still glued to the news, shook his head. "Get your own. Check out the fridge."

Crisp walked to a beat-up low-boy beside the television set, opened the door and shook his head. Not a plentiful selection. Two six packs of Coors Gold, a quart of Evian water for Cleveland, and a half bottle of seltzer. He removed two beers from the small fridge and slammed the door.

Alexis massaged her wrists to keep the circulation going. Dag winked as if to say, Simon's on the way. Dear God, if it were only true. But how could he find them if he didn't know where they were? Bless Dag for trying to cheer her up. Did he know how much she feared being tortured again?

A yawning Cleveland rose from his chair. "Yes sir, you two are going to fly the friendly skies with Mr Martins. Mr Henson is on his way here too. Wants to watch you and D'Agosta get the treatment. You best tell Mr Martins what he wants to know. That way you get the thing over with. Can't be handing the man a line of cheese, know what I'm saying?"

Alexis said, "You're saying if I tell Martins where my son is, I get to die quickly."

Cleveland nodded. "You got that right."

Brendal fingered his crotch. "Stop jerking the lady around.

199

Ain't like she's going to be able to pick up the shattered pieces of her life and move on. When Martins finishes carving up her and the ginzo, he's going to drop them out at twenty thousand feet. Straight down into the ocean. Don't you just hate it when that happens?"

Cleveland shook his head sadly, as though deploring being lumbered with crude help. "Much of what comes out of Mr Brendal's mouth is contrary to the human brain."

"Did I hear someone mention four million dollars?" Brendal said. "I think Martins will want to know what happened to his money. I think he's gonna be a one-man 'Wheel of Fortune' on this subject."

He leered at Alexis. "Hey, missy, how 'bout you and me having ourselves a lightning round before the plane gets here. Truck on over to daddy, and we'll play a little bouncy-bouncy. What do you say?"

Cleveland looked disgusted. "Man, you're a silver-tongued devil, ain't you? Don't mind him, Mrs Bendor. The man doesn't know the first thing about courtesy and respect."

Brendal grinned. "Old chickens make the best soup. Just kidding." Crisp looked down at the floor. He wouldn't fuck that old broad if there was money on the table. But he wasn't Brendal.

Cleveland's voice was suddenly softer, a change Brendal caught immediately. "I hope you're kidding," Cleveland said, "because you try and do the wild thing with Mrs Bendor, and I will be displeased. I suggest you solve your booty drought at some other time."

Brendal looked away. "Fuck you if you can't take a joke." Goddam Cleveland. Just another nigger trying to be a white man, not that Wayne Brendal was dumb enough to tell him. Few guys had whacked as many people or survived as many meanass prisons as Charles Parker Cleveland, named for some spade saxophone player Brendal had never heard of.

Brendal had a very clear picture of what happened when you jumped salty around Charles P. Cleveland. What came to mind was one of Henson's new men, a white guy fresh out of Folsom, a big shot in the Aryan Brotherhood, the baddest, all-white prison gang on the planet. Every time he saw Cleveland it was nigger this, nigger that until one day Cleveland shot him in the throat. "Now that's one way to educate a fool," Cleveland had said.

Meanwhile Cleveland stood over Alexis, her wig and handbag in his hands. "Never wear a wig," he said. "You have a hair problem, get a weave like black women do. There're some uncustomary items in your possession. Nine thousand dollars in cash, a little black book with White House telephone numbers. You're also carrying computer tapes."

Alexis looked away. "Ordinary tapes. Nothing special."

"Nothing ordinary about you, Mrs Bendor. File says you're an unusual lady. My nephew, now that little brother's only twelve and a genius with computers. I could ask *him* about these tapes."

"Why don't you?" Her voice was tight with anger.

"Now don't go getting hormonal on me, Mrs B. You don't figure to be the kind of lady who carries around useless objects. You've had intelligence training."

"Yes, and it was light years away from the nonsense you people are doing. It's disgraceful that a legitimate agency would even think of working with you."

"Times change. Nobody knows what's legitimate any more. Right and wrong ain't nothing but words on a street sign. There's winners and losers, and not much else in between."

"Whatever else you are, you're not patriots. All you've proven is your willingness to kill and be killed."

Cleveland shrugged. "All I know is this kind of work lets you break all the rules and get paid for it. This is America and they don't call it the land of opportunity for nothing. Me, I'm just happy to be a link in that chain of events. Meanwhile, how 'bout you tell your Uncle Cleveland what's on them tapes."

Alexis shifted uncomfortably in her chair. Every eye in the room was on her. She chewed her lip. Uncomfortable under Cleveland's gaze, she finally looked away.

He said, "You appear reluctant to confide the particulars. Well, we'll let Mr Martins pursue this little matter. And speaking of pursue, sooner or later we will catch up to that

201

son of yours. He's killed three of our people, and copped four million dollars belonging to Mr Martins." Cleveland grinned. "Your boy is awesome but he's got an attitude. You gotta love a man who's comfortable with who he is. But in the process of being himself your son has not left Mr Martins feeling a surge of pleasure, know what I'm saying?"

Alexis changed the subject. "Does Henson own this motel?"

Cleveland nodded. "This rathole and most of the empty land around it. Sometimes Henson lets cops keep witnesses out here."

"How long had you been watching us?"

"Weren't watching you at all. We got Mr D'Agosta's address from the dynamite man, the Italian dude who fixed him up with explosives down in Santo Domingo. Then we staked out Mr D.'s home and place of business. We still have men in both places waiting for your son to show up."

"He won't."

"And what makes you so sure he won't show up?"

"Because he doesn't follow me around. And I don't know where he is."

Cleveland straightened a pocket handkerchief. "That's between you and Mr Martins. He'll get to the truth, I'm sure."

He picked up a hand radio from a window-sill. "Check-in time. Let's see what's new in the wild and wacky world of Simon Bendor. You will excuse me, Mrs Bendor. Reception's not too good inside. Got to go outside to communicate. Anything you want before I leave?"

Alexis wiped perspiration from her forehead. The smell of the bug spray from the bathroom was getting to her. In addition to everything else, the mosquitoes were eating her bare arms.

She watched Brendal finish a beer and crush the can in a hammy fist. Now he was watching *The Tonight Show* and still smoking like a chimney. *Smoking, bug spray, drinking.* Dizzy with excitement, Alexis nearly leaped from her chair.

202

Impossible, she told herself. The idea would never work. She couldn't pull this off in a million years. But if she didn't, she was dead.

She looked at Cleveland. "I'd like to go to the bathroom, if I may."

"You may indeed. No lock on the door, but you can close it if you wish. There's no back exit and the only window's barred. Not that you would leave us suddenly."

"The hell I wouldn't."

She heard Dag chuckle.

Cleveland smiled. "Still feisty after all these years. I see where your son gets his sense of adventure."

Alexis rose, stood until the giddy feeling of nerves passed, then walked to the bathroom. Inside she switched on the light and closed the door. Covering her eyes with her cuffed hands, she started to cry. Just as quickly she shook her head. There wasn't time for self-pity.

Heart racing, she grabbed a handful of paper towels. A quick glance over her shoulder then she crushed the towels into a compact ball. God, don't let them come in before I finish. She looked at the toilet bowl. She nearly gagged at the overpowering smell of urine and faeces.

She shoved the paper towels into the dingy water. Into the base of the toilet bowl. She hadn't used enough. She needed more towels.

She rose, feeling the pain in her arthritic left knee. There were brown flecks on her bare arms. She was on the verge of vomiting. She grabbed more paper towels, dropped to her knees and pushed them into the hole. It took a third wad of towels before she had clogged the bowl.

On her feet, she raised the toilet top and cringed. What she saw was absolutely repulsive. The inside of the tank was corroded and half filled with brownish water. Reaching into the water, she gripped a thin piece of metal. This was the trip handle and looked breakable. Alexis pulled with all her strength. The trip handle didn't budge.

She pulled again. The trip handle remained in place. When she pulled a third time, the trip handle snapped, splashing her with water and sending her staggering backwards. Her right hand gripped a four-inch piece of rusty, jagged metal. The hand was bleeding.

Paper towels over the cut, she returned to the water tank and seized the flat bowl, a plastic globe the size of a small melon. She tugged. It came loose at once. The toilet was broken. And clogged. Alexis dropped the flat bowl in the tank and put the top down.

"Hey, missy, want me to wipe your thingy?"

Brendal.

Alexis picked up the bug spray. "Almost finished."

She sprayed the bowl, coating the water's surface until it glistened. She sprayed the sides of the bowl and the rim. Then dropping the bug spray on the floor, she grabbed more paper towels and wiped her blood from the tank top. She was drying her arms when Brendal opened the bathroom door.

He was drunker than ever. And still smoking. When Alexis tried to walk about him, he blocked her path.

She squeezed the wad of paper towels in her bleeding hand. "Out of my way," she said.

He looked her up and down. "Sure you don't want to party before take-off? We could do it like Smurfs. Fuck till we're blue in the face."

"I said, out of my way."

"Say please."

"I think I'll call Cleveland and have him say it for me."

Brendal's hands went up in surrender. "Oops." Still leering, he stepped aside.

In the bedroom Alexis eyed Brendal's .38, which was still on the night table. But Crisp was eyeing her. And so was Cleveland who'd left the front door open and was standing outside on a cracked, weed-infested sidewalk. Alexis walked past the night table and took her seat. Cleveland turned his back to the room and resumed radio contact.

Crisp went back to watching television. He sat on a metal folding chair, mesmerised by a radiant Dolly Parton who was telling Johnny Carson about Dollywood, her Tennessee theme park. Crisp's .45 Automatic was a heavy piece. He'd placed it atop the TV set. Alexis looked at Dag and whispered, "Get ready."

He frowned. What the hell was she talking about?

She was rigid as a board. D'Agosta wondered if the tension and heat had gotten to her. He followed her gaze and looked into the bathroom. All he saw was Brendal's back.

Brendal taking a piss. Brendal smoking.

When he finished pissing, Brendal took a final drag on his cigarette then reached to flush the toilet. D'Agosta heard Alexis inhale and he turned to look, wondering if she was having an asthma attack.

Her eyes were glued to Brendal. *Get ready.* Dag went back to watching Brendal, who was now jiggling the toilet handle. The toilet wouldn't flush. Brendal said shit, and threw his cigarette into the bowl. A wild-eyed Alexis leaped from her chair.

She'd taken two steps when flames shot up from the toilet bowl and seared Brendal's groin. Shrieking, he fell back into the hallway. Alexis raced to the night table, grabbed Brendal's .38, turned and fired three shots at Cleveland now staring into the room in response to Brendal's screams. Cleveland fell, disappearing from the doorway.

Crisp also reacted to Brendal's agony. He looked towards the bathroom but remained seated, a fatal error of judgement. Seeing the old broad move, he assumed she was running to help Brendal. By the time he figured out what she was really up to, he had a problem.

Alexis picked up the gun. Crisp's jaw dropped. What the fuck? As she got off three shots at Cleveland, Crisp leaped for his gun. He reached the television set where the .45 was and had his hand on the gun butt when the old broad shot at him. She missed.

The bullet passed his hip, missing him by inches. It shattered the TV screen, sending sparks and broken glass onto the carpet. Crisp got excited, thinking, Mama, you can't shoot for shit. Gun in hand, he started to turn and cap the old broad when her second shot hit him in the shoulder.

He dropped to his knees, back to Alexis. But he carried on, never mind the pain in his back. He turned to face Alexis and that's when she shot him in the head and chest. He fell face down into broken glass and onto old magazines.

Dag raced across the room, grabbed Crisp's .45, then ran to the front doorway. "Get down," he yelled to Alexis. "And watch the guy in the bathroom."

Alexis crouched under the bed, keeping her head and gun hand pointed towards the bathroom. Brendal lay in the hallway, writhing in pain. She looked at Dag who was all cop now; .45 in both hands, he sat on the floor and to the right of the door. A quick look at Alexis, then he took a deep breath and dived through the doorway, disappearing from sight.

Seconds later Dag returned to the bedroom. The .45 was tucked in his belt and he was uncuffing himself with a small key. "Cleveland's dead," he said. Alexis felt sick.

Dag stepped to her side. "You had no choice. You did what you had to do. And you were great. Absolutely, fucking great."

Alexis started to speak then turned to see a sobbing Brendal crawl towards her. She backed away as he entered the bedroom and collapsed onto his back. His thighs were charred and bloodied. Fire had also blacked his hands. "Christ, my dick! Need a doctor. Jesus, it hurts."

Alexis felt D'Agosta uncuff her hands. For the first time she noticed a second gun in his belt. Silver and elegant, it had belonged to Cleveland, a would-be elegant man. She almost felt sorry for him. Meanwhile a bright-eyed Dag was just starting to come down from an adrenalin rush.

He hugged Alexis. "I thought we'd had it. That's as close as I ever want to come. You're beautiful."

A trembling Alexis turned from him and threw Brendal's .38 on the bed. "I didn't know if it would work."

"It worked. Saved our butts."

"The beer was making him go to the bathroom. And he was a heavy smoker. I knew if he dropped a cigarette into bug spray, there'd be a fire. It's highly inflammable stuff."

"Simon couldn't have done better. Man, I thought we'd bought the farm. Now we've to get out of here before Martins and Henson arrive. I also have to get to my family. Henson's people might move on them."

"I'll call the widower," Alexis said, "and have him send

206

the FBI to your house. When I tell him about the tapes, he'll be glad to help."

She pointed to the stricken Brendal. "We've got to get him to a hospital."

"Outside," he said. His voice was icy.

A shocked Alexis couldn't believe his tone of voice. "We just can't leave him here."

"I'll take care of everything." Dag gently pushed her towards the door.

Too weak to resist, she stepped into the warm night. Cleveland's corpse looked small and vulnerable. His pain had ended; hers would go on for some time.

The other motel units were dark. Dag's van and the squad car were parked facing the airport fuel storage tanks. Alexis decided to wait in the van. She didn't want to set foot in the motel again. She started to weep, then she heard the shot.

It came from inside the motel. When she turned Dag was outside staring at her.

"Had to do it," he said.

She was disgusted. What kind of crazy would kill a defenceless man?

"You *had* to kill an injured man?" she said. "I don't think so. I really do not *think* so."

D'Agosta held out his arms. "Alexis, listen – "

"Stay away from me."

"Alexis, he could have gotten Simon killed or at least killed his plans. All he had to do was tell Henson and Martins about the tapes. He had to go. Believe me there was no other way."

A numb Alexis blinked away tears. Of course Dag was right. If Brendal had lived, Simon would have died.

21

Albert Martins sat in the library of a Fifth Avenue townhouse, sipping decaffeinated coffee while staring at an oversized bamboo ceiling fan.

The fan had once belonged to Ferdinand Marcos with whom Hugh Henson had enjoyed a business relationship for thirty years. Henson turned sentimental and teary each time he saw it. The fan reminded him of presidential parties where he'd accompanied Imelda Marcos on the piano while she sang "Don't Fence Me In", her favourite song.

The library's mirrored walls and green marble floors made it the loveliest room in the townhouse, headquarters of the Random Group, Henson's private intelligence agency. The building, with its stained-glass windows, had once been owned by J. P. Morgan.

It was nearly 8.30 a.m when Martins put down his coffee cup and picked up his nail file. He ignored Henson's apologies for last night's escape by Mrs Bendor and D'Agosta. There was little to be done about it now. D'Agosta's Queens home was under twenty-four-hour FBI guard, making him and Mrs Bendor untouchable.

Hugh Henson didn't share Martins' professional respect for Mrs Bendor. He downplayed her achievements, past and present. He saw her as some old biddy without sense enough to lay down and die. Last night's escape was sheer luck.

"You're wrong about Mrs Bendor," Martins said. "Her intelligence connections are still first-rate. That's how she learned about me so fast. Don't downplay what happened last night. She could find Elvis if she put her mind to it."

As a former field agent Martins could have told Henson how idiotic it was to generalise about women. Women were experts at using a man's weaknesses against him. And even better at turning their own weaknesses into weapons. Fabienne was living proof of that.

In the library Henson nervously scraped his feet on the marble floor and watched Martins file his nails. Martins let the silence unsettle Henson whom he blamed for last night's fiasco. After all, it was Henson's men who'd gotten themselves massacred while allowing their prisoners to fly the coop.

Losing Mrs Bendor and D'Agosta was tough to live with. But it was time to stop dumping on Henson. It was his money Martins was using to repay the Chinese. His connections and goodwill were necessary if Martins was going to outfox Charlie. Martins put down his nail file. No more nitpicking.

"Hugh, I'm sorry for coming down on you so hard, but I'm under severe pressure. We've still got a lot of money to smuggle into the country, and only five days to do it in."

"I understand." Henson looked relieved. "You were upset. I was upset myself. I was looking forward to watching you interrogate them."

Martins lifted his coffee cup in a toast. "To Mrs Bendor, a woman who can't stop being clever. Does a number on three of your men then gets the FBI to protect her. Now there's a lady to be reckoned with."

"As of now," Henson said, "she still hasn't reported the dead men to the FBI. The corpses won't be found. We made sure of that."

"Good. Mrs Bendor isn't telling all because it would call attention to her son. We know she gave the feds some kind of story. The question is, what kind?"

"You still say she and D'Agosta had no outside help?"

Martins shook his head. "I went over the motel last night with a fine-tooth comb. There was no sign of forced entry, no sign of a struggle. No sign of any vehicles in the area other than D'Agosta's van, the squad car, and your limousine.

Simon Bendor would have had to drive or bike to the motel. He didn't."

Martins pushed his coffee cup aside. "The toilet bowl had been booby-trapped. A nifty idea. Catch your enemy on the potty where he's at his most vulnerable. Brendal's balls were nearly cremated. Reminds me of OSS tactics used during World War Two."

Henson smiled. "Alexis Bendor was in the OSS."

Martins rubbed the back of his neck. "Brendal was killed last. That bothers me."

"How do you know he was killed last?"

"Charlie Cleveland was a first-class operative. He had to have been killed first. Otherwise, he'd have gotten off one or two shots. You don't catch a man like that napping. His gun hadn't been fired. Somehow he was caught off-guard."

Henson nodded in agreement.

"He and Crisp were killed with Brendal's .38," Martins said. "We found it in the motel. Which brings us to Brendal. He's the one who's left me puzzled."

"Why so?" Henson said.

"He was executed in cold blood. The other killings were self-defence, more or less. Not Brendal. He was out of it when somebody shot him point blank with a .45. To avoid being splattered by blood the killer fired through a pillow. That says he was experienced in these matters."

Henson grinned. "D'Agosta."

Martins began filing his nails. "A .45 is an awful lot of gun. Hard for a woman to handle. Bullet makes a hole the size of a quarter going in and the size of an orange going out. Except, why kill Brendal when he was already half dead?"

"To keep him from talking."

Martins examined his cuticles. "Keep him from talking about what? I'd give this year's wine crop to know why it was necessary to cancel his ticket."

"Why don't we tell the FBI it's a matter of national security and make them hand over Mrs Bendor and D'Agosta?"

"Lay that on the feebs and they'll eat you alive. We're private not federal. That kind of bullshit is overstepping our

210

authority and could bring an FBI probe. We do have federal backing, but it's limited and certainly not enough to confront the FBI."

Amateurs, Martins thought. Hugh Henson and his brother Random had started out selling hair driers and refrigerators in Nebraska until they'd made enough money to buy small electronic companies. They expanded into hand and power tools, computer technology and real estate. Both had been hard-headed businessmen and well-known supporters of right-wing causes.

Eight years ago Henson had turned fanatically anti-Communist when his brother had been among three hundreds passengers who'd died when a Korean airplane had been shot down by a Russian missile. He'd then formed a private intelligence company to fight Communism, naming it after his brother. It amused Martins whenever Henson acted as if he'd been in the spy trade for years.

Martins looked at his pocket watch. "Langway's late, as usual. And he still doesn't know about last night?"

Henson shook his head. "Neither he nor Charlie have been told a thing."

"Give Langway another ten minutes then phone his apartment. I want a new courier schedule drawn up before we hand over any money to the people in Chinatown. It has to look like we're taking precautions against future 'accidents'."

"Still think Langway's involved in the robbery?"

Martins' reply was cut off by a red telephone ringing near Henson who angrily snatched the receiver. "I said we weren't to be disturbed. Who is this?"

"Stephen Velez at the front desk. We've got a caller who says he has to speak to you. Won't give his name. Says it's about the fire in Langway's office and the four million we lost yesterday."

"One moment." Henson pressed the mute button and repeated Velez' remarks to Martins.

"Put a man on this door," Martins said. "He's to keep Langway outside until he hears from me. Then put this call on conference. And don't say you're with anyone."

Henson released the mute button. "Velez, send a man up here right away. I'll give him orders when he arrives. And put the caller through."

"Yes, sir."

Henson pushed the phone's conference button then returned the receiver to its cradle. Eyeing the ceiling, he cocked an ear towards the phone's speaker. "This is Hugh Henson. To whom am I speaking?"

"Mr Smith," said a rasp-voiced male. "Called the Waldorf and they told me you were here."

As Martins and Henson exchanged glances the caller said, "I torched Langway's office the other day and never got paid."

Martins leaned towards the phone, suddenly interested. The caller had a touch of Brooklyn in a voice that was being electronically distorted. Martins quickly scribbled the word *Why?* on a writing pad which he handed to Henson.

Bifocals on the end of his nose, Henson nodded. "Why are you calling us, Mr Smith?"

"I'm looking to get paid."

"Why should we pay you?" Henson said.

"Langway wants me dead. I need travelling money."

"And we're supposed to give it to you." Henson watched Martins write on the notepad.

"That's why I'm calling," Smith said.

Henson looked at the notepad. "Tell me something, Mr Smith. Why did Langway hire you?"

"The insurance. Why do you think he hired me? He's paying for an expensive divorce and he also likes to gamble. He screwed me and I don't like it."

"What were the terms of your agreement?" Henson said.

"Twenty-five thousand upfront. Another twenty-five after the job was done. He's holding back the second half and threatening to have his friends from Philly whack me if I don't go away. I can't take on those guys. So I'm coming to you because some papers in Langway's office said you two work together."

Henson shook his head in disbelief. "Mr Smith, we only have your word that something illegal may have occurred."

212

"Tell you what. Call the Fire Department and ask them about the contents of Langway's safe. Something else for you to think about. The Chinks believe the fire's tied to the robbery. Be talking to you."

"Don't hang up," Martins said. But the line went dead.

22

Avignon, France

Trach Dai had purchased a boning knife from a hardware store. He carried it in his backpack this afternoon as he walked along the empty corridor of a cheap hotel facing the railway station. His face was hidden by dark glasses and a baseball cap.

He had spent fifteen years penetrating Martins' mind while remaining masked and distant himself. As of today the mask was no longer required. He would pursue his revenge openly.

He was Chinese, tenacious and unrelenting, with a staying power beyond the comprehension of Western minds. His hatred of Martins was limitless, as was his patience. Outwardly he'd shown his gratitude at being rescued from Vietnam by helping Martins move drug money around the world. Inwardly, Trach Dai had never ceased calculating from within the darkest part of himself. He had never wavered in his determination to get even for having been mutilated.

In the darkened hallway he paused and looked over his shoulder. He saw a rat scurry along the base of a wall then disappear into a pile of old newspapers. He passed a room where a prostitute could be heard refusing sex with a client who wouldn't use a condom. A dog yelped as someone kicked it. Trach Dai wrinkled his nose at the smell of urine.

At the end of the corridor he stopped in front of a door decorated with magazine photographs of the Ayatollah Khomeni and Diego Maradona, the Argentine soccer player. He took a deep breath then pulled a pair of leather gloves from the backpack and put them on. He hid the boning knife behind his thigh.

He knocked on the door with a shaky fist. Inside the fist was a folded piece of paper.

"*Oui?*" A male voice inside was brusque.

Trach Dai knocked again.

"*Oui?*"

He was about to knock once more when he heard someone on the staircase. A vein throbbed on his forehead; a nervous tic suddenly appeared beneath his left eye. He couldn't afford to be seen in the hotel. Not by whores, Arabs or any of the scum frequenting this flea-pit.

Before he could knock again the door opened. Trach Dai entered quickly, finding himself in a small, seedy room occupied by Saad Selim. Selim was a tall, twenty-eight-year-old Moroccan who was a guard at Martins' castle. An ex-Legionnaire, he'd lost an eye in a barracks brawl and now had trouble recognising Trach Dai. The Moroccan, in fact, was about to knock the intruder on his ass. The hotel was full of drug addicts, all of them thieves and trouble-makers.

Trach Dai lifted the bill of his baseball cap. Selim lowered his fist. He closed the door then took the folded note from Trach Dai. The guards' nickname for the little Chinese was Mr Mum, as in *Mum's the word*. In Selim's six months at the castle this was his first visit from Mr Mum. It would be at least a year before Selim would be eligible to live at the castle where he wouldn't have to pay rent.

He wondered why Mr Mum hadn't had the desk clerk page him on the house phone. Maybe Mr Mum was here to explain why the guards had been ordered to be more alert. If they wanted Selim back at the castle, they'd better be ready to pay him overtime. The Moroccan brought the note up to his good eye.

The piece of paper was blank.

Leaping forward Trach Dai drove the boning knife into Selim's stomach up to the hilt. The Moroccan doubled over, in agony. Trach Dai quickly slit his throat, silencing him forever. As Selim lay dying, Trach Dai slipped out of his backpack and placed it on the floor. The blank piece of paper was returned to his shirt pocket.

From the backpack, he removed a large garbage bag and slipped it over his head, arms and legs going through slits. Then he took a tin of green camouflage paint from the backpack, and carefully smeared paint on Selim's forehead, cheeks and chin. Laying the paint aside, he picked up the boning knife and made an incision below Selim's right rib. As Trach Dai began removing his liver the Moroccan died.

When the liver had been severed, Trach laid the knife aside. Then he bit into the liver.

23

When the red telephone rang at 10.22 a.m. in the library of the Random Group townhouse, Martins and Henson eyed it in silence.

"Smith," Henson said finally. "About time."

Neither man had left the library since Smith's first call two hours ago. Fuelled by coffee and cigarettes, they'd spent the time drawing up a new courier schedule. They'd also ignored Langway's tantrums which could be heard just outside the door. The lawyer was furious at being kept under guard without being told why. He'd been told only that he was being detained on Martins' order.

As for the phone, it wasn't Smith calling. An anxious Fabienne was telephoning from France.

She and Martins spoke in French. "Simon Bendor's in France," she said.

Martins covered his eyes with one hand. He should have seen it coming. Bendor was planning a hostage swap. Fabienne for Erica Styler. It was a faster way of getting Styler back than knocking off couriers.

Except Styler wasn't Martins' to exchange. Not at the moment.

"How do you know Bendor's there?" he said. "Has anyone seen him?"

"The police are here asking questions, interviewing guards. I've just finished speaking to an inspector. Albert, I thought I'd left these things in Saigon."

"Left what? Why are the police there?"

"One of the guards, Selim, was murdered in his hotel. It was awful."

"That's no reason for you to get worked up. You didn't know the man."

"Albert, Selim had his face painted green and his liver cut out. And there was an ace of spades left on the corpse."

"I see. Was anything else done to the body?"

"Police say the killer took a bite out of the liver. Do you know what that means?"

"Yes, I'm afraid I do."

American special forces units in Vietnam would sometimes mutilate dead Vietcong in order to frighten the living. According to Buddhist belief, a mutilated corpse could not enter heaven intact. Mutilation was an impurity and the impure could never find happiness, not even in nirvana. For many Vietnamese there was no more horrifying sight than that of a loved one left painted, butchered and defiled for the afterlife. Camo paint was left on the corpse to identify his killers. The ace of spades, a calling card, simply added to the drama.

Fabienne said, "What does Bendor hope to gain by killing one of our guards?"

"He wants to scare us," Martins said. "He's certainly going to make the guards uneasy."

"Can you come home at once? I'm frightened. Trach Dai thinks Bendor will try to kidnap me, then make an exchange for his lover."

"He's right. I'll be home tomorrow, next day at the latest. I can't ignore the deadline on this Chinese deal. One of Hugh's planes will fly me back as soon as I finish working. Stay close to Trach. He's not to let you out of his sight. I'll fax him a photograph of Bendor. Have him distribute copies to everybody. Damn Bendor. He would pick now to show up in Avignon."

Each summer Avignon produced a summer arts festival to celebrate a tradition of cultural excellence. The event ran through July and August, and featured plays, street theatre, film workshops, concerts, dance, mime, and café cabarets. During that time Avignon's population nearly doubled. Bendor could easily lose himself among 200,000 people.

"Albert, I'm terrified. I know how Bendor hated us."

"If I have Miss Styler, he'll think twice about doing anything. And I'm going to get her."

After hanging up, Martins repeated the conversation to Henson. Bendor was a mad dog, he said. And you dealt with mad dogs by killing them. The red phone rang as Martins nodded. This time it was the raspy voiced Mr Smith. Henson pressed the conference button.

"This is Hugh Henson."

"What did the Fire Department have to say?"

"Mr Smith, I'm going to bring in an associate of mine."

"Mr Smith," Martins said, "I work with Mr Henson. My name is Martins."

Smith sounded annoyed. "Henson, I don't like surprises."

Martins squeezed the nail file. "Don't hang up, Mr Smith."

"New players make me nervous," Smith said.

Martins said, "You'll learn that I can expedite matters faster than Mr Henson, which could be to your advantage. We spoke to the Fire Department. You were right."

"Was I now?"

Martins turned up the volume on the speaker phone. "The safe contained blank tapes, just as you said. And its burglary and fire ratings were low."

Mr Smith snorted. "I saw Langway take tapes out of the safe and put back blanks."

Martins smile was brief. "The Fire Department said the safe was at least ten years out of date, perhaps more."

"Langway wanted something that would burn," Smith said.

Langway wanted to make money, Martins thought. The esteemed attorney collected from the insurance then arranged to be robbed of four million in Triad money. Bendor was in France and had nothing to do with the fire or the robbery. The blank tapes, bad safe, and a torch who'd gotten stiffed had all come back to haunt Langway.

"So Langway threatened you," Martins said.

"He said he'd send some of Altabura's crew around to see me. I can handle Langway. Handling his friends is something else."

"You said the Chinese have tied the fire to the robbery. Could you be more specific?"

"I could, but I'm not going to. Not until you people give me fifty grand. What I've got to say is worth at least that."

Martins dug his nail file into the notepad. "Fifty thousand. For what, Mr Smith?"

"For telling you where Langway hid the shit he took from his office before the fire started. I watched him walk out with files, his divorce papers, and a brown envelope with the name Andy Lam on it. The same Andy Lam you owe four million dollars to."

Martins and Henson exchanged glances.

Mr Smith said, "Listen up, because I'm only saying this once. The Chinks aren't dumb. They smell a rat. How do I know? Because they want to talk to me."

"Why you?" Martins said.

"Because there're only three or four good torches in town and the Chinks have already talked to most of them. They're asking about the fire and the robbery. Sooner or later they'll get around to me."

Martins froze. "They're looking for you?"

"That's why I have to leave town."

"About the robbery," Martins said. "Tell me – "

"No, Mr Martins, you tell me. Tell me if you're going to come up with some money and if you want to know where Langway hid what he took from his office."

"Fifty thousand is a lot of money."

"So's four million."

Martins nodded. "And you'll tell me about the robbery."

"No, just the fire. You have to ask Langway about the robbery. I only know what another torch told me, things he learned from being questioned by the Chinks."

Martins wrote Langway's name on the notepad. The lawyer could have had Altabura's crew grab the four million dollars. That money plus the fire insurance would clear up Langway's financial problems. Unless Martins dealt with Langway quickly the Triad would come poking around. Among other things, it would learn that Fabienne and Erica Styler were the root cause of its troubles.

There was always the chance that Mr Smith was bogus, a scam artist out to profit on Martins' misery. He could even be a courier calling from within the building. Unfortunately, the deadline and the violent nature of the Triad made it impossible for Martins to ignore Smith.

As though reading his mind Smith said, "I could always go to the Chinks."

"What do you mean?"

"For a price, I could point them at Langway. They could ask where he hid certain papers and computer tapes so they wouldn't go up in flames. They could ask why he wasn't beaten up like the two couriers. Who knows what that could lead to? I don't like working with the Chinese. But for fifty grand, it's worth a shot."

"We have a deal," Martins said quickly. "Fifty thousand dollars for information on items Langway took from his office prior to the fire."

"Smart move. One hour from now you have a man downstairs in front of the building with the fifty grand. He's to be alone. Dick me around and we're history."

"We'll follow your instructions to the letter."

"Put the money in a shoebox then seal the box with duct tape. All hundreds. Tape it good then put the box in a small plastic bag with handles."

Martins was writing on his pad. "Plastic bag with handles."

"The person making the pickup will give you a blank domino in exchange for the shoebox. Don't bother asking him questions. He won't know who sent him and he won't know what's in the package. You just make the exchange."

"It'll be done."

"Marking the bills is a waste of time. I can launder the money through any race track in town. Put a homing device in the shoebox and I'll dump the money. I'll be long gone before you get anywhere near me."

Martins lit a cigarette. "You'll call after you get the money?"

"If the money's there, you'll hear from me."

"Suppose we persuade Langway to give us your name."

"He doesn't know my right name. Far as my looks go, I could be in the same room with you and you'd never notice me. In any case, you got the Chinks breathing down your neck. You don't have time to waste."

Martins exhaled. "One hour from now. Downstairs in front of the building."

Smith hung up.

"Get the money ready," Martins said to Henson.

Henson leaped from his chair. "Are you going to let him get away with this?"

"What do you think?" Martins said.

24

This morning seventeen-year-old B.W. pedalled his bicycle through Manhattan's crowded streets as fast as his legs could pump. His bike had no brakes. Brakes added weight, reducing his speed.

The heavy traffic didn't surprise B.W., born Carmel Gavin Lynch. Today was Wednesday, the favourite day for shoppers and theatregoers. The city was also full of tour buses, bargain hunters, and vendors crowding sidewalks, forcing pedestrians into the gutter. B.W. also had to contend with cabbies out to run over his black ass for no reason.

He rode for *Kwik-N-Ezee* Messengers, run by the old Jew Orbach who'd gotten himself arrested one time for selling fake birth-control pills. B.W. liked the job because he could work outdoors and set his own hours. He was working a *special*, a job Orbach gave his fastest bikers who also had to be able to keep their mouths shut. B.W.'s special was taking him to Grand Central Station where he was to deliver a shoebox to somebody whose face he wasn't supposed to see.

He hadn't been told the box's contents. Nor had he asked. He cared only about the fifty dollars he'd make for getting his buns to the station in fifteen minutes. Get there late and he'd get only ten bucks from Orbach. Fifty bucks was a day's pay. And he stood to make that in just fifteen minutes. Fantastic.

Fifty bucks was his final payment on a new surfboard. He'd been putting money down on a six-foot, three-finned thruster he planned to use in a surfing contest at Rockaway Beach. He'd gotten the nickname B.W., short for *Born To Be Wild*, the first time surfers had watched him "air". Watched him speed up the face of a wave then go airborne before dropping back onto the wave and racing towards shore.

He raced up Fifth Avenue in Spandex shorts, knee-pads, crash helmet, and Ray-Bans. He had a beeper clipped to his belt and a whistle in his mouth, allowing him to warn fools to get out of his way. Travelling up Fifth against traffic was illegal. Anybody who didn't like it would have to catch B.W., except he was too fast to be caught.

Traffic cops and meter maids yelled for him to come back so they could ticket his butt. Fucking people had to be crazy. A pot-bellied white cop screamed, "Pull over." B.W. yelled, "Your mother shaves her ass," and never slowed down.

Going against traffic had been Orbach's idea. He hadn't said why and B.W. hadn't asked. Just go where Orbach sent you, and don't say nothing when you returned. Riding into traffic made it hard to follow B.W. in a car. And he was too fast to be followed on foot.

On Fifth Avenue he slowed down and edged his way past a Haitian parade heading downtown towards the UN. At 61st Street he turned right and pedalled one block to Madison Avenue. Ignoring a red light, he turned right and headed downtown. He kept near the kerb, cycling into traffic. His eyes gleamed with an unbroken concentration. His massive brown legs pumped frantically. A knee brushed against the plastic bag which was taped to the handlebars.

He hung a left on 57th Street, going with crosstown traffic until he reached Park Avenue. A right turn and he was heading downtown, dodging a school bus, a hot-dog vendor's pushcart, a squad car with two cops. As he neared the Waldorf-Astoria he blew on his whistle, warning a uniformed driver who'd stepped from a parked limousine into his path.

The driver, big and black, a brother who hated being hassled, prepared to stand his ground. Something about B.W. made him reconsider. He leaped backwards and B.W. missed him by inches. He cursed B.W.'s mother, sounding on her like only a brother could. Without looking back, B.W. gave him the finger.

Orbach had allowed him some leeway. "The last five

minutes get there anyway you can," he'd said. At 48th and
Park, B.W. turned left. Gonna go with the flow. Travel with
traffic until reaching Grand Central Station. He was in the
home stretch. He pedalled one block to Lexington Avenue and
turned right into traffic. He looked at his watch. Six blocks
to Grand Central. And just six minutes to get there.

He hated Lexington Avenue. It was a skinny-ass street,
lined with highrises blocking out the sun. In the low forties,
where Grand Central was located, the area was filled with
commuters. If B.W. was going to have a problem, it would
be here. Traffic was closing in on him. He slowed down by
turning the front wheel slightly, and letting the bike drag. His
unblinking eyes had a laser brightness.

With two blocks to go, traffic stopped moving. Cops were
everywhere. Damn people were playing with B.W.'s money.
He wondered if someone had tried to rob a bank. Then he
saw two fire engines blocking the street. Saw the fire marshals'
cars, squad cars, and people pouring out of a high-rise, and
more people packing the sidewalks. How was he going to get
through that shit?

He wiped sweat from his forehead with a gloved hand. Had
to be a way round this problem. Grand Central Station ran
three blocks, 42nd to 45th Streets between Vanderbilt Place
and Madison Avenue. Lots of entrances and exits.

Dismounting, he walked his bike towards Grand Central.
He kept to the right, on the sidewalk, blowing his whistle to
clear a path. Letting these suckers know he was in a hurry.
Giving 'em his crazy nigger look. They moved.

One block and he was at one of Grand Central's Lexington
Avenue entrances. He entered a passageway lined with shops,
newsstands and homeless men panhandling or sleeping on the
ground. B.W. worked too hard to give his money away. Any
nigger who got in his face was looking to get stomped.

From the passageway he stepped into the main concourse,
the biggest room he'd ever seen. Blew him away every time
he came here. It was five hundred feet long, with a ceiling
150 feet high and painted to look like a winter night sky
with thousands of stars. Only a few of the ticket windows
had people waiting in line. He could have done without

225

the billboards and advertising. Couldn't stick your nappy head out of your house without somebody trying to sell you something.

He walked his bike to a row of six telephone booths facing the shopping arcade. The first three were occupied, the last three were empty. He ignored the empty booths. Instead he waited until a chubby white man with a briefcase in the first booth finished talking on the phone and left. B.W. slid in behind him, sat on the still warm seat, and placed the receiver to his ear. His other hand remained on the bike, keeping it upright.

Phone between chin and shoulder, he reached for the touch tone dial just as someone tossed a domino into his lap. B.W. picked it up. *Double six.* He took his hand off the bike, letting it lean against the phone booth. He'd just begun dialling the office, punching in *Kwik-N-Ezee*'s number, when someone rolled the bike from view.

B.W. stayed cool. A second later, a hand dropped an envelope into the phone book. B.W. relaxed. Seconds later, the bike was rolled back into view. The plastic bag was missing from the handle bars.

When the phone rang at the other end, Orbach answered.

B.W. said, "Cherry-pie, my man, cherry-pie. Smooth sailing all the way." Then he hung up and sat in the booth looking at the fifty-dollar bill.

At 12.48 that same Wednesday afternoon, Martins was in Random's library, eyes closed in anger, as he sat in front of the conference phone talking to Gavin McBee, a kindly-looking Irish operative wanted by Interpol for killing a British army officer in Germany.

Martins said, "When did you lose him?"

"Early on, I'm afraid. Crafty little bugger. Flew up Fifth Avenue the wrong way. Rode down Park Avenue like a madman. Could never position ourselves to follow him. Sorry."

"You're saying a boy on a bicycle outwitted two carloads of trained operatives."

"I'm afraid so. We tried to intercept him but failed. One

226

car did spot him heading downtown on Lexington. Actually got on his tail. Nearly had him."

"And then what?"

"Some sort of disturbance. Fire engines, police, ambulance, crowds. They blocked the street. Our lad got off his bike, walked into the crowd and disappeared."

"Did you attempt to follow him?"

"That we did. No luck, I'm afraid. Took us forever to make our way through the crowd. Things didn't improve in Grand Central. Damn place is huge. We tried searching the area, but we didn't have enough men to cover all entrances and exits. The boy could have dropped off the money or gone through the terminal and continued downtown. We have no way of knowing."

Martins looked at an attentive Hugh Henson then said to McBee, "Pack it in. All we can do now is wait to be contacted. Don't bother with a written report. One more thing."

"Yes, sir."

"Stay out of my sight until I leave New York. I don't want to see your face any time soon."

The Brooklyn hotel room was pitch black. Eyes closed, Simon sat on the bed. His legs were folded in the lotus posture. His hands, palms up, rested on his thighs. The shoebox with Martins' money lay open and forgotten on a night table.

He sought to calm his mind, which had grown edgy with worry. His objective was to set Martins against Hocq and bring Erica out of hiding. Provided she was still alive. If she was dead, a part of him would die as well.

Know yourself and your enemy, John Kanna had said, and you will win every battle. Simon knew Martins couldn't be trusted so he'd phoned in a false fire alarm near Grand Central. The chaos that followed had prevented Martins' men from grabbing the messenger who worked for a service owned by a friend of Dag.

Simon would never forgive Hocq and Martins for what they'd put Erica through. Whether she was alive or dead, they were going to pay. And so would Hugh Henson, the man who'd wanted to see Alexis tortured. She was safe

227

now, under FBI protection at Dag's house. If Alexis and Erica died, he would have failed. He sat in the darkness, uneasy and silent.

He would have to remain unknown, undetected. He must draw no attention to himself or to his purpose. Let him fight fire with fire. Use the enemy against each other. He remembered past conflicts with Martins and knew what to expect. His own tactics, however, must remain hidden and unpredictable.

He opened his eyes. It was time to lead Martins to the stolen four million dollars.

25

Abby Langway stood in the living room of his Sutton Place duplex, trying to hold Martins' gaze. Seconds later he dropped his eyes and walked to the Frank Stella print hiding his wall safe.

He considered defying Martins. Just stand his ground and refuse to open the safe. Martins, however, was in a foul mood. And he had two men with him. If he turned violent, Langway was history.

It was late afternoon. Since early this morning Langway had been kept under guard, his freedom restricted on Martins' orders. He hadn't been allowed to telephone his associates, girlfriend or Charlie Hocq. For the past eight hours Martins had treated Langway like shit, refusing to tell him what was going on. Being held prisoner made Langway understand what Erica Styler must be going through.

He was dialling the safe's combination when someone called out to Martins. Malcolm Hoey, a big forty-year-old ex-cop from Kansas, announced he'd just concluded a search of the apartment. "Nobody home," he said.

"Nobody home in your head either," said Reggie Lau, a balding thirty-five-year-old black. The guards grinned like schoolboys. Langway shook his head. These fucks were treating this thing as a game. Sooner or later Martins would have to let him in on the joke. He'd never liked him, finding Martins cold and unemotional. Langway wouldn't warm up to him if they were cremated together.

Martins crushed a half-finished cigarette in an ashtray. "You and Charlie talk often?"

"Almost every day," Langway said. He spun the safe's dial. "Twice a day sometimes. Got a problem with that?"

"Should I?"

Langway was blunt. "I don't like being jerked around. Since I can't get that across to you, maybe Charlie can. Maybe you can tell him why you've kept me cut off from everybody for the past eight hours. Even prisoners get one phone call."

"If you're finished dialling the combination, open the door and step aside."

"Whatever you say, *Mister* Martins."

A telephone rang. "The service will pick up," Martins said.

Langway said, "Could be Charlie wanting to know why he hasn't heard from me."

"Open the safe."

"I take it you gave Andy Lam his money this morning. Or should I say you gave him Henson's money?"

"Open the safe."

"By the way, what happened with Mrs Bendor and D'Agosta? Strange no one's mentioned them. Why's that, I wonder?"

"You're wasting time," Martins said.

"I'm not the only one." Langway noticed that Martins had lit another cigarette. His eyes were baggy and he looked bone tired. Something had cracked his cool.

Langway thought, there's a reason for Martins being so tight-lipped. Has it anything to do with Bendor's mother and D'Agosta? Or with Simon Bendor whose sudden reappearance in Martins' life had him wetting his pants. Langway would give his new boat to know what was going on.

He opened the safe then stepped aside. "All yours, big guy. Don't steal the stamps, will you?"

Martins walked to the safe. Langway removed his tie and sat on a sofa, debating whether to fix himself a martini or settle for Mexican beer. He could also use a week in Bermuda.

"Explain these," Martins said.

"Explain what." Langway looked over his shoulder to see Martins holding a handful of computer tapes.

"These," Martins said. "They were supposed to have been destroyed in your office fire."

"Let me see them." Langway rose, but a look from Martins stopped him in place.

"Tear this place apart," Martins said to his men. "Start with this room then move upstairs."

"What are we looking for?" Reggie Lau said.

"Four million dollars," Martins said.

Langway threw up his arms. "Are you out of your mind? You're not going to find four million dollars here. Is that what this is all about?"

Martins placed the tapes atop the Stella print. "Mr Smith wishes you would pay your bills."

"Smith? What the hell are you talking about?"

Martins reached inside the safe. "He torched your office so you could collect the insurance. Let's see what else you've got in here."

"The fire in my office was an accident. I didn't hire any torch. Look, if that's what's bugging you – "

"Now *this* bugs me," Martins said. He reached inside a large brown envelope taken from the safe and withdrew several typed pages. He glanced at the pages before returning them to the envelope. Andy Lam's name was on the envelope's front.

A tense Langway said, "May I see that?"

Ignoring him, Martins peered into the safe. "This envelope contains information about Andy's purchase of an Atlantic City casino on behalf of the Golden Circle. What did you intend to do with it?"

Behind Langway, Reggie Lau was on his knees looking under the sofa. Malcolm Hoey was moving the Chinese lacquer screen away from the fireplace. A dazed Langway shouted at Hoey, "Be careful with that. It's priceless."

"Yeah, right," said Hoey.

Langway turned towards Martins now reading other documents from the safe. "So Charlie's in contact with Vietnamese intelligence," Martins said. "Says here he might be able to help them locate a certain American intelligence officer and his Vietnamese wife. Seems Vietnamese intelligence has been hunting this couple for the past fifteen years."

231

Langway shivered under Martins' gaze. He felt like screaming. He was on a roller-coaster car that had left the tracks at the peak of its climb, and was free-falling towards the ground.

Martins looked at the letter. "Apparently Charlie's offering this assistance in exchange for certain off-shore oil drilling rights in Vietnam."

Langway found his voice. "I swear I don't know how that stuff got in my safe."

"This letter has your signature on it."

"Well, lookee here," Malcolm Hoey said. "Mr Martins, Reg, check this out."

Everyone, Langway included, walked to the fireplace where a grinning Malcolm Hoey knelt on a sofa cushion to protect his knees from the hearth. His soot-blackened hands were filled with hundred dollar bills. He pointed to a plastic trash bag crammed with hundred dollar bills. "Found this up the chimney. Bag's chocked full of money."

Reggie Lau whispered, "Jesus, sweet Jesus."

Martins looked at the money. "I could be wrong on this but something says there's four million dollars there."

He looked at Langway. "What's your opinion? Inquiring minds want to know."

Langway held out his hands. "Believe me, I don't know how that money got here."

"I suppose you and Charlie planned to invest this in your new oil venture," Martins said.

Langway stepped towards Martins. "Hear me out. I swear I don't know what's going on. Look, if I'd taken the money, I wouldn't have hidden it here. I'm not that stupid."

"No, but you are desperate. Expensive divorce, expensive apartment, and a new lady to warm your heart. And let's not forget your new career as an oil magnate. All that costs money."

Martins weighed a packet of hundreds in one hand. "Let's review. For starters, you probably didn't have much time to plan the robbery, which is why the money ended up here."

"I told you I didn't steal a damn thing."

"Altabura's people probably helped you pull the job.

232

Wisely you decided not to allow them to hold the money. That would be like setting a rabbit to guard a lettuce field." Martins nodded. "You certainly couldn't launder four million dollars without calling attention to yourself. You were forced to stash it here, I'm afraid."

A terrified Langway saw where the argument was heading. "Albert, we've worked together for a long time – "

"Not really, but go on."

"I know how you act when you think you've been cheated. I couldn't survive being tortured. Just the thought of it – "

Martins dropped the hundreds back in the garbage bag. His voice was soothing. "You've got the wrong idea."

He put a hand on Langway's shoulder. "No torture. Put your mind at rest."

Suddenly taking a hand from his pocket, he jammed a Beretta against Langway's temple, and shot him in the head. Langway fell back onto the floor. Surprisingly there was little blood.

Using a handkerchief Martins wiped the Beretta clean of prints then placed the gun in Langway's right hand.

"Finish up here," he said to Reggie Lau. "And make it look good. I have to arrange for Charlie's trip. He doesn't know it yet, but he's going to be my guest in Avignon."

The telephone jolted Erica Styler out of a troubled sleep.

"Jesse Borrega. Did I wake you?"

"Yes."

"I'm sorry. Start packing. We're leaving the ship."

She sat up in bed. "We're what?"

"Hocq, Tautz, you, me. We're going to France. We'll be staying with Martins for a while."

"Why?"

"There might be trouble on the ship."

"Simon?" Erica gripped the phone.

"We're flying to Marseille right away. Get packed as soon as you can."

"Can't you tell me anything?"

Borrega hesitated then, "I can tell you Abby Langway's dead. Hocq just got the news from Martins in New York."

233

"Oh no. How did it happen?"

"He was shot to death. Someone tried to make it look like suicide. Hocq had to be sedated."

"Someone tried to make it look like suicide?"

"Martins says Simon Bendor did it. Shot Langway then tried to make it appear he killed himself."

Erica shook her head. "He had no reason to kill Abby."

"He was seen leaving Langway's apartment building."

"Seen? By whom?"

"Hocq didn't say. He's taking Langway's death hard. He wants Bendor dead as badly as Martins does. Maybe Bendor killed Langway to shake Hocq up. Maybe he went crazy because his mother's dead."

Erica was out of the bed. "Alexis dead? When did that happen?"

"Last night. Martins' people got her and D'Agosta in New York. I guess they couldn't survive Martins' interrogation. I'm sorry. I know they were your friends."

Face hot with tears Erica stared at the night sky through a porthole. "Poor Alexis. She and Joe were only trying to help me."

"Martins claims Bendor had intended to kill him, but ended up getting Langway instead. Before she died Bendor's mother said the yacht was going to be attacked."

"Attacked? When?"

"Next couple of days, apparently. Bendor's getting some Vietnam buddies to attack the yacht with a fighter plane. Martins was in Vietnam and swears these guys are killers. We can't defend against planes so we're leaving right away. Looks like Bendor is serious about getting even for his mother."

Something's wrong, Erica thought. Something Borrega said didn't make sense.

The Cuban had more bad news. "Bendor's men are planning a world-wide attack on Hocq. They're going for his homes in Manila, Hong Kong, all over. They're even planning to poison any food and water we bring on board."

"You say Simon's friends intend to do all this?"

"His CIA friends, yes."

Erica exhaled. Simon worked alone. He believed the more

234

people involved, the more chances of something going wrong. Furthermore, if he'd gone after Martins, Martins would be dead. As for Simon being seen leaving Langway's apartment building, that never happened. Simon was too slick. And his reaction to Alexis' murder would have been to go after the murderer. Not after Langway or Hocq.

Martins was lying. Erica thought, Maybe Alexis and Joe aren't dead after all.

"I'll call for you in twenty minutes," Borrega said.

An excited Erica said, "I'll be ready."

26

Vinnie DeCarlo peered through the binoculars and said, "Holy shit."

A long list of famous people passed through Tampa International Airport every year. DeCarlo, a fifty-year-old retired New York cop, had managed the airport's main gift shop for the past five years. In that time he'd come face to face with more presidents, kings, movie stars and generals than he could count.

This afternoon he stared at a face that topped them all. He focused the binoculars, bringing the face closer. "Come to poppa."

He sat in a security car parked behind a cargo terminal in the south-west corner of the airfield. The area was restricted to private planes, allowing them to land away from major terminals, press and the public. DeCarlo's binoculars were trained on a man who positively craved privacy. He was staring at Charles Hocq, the world's most famous thief.

Mr Hocq was wanted in a dozen countries for walking off with half a billion dollars. Wearing a white suit and shades, he'd just stepped from a helicopter and was following a coffin being wheeled towards a waiting 747. The plane was marked with the *Always There* logo.

DeCarlo lowered his binoculars. "D'Agosta, what the fuck have you gotten me into?"

Simon Bendor entered the International Terminal at Kennedy Airport shortly before midnight. He wore horn-rimmed glasses and a clergyman's Roman collar. He carried a shoulder-bag and one suitcase.

He walked to an Air France ticket counter. Standing ahead of him was a squarely-built, middle-aged Pakistani and his equally chunky wife. Both rattled off questions about seating arrangements, in-flight meals, and arrival times in London. A young black clerk, pushed to the edge of her patience, answered without looking at the couple. This information, she said, could be obtained at baggage check-in. The Pakistanis persisted until she said to Simon, "Next."

The terminal was almost empty. Most ticket counters had closed for the night. A young pony-tailed Latino backpacker stood alone, staring at a flight information board while drinking from a bottle of Evian water. Several yards away, a uniformed security guard stopped a homeless man from panhandling. Simon counted less than a dozen passengers in the terminal.

Waiting for him at the desk was a ticket to Marseille in the name of the Reverend Jim Tyrone, a name suggested by Alexis who'd taken it from a Eugene O'Neill play. Still upset at the Pakistanis, the ticket clerk worked in sullen silence. She handed Simon his ticket without a word.

His flight took off in two hours.

He checked his suitcase through to Marseille, received a boarding pass then walked to the currency exchange counter and converted a thousand dollars into French francs. At a security check a stoop-shouldered Puerto Rican swept his body with a hand-held metal detector, inspected his shoulder-bag then ran it through an X-ray machine. A chubby Asian lady stamped Simon's passport and said, "Have a safe trip, Father."

He walked to a book store facing a bank of telephone booths. He was expecting a phone call, leaving him twenty minutes for book browsing.

He left the book store after eighteen minutes, a copy of the New Testament in one hand. In a telephone booth nearest the book store he sat in with a hand on the receiver. Ninety seconds later the phone rang.

"Father Tyrone?" The caller was Joe D'Agosta.

"Bless you, my son," Simon said. "How's it going?"

"Couldn't be better. Mets are winning for a change. Want to speak to Alexis?"

"When we're finished. Where are you calling from?"

"My back yard. Don't worry about a tap. I'm using a cellular phone."

"How's life with the FBI?"

"Not bad," Dag said. "Maybe I'm just getting old, but the agents are looking younger and younger. Get the ticket OK?"

Simon tapped his jacket pocket. "No problem. Any more from DeCarlo?"

"He confirmed that Hocq's plane took off for Marseille."

"And he definitely saw Hocq and Erica?"

"If DeCarlo says he saw them, he saw them."

For Simon, DeCarlo's sighting was good news and bad news. The good news: Erica hadn't dropped out of sight. She was on her way to France. The bad news: Martins' security would be tougher than Hocq's. Martins, aka Edwin Morell, hadn't survived this long by being sloppy.

"Why are Martins and Hocq going to France now?" Simon said. "The Triad has them on a tight deadline with this casino deal. You'd think they'd stick close to this country, at least for the next week."

"Alexis might have the answer," D'Agosta said.

"Anything new on Langway's death?"

"No. Cops still say it's suicide even though he didn't leave a note. Most people don't leave notes, except in movies. He had no drug problems, no mental illness. There's also no record of gun ownership. Which doesn't mean he didn't find a gun from somewhere. Friends say he wasn't the type to kill himself, but right now that doesn't mean shit."

"Divide and conquer," Simon said. "That was the plan and so far it's working. Now let's see if we can get Martins to kill Hocq. Losing Langway's going to hurt Hocq."

"If Hocq learns Martins killed Langway, he's going to be hurt even more."

"You're sure the cops didn't find any money in Langway's apartment?"

238

"Homicide guy says they found eight hundred dollars in the safe, nothing more. They definitely didn't find any four million bucks. Computer tapes, the papers you left in the safe. All gone. What you're doing to those people is disgusting and devious, and truly worthy of admiration and respect."

Simon frowned. "I get the feeling Hocq and Martins are running scared. Hocq wouldn't leave the yacht without a very good reason. Not now."

"Alexis wants to talk to you. Here she is."

"Simon, are you all right?"

"I'm fine. How's things with you?"

"I love Joe, but I can't stand being cooped up. I spoke with the White House today. The Vice-President's resigned from Henson's charity but it won't be announced for a week. The administration wants it to appear he bailed out before the FBI closed in. Speaking of which, the FBI's studying those tapes you took from Langway. Don't bet on the casino deal going through."

She paused. "Simon, listen. I think they know you're on your way. I think they expect you in France."

"What are you talking about?"

"Martins and Hocq. They're waiting for you in France."

Simon shook his head. "No way. Only we three know I'm going."

"This afternoon Joe and I drove into Manhattan with the FBI. I wanted to get out of the house, so Joe suggested we drive past your apartment and the health club so he could show the FBI the surveillance Martins had on you. Simon, Martins' men weren't there. They'd all gone."

"What are you saying?"

"I'm saying they've stopped looking for you here. They're looking for you in France."

A bummer, Simon thought. He'd hoped to surprise the castle while Martins was in the States. Maybe snatch Fabienne and make a swap. If his mother was right, he wasn't going to surprise anybody. "Are you sure they know I'm coming?"

"Listen to me," Alexis said. "Hocq wouldn't leave his yacht unless it wasn't safe. He's not afraid of the Triad. Not yet, anyway. And he's not afraid of Martins. Otherwise, why go to France? That leaves you. No one else has the power to frighten him but you. He's dragging Erica around as protection against you."

Simon shook his head. "I haven't done anything to him. Not directly."

"Langway's dead. We know Martins did it. Suppose, just suppose, he's convinced Hocq you killed Langway."

Simon nodded. "And now I'm coming after Hocq."

"Right. Joe said his Florida friend saw a coffin being loaded onto the plane taking Hocq to Marseille. That would be the corpse of Hocq's sister. I'd bet Martins conned Hocq into thinking you killed Langway and are planning to attack the yacht."

Simon nodded. "You've been right before."

Alexis said, "You've given Martins reason to distrust Hocq. How else can you explain this sudden rush to France?"

Simon closed his eyes. He'd lost the element of surprise.

Alexis sounded frightened. "They know you'll come for Erica. They're waiting for you."

27

Avignon, France

Martins knew that Hocq couldn't be fooled for long.

Eventually Charlie would learn that Martins had tricked him into coming to Avignon and all hell would break loose. Charlie's loony act was just that, an act. If betrayed, he could turn homicidal in an instant.

At sundown Martins and Trach Dai stood in the castle's dry moat surrounded by the wolf-dogs. Both men drank from wine glasses as the white wolves suddenly sprinted to an abandoned power mower and back. The dogs milled around Martins and Trach Dai in self-congratulatory joy then launched a second race.

"The way they run," Martins said, "you'd think they were doing it for money. If I'd been that fast as a college football player I'd have made All-American."

He winked at Trach Dai who smiled shyly, bowing in a deferential and respectful manner. Martins refilled their glasses then sighed contentedly. It was good to be home again, to feel the warmth of the Provence sun and enjoy wine he'd made himself. He stared at the distant ramparts of Avignon now reddened by twilight. Behind his back, Trach Dai's face hardened. The look disappeared seconds before Martins faced him again.

Martins said, "Is he still watching us?"

Glass to his lips, Trach Dai nodded.

"The man just won't give it a rest," Martins said.

Jesse Borrega was looking down at them from the castle ramparts. Unless the Cuban was eliminated he could spoil

Martins' plans for Hocq. Borrega had brought three Cubans with him. His best men, probably. They'd have to be killed as well.

On arriving here they had painstakingly checked the castle and its grounds from ramparts to dungeon. A tense Martins had watched the Cubans interrogate his staff and as much as he'd wanted to stop them, he hadn't. To do so would have aroused suspicion.

Borrega wasn't stupid. Eventually he'd learn that a castle guard had been murdered, at which point the shit would hit the fan. The guard's half-eaten liver and painted face would point to Simon Bendor as the killer. It would also indicate that Martins had led Hocq into a trap.

Martins' guards were noticeably edgy, something Borrega had probably picked up on. This morning an Algerian patrolling the front gate had shot and killed a stray dog. With effort, Martins had restrained himself from sacking the bastard. Borrega might want to know why.

Martins' staff were under orders to keep quiet about Selim's murder. He'd hinted that Hocq might be involved in the crime. Everyone was to treat Mr Hocq with the usual respect. At the same time, there was to be no idle chatter in his presence.

In the moat Martins turned his back on the castle and faced Trach Dai. "Borrega has to die first. Otherwise we can't get to Hocq. I think I know how to rid ourselves of *el señor*. But let's put that aside for the moment. Right now we deserve a pat on the back for our accomplishments today."

Trach Dai nodded in agreement.

"Even Charlie worked, for a change," Martins said. "No sex during business hours, no poker games. I purposely put Miss Styler in a guest room near me and Fabienne to keep an eye on her. She's my hole card."

A smiling Trach Dai lifted his glass, seconding his mentor's wisdom.

Martins brought his wine glass to his nose and inhaled. "We've assured the Chinese that the pay-off money is arriving in the States on time. All of it's coming in at once, making up for lost time. I'd say it's been a good day."

Trach Dai signed, *The plan's too dangerous.*

"I know," Martins said. "It's not wise to put all your eggs in one basket. But I have no choice. Thanks to Hocq and Miss Styler, we're behind schedule. Re-routing the couriers has only added to the delay. To make the deadline, I've got to gamble. Besides, this was your idea."

I almost wish I hadn't mentioned it.

"The idea makes sense. Henson's planes brought us here and they're still in Marseille. So why not use them to take the money back? Your idea was a good one."

Trach Dai bowed.

Martins said, "In the morning I'm driving to Marseille to see the couriers safely on the planes. I should be back by dinner. Fifteen million dollars. That's an awful lot of money to send at once, even if it is going on two planes."

Trach Dai's fingers flew furiously. *Henson?*

"When the money arrives in the States, it's his responsibility. Fuck up and I've told him the Triad will have his balls. I'll need him when Charlie's gone."

When will you kill Hocq?

Martins looked at the ramparts. Borrega had disappeared. "Tomorrow evening when I get back. Wait any longer and he'll know something's wrong. Once the money's in the States, I won't need him any more. At that point the deal becomes all lawyers anyway."

He turned to Trach Dai. "I want Charlie's telephone calls monitored while I'm gone. When I return I want to know who he's spoken to and what they talked about. His scheme to hand me and Fabienne over to the Vietnamese has me paranoid. I don't trust him any more."

Martins looked towards Avignon. "Tomorrow morning drive into town and see if the police have had any problems with visiting Americans. I want everyone on the lookout for Bendor."

He shook his head. "No phones. I don't want Charlie or Borrega overhearing this particular conversation. If Charlie knew Bendor was around here, he'd have a heart attack."

Count on me to say nothing.

Both men laughed. Trach Dai's laughter was the sound of a trapped animal. But his eyes weren't laughing at all.

Avignon

At 11.33 p.m. a bare-chested Simon stared from a hotel window overlooking Clock Tower Square. Once an ancient Roman forum, the large square was shaded by giant plane trees and lined with open-air cafés and souvenir shops. The summer festival was in full swing; Avignon was one big party and tourists would fill the square until dawn. Simon had been here thirty-six hours and still hadn't gotten a decent night's sleep.

Across the hall a party was in full swing. Complicating matters, his room lacked air-conditioning. An electric fan didn't help and opening the windows only let in noise and mosquitoes.

He considered checking out of the hotel. He'd signed himself into three hotels, paying cash a week in advance. Three hotels permitted him to move around before his face became too well known. He couldn't wait to tell Alexis that one hotel was called the Hotel de Sade, a sixteenth-century mansion said to have been owned by the Marquis de Sade.

In the square a mime was performing to dozens of spectators. He was a thin-faced young Frenchman in baggy pants, black derby, false nose and moustache. His act consisted of sneaking behind passers-by and imitating them to perfection. Spectators applauded, contributing when he passed the hat. Simon drank warm Perrier from a bottle, thinking, Maybe this was the way to get into Martins' castle. Walk in behind a guard and pretend you were both the same guy.

He'd just swallowed more Perrier when someone pounded on his door. It was a woman calling for help in English and French. Someone was smacking her around.

I don't need this, Simon thought. The woman's screams were ear-piercing. She sounded as though she were being beaten by two men. Simon walked to the door. He liked the hotel's view of the square with its backpackers, old French priests, and Swedish girls in minis. But after he checked out this disturbance, he was out of here.

He opened the door and saw two half-nude young men standing over a naked teenage girl who lay weeping on the hallway floor. Before Simon could move, one man deliberately broke the girl's thumb. She shrieked in pain.

The girl, a round-faced Scandinavian, had cigarette burns on her breasts. Her scalp was pink where hair had been pulled out. The second Frenchman, stocky and bearded, casually let the girl's loose hair fall from his fingers onto the floor. He looked at Simon while speaking in French to the thumb-breaker. Both Frenchmen laughed.

A third young male and a second teenage girl watched from the room doorway opposite Simon. Simon figured the girls for tourists, out-of-towners who had decided to party with locals and gotten in over their heads. He smelled marijuana and alcohol. And unavoidable trouble.

The thumb-breaker, who was drunk, looked at him with contempt. He spoke in French and when Simon didn't answer he said in English, "What are you looking at, Mr Tourist? You fucking bastard."

"Let the girl alone," Simon said.

Thumb-breaker spat on the weeping teenager now in a fetal position on the floor. His small eyes were unwilling to compromise. He wanted to hurt somebody. He stepped towards Simon. His bearded friend brushed the last of the girl's hair from his hand and eyed Simon with a predator's hunger. Simon waited calmly, knowing neither Frenchman would let him walk away without a fight. His best bet was to end it quickly then disappear.

Thumb-breaker said, "You want trouble, Mr Tourist? I give you trouble."

He threw a round-house right at Simon's head, a street fighter's attack with a drunken man's clumsiness. Bearded-man slid to Simon's right. He'd attack when Simon's back was turned.

Simon ducked, letting Thumb-breaker's punch go over his head. Still crouched, he grabbed Thumb-breaker's balls and squeezed. The Frenchman screamed and when he doubled over, Simon slammed a forearm into his face, hooked a left to his temple then quickly spun around to face the bearded man. Behind Simon, Thumb-breaker fell backwards to the floor, landing glassy-eyed and gasping for breath. In front of Simon, Bearded-man backed away with a weak smile on his face.

The other partygoers stood rooted to the spot.

Back in his room, Simon hurriedly packed. Finished, he put on his Roman collar, black dickey and horn-rimmed glasses. He slipped his Father Tyrone passport into a shirt pocket. He took one last look around then opened the door to find three uniformed policemen waiting for him.

One aimed a pistol at Simon's head.

28

It was nearly 10 a.m. when Trach Dai sat doodling on a notepad in Avignon's police station. He was in an empty office awaiting Inspector Bonnieux's return. After thinking it over he had decided to warn Hocq of Martins' plan to murder him.

He would tell Hocq that Martins had murdered Langway and hand over documents taken from Langway's safe, saying they were forgeries created by Martins to discredit Hocq. He would also tell Hocq that Martins had stolen the Triad's four million dollars then tried to place the blame on Langway. Tonight when Martins returned from Marseille his life would be measured in seconds.

Mr Smith, the arsonist, had been a gift from heaven, a delicious rice cake that fell into one's mouth when least expected. Thanks to him Martins was now determined to rid himself of Hocq. Trach Dai closed his eyes. He was staring into Martins' coffin.

He heard footsteps along the station house corridor. When the door opened he looked up from his doodling to see Bonnieux and a uniformed cop escort a handcuffed young priest into the room. An atheist, Trach Dai glanced at the clerical garb then turned away.

As Inspector Bonnieux settled behind his desk, Trach Dai paused in his drawing of an elongated petal. The priest's calm was extraordinary. Everything about him, in fact, was controlled. Calculating, Trach Dai thought. The trained agent in him marked the priest as a man selective about his words and actions. Here was a person with something to hide.

Suddenly Trach Dai's heart began beating faster. A neck vein quivered. He felt a growing dizziness. He frantically sought a logical explanation for the thought now creeping into his brain. Finding none, he accepted what his mind said must be accepted. The priest was Simon Bendor.

With effort Trach Dai remained seated. He dug the point of his pen into his palm, focusing on the pain and thus controlling himself. Finally he turned from Bendor to stare through a barred window. He was afraid and excited at once. He looked at Bendor again.

He took in the American's glasses, dyed hair and clerical garb. There was nothing frightening about him until you looked into his eyes, the same unmerciful eyes Trach Dai had seen on a young CIA assassin in Vietnam. Incredible. Fate had presented Trach Dai with Martins' most feared enemy.

The uniformed cop left Bonnieux' office, closing the door behind him. Trach Dai noticed that Bendor appeared more amused than terrified. The Vietnamese prided himself on staying unruffled in moments of crisis but Bendor left him feeling inept. Didn't the fool realise his life hung by a thread?

Bonnieux handed Bendor's passport to Trach Dai. The name on it was phoney, of course. An immigration stamp indicated that Bendor had passed through Marseille customs two days ago. "He has three passports," Bonnieux said in French. Trach Dai nodded. Credit that to Bendor's CIA training.

Martins' orders to check on Americans in Avignon had turned up Bendor. Unfortunately, the same order could also lead to Trach Dai's death. Should Martins learn that Bendor hadn't been in France when Selim was murdered, he'd realise he'd been lured from America under false pretences. The blame would fall on Trach Dai who had encouraged Fabienne to have Martins return as soon as possible.

To save himself Trach Dai had to think fast. He did. He instantly conceived a new scheme for killing Martins. A scheme using Bendor, a trained assassin with good reason to see Martins dead.

Frederic Bonnieux, a snub-nosed forty-year-old inspector with *Sûreté Nationale*, the national police force, gave Trach Dai a rundown on the arrests of four American tourists. Two female college students had kidnapped a Macaw from a local pet shop. A retired US Army sergeant had gotten drunk then stolen a motorised wheelchair from Notre-Dame-des-Doms Cathedral. And a priest had beaten up one of Avignon's leading citizens.

Bonnieux read from a typed page and pointed at Simon. "A teenage girl says our Father here stepped in when she was being beaten by two local males."

Bonnieux looked at Trach Dai. "The good Father walloped Jackie Sainte-Claire."

Trach Dai raised an eyebrow. He knew Sainte-Claire. Bendor had performed a public service.

Bonnieux said, "Jackie belongs in a mental hospital. His mother owns department stores all over Provence so he thinks he has the right to do as he pleases. The girl he knocked about was one of two Danish sisters here for the festival."

Bonnieux continued reading. "The girl who got worked over is seventeen. Jackie invited her and her sister to a party. The party consisted of three males and the girls."

Bonnieux chuckled. "Father Tyrone nearly pulled Jackie's nuts off. One of Jackie's partygoing friends phoned the hotel night manager who stepped outside and called the cops. We don't care what happens to Jackie but his mother carries a lot of weight in this town."

Bonnieux couldn't sign so Trach Dai wrote on his notepad and tore off the page.

Bonnieux read in silence. Then, "He's one of yours?"

Trach Dai nodded.

Bonnieux shook his head. "That explains why he's such a tough guy. Are you using him on this Chinese deal?"

Again Trach Dai nodded.

To give himself time to think Bonnieux lit a cigarette. Martins was paying him for police intelligence. Let him pay to get the priest who wasn't a priest out of jail. Whatever cost nothing had no value.

Bonnieux tapped the typed page on his desk. "If I let this guy walk, Jackie's mother will kill me."

Trach wrote, *When girls testify, he'll be turned loose.*

"French law says he can be held in jail until an examining

249

magistrate decides if there's grounds for a trial. That could take months."

Five thousand dollars if you fix it.

"I'll have to talk to the magistrate's office."

Do it.

"I could tell Jackie's mother the Danish girls intend to accuse him of rape. I'll say their testimony plus that of the priest could send him to prison. I'll say we let the priest go to protect Jackie."

Bonnieux suddenly felt a chill. It had nothing to do with the air-conditioning. The priest had been watching him with the coldest green eyes imaginable. Bonnieux rose from behind his desk. "I'll go clear the paper work. Back in a few minutes."

When the door closed behind Bonnieux, Trach Dai handed Simon a short note. *Welcome to France, Mr Bendor.*

Simon nodded. "Trach Dai. You use to be a Vietcong agent. From what I read in Langway's files, you're working for Martins these days. Or should I say you're working for Morell, the man who cut out your tongue."

I want you to kill him.

"I had the feeling you and the cop were cooking up something. Why don't you kill Martins yourself?"

Promised Fabienne I would not.

"So you want me to do your dirty work. Fabienne always could convince men to see things her way."

Simon looked at the note pages in his hand. "All these years and Martins thinks you've forgotten what he did to you. Doesn't he know the Chinese never forget?"

Trach Dai's face hardened.

Simon said, "Me, I'd have killed him a lot sooner."

I'll help save Erica Styler.

Simon took his time answering. "Will you, now?"

No trap. Police could kill you here.

"Nothing personal, but you'd sell me out to get Martins and we both know it."

Trach Dai handed Simon another page from the notepad.

Simon read it carefully. "Martins is sending fifteen million dollars from Marseille to the States? Are you sure?"

The Vietnamese nodded, then wrote, *It's yours.*

29

At 8.22 that evening Martins, in a freshly pressed white suit, crossed the castle courtyard and climbed a flight of stone steps to the chapel. He entered an austere stone room with arches and a curved vaulted ceiling. The chapel was now a communications room whose stained-glass windows looked down on computers, high-powered radio and automatic switchboard.

The trip to Marseille had been exhausting but satisfying. The last of the Triad's money was on its way to the States. Martins had remained at the airport until both planes were in the air. Tonight's dinner with Fabienne, Trach Dai, and Charlie would be a celebration of a job well done.

For Charlie, this would be his last supper. Before the meal ended he and Borrega would die. With the last of the Triad's money now airborne, Charlie's services were no longer required. His pink slip was in the mail.

Dinner would have to wait a while. Martins had been summoned by his top accountant, a curly-haired, fifty-year-old Frenchman named Marcel Thomassin. The matter was urgent. Thomassin was not given to embellishment or overstatement.

He said to Martins, "You told me to keep an eye on Hocq and his people so now I tell you."

He pointed to a safe resting on the chapel altar. "Werner Tautz just walked out with a hundred thousand dollars. He said Charlie needed the money for a poker game with Miss Styler. I thought there was to be no poker until the planes landed in New York."

Martins said, "Charlie never mentioned any game to me."

"So what's Tautz want with a hundred thousand dollars?"

Werner Tautz locked himself in the small room facing the castle courtyard against the oaken door, trembling. Then he raced to Rachelle Hocq's coffin and began looting the corpse. He intended to fill his flight bag with jewellery then head to Marseille and the first plane to Germany.

He had his passport. He also had jewellery given him by Charlie, plus a few choice pieces belonging to Charlie himself. And there was a hundred thousand dollars of Charlie's money in a money belt around his waist.

Two days in this concrete rathole was enough. The place was damp, musty, spooky. It took hours to walk from one part to another. Nor did Tautz feel secure around Martins' trigger-happy guards. One had shot a stray dog, thinking it was about to attack the castle.

And then there was Bendor's threat to unleash aerial bombings on Charlie anywhere in the world. Why should Tautz die just because Hocq wanted to play cards with Bendor's girlfriend? The good times with Charlie had come to an end.

Yesterday any reservations about leaving the castle had vanished after a talk with Nicola Pitti, the twenty-year-old Italian maid who cleaned Tautz' room. From the moment she'd laid eyes on Tautz, fat-assed little Nicola had gotten sexed up over his good looks.

She owned a car and had offered to drive him around should he want to go sight-seeing. While Charlie had involved himself with business, Tautz had fast-fucked Nicola in an ornate four-poster bed, going up her like a rat up a drain, making her shriek with joy.

Nicola was now waiting for him in the courtyard. After he grabbed the jewellery they'd have dinner in Avignon and go back to her flat. When she'd fallen asleep, Tautz intended to steal her car then drive to the airport in Marseille.

Nicola had told him about the murder of a guard by Simon Bendor, something Martins had kept secret. Murder, however, was a hard secret to keep. Tautz knew Bendor couldn't have killed Langway in America and a castle guard in France at the same time. A man didn't need to be Einstein to realize that Martins was up to no good.

Rather than risk Martins' anger Tautz had kept quiet about the guard's murder. Only a fool would challenge a king in his own castle. As for Nicola, the murder had left her nervous but not nervous enough to quit work. Jobs were scarce, and besides she was making payments on a new Fiat.

Tautz removed a diamond tiara from Rachelle Hocq's hair then yanked an emerald pendant from her neck. Did her chest rise and fall? Christ, he couldn't wait to get out of here. Two emerald brooches went into the flight bag. One was worth a hundred thousand pounds. Tautz had been with Charlie when he'd bought it in London.

Rachelle looked so lifelike that Tautz half expected her to stick her tongue in his ear. He grinned, remembering the time he'd gotten sloshed and seriously thought about smearing shit on her teeth. And then there was the night he'd considered fucking her just for the hell of it. Charlie would have loved that.

Tautz yanked off Rachelle's diamond earrings, scratching her skin, and mussing her hair. Her flesh was cool. He took her rings, one with a diamond the size of a walnut. He considered giving a ring to Nicola then decided that would be a mistake.

He turned to leave the coffin then stopped dead. He'd almost forgotten the tape. This was to be his diversion. It would take Martins' mind off Tautz and point him in Charlie's direction. And it would unsettle Fabienne, a lady who acted as though her ass was ice cream and everybody wanted a bite. Who was she kidding? She was a motorcycle and any man could ride her for the asking.

Tautz dropped the cassette into his flight bag. He'd mail it to Martins from the Marseille airport.

He blew a farewell kiss to Rachelle Hocq. Then he opened the door and nearly screamed.

In the doorway a smiling Martins looked up from filing his nails.

30

That same evening Erica Styler stared at her uneaten dinner which had been brought to her room on a silver serving tray. Dinner was culinary perfection. It had been prepared by an eighteen-year-old French chef, a prodigy from a three star Avignon restaurant owned by Martins.

On a night table a radio station offered an eclectic mix of jazz, classic, and pop. Erica drank red wine and listened to Bobby "Blue" Bland sing, *If You Must Step On My Love, At Least Take Off Your Shoes*.

She was confined twenty-fours a day to a large bedroom overlooking the castle courtyard. A guard stood in front of her door at all times. She was on Martins' turf and he was calling the shots. She was his bargaining chip, not Hocq's.

With Charlie working around the clock, there hadn't been any poker in France. Borrega had also been busy. However, he had found time to phone Erica and ask if she was being well treated. She was, but she still wanted her freedom.

She spent much of her daylight hours staring down into the courtyard, watching guards check the front gate and Martins play with his wolflike dogs. Borrega and his Cubans prowled the grounds like caged tigers. She sensed Martins was expecting trouble. *Simon?*

The longer Erica waited for him, the more depressed she became. The worst part was knowing she had only herself to blame for being here. Ice Princess had taken one chance too many. Screwing around with Hocq had cost her big time.

There was a knock on her door. She hoped it was Jesse come to cheer her up. She could use the company. She'd even welcome Jehovah's Witnesses. "It's Albert Martins. I want to come in."

She opened the door. The first thing she noticed was the blood spots on Martins' white suit. Then she saw jewellery glittering in a flight bag hanging from his shoulder. His left hand held a video tape. A surgeon's scalpel was in his right hand. A frightened Erica backed away from him.

Martins followed her into the room. "I'd like you to invite Jesse Borrega here. Now, if you please."

"Why?"

"Because I said so."

She turned her back to him. "I won't do it."

"Yes, you will."

"You're planning something. I don't know what, but it's not good for Jesse. Otherwise, you'd have phoned him yourself."

Martins stared down at his white shoes. "Miss Styler, there's a Vietnamese working for me. I'm sure you've seen him from your window. He has no tongue because fifteen years ago I cut it out. Now if you don't call Borrega, I'll cut out your tongue."

Erica, her back still to Martins, began to tremble.

Martins barked a command in French. Instantly, two men with pistols entered Erica's room. Martins said, "I won't ask again, Miss Styler."

Charles Hocq sat slumped in an oaken chair in the castle banquet hall, his fingers drumming on an extended dining table. Where in God's name was Albert? Hocq was certain that Fabienne and Trach Dai, sitting across from him, could hear his growling stomach. He was hungry enough to gnaw a bone.

He watched Fabienne and Trach Dai sign to each other, their fingers reminding him of South American pickpockets in action. As usual Fabienne was an ecstasy, beautiful and elegant in a simple black dress and pearls. She had nothing going for her except beauty. But such beauty.

Occasionally she and Trach Dai would include Hocq in their conversation, Fabienne translating Trach Dai's signing into Vietnamese. But for the most part Hocq felt he was being deliberately ignored. Perhaps they blamed their current troubles on his preoccupation with Erica Styler. They didn't understand his need to win at all costs.

He wouldn't be here much longer. Tomorrow morning he was leaving the castle and returning to his yacht. Don't tell Martins, Jesse had said, until we're ready to leave. This way he wouldn't have time to talk them out of going. Since Werner was a gossip, he hadn't been told either.

Jesse had advised against leaving the yacht, preferring to make a stand on familiar territory rather than on someone else's home ground. Stay on the *Rachelle*, he'd said, and force Bendor to chase them from country to country. Too frightened to think straight Hocq hadn't listened. He'd let Albert persuade him the castle was impregnable. Too late he'd learned that being bored was as upsetting as being killed.

He bit into an olive, wondering when the Happy Hormone, his name for Tautz, would show up. Was he giving that Guinea maid a poke? If so, Hocq wanted all the gory details.

He dipped a radish into mayonnaise. No more of this rabbit food. He'd worked up an appetite and deserved a decent meal. If he didn't get one soon, he was going downstairs to eat with Borrega and the other Cubans. He was leaving this penitentiary tomorrow morning as scheduled. He missed his yacht and those delicious young *Latinos*.

He'd popped the radish in his mouth when he heard the dogs, the hounds from hell. The sound was coming from the courtyard where they were barking loud enough to wake the dead. Only someone like Albert would keep such vicious animals.

Fabienne and Trach Dai ignored the barking and stuck to their sign language. Hocq rose from his chair. Curiosity about the dogs had won out. He stopped when he saw Martins stride into the banquet hall. Forget the hell hounds. It was time to eat.

Martins placed a video cassette beside Hocq's place setting. "Sorry about the delay."

A flight bag hung from his shoulder. At the sight of blood

256

on Martins' white suit, Hocq shook his head. Not the sort of thing one expected from finicky Albert.

Martins smiled at Hocq. "Sorry, Charlie, but something came up. I couldn't let it go."

Hocq eyed the suit. "Cut yourself shaving?"

Fabienne frowned. "Albert, your clothes."

Martins looked at her. "I'll explain everything in a minute, darling."

He removed a scalpel from the flight bag and slipped it into a jacket pocket. "I didn't cut myself shaving, Charlie. But I have been cutting, that's for sure. Anyway, I promised you a gem of a meal. First course coming up."

Martins removed a tiara from the flight bag and placed it on Hocq's plate. Then he added a jewelled pendant and an emerald brooch.

"Charles doesn't find this amusing, Albert."

Hocq felt his anger rising. Albert had never gone near Rachelle's coffin before. So what kind of shitty game was he playing now? And then a terrifying thought entered Hocq's mind. He grew dizzy with fear. Biting a thumbnail, he glanced at the video tape.

Martins pointed to the tape. "It's embarrassing seeing yourself onscreen, banging away like a shithouse door in a thunderstorm. You managed to get plenty of 'pickle shots'. That's what movie people call shots of the male sex organ. Tautz told me you two would watch the tape then fuck like rabbits."

Hocq's voice was nearly inaudible. "What have you done with Werner?"

Martins looked at Fabienne. "Remember that business in Manila with Lisa Rizal? Apparently, there was a video camera in our bedroom."

Fabienne's jaw dropped.

"I haven't seen it all," Martins said, "but what I have seen can get us tried for murder."

He upended the flight bag, dumping jewellery at Hocq's feet. Tautz' passport and money belt also fell out. From a side compartment of the flight bag, Martins removed a white envelope. It was sealed and blood-stained. He tossed the envelope at Hocq and said, "Tautz told me you'd hidden the tape in Rachelle's coffin."

Hocq whispered, "He didn't."

"His closing statement."

"Closing statement? What's that supposed to mean?"

"Tautz was leaving you, Charlie. Simon Bendor had him scared shitless."

"You're lying. He wouldn't leave me."

"He was walking out with every rock Rachelle owned. I'm surprised he didn't slice off her tits and throw them in the bag as well. We ran into each other as he was coming out of her room. That's his passport and money belt on the floor. There's a hundred thousand dollars of your money in that belt."

Hocq hugged himself. "You're being spiteful and Charles doesn't like it. Werner loves me. He'd never leave. You tricked me into leaving the yacht, didn't you?"

"You and Langway hit the courier in New York."

"You're mad."

"I understand you're planning to go into the oil business."

"What are you talking about?"

"Next thing you'll tell me is that you never made a video of Fabienne, me and Lisa Rizal."

Hocq closed his eyes. "Bendor didn't kill Abby. You did. I should have listened to Jesse. But I panicked. *Panicked.*"

"Jesse knows his stuff, I'll say that. Unfortunately, he can't help you now. You're on your own, *mon ami.*"

He pointed to the blood-stained envelope at Hocq's feet. "Open it. Pretend it's Christmas morning and you're about to open a special gift, your little eyes bright with innocent wonder."

Hocq picked up the blood-stained envelope with two fingers. He looked at Martins, and saw no mercy in his face. Hocq tore open the envelope and stared at the contents without speaking. Suddenly his eyes widened with recognition. He dropped the envelope as though it were on fire.

Martins said, "I promised myself I'd cut out Werner's tongue one day. Face it, nobody likes a wiseass."

Hocq pointed to the floor. "That's Werner's tongue? Is he dead?"

"Dead as can be."

At the table Fabienne looked at Trach Dai who stared at Martins. She hadn't seen such hatred in Trach's eyes for a long time. When Fabienne touched his arm Trach shook her off.

Taking a stunned Hocq's elbow, Martins guided him to a window. "Something in the courtyard I want you to see."

At the window they were joined by Fabienne. Trach Dai remained seated alone at the table. He didn't move, not even when Hocq shrieked at the top of his voice. Down in the floodlit courtyard the white wolves were tearing Rachelle Hocq's corpse apart.

"Make them stop!" Hocq screamed.

Martins blew on a whistle. Immediately the dogs paused to look up at him. He brought the whistle to his lips again. The dogs trotted into the castle.

They left behind a savaged Rachelle Hocq, her arms ripped off and her face nearly chewed away. Hair, pieces of clothing, and chunks of flesh were scattered about the floodlit courtyard where guards and household staff stood in silence, their gaze going from the corpse to Martins and Hocq.

Martins turned from the window. "Here comes the A-Team."

Tongues lolling from their mouths, the white wolves trotted towards him. One of Martins' hands came to rest on his thigh. The dogs saw the gesture, and immediately surrounded Martins and Hocq.

Martins put one arm around Hocq's shoulders. "We're going to walk over to that small wooden door. Don't run or the dogs will tear you apart. Remember what they just did to little sis."

Trailed by the white wolves, Martins guided Hocq across the banquet hall. He smiled, visualising two tons of rocks descending on Charlie.

Martins opened the small door and leaped backwards, shocked at what greeted his eyes. He was staring at a green-faced corpse. The throat had been cut and there was a bleeding incision below the left rib. The ace of spades was pinned to the corpse's shirt. The dead man was Boris Neilsen, a big Swede who'd been with Martins for five years.

Martins felt a painful pounding in his right temple. "Bendor," he whispered. He turned to speak to Trach Dai but the Vietnamese had left the room. Fabienne stood alone.

Hocq stared at the corpse. "Bendor's in the castle?"

Fabienne hurried towards her husband. "Albert, what is it?"

Martins' hand shot up in a stop signal, freezing her in place. A hand radio clipped to his belt began to squawk. He brought the radio to his lips. "Martins."

"Hendrik Speke," said a South African voice. "We just found Pascal's body in a parked car. Throat's been cut and his face is painted green. Could be his liver's missing, but we can't be sure. Whoever did it might still be here in the castle."

Martins squeezed the radio. "Speke, keep this quiet or we'll have a panic on our hands."

"Too late for that, I'm afraid. Word's already out. Three guards have walked off. At least three, maybe more. They're not ready for this sort of thing."

"You've got to keep this quiet."

"Can't be done, I'm telling you. They're leaving in droves. It's a bloody madhouse down here. How the hell could Bendor have gotten in? We checked every vehicle entering the gate."

"Stay calm. Bendor's just trying to scare us."

"He's doing a bloody good job, let me tell you. I've got the willies myself. Taking him on is a bit more than we bargained for."

Martins ran a hand through his hair. "Shoot deserters if you have to, but keep the men here."

"I've been in a dozen wars and when you shoot deserters, you're admitting you've lost the fight."

Martins was about to insist that Speke carry out his orders when he heard the *pop-pop of* a handgun. Gunshots and a man's scream had come from Erica Styler's room. Martins felt Fabienne squeeze his hand and then the castle went dark.

260

31

It was 9.16 at night when Erica abandoned a game of solitaire in her castle room. Under Martins' icy stare she had just phoned Jesse Borrega to say that Tautz was threatening her again. Jesse was now on his way. Martins was gone, having left behind two armed men to kill the Cuban.

A jittery Erica squeezed the deck of cards as she listened to the noise made by the dogs in the courtyard. The animals terrified her. Only Martins seemed able to handle them. Probably because he and they had a lot in common.

Still squeezing the cards, she rose from the writing desk. She needed to be alone. The presence of the armed goons by the door was upsetting. "I'm going to the bathroom," she said.

"Make it quick," said a young Englishman with receding blond hair. "If you're not back when your friend comes to call, we'll shoot him through the door." His partner, a grey-haired Frenchman, nodded in agreement.

Erica locked the bathroom door with shaking hands. She had no idea why Martins wanted Jesse killed. With Jesse dead, Hocq was vulnerable. Maybe that's what Martins had in mind.

It might explain why they'd left the yacht in such a hurry. How could Erica warn Borrega without getting herself killed?

She stared at her reflection in the bathroom mirror. She looked wasted. There wasn't enough make-up in the world to hide the bags under her eyes. *Make-up*. To keep from shouting, she covered her mouth with both hands. There *was* a way to warn Jesse. If it failed, they were both dead.

Using an eyebrow pencil she wrote something on a card and returned it to the deck. Then she turned on the basin taps, closed her eyes, and listened to the water. Suddenly, she opened her eyes. When Jesse arrived she had to be at the door or he didn't have a chance. She doused her face with cold water, then dried it and flushed the toilet. Be lucky, she told herself.

In the living room she sat restlessly shuffling the cards. She was about to pour herself a glass of wine when she heard a knock on the door. *Be lucky*.

Erica rose from her chair. "Jesse?"

"Yes. You OK?"

"Just a minute."

Deck of cards in one hand, Erica walked towards the door and Martins' men. As she reached for the door handle, the young Englishman grabbed her wrist and pointed to the cards. "Hand them over," he whispered.

"One minute, Jesse," she said.

A smiling Erica held out the deck. But as the Englishman reached for them she executed a one-handed cut.

Then she cut again, mixed, and cut again, her supple fingers moving faster and faster as she continued to handle the cards with one hand. Both guards were mesmerised.

She finished with a triple cut then sprayed the cards at the guards, filling the air with diamonds, clubs, and spades, forcing the guards to shield their faces with their arms.

She quickly took advantage of the diversion she'd just created. She opened the door and offered her hand to Borrega. He took it, along with the card she'd palmed. "Nice to see you," he said. Too nervous to speak, Erica could only smile.

He glanced at the card hidden in his palm. "Tautz here yet?" The Cuban was holding the ace of spades, the death card. On it Erica had written – *A trap. Two men inside.* Borrega watched her eyes flick left then right.

"He's on the way," she said. "Can you stay until he arrives?"

"My pleasure." Borrega slowly drew his .357 Magnum from its shoulder holster. Then he seized Erica's wrist, yanked her from the doorway and dived into the room.

She landed on the corridor's stone floor. Looking into the room, she saw Borrega lying on his back, firing at Martins' men. When a bullet hit Borrega in the side, Erica screamed and the castle went dark.

Simon had entered the castle grounds hidden on the floor of Trach Dai's Mercedes, a car which was never searched. He wore sunglasses, false beard, baseball cap and backpack. He carried an automatic rifle. A K-bar knife hung from his belt. Trach Dai led him inside the castle and to an empty stone tunnel hidden behind an old wooden door. No one came here. Simon could hide in safety.

Left alone, he carefully examined the tunnel. There was no escape route. He didn't like that. A second door, this one at the far end, was locked from outside. The door through which he'd entered had been left unlocked by Trach Dai. That would have to be Simon's escape route, provided no one blocked it.

Nothing had been said about the massive rocks hidden behind the ceiling. Trach Dai was keeping secrets. I'm safe from him, Simon thought, until after I take out Martins.

He sat on the stone floor in total darkness and studied a castle map through night vision goggles. He circled his targets – the generator room, parking lot, banquet hall. He also circled the second-floor room where Erica was being held.

According to Trach Dai, the locked door in this tunnel opened into the banquet hall where Trach, Martins, Fabienne, and Hocq would be dining tonight. Did Simon plan to kill Martins here? No. First, the guards must be discouraged. After that Martins would be isolated.

After studying the map Simon used his backpack as a pillow and went to sleep on the stone floor. He awoke at 7.30 to a wrist alarm and ate a light supper of fruit and cheese. He then put on the backpack and walked to the unlocked door. He listened and when he heard nothing, Simon peered into the castle passageway. It was empty.

He stepped outside. Martins had to be weakened by fear. Fear made a man anticipate the worst.

*   *   *

Flashlight in hand, Trach Dai raced along a darkened castle corridor and towards the chapel. In the banquet hall the sight of Tautz' severed tongue had left him paralysed. He'd sat stunned, his reason destroyed by memory. The response had been costly since it had left him pressed for time. Now he couldn't destroy both the radio and the back-up generator. He'd have to choose.

The darkened castle said that Bendor had destroyed the main generator. Hopefully, he'd also taken out the telephone lines. Trach Dai decided to destroy the radio. Without communications, Martins was cut off from the outside world.

He thanked the gods for having sent Bendor to him. Meeting the American this morning had been the equivalent of being struck by a thunderbolt. Martins' heart was made of iron but Bendor was a furnace. Regretfully, Trach Dai would have to kill Bendor when this was all over. As long as the American lived, Fabienne would have no peace.

In the darkened passageway Trach Dai dodged men and women rushing past him with flashlights and candles. All were heading for the courtyard and safety. Some men brandished broadswords and battle axes taken from castle walls. An hysterical woman recognised Trach Dai and clung to his arm. Shoving her aside, he continued running.

He was nearing the radio room when the castle lights went on. The sudden glare hurt his eyes. Cursing, he stopped to give his eyes time to adjust to the light. The back-up generator was in operation.

Around him people cried out with relief. All, however, continued to run towards the courtyard. Would Bendor think Trach Dai had double-crossed him? Pulling a Luger from his waistband, the Vietnamese ran towards the chapel.

Martins blinked as the lights came on in the banquet hall. His men had reached the back-up generator. He radioed them to stay put, to protect the back-up against Bendor. The main generator, however, wouldn't be operational for days. Cables had been cut and sugar poured into the motor. Telephone lines had also been cut and guards were deserting. Hand radios weren't powerful enough to reach Avignon.

Martins needed the short-wave radio to call for outside help — unless he decided to run, to pull out of the castle at once.

Forget about using Erica Styler as a human shield. After radioing her room and receiving no response Martins decided that Borrega or Bendor had killed the men he'd left with her. Either way, it made no sense to send more men after her and lose them too. For now, Styler was on hold.

In truth, Martins didn't know how many men he still commanded. The bastards were deserting in droves. His place was with Fabienne. To leave her and go looking for Erica Styler was unthinkable. His only choice was to run from Bendor as he had fifteen years ago.

First, he had to deal with Charlie who stood surrounded by the white wolves. Flanking Charlie were two guards — Henrik Speke, the big forty-year-old South African, and Dwayne Knuckles, a young, sleepy-eyed Mormon. Martins wondered if he could rely on them.

He pointed to the secret corridor. "In there, Charlie. And don't trip over Neilsen's body."

"Albert, please. I don't want to go in there."

"Inside."

"I'm sorry about the tape. Really sorry."

"Charlie, it's no use tightening your ass after you've farted. If you hadn't kidnapped Erica Styler I'd never have known about the tape."

Martins tapped his thigh twice. Growling, the white wolves inched towards Hocq. The weeping embezzler stumbled backwards into the corridor. The dogs followed.

Martins blew on the whistle and the dogs backed into the banquet hall. A nod from Martins and Dwayne Knuckles slammed the door on a screaming Hocq. Martins pulled a loose stone from the wall, reached into a small crevice and hesitated briefly before yanking on a steel lever. *Au revoir, mon ami.*

The rumble of falling rocks in the tunnel was ear-shattering. Dust floated from beneath the ancient door and the stone floor vibrated beneath Martins' feet. The white wolves milled around in circles before hunkering down near Martins to gaze at the wooden door. Fabienne, Speke and Dwayne Knuckles covered their ears.

As the rumbling wound down, Martins held out a hand to Speke. "Your pistol." The guard handed over a Smith & Wesson 9 mm.

Martins said to Fabienne, "I don't want Bendor to get you, so we're clearing out."

"We run from him again."

"We've no choice. I'm sorry."

"Trach Dai must come with us."

A vein throbbed on Martins' forehead. "Let's find him, shall we?"

He took Fabienne's hand. "Stay close. We're going to the safe to get money. After that, we're leaving. No luggage, no jewellery. No time for that. I'll take care of you. I always have."

She brought his hand to her lips. "I know."

Martins looked at the guards. "I'll pay you each fifty thousand dollars if you see us to Marseille."

Knuckles and Speke nodded.

Martins signalled the guards to move out. Then he and Fabienne followed. Trailing them were the white wolves, ears flat against their skulls, their reddish eyes bright and alive.

Simon raced along an empty corridor lined with suits of armour and high-backed medieval chairs. The automatic rifle hung from his shoulders. The bloodied K-Bar was in one hand and the night vision goggles hung from his neck. He didn't need the goggles now; the castle lights were on. Why hadn't Trach Dai taken out the back-up generator? The Vietnamese had either pulled a double-cross or run into trouble.

Simon was hurrying to destroy Trach Dai's targets himself. His destination: the radio. It was nearer than the back-up generator. Destroying the radio would prevent Martins from calling for reinforcements.

The castle seemed empty. He was running into fewer and fewer people. Meanwhile, the courtyard was a madhouse as people clogged the front gate in cars and on foot. Because of the dead guards everyone now saw fear in every shadow. The castle was lit again but no one wanted to become one of the green men.

Simon considered going to Erica, but decided against it. If Martins were dead, the castle would be without a leader. Cut off the head, and the snake – Krait – dies. First Martins, then Erica.

Rounding a corner, Simon entered a narrow passage leading to a stone staircase. His map said the radio room was at the bottom of the staircase. Halfway into the passageway, he froze. Someone had gotten to the radio room first and was tearing the place apart. Trach Dai? Maybe.

Simon tiptoed to the top of the staircase, and peered down into the radio room. Inside Trach Dai was smashing a chair into a computer. He'd already destroyed the radio. He'd also killed the radio operator who lay face down near the altar, blood seeping from beneath his head. A Luger rested atop a nearby safe.

Did Trach Dai intend to kill Simon now or later? Suddenly Simon dropped to the floor and listened with an ear to the timeworn stones. His hearing was extraordinarily keen. He'd just heard footsteps, which Trach Dai couldn't hear over the noise. At least three people were heading towards the radio room. The dogs were with them, meaning that Martins was heading towards Simon.

He stood up. At the bottom of the staircase Trach Dai swung the chair into a computer. The radio room looked like the South Bronx.

Simon was trapped, caught between Trach Dai, whom he didn't trust, and Martins who'd kill him on sight. He couldn't go forward and he couldn't retreat.

Ninja. Closing his eyes, Simon concentrated his mind on a dead man. The dead man was himself. Opening his eyes, he appeared to have changed drastically. His eyes were glazed, his facial muscles lax. He moved away from the staircase and sat with his back to the wall. As Martins and the dogs drew closer, Simon covered his face with green camo paint then rolled up a shirt sleeve. With a steady hand, he touched the K-Bar's cutting edge to his forearm. Blood appeared at once.

He rubbed blood on his face and neck. The voices of Martins and his men could now be heard clearly. Opening his shirt, Simon touched his ribcage with bloodied hands. Then he closed his eyes, withdrawing his mind from the outside world and plunging into the unlimited world within. His body became slack. His breathing turned shallow. As his heartbeat slowed he slumped against the wall and assumed the appearance of a dead man.

Speke pointed to the body near the staircase and called a halt. "Christ," he whispered, "another one." Dwayne Knuckles unloosened the safety on his rifle. Bendor was a psycho, worse than any serial killer. He could be sneaking up behind Knuckles right now, planning to cut his throat and eat his liver. Knuckles didn't want to die that way. He didn't want to die at all.

A hand signal from Martins and the white wolves sat. Fabienne eased closer to her husband. Ahead in the radio room, someone was smashing equipment.

"This is as far as I go," Speke whispered.

Knuckles nodded. "I'm with you."

Martins pointed to the radio room. "If that's Bendor, we've got him. There's three of us and the dogs."

Speke covered Martins with his rifle. "You sent three men after him in Hawaii and they didn't do too well. As for the dogs, Bendor's proven he's no easy target. Money's no good if you can't live to spend it. You keep your fifty thousand and I'll keep my liver."

Knuckles said, "Bendor's king of the mindfuck. Who knows what's inside that room?"

Martins narrowed his eyes. "You're free to go. Both of you."

Speke backed away, rifle still on Martins. "No hard feelings, but this just isn't my fight." Knuckles, eyes on Martins, followed the South African.

The guards turned the corner and disappeared. Fabienne dug her nails into Martins' arm. "What do we do now?" she whispered.

"Protect our rear," Martins said. He jerked his head in the

guards' direction. "They're waiting for us. They know we'll be carrying money."

Fabienne said, "Are you sure they're waiting?"

Martins nodded. He'd played the treachery game all his life. He knew what to look for. He blew on his whistle. Eager for action, the dogs raced after the guards. In seconds they'd turned the corner and were out of sight. A man's screams said the dogs had caught up with their prey.

Martins, 9 mm in his hand, led Fabienne past the green-faced corpse and down the stairs. They paused at the entrance to the radio room. Inside, Trach Dai was dialling the combination to the safe. Except for the dead radio operator, he was alone. Martins entered the chapel.

"Trach," he said.

The Vietnamese looked at the Luger resting on the safe.

Martins shook his head. "Don't try it. Where's Bendor?"

Fabienne felt the tension. Her eyes raced from her husband to her friend. She sensed an even stronger hatred between the two than she'd experienced in the banquet hall. Trach Dai appeared the more relaxed. He stood proudly, arms across his chest, a smile on his face.

Martins sighed. "You were good, *mon ami*. You waited fifteen fucking years before making your move. And I never saw it coming. I'm impressed."

Fabienne touched his arm. "Albert, what are you saying?"

"I'm saying Trach Dai and myself were the only people to come through the front gate without being checked. Trach also knows about the rock tunnel. He brought Bendor into the castle and hid him there." Martins smiled sadly. "I let Fabienne talk me into letting you live. Big mistake on my part."

A tearful Fabienne looked at Trach Dai. "You promised not to lift a hand to Albert."

Trach Dai signed, *Bendor's hand, not mine.*

"You can't kill him," Fabienne said to Martins.

He pushed her aside. "Watch me."

He brought up his gun hand. In that instant Fabienne threw herself between the two men and Martins' shot struck her in the chest. She spun around to face Trach Dai who caught

269

her and gently lowered her to the floor. A stunned Martins stared at his wife whose black dress was shiny with blood.

A solemn Trach Dai eased himself from under Fabienne. Then he lunged for the Luger. Recovering, Martins emptied his gun into Trach Dai's back. The Vietnamese clung to the altar before releasing his grip and falling face down on the floor. The altar front was smeared with his blood. He lay motionless, one hand within inches of the dying Fabienne.

Dropping to the floor Martins took his dying wife in his arms. His tears fell on her face. She started to speak, but her eyes grew brighter and she died. In his grief, Martins lost sight of the world forever.

He never saw the bloodied, green-faced man enter the chapel. K-Bar knife in one hand, he stood behind the sobbing Martins and watched him hold the woman who had been his life. Sorrow was in every corner of the room. Martins had never seemed more lonely, more powerless. Pain was the price for loving Fabienne, the green man thought. He slipped the knife into his waistband. He wouldn't be needing it.

Martins sensed someone behind him. Looking up at Simon he said, "She's dead."

Removing his beard, Simon let Martins see his face. "If I was in the same room with you," he said, "you wouldn't even recognise me."

Martins frowned. He'd heard those words before. "Mr Smith," said Simon.

He watched Martins think. Watched the enormity of the horror creep over his face. Watched him become aware of the deception enacted upon him. A deception that had cost him everything, including Fabienne.

"For Pete Sanchez," Simon whispered. And with his bare hands he strangled Martins to death.

He found Erica in a second-floor bedroom overlooking the empty, darkened courtyard. She sat on the floor, cradling a man's blood-stained body in her arms. The man, who'd been shot twice, was alive but bleeding heavily from a wound in his right side. Two dead men lay just inside the door.

When Erica saw Simon she reached for a Magnum. He

froze and spoke softly. "It's me, Simon. I've come to take you home."

She stared at him a long time before laying the gun aside. Then she rose and rushed into his arms. For a long time neither spoke. Finally she spoke through her tears. "I knew you'd come. I knew you'd come."

32

Honolulu, July

When the grey Datsun entered Chinatown, Erica Styler was dozing in the back seat. Simon sat beside her reading the *Wall Street Journal*.

She awoke to see Alexis Bendor driving through Chinatown without stopping. They'd planned to eat lunch here. Instead Alexis drove past red pagodas, Vietnamese gambling halls and Thai massage parlours until she reached Nimitz Highway, named for the American admiral who commanded the US Pacific Fleet during World War II. Why the change in plans?

Simon was engrossed in Wall Street's closing prices. Alexis' choice of a restaurant meant nothing to him. No matter where they ate, he'd have salad and Evian water.

"I was right about Muriel Hostetler," Alexis said. "She worked for the State Department until retiring here last year. Had her face lifted so many times there's nothing inside her shoes. Ten years ago she and Hugh Henson were playing footsie. Mrs Henson found out about it and started using words like divorce and property settlement. That was the end of Muriel Hostetler. We belong to the same bridge club. Made it easy for her to spy on Simon and report back to Martins."

Alexis eyed Erica in the rear-view mirror. "You look better. The tan suits you."

Erica patted her stomach. "I've put on five pounds in two weeks."

Alexis said, "The widower called to convey the White

House's gratitude for saving the Vice-President's butt. He also offered me a lot of money."

"So marry the old fart," Simon said.

"He was offering me ten per cent of the Triad money confiscated by the FBI. That's the usual fee for informing on law-breakers. I turned down his offer. You have to pay taxes on the money and I didn't think you'd want the FBI and IRS knowing too much about your private life."

"Thanks," Simon said. "The widower say anything about Henson?"

"Henson's going in front of a grand jury. Andy Lam's already been indicted and is looking at three hundred years if convicted. Dag thinks it couldn't happen to a nicer guy. The FBI is taking credit for killing the casino deal. Which means you don't get invited to the press conferences when the FBI tells us what great crime fighters they are."

Simon shrugged. "I can live with that."

"The media are comparing this to the Iran-Contra deal. In both cases, you have the same intelligence groups doing stupid things."

Erica squeezed Simon's hand. "The Chinese have no money and no casino."

He folded his newspaper. "If Martins and Hocq were still alive, their days would be numbered. The Triad's blown thirty million in bribes and also lost face. Somebody has to pay for that."

"Glad it isn't me," Erica said. She looked through the window. They were approaching Honolulu International Airport. And just like that, she knew. Nothing had been said but she knew.

She released Simon's hand. "Whose idea was this?"

"Mine," Alexis said. "And you're going through with it. If I have to personally drag you on the plane, you're going."

Erica shook her head. "I'm not up to playing cards. Maybe later, but not now."

Alexis said, "Downtime's over, kiddy. Hocq might have scared you, but you didn't lose your nerve. If you had, you would be dead."

Simon handed Erica an airline ticket. "They want you in

Vegas for the Million Dollar Challenge. Fifty players are coming in from all over the world. Some are showing up just to take you on."

She forced a smile. "Just to take me on." She nodded. "Really?"

Simon took her hand. "Really."

"I don't have a bankroll."

"There's three hundred thousand in your Vegas bank," Simon said.

"Isn't that the money you took from Hocq's safe?"

"It's yours. Hocq owed you. You had him beat before he weirded out. I only took what belonged to you. That's all I took."

Erica looked in the rear-view mirror at Alexis. "You wouldn't be trying to get rid of me, would you?"

Alexis raised an eyebrow. "Perish the thought."

Simon said, "I'll join you in a few days. Walk into the game on your own like always. No reason to do it any different."

She kissed his cheek. "If you don't show up, I'll come looking for you."

Alexis looked at Simon. "You going to follow through on Henson? I wish you wouldn't. Not that anything I say will influence you."

"I'm finished with him."

"Are you serious?"

"Like I said, the Chinese don't like losing face. Henson will get what's coming to him. And I won't have to lift a finger."

Hugh Henson left Manhattan in a limousine at 4.45 p.m., got stuck in traffic on the Long Island Expressway at 5.14, and cursed his Jamaican driver for choosing this route during rush-hour travel.

He'd been indicted this morning in Manhattan Federal Court on 322 counts of laundering money for drug traffickers over the past six years. The FBI had linked his name with heroin dealers, shady bankers, right-wing loonies, Mafia controlled unions, and corrupt politicians. He'd never been so humiliated in his life. He'd formed his own intelligence agency for excitement, not to be buried up to his hairline in sleaze.

He'd tried to have the indictment set aside, telephoning friends in Washington for help. But his calls to the White House, Justice Department, and the CIA had gone unanswered. The indictment went forward as ordered, with Henson's so-called friends ducking him at every turn. He was on his own.

He had a net worth of two billion dollars, more than enough money to keep him out of prison. Should he be found guilty, he could keep the appeals going for years. He'd never go to prison. With money he could guarantee his freedom.

The federal prosecutor, a plug-ugly spic named Bolivar Infante, was hot to make a name for himself. He'd zeroed in on Henson, the biggest name in the bunch, making sure the billionaire had taken the prime hit. Thanks to him, Henson was facing fifty to life in a federal penitentiary prison plus a twenty million dollar fine. Mr Bolivar better not hold his breath until that day arrived. Henson had money enough to write his own future.

He didn't need to be a genius to figure out that Simon Bendor had taken care of Martins, Hocq, and rescued his girlfriend in the process. Bendor was a man he wouldn't mind meeting. Anyone who could kill Martins was worth knowing. Unfortunately, Henson couldn't tell anyone about Bendor without implicating himself in a swarm of unlawful practices.

Meanwhile, he was the media whipping boy, his name and face on the cover of every supermarket tabloid known to man. Reporters from Europe, Asia and South America had joined the media frenzy, pestering his family, friends, employees. The court had been packed this morning when he'd pleaded not guilty before Federal Judge Ruth Crowe who'd released him on two million dollars bail pending a September hearing. Crowe, set to try the case, was called Maximum Ruth for handing out long prison sentences. If convicted, Henson could expect her to hit him with everything the law allowed.

He was off to spend the weekend with his trial attorney Abraham Levin, who lived in Cold Springs Harbor, a Long

Island town that still retained the quaint flavour of the nineteenth-century whaling village it once was. Henson had dozens of corporate legal wimps on his payroll but none knew criminal law.

So he'd gone to Levin, a superstar among criminal lawyers and so good he could have won Hitler an acquittal in Tel Aviv. Levin didn't work cheap; he'd insisted on a million dollar retainer up front. Presumption of innocence, Levin said, began with payment of the fee.

This case had already cost Henson fifty million dollars, the price of two planes confiscated last month by FBI and customs agents when they'd arrested Martins' couriers coming in from Marseille. The Golden Circle's fifteen million in cash had also been confiscated. All of the Triad bribe money, in fact, had been confiscated, bringing its losses to thirty million dollars. As for that casino the Chinese had worked so hard to buy, it was still on the market.

Henson wasn't the only one in need of a good trial lawyer. The FBI was handing out indictments to gaming officials, politicians, gangsters and union chiefs. Some would undoubtedly cooperate with authorities in hopes of avoiding prison. Their cooperation would consist of betraying anyone they could, including Henson.

He'd had a slight problem with the Chinese who had decided to hold him responsible for their financial losses. With no Martins and Hocq to kick around, somebody had to be the fall guy. Andy Lam had requested that Henson pay thirty million dollars to the Triad as compensation for its losses in the casino deal.

Henson had laughed in his face. Who did Lam think he was talking to? Martins and Hocq had been responsible for moving the money into the States. Henson had furnished the transportation, nothing more. He wasn't about to hand over thirty million dollars merely because the Chinks requested it.

Lam didn't see things that way. Martins and Henson had been associates. Martins had made a commitment which Henson must now carry out. He could either pay the Triad thirty million dollars or arrange for a stock transfer in this amount.

"Working with the Chinese is like dancing with a bear," Martins had said. "You don't stop dancing when you get tired. You stop dancing when the bear gets tired."

Henson didn't give a shit about dancing bears. He hadn't made his fortune by bowing to pressure. You don't make two billion dollars by giving up the store. Andy Lam and his friends were getting nothing. Henson would sooner cut an inch from his dick than sell the Chinks a single share of stock.

He was more concerned with other consequences of his indictment. He'd been dropped from the White House guest list. The Vice-President and his wife had resigned from *Always There*, and were refusing to return his calls. Rejection also included having New York, Washington and Palm Beach society strike him off its guest lists. Nobody came to see you in the hour of your disgrace.

In the limousine he swallowed brandy and thought about how naïve the Triad was. Did they really think he would hand over millions of dollars for a disaster that hadn't been of his making. The Chinese were living in a dream world. If they wanted to operate in America, they would have to understand that business setbacks were common.

Henson was certain the Golden Circle would eventually see things his way. In time they would put this little affair behind them. They would forgive and forget. Henson was willing to bet his life on it.

Avignon

From a hospital window Jesse Borrega stared at a chapel whose facade offered two stone angels bearing a dish containing John the Baptist's head. He wore a grey sweat suit and leaned heavily on a cane. The door to his room was open.

A knock on the door caused him to look over his shoulder. Entering the room was Doctor Clement Pertuis, a strapping, fifty-year-old hospital administrator. He carried a clipboard and a sealed manila envelope. Borrega was being released after a three week stay.

Pertuis handed Borrega the clipboard and a pen. "Sign all

six copies." He spoke in French, one of four languages spoken by Borrega.

Pertuis tossed the manila envelope on Borrega's bed. "Sign by the X. There are two policemen outside."

"I know." Borrega began signing the forms. The cops were here to escort him aboard a Czech airliner flying to Havana. And to keep him incommunicado. Cops who'd been on Martins' payroll wanted Borrega out of the country before he could talk to anyone. He was leaving France with the clothes on his back and the contents of the manila envelope, nothing more.

Borrega handed the signed releases to Pertuis who said, "Lucky the priest and woman found you in the park when they did. They got you to the hospital just in time."

Borrega sat on the bed, a hand on his wounded side. The woman was Erica. He owed her his life. The priest had been Simon Bendor and he'd lived up to his reputation. He'd turned the castle upside down, killed Martins and got his woman back. That made him better than Borrega. A lot better.

The French police and American FBI were looking into Martins' affairs. To avoid being dragged into the investigation, Bonnieux suggested Borrega claim to be a mugging victim. Just say a priest and a woman found you in a public park, then brought you to the hospital. Follow orders and Borrega would get a one-way ticket to Havana. Otherwise, he could end up in prison.

Pertuis said, "You'd have bled to death had it not been for the priest and the woman. Your leg wound was bad, the side wound was worse. Arabs probably mugged you. We should deport them before they kill us all."

Borrega picked up the envelope Pertuis had tossed on the bed. The Cuban's name was on it. But he couldn't remember what was inside. He decided to take a piss then check the envelope.

Pertuis began initialling Borrega's release forms. "The police give us one story and those at Martins' castle give us another. A barmaid told my cousin that one of Mrs Martins' lovers, a crazy German, was a dinner guest at the castle. He killed her when she wouldn't run away with him."

Borrega smiled. "Really?"

"Killed her husband too. When people tried to stop the German, he turned into Rambo. Killed some dinner guests then took his own life."

Pertuis made ready to leave. "We'll probably never know the truth. Maybe there's a serial killer on the loose. You never know. Any trouble, just drop in and we'll look at those wounds of yours."

"Thank you, doctor." Alone, Borrega carried the envelope to a tiny bathroom where he locked himself in. His wounded leg wasn't too bad but his side was killing him. Dropping his pants, he sat on the toilet. He couldn't stand on the leg too long.

He hated going home to his family empty-handed. Cuba was poor and with the Russians pulling out things weren't going to get better. Borrega couldn't start looking for work until his wounds healed. Meanwhile, he had to feed his family.

He tore open the envelope. There was a money belt inside. Couldn't be his because he didn't own one. It belonged to someone else. The hospital had made a mistake.

He looked inside. *Madre de dios*. He was looking at thousands of hundred dollar bills. Nice new ones. Borrega pulled the hairs on his arm. He wasn't dreaming. There had to be more than fifty thousand dollars here. Maybe even a hundred thousand.

He could use the money, but it wasn't his. He didn't know whether to turn it in, or keep it. Instantly the decision was made for him. A playing card, the queen of hearts, had been included with the money. On the card was a single word written with an eyebrow pencil. *Thanks*.

A smiling Borrega brought the card to his nose and inhaled, smelling traces of her perfume. He remembered her eyes, eyes that could make a man forget everything. He kissed the card.

"*Gracias*, Erica," he said. "*Gracias, mi querida*."

MARC OLDEN

KISAENG

Park Song, aka the Laughing Boy, made money. Probably the finest counterfeiter in the world, his speciality was the US $100 bill.

Park Song also bought girls.

Manny Decker was a cop who investigated cops.

Corruption, brutality, links with organised crime: undercover work, dangerous and lonely. He liked it.

Tawny DaSilva was missing.

Daughter of the one love of Decker's life, she had set off for school and vanished.

Decker was about to head down into an international underworld of expensive vice and ruthless cruelty that would shock even him.

'Tough, realistic, sadistic and erotic, *Kisaeng* combines the traditions of Lustbader and Clavell, but outstrips them with sheer energy of narrative' *Fear*

HODDER AND STOUGHTON PAPERBACKS